THE LANGUAGE

OF THE BIRDS

The Language of the Birds

A NOVEL

K. A. Merson

BALLANTINE BOOKS

NEW YORK

Ballantine Books
An imprint of Random House
A division of Penguin Random House LLC
1745 Broadway, New York, NY 10019
randomhousebooks.com
penguinrandomhouse.com

Hardback ISBN 9780593874523
Ebook ISBN 9780593874530

Printed in the United States of America on acid-free paper

2 4 6 8 9 7 5 3 1

FIRST EDITION

BOOK TEAM: PRODUCTION EDITOR: *Ted Allen* • MANAGING EDITOR: *Pam Alders* •
PRODUCTION MANAGER: *Angela McNally* • COPY EDITOR: *Kathy Lord* •
PROOFREADERS: *Addy Starrs, Cathy Sangermano, Al Madocs*

Book design by Barbara M. Bachman

The authorized representative in the EU for product safety and compliance
is Penguin Random House Ireland, Morrison Chambers, 32 Nassau Street,
Dublin D02 YH68, Ireland. https://eu-contact.penguin.ie

To Kristi.

When I try to express my love and gratitude,
words fail me.

THE LANGUAGE
OF THE BIRDS

HIJKLMNOPQRSTUVWXY
L   KMN   WXY

NLHTHDTQGKHRHKCGKH
THE   E   RE ER   RE

GTNLHBDMNNLHEHMNGQ
   THE   STTHE   EST

NLUMCGKNDBSGOKFHYH
TH S   RT   R   EYE

VHDLGMNAGCHMMCUBUF
 E H   ST   ESS

LHPKHHNMOMGFNLDNNK
HEGREETS   S   TH   TTR

JKLMNOPQRSTUVWXYZ
           KMN   WXYZ

PART ONE

All the secrets of the world are

contained in books.

Read at your own risk.

—LEMONY SNICKET

HTHDTQGKHRHKCGKH
E E   RE ER   RF

NLHBDMNNLHEHMNGQQKUHF
THE   STTHE   EST   R E

UMCGKNDBSGOKFHYHIM
 S   RT   R   EYE   S

DLGMNAGCHMMCUBUFPNGNI
 H ST   ESS   GT TI

PKHHNMOMGFNLDNNKDFJOU
GREETS   S   TH   TTR

LHKIUIUFPEUKTFGKIHHIL
HER   G   R   R   EE

HIJKLMNOPQRSTUVWXY
           KMN   WXY

NLHTHDTQGKHRHKCGKF
THE   E   RE ER   RE

GTNLHBDMNNLHEHMNGC
   THE   STTHE   EST

NLUMCGKNDBSGOKFHYH
TH S   RT   R   EYE

VHDLGMNAGCHMMCUBUF
 E H   ST   ESS

LHPKHHNMOMGFNLDNNK
HEGREETS   S   TH   TTF

JNLHKIUIUFPEUKTFGK

Arrested Decay

California • October

ARIZONA CRADLES THE FIGURE-EIGHT PENDANT BETWEEN her thumb and finger and counts the days since her dad died—seventeen, the same as her age, and a prime number. A cold wave rolls from the pendant through her fingertips, up her arm, past her heart. Her chest rises and the wave breaks, coming out as a gasp, a breath cut short by pain. At once she's in a memory, sea-kayaking with her father. The swell is so deep that she glimpses him only when they are both on crests of the giant waves. All she sees are walls of water, as if the ocean has swallowed her dad along with the rest of the world.

Back in the present, her throat feels thick, her mouth gummy, so she turns from feelings to thoughts. To the soothing power of facts. Waves break when the ratio of wave height to water depth is approximately 3:4, so a six-foot wave breaks in about eight feet of water. How high is this wave? Will it ever break? Is she even getting closer to shore? Red sky at night, sailor's delight. Red sky in morning, sailors take warning. She looks out the window of the truck, but there is no red in the sky at all. Just gray.

Mom drives the black F-150 while Arizona's boxer, Mojo, sleeps on his dog blanket in back. They turn off Highway 395 and head east, past a sign that reads BODIE—13 MILES. Dad had loved ghost towns, especially Bodie.

"What's on your mind, honey?" Mom says to cut through the fog of silence that fills the truck.

"Waves," Arizona says, then to avoid an explanation adds, "but before that I was thinking about the gathering last week."

"The celebration of life? What about it?"

"It's such a stupid name. Who wants to celebrate after someone dies?"

"It wasn't about death. It was about celebrating the time we had with him. And sharing the burden of pain."

"Sharing pain doesn't make sense. It doesn't add up, literally. When you get ten people together who are in pain, it's just ten times the pain. It's basic math."

"Feelings don't always work like math. Shared joy can be greater than the sum of its parts. And when pain is shared, the result is actually *less* pain. Trust me on this."

Arizona scoffs. Trust is a stone that slips midstream. She trusted her teachers, but they didn't stop the bullying. She trusted Dad when he promised to always be there for her.

"I think he'd be happy that we're back on the road, spreading his ashes in places he loved." Mom hesitates. "It's been nice so far, don't you think?"

Arizona wants to say yes but doesn't like to lie, so she nods instead—somehow, nonverbal lies don't count. At home, the rambling house and property afforded them space to process the loss in their own ways. But now traveling in the Airstream trailer, it feels like the shiny silver walls are pressing in.

She turns away from her mom and retreats into nature, a world that never lets her down. She watches the landscape change as they climb the winding canyon road, past black cottonwoods thriving in arroyos, through stands of stunted piñon pines, until they emerge into a landscape of barren scrub-flecked hills. In the distance, wooden buildings rise and grow, their weathered sides barely distinguishable from the gray earth and sky. She breathes it all into her lungs—not the scent or the air but the trees themselves, the hills, the very earth—and holds it there close to her heart.

———

THEY PASS ANOTHER SIGN—BODIE STATE HISTORIC PARK, ELEVA-
TION 8,379 FEET—and pull into the dirt parking lot. Arizona puts
Mojo on leash and grabs her daypack from the bed of the pickup.

"Can we explore together?" Mom says while she pulls her hair back
through a scrunchie.

"You said you wanted to take the tour of the stamp mill. They don't
allow dogs on that."

"I know, but there's plenty of time before it starts."

Arizona shakes her head. "I could use a little more alone time."

"Your dad needed his space, too."

Arizona deepens her voice to impersonate her dad. "Sorry, honey,
but the apple doesn't fall far from the tree."

Mom forces a chuckle, as if testing out the sound. "All right. Where
will you go?"

Arizona shrugs. "Just wander. Find a place to read. Maybe check
out the cemetery."

"Do you think that's a good idea? You know, so soon after . . ."

Arizona rolls her eyes and sighs. "I like the quiet."

"This is a ghost town, honey. The whole place is quiet."

"Why do you always have to question what I do? Like you don't
trust me to make my own decisions."

"I'm just trying to protect you."

"Just because I have some disorders—"

"Differences," Mom says, "not disorders. And everyone is different."

"Whatever. I don't need to be protected. I'm not your sister. I'm not
going to kill myself."

Mom sighs, looks at the ground, and dons her sunglasses. "Okay,
sorry. How 'bout we meet at the Methodist Church at four? Then we
can find a nice spot for . . . the ashes."

"Sure."

As her mom walks away, Arizona wonders if maybe she shouldn't
have snapped at her. But Mom's been so friggin' clingy since Dad died.

And Mom apologized, so she obviously knows she was in the wrong. Right?

Arizona sets her phone alarm and leads Mojo straight for the cemetery. They stroll through a sea of gray-green sagebrush scrub, its cool minty aroma heightened by nocturnal rain, the first of the season and so light that Arizona can count the raindrop pocks on the trail.

As they roam through the 150 marked graves, Mojo's tail says he's happy to be sniffing new things, even if they're headstones instead of hydrants. Cemetery tour complete, Arizona removes her pack and sits against a large monument.

"I need kisses, buddy," she says.

Mojo licks her face and she kisses his forehead. He curls up by her side, a contented look in his eyes.

"Good boy."

She opens her dad's worn paperback copy of *Brave New World*. Given the circumstances, the sardonic title feels downright contemptuous. But it's a way to keep Dad close, not to mention a darn good read.

LOST IN THE BOOK, as usual, she doesn't know how much time has passed when a movement catches her eye. She watches the majestic bird alight on a headstone, feathers lustrous black, talons latching to miniature dimples in the wind-worn Sierra granite. "*Corvus corax*," she murmurs, before scowling at the more familiar name, common raven. There is nothing *common* about corvids, with a brain-to-body ratio that rivals that of the great apes.

The raven's goiter of shaggy throat feathers bobs, its beak opening and closing in silence—as if it whispers to the dead. How ironic that the world's largest songbird would whisper, but she understands. Cemeteries are sanctuaries, like libraries. She puts her book away, opens her pocket notebook, and writes.

> Cemeteries are sanctuaries,
> like libraries—
> quiet, solitude, full of history.

Permanence of stone
to mark the impermanence of life,
like the written word does
for the fleeting spoken word.

Even though she is comfortable in sepulchral settings, this time *does* seem different. She scans her body, tries to determine what it is, where it comes from. She feels cold and . . . fragile? Like the veil of ice on a pond in early winter. Is it the cool stone behind her back? Or the wind? Certainly it's not that her mom was right.

Her thoughts are interrupted by her phone alarm. 3:14 P.M.—pi time. One last look, one last breath in this quiet place. She rises and turns in place, surveys the headstones, the desolate hills, the weathered buildings frozen in time. The empty spaces where fires razed nine-tenths of the town, now blanketed with low brush and dotted with an incongruous mix of abandoned vehicles—wooden wagons and rusted panel trucks—like an open-air transportation museum. She multiplies the number of buildings by ten and visualizes the town in its heyday. Eight thousand people seeking gold and opportunity, until the mines ran dry, and they left as quickly as they had come. That's way too many people. She prefers it like this. Dad did, too.

She walks Mojo down the path against a chill wind that kicks dust off the dirt streets of the ghost town. Preserved in a state of arrested decay. Like her family.

They pass the church, where they will meet Mom at four, and amble down Green Street. Past the park office, surrey shed, and morgue, to the schoolhouse. Arizona peers through the windows and listens. It's so quiet, unlike the school she'd known, with its cacophonous din and jeering voices. She looks at the rows of desks still laden with books, pictures the ghosts of children returning from their eternal recess, and wonders if, in a different place and time, she could have fit in.

They take the long way back, up Wood Street. The stamp mill, its corrugated blue-gray metal siding just two hundred feet away, looms large behind small wooden buildings with sagging rooflines. A brown sign with white lettering reads HAZARDOUS AREA, CLOSED TO PUBLIC.

Wearing a crooked smile, she imagines herself and Mojo as they navigate old mine shafts and clamber up loose piles of mercury-laden tailings.

They continue around the block to the corner of Main and Union, the site of the former Sawdust Corner Saloon. Arizona hears the ghost of the bar's calliope and wonders how it had ever competed with the thunderous ore-crushing pistons of the stamp mill. Maybe the saloon was open only when the mill was closed? The two sound wraiths begin to battle inside her head, so she moves on before they can possess her.

They wander down Prospect and Park streets, through the section that best survived the fires—more or less intact—and reach the Methodist Church at exactly four o'clock.

Mom is nowhere to be seen.

2

Occam's Razor

ARIZONA SEES A GROUP OF TOURISTS COMING DOWN GREEN Street, accompanied by a young park ranger. Mom isn't among them. She scowls. Tardiness is disrespectful, and Mom knows that. Her body is still while her brain scurries. She looks at her phone—no service. Next idea. Search? No, Mom isn't *that* late. Ask the ranger? She feels her pulse in her temples. She inhales and exhales, slowly, three times, from the diaphragm like Mom taught her. The ranger is only one person. No big deal. She swallows, takes one more breath, and approaches him.

"Excuse me," she says, making momentary eye contact. "My mother went on the three o'clock stamp-mill tour. We were supposed to meet at the church at four, but she's not there."

"That tour probably just finished," he says, looking at his watch. "Not a fan of stamp mills?"

"My dog couldn't go."

"Oh, right. Give your mom a few more minutes. I'm sure she'll show up."

Arizona gives a perfunctory nod. She thinks about saying thanks, but she isn't thankful. She walks Mojo in laps around the church, again and again. Half an hour passes. She looks at Mojo, whose expression is as clear as words—*why are we walking in circles, and where the heck is Mom?*

"I know, right?" she says. She feels a flutter in her chest and wonders what it is. Annoyance? Confusion? Worry? Probably just annoyance.

She fetches the park brochure from her pack and flips to the map. Her eyes dart back and forth, look for patterns—search patterns. She pulls out her notebook and writes.

> Each search grid larger, yet incorporating the previous.
> Self-similar supersets of Euclidean space.
> Fractals? No, unnecessarily infinite.
> Tiles that combine to self-replicate. Rep-tiles.

She looks at the map and visualizes a set of self-replicating tiles. First, a set of simple shapes conjured from the dusty streets.

She thinks of the homonym, *reptiles,* and briefly considers ones that would fit each tile—two snakes, a turtle, a lazing lizard. Then combines them to create larger versions of the same basic shapes.

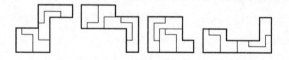

And again . . .

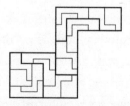

She leads Mojo around the block across the street, past the sawmill and park office. Then the larger block to Union Street and back. Larger still, through the parking lot. As she searches, she contemplates possibilities, calculates probabilities. Head injury. Amnesia. Stroke. Altered state. No. Occam's razor—she probably just fell.

The hands of Arizona's watch race around as her search expands. North to King Street. East past the schoolhouse. Wind whistles through weathered clapboards. Its pitch plagues her, mocks her feeble efforts to tune it out.

They traverse west again, through town and beyond, back to the cemetery knoll. At a large monument with a good view of town, she fetches the binoculars from her pack and scans for Mom—white shirt, jeans, medium height, dark hair in a ponytail. She recalls the red fleece jacket tied around her waist and starts over. Past the schoolhouse she scans, into the area closed to the public, to the stamp mill. She can barely make out the tiny ant people half a mile distant. Three of them, in a tight group. As if two are helping the one in the middle, the one in the white shirt. Mom? Arizona's insides twist. Her eyes strain to see a red jacket around the waist, but the ant people are too far away.

She races back through town, dragging Mojo whenever he stops or goes the wrong way. But when they arrive, she doesn't see anyone. She runs along the verge of the closed area and tries to fend off the unbidden sensations—weighted chest, prickled skin—but none of her safety poems will come to mind.

As she approaches a dilapidated shack that lists like a small boat in heavy seas, an older ranger steps around the corner and startles her. "Hello, miss," he says with a deep voice. "Are you looking for someone?"

She takes a deep breath, braces for the interaction. Maybe he'll be more helpful than the last ranger.

"Yes, my mom." She glances up at the tall man's caterpillar eyebrows. "We were supposed to meet at the church at four and it's almost six now." Arizona recounts the details of her search (though not its Euclidean structure) and the three people she had seen from the cemetery.

The ranger fetches the radio from his belt, steps four paces away, and relays everything. Arizona's eyes are drawn to him. First to his eyebrows, then to his light-blue eyes—as if his eyebrows are lures and his eyes the hooks. Looking at people's eyes is okay as long as they're not looking back.

He signs off and comes back. Her eyes return to his top button.

"Nobody has reported finding an injured person. But the park closes in a few minutes and we can conduct a search once all visitors have left. Do you live locally?"

Arizona doesn't reply. She looks around, as if searching for the answer.

"Miss, do you live locally?"

"No, we're camping in our trailer, down in the valley."

"I see," he says. "Do you want to wait at park headquarters while we search?"

"Can we help?"

"No, I'm afraid not. Sorry."

Arizona nods. Mojo whines.

"What's your dog's name?"

"Mojo."

"Is he hungry?"

"Probably. He's usually had dinner by now. And it's been dog days since he ate."

"Dog days?" he asks.

"Yeah, if one year is like seven years for a dog, then one day is like seven to him. He eats twice per human day, but it's probably been like three dog days since he had breakfast."

"That's funny. I never thought of it that way."

Of course you haven't, she thinks. Nobody thinks like her, except her dad. "You probably wouldn't think it was funny if you were a dog."

"No, probably not." He chuckles. "Do you have cell service at camp?"

"Two bars. Why?"

"If you give me names and numbers for you and your mom, and your camp location, then you could go back and feed Mojo. You'll probably be more comfortable waiting there anyway. I promise we'll call as soon as we find her."

Arizona thinks about it—four breaths pass—but she can't come up with any alternatives, so she pulls out her notebook. She asks the ranger's name—Stephen Gordon—jots it down, writes their information on a separate page, tears it out, and hands it to him.

"I'm sure we'll find her shortly," he says.

Arizona glances at his face, wonders if his expression is meant to reassure.

Several seconds pass before it occurs to her what to say. "Thank you."

BACK AT CAMP, ARIZONA parks the truck and follows Mojo inside their silver Airstream trailer. She thinks about calling someone. But who? She performs a genealogical inventory, but it takes only one breath. She has no siblings. There are no grandparents in the picture—Dad's parents died when he was in college, and Mom is estranged from hers. No aunts, uncles, or cousins, either—Dad was an only child, and Mom's only sibling died as a teenager. Her last words to her mom spring to mind. *I'm not your sister. I'm not going to kill myself.* Maybe she shouldn't have said that. Crap.

Mojo lies down in his backward fashion, chest first, then butt. She turns to look at him.

"Our family tree is a friggin' stump. But the park rangers are looking for Mom now, so it's out of our hands anyway."

She thinks Mojo looks relieved, too. Searching never should have been her responsibility. And if the first ranger hadn't been so dismissive, they could have started searching two hours earlier. She summoned all that courage to talk to him, too. Whatever.

She goes to the bathroom but doesn't look in the mirror. She doesn't like to look at herself. Besides, mirrors remind her of the school bathrooms, where she would go to hide. She finishes the roll of toilet paper, then smiles as she slides its naked cardboard tube through the two-inch gap beneath the bathroom door, where it is gently appropriated by soft black jowls. She sighs. Even this small thing reminds her of Dad, who called Mojo's tubes *fruit from the tree of a thousand wipes.* A tear rolls down her cheek. How she misses that dork, the only one who truly understood her. *That's probably not fair,* she tells herself. Mom may understand her pretty well, too. It's just that Dad didn't need to protect her. He trusted her to find her own way.

As Arizona exits the bathroom, Mojo looks to his bowl, back to her, then to his bowl again.

"Okay, buddy. I hear ya."

She feeds him and takes him for a walk by headlamp. She considers making dinner for herself but isn't hungry. Tries to read but can't focus. Every set of headlights she sees is another jab of hope. Is it the ranger bringing Mom home? But all the cars drive by or pull into other campsites. She does what she always does to calm the confused seas of her mind—she opens her notebook and writes.

> Orange glow of campfires,
> Smell of woodsmoke,
> Dry pine crackling,
> Laughter.
> Sights, smells, and sounds
> Of happy families.
> It's not fair.

But writing doesn't help this time. She closes the windows to tune out the sounds and smells, the cruel reminders of happier times. Where the hell is Mom? Dad would have known what to do. *Let's review the facts,* he would say. *Let's not jump to conclusions.* She replays her search in her mind. Thinks about the ant people half a mile distant. The red jacket she couldn't see. Was that Mom? She thinks about rep-tiles and reptiles and wants to turtle her dizzy head into her shell.

She curls up on the bed with Mojo, for comfort rather than sleep— knowing that the latter won't come.

"Sometimes you're the only thing that makes sense to me," she whispers.

Mojo smacks his lips repeatedly, like an old man deep in thought.

The unconditional love of a dog, of *her* dog, is all that keeps the weight of loss and confusion from crushing her. She holds him, his short tail twitching as he dreams.

3.

Sam Yeats

ARIZONA RUBS HER EYES, FOGGED BY A SLEEPLESS NIGHT. The black velvet curtain of Mojo's jowls lies draped across her calf. The sun is up. She checks her phone, nerves fluttering in her stomach. Why hasn't Stephen Gordon called? She phones the park but gets a recording. She feeds Mojo breakfast and makes herself some instant oatmeal to appease the hunger she can no longer ignore. But a sour taste in her mouth overwhelms the apples and cinnamon. She throws the dishes in the sink and they head for the truck.

A few miles from Bodie she passes a yellow warning sign, PAVEMENT ENDS, but doesn't slow down. They pull into the park five minutes after it opens.

She marches Mojo into park headquarters.

"Can I help you?" says a ranger.

Arizona doesn't reply. She doesn't look up to confirm, doesn't need to. That flicker, and the sound. She grimaces. Her eyelids quiver. She finds the switch by the door and turns the lights off.

"What are you doing?" the ranger says.

"I can't concentrate in fluorescent lighting. The buzzing sound triggers my misophonia." Arizona doesn't look up from the rough-planked floor.

"Okay," the ranger says, with a tone indicating it isn't. "I don't know what that is."

"It's a hypersensitivity to certain sounds, like people chewing. Regardless, I need to speak with the head ranger," Arizona says. "Please," she adds as an afterthought.

"I'm the supervising ranger, Samantha Yeats. But everyone calls me Sam."

"Any relation to W. B.?" Arizona asks as she writes in her notebook.

"Actually, yes," Sam says, with an eye on Arizona's note-taking. "He was my great-great-great-grandfather, give or take a great. What can I do for you, young lady?"

"Nobody called me after the search last night."

"I'm sorry, what search is that?"

"The search for my mother."

"I have no idea what you're talking about."

Arizona tastes copper. Wonders if she is going crazy.

"But yesterday I reported that my mother was missing. You conducted a search."

Sam arches her eyebrows. "Who did you report this to, and when?"

"Ranger Stephen Gordon, just before the park closed, at five fifty-five P.M. He called it in on his radio, said you'd conduct a search after all the visitors had left and that he'd call me. But he never called."

"Did you say Stephen Gordon?" says Sam. "Perhaps you got his name wrong?"

"I did *not* get his name wrong. He didn't have a name badge, so I asked him. I even had him spell it for me. And I wrote it down. Look." She flips back a page and holds the notebook for Sam to see. "Why did you think I got his name wrong?"

"Because we don't have a ranger by that name."

The world tilts, like in an old noir movie. "What?"

"I said we don't have a ranger by that name."

How can that be? Arizona's head is spinning. She puts a hand on the back of a chair.

"Are you okay?" Sam asks.

But the question is just noise. She takes two breaths. In through nose, out through mouth. She repeats herself, in silence. She asked his name. Had him spell it. Wrote it down. She looks at the page again, thankful that the name is still there. He was real. She can picture him.

"Pictures," she says.

"What's that?" Sam says.

"Do you have pictures of your rangers?"

"There's a group photo on the wall behind you."

Arizona examines the picture. Seven rangers, a prime number. They're not organized by height or in any other way as far as she can tell. "He's not here. But I also talked to this one, at around four."

Sam walks up to the photo. "That's Eric," she says. She returns to her desk and picks up a two-way radio. "Eric, come to HQ, please. Over." She turns back to Arizona. "Can you tell me everything that happened yesterday, starting with your name?"

Arizona grimaces at having to do this again, then recounts the events of the previous day in detail—leaving camp, separating from her mom, setting her phone alarm for pi time, her search, and her conversations with Eric and Stephen Gordon. Eric comes in while she is partway through and nods in agreement as she describes their conversation. Arizona wonders if her green eyes betray relief that Eric is real.

Sam listens without interrupting, which Arizona appreciates. Most people are far too eager to speak.

"Pi time?" Sam says. "Is that three-fourteen?"

"Exactly." The clouds in Arizona's mind part briefly, and she feels the warmth of being understood. The shadow of a smile passes over her face and then is gone.

"Eric, why didn't you report your conversation with Arizona?"

"Well, uh, I guess I figured that her mom showed up shortly after that. You know, otherwise she would have followed up with somebody."

"But I *did* follow up with somebody."

"Sorry, I didn't mean—" says Eric.

"All right, Eric. You can go, thanks." Sam returns her attention to Arizona. "What else can you tell me about this ranger Stephen Gordon?"

"He was tall, probably six foot four, medium build. Brown hair with a little gray on his temples. No facial hair. Bushy eyebrows. Dusty-blue eyes." Her quick breath fractures her speech. She pauses, tries to recall other details. "I didn't notice anything else. His uniform looked just like yours."

"Okay. I'll have to report this to the chief ranger. He oversees all law-enforcement aspects of the district. And he'll probably want to get the sheriff involved, too. Meanwhile, I'll get the search started for your mom." She tilts her head. "It's October. Shouldn't you be in school?"

"I'm homeschooled—or trailer-schooled, technically. We've been traveling almost full-time for the last three years. My dad used to call me a road scholar."

Sam chuckles, then wipes the smile away as the past tense sinks in. "Used to?"

"He died recently." Arizona keeps the rest of the thought to herself—*eighteen days ago.*

"I'm very sorry to hear that."

Arizona keeps her head down but nods. She is sorry, too. She raises a hand to her neck and cradles the figure-eight pendant her father had worn. Mojo whines, as if he knows her thoughts.

"No siblings?" Sam says.

She shakes her head. "It's just Mom, me, and Mojo now."

"How old are you, fourteen?" Sam says.

Arizona hesitates. What if they find out she's only seventeen? Will they turn her over to child protective services? "Eighteen." It's a small lie, but still it elicits a thorny feeling, like a bramble in her throat.

Even with her head down, Arizona registers the surprised look on Sam's face. Or is that suspicion rather than surprise? Is she about to get caught in a lie? "I don't suppose I can help with the search?"

"Sorry, no. You should probably go back to your camp. Hopefully we'll find your mom soon, but will you be okay on your own till then? Would you like someone from the sheriff's office to check on you?"

"I'll be fine." She doesn't look up. "Besides, I won't be on my own. I have Mojo."

"Okay." Sam pauses. "You don't look at people much, do you?"

"Why would I need to look at you when I know where you are?" Arizona raises her head briefly.

"Fair enough," Sam says with a wry smile. She slides a pad and pen across the desk. "Could you give me your phone number and camp location? Please."

Arizona scribbles the information for the second time, edits for legibility, and slides the pad back.

"Thanks." Sam stands up and extends a hand to Arizona. "I'll call you soon."

Arizona hesitates, then shakes Sam's hand because she knows it's expected. She leaves headquarters and lets Mojo finally pee on the dirt street. As they walk back to the truck, her mind is still racing—all questions and no answers. Can she trust Sam Yeats? After all, she went out on a limb with two other rangers, and see how that worked out. The friggin' limbs snapped right off. Eric dismissed her concerns, and then Stephen Gordon lied to her. Why would anyone pretend to be a ranger anyway? And where the hell is Mom?

4 •

The Airstream, the Note,
and the Mossberg Pump

ARIZONA ROTATES THE DEADBOLT KEY IN THE DOOR OF THE
Airstream but doesn't notice the lack of resistance. She holds
the door open for Mojo. He doesn't go in. He *always* goes in first.

She steps up into the doorway but can go no farther. The floor and
counter are seas of jetsam, littered with the contents of drawers, cup-
boards, pantry, and wardrobe, most of which still hang open. Twenty-
eight feet of chaos from the table at the back to the bed at the front.
The dining and daybed cushions lie askew like giant fabric-covered
jackstraws.

Arizona pushes debris away with the side of her foot, puts the
cushions back in place, and beckons Mojo onto the daybed. She sits
down at the table and calls her mom. Straight to voicemail. She assumes one of her many thinking poses—fingers interlaced, thumbs
against her chin, index fingers steepled. But it doesn't help. Tears fall
onto her folded hands. In the wake of her father's death, she has tried
to hold on to hope, but now it has slipped through her grasp.

She dries her face with a T-shirt sleeve, then begins straightening
up. She focuses on one storage space at a time, groups the items, then
rearranges the groups by relationship. Organization comes naturally to
Arizona. Elementary set theory. She can see the Venn diagrams in her
mind's eye.

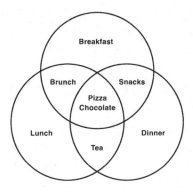

But the overlapping circles remind her of Dad's tattoo. She can't escape, haunted by degrees of separation.

Her eyes drift across the remaining mess and lock on to something she doesn't recognize—a folded piece of paper on the counter. She slides it from beneath its Coke-can paperweight and unfolds the typewritten note.

> **Your father should have provided us with the information that we seek. His death could have been avoided. Now we have your mother. With your father gone and your mother unable or unwilling to help us, it is up to you. Attached is a test. If you're of no use to us, the same is true for your mother. You've already lost one parent. It would be tragic to lose the other. We'll be watching.**

"Kidnapped?" she says aloud, as if questioning her own comprehension. Mom was kidnapped. What the frick. What information? Dad's death was just an accident. Who . . . But the question doesn't even finish forming in her mind before the answer comes. Stephen Gordon. But who is he?

She looks at the second page of the note:

```
QAUVGTUJCXGDGCTFUUCKFNCFADKTF
UKPIHNKGUUKPIHTQIUUKPIHKFFNGUVTKPIU
LORYHWKHPIRULNQRZ
WKHBQHYHUFKDWWHUVR
YMJDBTZQISTYXFDTSJXNSLQJBTWI
STYNKDTZHWTBSJIYMJRPNSLX
DVYKZOHCLWVDLYZHPKSHKFIPYK
ZPUNZSHNZZPUNZSBNZZPUNZPUALYLKJSHF
QZCESPTCCTRSEDEZLXPYO
XLRYFXZAFDSPAPYYPO
LRGGJBFPBERNAQCNEGBSNGUVEQ
CNFFRQSBEROVEQFUNQGURVEFNL
WZIVYRJCZWVJRZUCRUPSZIU
JZEXAZXXVIPGFBVIPAVVIZEXAZSV
YNLXWPBMAPTMXKBMUEHHFL
TFHGZIBHGXXKMHFUL
XQLHBKLKPQLKBPLXSBOOBA
CLOJBPPBKDBOXKAPZOFYB
```

The ransacking wasn't a robbery. They were looking for something.

She goes to the nearest window. Hunched over, eyes just above the sill, she scrutinizes the scene. Are they still there, watching her? Not seeing anyone, she closes the window and the blind and goes to the next window. The sweet smell of sagebrush wafts in. Her stomach roils. She recites one of her safety poems as she scans her surroundings and closes windows and blinds.

'Twas brillig, and the slithy toves
Did gyre and gimble in the wabe;
All mimsy were the borogoves,
And the mome raths outgrabe.

But the anxiety can't be tuned out. She gets through five verses before her oatmeal comes galumphing back.

As she cleans up—herself and then the rest of the trailer—her eyes mushroom with recollection. She rushes to the bedroom and stumbles over the remaining debris. On her knees, she opens the secret panel below the TV, behind a magazine rack. There, under the floor of the shower, is Dad's shotgun.

Arizona pulls out the Mossberg 590 and a box of shells. She finds the action-lock lever, to the left rear of the trigger guard, presses it, and slides the forearm back to open the ejection port, just like Dad taught her. The chamber is empty, but the butt end of a shell is visible in the tubular magazine. She pushes on the end of the shell, compressing the spring at the other end. It moves a short distance and stops—the magazine is still fully loaded with eight shells. She puts the box of shells back, closes the compartment, and double-checks to make sure she locked the Airstream door. She did.

She sits down on the edge of a cushion and thinks. The note said that Dad's death could have been avoided, but the authorities said his motorcycle accident in Titus Canyon was just that, an accident, most likely brake failure. Are the kidnappers implying they killed him? Or are they just trying to scare her? If so, it's working.

Who can she trust? She asks herself the question but already knows the answer. Nobody but Mojo. She replays her list of betrayals. Kids. Teachers. Dad. She trusted Mom to meet her at four. She trusted Stephen Gordon and told him where they were camped. She also told Sam, who will involve the sheriff. And if they find out that she's only seventeen, with Dad dead and Mom missing, the sheriff will call child protective services.

"Foster care for me and the pound for you, buddy? No, we have to find Mom on our own. It's time to run."

She walks out to the truck and slides the shotgun under Mojo's blanket in back—hidden but within reach. It's illegal to drive with a loaded gun in California, but she doesn't care. She backs the truck up to the trailer (even with the backup camera it takes five tries), hitches up, and removes the wheel chocks. She tosses the WIPE YOUR PAWS welcome mat into the rear of the truck, tightens the straps holding her sidecar motorcycle to its custom rack in the pickup's bed, and walks around the campsite to make sure she hasn't left anything.

Mom's plastic pink flamingos stand right where she perched them the previous morning, before they left for Bodie. Lawn kitsch owned by a woman with a master's degree in fine art. The incongruity, the quirkiness, is part of what makes Mom special. Arizona stares at the flamingos for five breaths. She's standing still but feels like she's stumbling through fog. No control. No clarity. A tear rolls down her cheek as she recalls their last exchange with a pang of guilt.

She puts the flamingos away with care, as Mom would have. As she does, she notices that each flamingo stands on two thin metal legs. How curious. Wouldn't a single leg be more appropriate? Then she wonders why she's never wondered that before. After fetching Mojo and a can of Coke, she folds up the Airstream's steps and locks the door, and they head for the truck.

Arizona pulls up to the stop sign at Highway 395. She knows the east side of the Sierras well from traveling with her parents. She looks past the converging painted lines to the north—Bridgeport, Topaz Lake on the California–Nevada border, the Carson Valley, and, if she turns west and keeps going, Lake Tahoe, the Sierra crest, and eventually the family home in Gold Country, the foothills of the western slope. But home seems too far away. She just needs to feel safe, to be able to think clearly.

She turns and looks south—Lee Vining, the June Lake loop, Mammoth Lakes, Bishop, and Big Pine. Even farther south are Lone Pine and the Alabama Hills, one of her favorite places on the east side. The good memories pull her heart south, like a rubber band stretched to the breaking point. But, like home, the Alabama Hills are too far away.

She turns north and accelerates to 55 mph, the towing speed limit. As the miles bleed into one another and the lines on the tarmac blur, thoughts swirl inside her head like mist. A painful, dangerous mist, like something out of a Stephen King story.

Dead father.

Kidnapped mother.

Fake ranger.

Ransacked trailer.

Ransom note.

And a cryptogram, a cipher. Her thoughts turn to the past.

5

A Puzzling Present

THE MORNING OF HER FIFTEENTH BIRTHDAY HAD STARTED like most. Arizona scanned her shelf of favorite books, arranged alphabetically by author—Agatha Christie, Arthur Conan Doyle, Rudyard Kipling, Edgar Allan Poe, Mary Shelley, Robert Louis Stevenson, Mark Twain, Jules Verne, H. G. Wells—as she ran her index finger across the worn leather spines of each volume. They had been her dad's (and his father's before that), and his favorite authors had become hers, too. Written when the American West was still the Wild West. Written in formal, fastidious language that felt so natural to Arizona.

She had all of these books and more on her iPad, too, but preferred the physical over the digital. The feel of a real book in her hand. The weight of it and of the wisdom within. The whisper of the pages. The aroma of ink, of paper, of time itself.

She stuffed a book into her pack and began her bedroom-departure ritual, touching each Airstream in her collection—the Airstream cookie jar, the Airstream and station wagon salt-and-pepper shakers, the Matchbox-scale Airstream, the larger-scale Franklin Mint Airstream with awning deployed, and—her favorite—the Lego Airstream. Last, on her way out the door, she ruffled the mop of white hair on the Albert Einstein marionette, which her parents had given her when they realized that she was a visual thinker, like Einstein. She thought in images and visual patterns, allowing her curious mind to see things that others would miss—be it in the everyday or in the extraordinary. The dapper marionette in a white lab coat had starred in a puppet show explaining the theory of relativity to Mojo, who had listened attentively between snores. But visual thinking wasn't all that Arizona shared with Einstein. Pinned to the coat of the marionette was her membership pin from Mensa.

She rushed to the breakfast table, hoping to see a mountain of presents, but there was only an envelope. Her stomach grumbled at the aroma of fresh pancakes while her parents wore sly grins.

"Go ahead, open it," said Mom, as Dad nodded in agreement.

Arizona picked up the envelope and turned it over. On the front was written *The Case of the Puzzling Present*. Eyes wide, she tore the envelope open. Inside was a card that read:

> mdtrop dtngu tremns etneh iaraor
> eauhso eglgo fefsdm tieru pnfrsf
> sauihr foiot uuoudo htueb klhoee
> nmyeet heddg swvkon fsntw rnuila
> ameaue uoaao hlhsnh sevos ygbtae
> eoweso yddns wmwnyd matrn uorool
> ronoem oarle ndlaga clofg oshkea

She always enjoyed a good puzzle, so sometimes her parents made her work for her presents. Not every birthday, not every Christmas. The timing was unpredictable, like the puzzles and the presents.

She ran back to her room, typed the message into a new document on her Mac laptop, and double- and triple-checked to make sure she hadn't made a mistake. *That's weird,* she thought, while gnawing on her lower lip. Every word had five or six letters. She changed the font to Courier so that every letter would be the same width:

```
mdtrop dtngu tremns etneh iaraor
eauhso eglgo fefsdm tieru pnfrsf
sauihr foiot uuoudo htueb klhoee
nmyeet heddg swvkon fsntw rnuila
ameaue uoaao hlhsnh sevos ygbtae
eoweso yddns wmwnyd matrn uorool
ronoem oarle ndlaga clofg oshkea
```

Not only was every line the same length, but all the spaces lined up in perfect columns. That certainly wasn't normal, and it probably wasn't coincidence, either. The words couldn't all be the same length, so were the spaces a red herring, meant to mislead her?

She deleted the spaces between the words, but then it was just a jumbled mess, so she added spaces between each letter to help her look for patterns:

```
m d t r o p d t n g u t r e m n s e t n e h i a r a o r
e a u h s o e g l g o f e f s d m t i e r u p n f r s f
s a u i h r f o i o t u u o u d o h t u e b k l h o e e
n m y e e t h e d d g s w v k o n f s n t w r n u i l a
a m e a u e u o a a o h l h s n h s e v o s y g b t a e
e o w e s o y d d n s w m w n y d m a t r n u o r o o l
r o n o e m o a r l e n d l a g a c l o f g o s h k e a
```

Now it looked like a word-search puzzle, so she wrote down the words she could find:

port, tits, she, lid, god, tier, up, don, hub, yew, dad, sea, seal, use, soy, lend, lag

But that didn't help. With pursed lips and an exaggerated grimace, she counted the letters. Seven lines of twenty-eight letters. One hundred ninety-six.

"The square of fourteen?" she muttered. It was possible that was just coincidence. But considering the odds, not likely. And a square number meant the letters could be arranged into a perfect square. She split the seven lines into fourteen, creating a fourteen-by-fourteen square:

```
m   d   t   r   o   p   d   t   n   g   u   t   r   e
m   n   s   e   t   n   e   h   i   a   r   a   o   r
e   a   u   h   s   o   e   g   l   g   o   f   e   f
s   d   m   t   i   e   r   u   p   n   f   r   s   f
s   a   u   i   h   r   f   o   i   o   t   u   u   o
u   d   o   h   t   u   e   b   k   l   h   o   e   e
n   m   y   e   t   h   e   d   d   g   s   w   v
k   o   n   f   s   n   t   w   r   n   u   i   l   a
a   m   e   a   u   e   u   o   a   a   o   h   l   h
s   n   h   s   e   v   o   s   y   g   b   t   a   e
e   o   w   e   s   o   y   d   d   n   s   w   m   w
n   y   d   m   a   t   r   n   u   o   r   o   o   l
r   o   n   o   e   m   o   a   r   l   e   n   d   l
a   g   a   c   l   o   f   g   o   s   h   k   e   a
```

She searched for words again:

gut, mess, sum, hire, oft, dad, nib, sunk, old, mom, sue, sues, ray, nag, hew, sod, soy, won, mod, mat, tog, ode

Two words leapt out—*dad* and *mom*—spelled vertically, back-to-back, in the second column. She scanned the next column for another word, but that didn't help. *Tsumu, nehwd* . . . just nonsense. But *dad* and *mom* couldn't be a coincidence on a birthday puzzle. She pondered for a couple of seconds.

Dad and *mom* were both palindromes. Which meant you could read them from bottom to top, as well as from top to bottom. Arizona tilted her head to the left and sounded out the words starting with *mom*, from bottom to top.

"Mom, dad, and . . ."

She tried the third column, again from bottom to top.

"And when you must . . ."

Okay, what about the first column?

And then she saw it.

"Arne Saknussemm!" she shouted.

"I told you we should have made it harder," Dad said from the kitchen.

At the beginning of one of Arizona's favorite books, Jules Verne's *Journey to the Center of the Earth*, the main characters found and decoded a puzzle from Arne Saknussemm, a cryptogram written vertically and backward.

She opened the complete works of Jules Verne on her iPad, searched for *Saknussemm*, and copied a quote into her notebook.

"Arne Saknussemm!" he cried in triumph. "Why that is the name of another Icelander, a savant of the sixteenth century, a celebrated alchemist!" . . . "Those alchemists," he resumed, "Avicenna, Bacon, Lully, Paracelsus, were the real and only savants of their time. They made discoveries at which we are astonished. Has not this Saknussemm concealed under his cryptogram some surprising invention? It is so; it must be so!"

Arizona returned to her computer screen and, starting at the lower right of the square, read aloud vertically, continuing with each column until she had sounded out the entire square. She smiled, typed the decoded message into her computer, and added punctuation:

All we have of freedom, all we use or know,
This our fathers bought for us long and long ago.
—RUDYARD KIPLING

And so we bought for you the freedom to venture on.
Please use this to come safe hither and, when you must,
go yon.
—MOM, DAD, AND
ARNE SAKNUSSEMM

She couldn't recall which Rudyard Kipling poem the first two lines were from, but she appreciated the nod nonetheless.

It had been a fun puzzle, but now it was a riddle. The freedom to venture on? Come and go, hither and yon?

She grinned. Arizona had been dropping not-so-subtle hints that a mountain bike would allow her to explore much farther from home. But her dad had argued that Mojo wouldn't be able to keep up over the distances she liked to explore (and that he was too big for a bike basket or backpack).

She wondered why they had changed their minds. *Who cares?* She ran back to the kitchen, slid across the tile floor and past the breakfast table with Mojo in tow.

"Where are you going, dear?" said Mom.

"To find my new mountain bike, of course." Arizona ran out the kitchen door and headed for the detached garage, its aging cedar-shingled roof not quite steep enough to shed the thatch of needles from sheltering ponderosa pines.

By the time her parents were outside, Arizona had swung open the barn-style doors of the old garage. She bumbled around for the poorly placed light switch as the pungent smell of fresh-cut grass wafted from the lawnmower. Next to her dad's Ural sidecar motorcycle was something covered with a worn canvas tarp, besmirched with a decoupage of paint stains and topped with a red bow. It was about the height of a bike and wider at one end, where the handlebars would be. She thought they could have disguised it better.

"What are you waiting for? Go on, dear," Mom said from the garage doorway.

Arizona rushed forward, grabbed the tarp, and flung it off. She stood still, blinking in disbelief. It wasn't a mountain bike but a motorcycle. She turned to face her parents.

"You bought me a motorcycle? But your objection to the mountain bike was that Mojo wouldn't be able to keep up. How's he going to keep up if I'm on a motorcycle?"

"You haven't finished yet, honey," said Dad, with raised eyebrows and a smile as he pointed toward a corner of the garage that was still in shadow.

Eyes wide, Arizona spun around so fast it startled Mojo. She squinted into the shadows, past the shelf of dust-covered tools and the scarred surface of the wooden workbench, its vise a miniature ghost under a greasy rag. In the far corner was another tarp with a bow but shorter, lower to the ground. She rushed over and tore off the tarp, exposing a sidecar.

"It's just like yours, Dad," she said.

"Yes. It's used, of course, but in pretty good condition all things considered. After *the adventure gone a little long,* we thought this would help you explore farther but still get home before dark."

Arizona straddled the seat, put her hands on the grips, and worked the clutch and front brake as if zipping along under the power of its twin-cylinder engine.

"Aren't you forgetting something?" said Mom, as Dad moved the sidecar next to the motorcycle.

"Mojo, sidecar," Arizona said to her best friend, who eagerly complied. Her parents had even put a blanket in the sidecar for him.

Arizona beamed. Mojo wagged his short boxer tail.

6.

The Cipher Disk

B Y THE TIME ARIZONA GETS TO THE NEVADA BORDER, SHE has a destination in mind—a small state park where the family camped once, just north of Carson City. Far enough for safety, familiar enough for comfort. The park has a shallow lake that was completely dry when they visited before, and they had hiked out into the middle of the dusty basin. That was during the drought years, and she wonders if the lake will have water this time.

As she and Mojo drive past the piñon forest between Topaz Lake and Gardnerville, she thinks about numbers again. Of more than one hundred species of pine trees worldwide, single-leaf piñon is the only species with single needles borne on the branches. All other pine trees have needles in bundles of two, three, four, or five. She can understand two, three, or five needles, since they're all prime numbers, but who thought four was a good idea?

They pass Carson City and she pictures the legendary frontiersman Kit Carson, whose many namesakes pepper the area. As they approach the state park, quaking aspens and arroyo willows mark the springs— both hot and cold—of the Carson Range.

The small campground is mostly empty and she finds a pull-through site, a welcome reprieve from the anxiety of trying to back the trailer up. More anxiety is the last thing she needs. She practiced backing up in a parking lot with traffic cones once, but it didn't go well for the cones. Unsure how long they'll stay, she leaves the trailer hitched up.

She takes Mojo for a walk around the campground, through the dappled shade of young cottonwood trees, past the few other campers. As they finish the loop, they approach an old VW camper van. Arizona doesn't remember it being there when they pulled in. Was she just too focused on parking the trailer? They walk by and its curtains tremble. The last words of the note race through her mind. *We'll be watching.*

She strides across the sand-ringed tarmac of their campsite, retrieves the shotgun from the truck as discreetly as possible, and unfolds the steps of the trailer with a loud metallic clap that she immediately regrets. It's best not to draw unnecessary attention when carrying a gun. She follows Mojo inside and locks the door. Fills Mojo's water bowl, sits down, and looks at her phone. She has voicemail.

"Hello, Arizona. This is Sam Yeats at Bodie State Park. Please call me back as soon as possible. This is my cell number. If you need to reach me during park hours, call the park directly, since cell phones don't work there. Thanks, Arizona. Hope to talk to you soon."

Arizona hesitates, then taps CALL BACK.

Sam picks up on the third ring. "Sam Yeats speaking."

"Hey, Sam. It's Arizona."

"Hi, Arizona. Thanks for calling me back."

Arizona's not expecting Sam to have any answers, but still her breath catches in her throat as she asks, "Have you found her?"

"I'm sorry," Sam says. "I wish I was calling with better news. But there's no sign of her here. We've searched most of town and near the stamp mill where you saw someone you thought could be her, but we still have to check the outlying areas."

Arizona sighs, not from the news but from withholding the truth. Of course they haven't found her. She didn't just fall and hit her head. She was taken.

"I do have one minor update. Eric thought to check our uniform inventory and found that an extra-large uniform was missing."

"Extra-large," Arizona says. "Stephen Gordon's size."

"Exactly. Unfortunately, the missing uniform has me wondering who I can trust, other than Eric, of course."

"Okay," Arizona says. It somehow feels inadequate, but she doesn't know what else to say.

"Well, I'll check in again when the search is complete. Be careful, Arizona."

"Thanks."

Arizona's mouth forms a lopsided moue. Sam mentioned trust. A part of her wants to trust Sam, but a bigger part can't.

She takes three deep breaths and switches her focus to the cipher, which she hopes will be a productive distraction from her feelings—or, more accurately, from the physical symptoms that help her identify her feelings (sometimes). Usually she can switch off and concentrate, at least if she is alone or with Mojo, but the stupid switch has been sticking of late.

Her birthday puzzle had been a transposition cipher, the letters merely rearranged. But transposition ciphers are neither common nor particularly secure. She expects that the cipher attached to the kidnapper's note is a substitution cipher, with letters representing other letters. She scratches her head, refreshes her memory. If each letter is encoded by a different substitution alphabet—a polyalphabetic substitution cipher—then she'd need a keyword, but she doesn't have a friggin' keyword. She thinks about using online decryption tools, but her parents taught her to think twice before sharing information online. And stuff that people are willing to kidnap for doesn't seem like it should be an exception.

"Etaoin shrdlu," she murmurs. The twelve most common letters in the English language, in order. She opens Arthur Conan Doyle's complete works on her iPad, finds a quote, and copies it into her notebook.

As you are aware, E is the most common letter in the English alphabet, and it predominates to so marked an extent that even in a short sentence one would expect to find it most often.

—SHERLOCK HOLMES,
"THE ADVENTURE OF
THE DANCING MEN"

In other words, if the cipher uses a single substitution alphabet—a monoalphabetic substitution cipher—whatever letter occurs the most in the cipher text *should* equate to E in the plain text.

She wakes up her MacBook, creates a new spreadsheet with columns labeled *Letter* and *Count,* and types the alphabet in the left-hand column, one letter per row. She counts the number of times the letter A appears in the cipher text, then B, and so on. When she is done, she sorts it by count, with the largest count at the top.

Letter	Count
P	28
U	26
Z	26
K	24
F	22
H	21
B	21
L	20
N	19
X	18
S	18
Y	17
T	16
I	16
V	15
R	15
Q	14
G	13
C	13
A	12
J	12
E	12
D	11
O	10
W	10
M	6

The most common monoalphabetic substitution cipher is called a Caesar shift, where each letter is shifted right or left in the alphabet by the same number. For example, if A moves over two letters to become C, then B becomes D, et cetera.

In that case, the easiest decryption tool is a cipher disk, made of two concentric rings, each labeled with the alphabet, and one of which rotates. She thinks of the cipher disk she has at home, made of brass. Dad gave it to her after she read "The Adventure of the Dancing Men" and wanted to do more cryptography. Home. Parents. It's where all thoughts lead. Only the degrees of separation change. She counts. Cipher disk, home, parents. Only two degrees of separation. So much for distraction.

She finds a cipher-disk template online, downloads and prints it. After cutting out the two circles, she tapes the larger one to the bottom of a cardboard box, centers the smaller circle on top, and inserts a pushpin through the center. She picks up and admires her makeshift cipher disk, her fingers curled gently beneath the box that Mojo donated from a case of canned dog food. A smile passes over her lips like a shiver, bequeathed by a ghost of happier times.

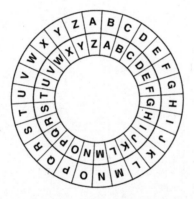

Since P is the most frequent letter, she rotates the inner disk until P lines up with E on the outer disk.

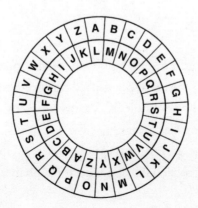

She writes down the first six letters of cipher text, spaced out, finds each letter on the inner disk, and writes the corresponding letter from the outer disk below.

Q A U V G T
F P J K V I

Gibberish. The letter U is the next most common, so she rotates the inner disk until U lines up with E and decodes again.

Q A U V G T
A K E F Q D

Just more nonsense. She continues searching for the elusive E, going down through her frequency list. She tries Z, F, K, H, L, N, B, X, Y, I, and S, all with no success. How could the letter E be so infrequent? Not knowing what else to do, she keeps going down the list. After three more attempts, she rotates the inner disk until G lines up with E and tries again.

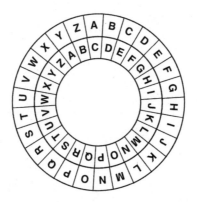

Q A U V G T
O Y S T E R

"Oyster?" Arizona says, waking Mojo from a nap. "Oh, sorry, buddy."

But *oyster*? What sort of secret message starts with *oyster*? She wonders if it could just be a decoding coincidence. She writes out two full lines of the cipher text, giggles at the FUUCK she hadn't previously noticed, and tests it.

```
Q A U V G T U J C X G D G C T F U U C K F N C F A D K T F
O Y S T E R S H A V E B E A R D S S A I D L A D Y B I R D


U K P I H N K G U U K P I H T Q I U U K P I H K F F N G U V T K P I U
S I N G F L I E S S I N G F R O G S S I N G F I D D L E S T R I N G S
```

Oysters have beards, said Lady Bird.
Sing flies, sing frogs, sing fiddle strings.
She knows those words. But from where? She writes out another line of the cipher text and tries to decode it.

```
L O R Y H W K H P I R U L N Q R Z
J M P W F U
```

Rubbish again. Crap.

7 ·

The Captive

A DOOR CREAKS OPEN. SHE OPENS HER EYES, DISORIENTED. She is seated in a chair, hands bound behind her to something rough and wooden. She wriggles her fingers and rocks the chair, to no avail but increased pain. As her vision adjusts to the dim light, more details come into focus. She is in a narrow room, facing a wall with no windows or doors. Light streams through cracks between old wall boards, highlighting the dust motes that tickle her throat. The planked floor is dirty and uneven. There is a cot in the corner. Against the far wall are a bucket and a roll of toilet paper, but it's not clear how she's supposed to reach them.

"Hello," says a male voice from behind her. A tall man wearing a black balaclava walks past and turns to face her. He is holding some papers. "How do you feel?"

"Like I've been drugged," she says. "Who the hell are you, and where is my daughter?"

"The effects of the sedative will wear off soon enough. You can call me Mr. Gordon. Your daughter is fine and free. If we wanted her here, she'd be here."

"Why should I believe you?"

"Would you rather believe that your daughter is in captivity?"

She doesn't answer, doesn't want to give him anything. Besides, her mind is still muddled. But she can feel her temperature rising, her chest tightening.

"I didn't think so," he says after several seconds. "As you can no doubt discern from the spartan accommodations, you're in a very remote location. Trying to escape would be pointless, because there's nothing around for miles."

That won't stop me from trying, she thinks.

"Likewise, nobody will hear you if you scream. But keep in mind that the lack of gag is a courtesy. If you start screaming, we'll gag you just to eliminate the annoyance. Understood?"

Her heart races, but she doesn't respond, not even with a nod. What the hell is happening?

"Is that understood?" he repeats. "Or should I just gag you now?"

"I understand." She sighs. "What do you want from me?"

"We have reason to believe that your husband had the key to a closely guarded secret."

Her eyebrows and forehead scrunch into a corduroy of confusion. "I must have misheard you. A closely guarded secret?"

He nods. "Guarded by powerful people in the United States government. Your husband worked for the U.S. government, did he not?"

She blinks. "Yeah, he was a cartographer for the U.S. Geological Survey. But the USGS isn't exactly in the secret-keeping business."

"Maybe he didn't work for the USGS at all. Maybe that was a cover."

"Do you know how ridiculous that sounds? I'd laugh if I wasn't fucking tied up."

She thinks he smiles, but it's hard to tell through the balaclava.

"Look," she says, "you've clearly got the wrong person. I'd know if my husband had any secrets. But even if he did, the secrets died with him."

"That would be most unfortunate for you, because this secret is the price of your freedom."

"I don't understand."

He holds one of the papers in front of her eyes. "Do you recognize this?"

"You're kidding, right? It looks like nonsense."

"It's a cipher. Do you think you could solve it?"

"No, my husband was the one into codes."

"I understand that your daughter is pretty good with codes, too."

How could he know that? "No, not really," she says, but she wonders if her flushed face betrays the lie.

He pulls the paper away. "We've been watching your family for some time. Your husband's death was most . . . untimely."

"I'm sorry that he inconvenienced you." Her eyes are on fire.

"We believe your husband was actively pursuing the secret at the time of his death."

"What are you talking about? He wasn't pursuing anything, except fun. We were camping. He went for a motorcycle ride through a desert canyon and crashed."

"What were you and your daughter doing in Bodie?" he says.

"Primarily just visiting, same as everyone else. But, also, my husband loved Bodie and requested that some of his ashes be left there. Not that it's any of your business."

"So your husband just happened to be in that very particular place when he died, and weeks later you just happen to show up in Bodie? You expect me to believe that it's merely coincidence?"

"I didn't say it was coincidence. My husband asked us to leave some of his ashes there. Listen much?"

"And you also happen to live near Nevada City? So that's just another coincidence?"

"What does Nevada City have to do with anything?" Her eyes are the size of coasters. Where is he going with this?

He walks behind her. Floorboards creak. She feels breath on her neck. Her feet are swept backward beneath the chair, so fast and far that she would fall forward if she wasn't bound.

"Hey! What the fuck?"

"I don't think you're being forthcoming, so you're losing the chair. I'll free your hands in a minute, but first I'm going to bind your legs to this post. It's going to be very tight, so if you struggle, you're just going to hurt yourself."

Cable ties zip closed, the pressure around her ankles increasing with each zip. When her hand restraints are cut, she swings her arms forward and massages the reddened skin on her wrists.

"Now get down on your knees so I can remove the chair."

"Is that really necessary?"

"Move."

She tries to move to her knees gracefully, but it's impossible with her legs bound to the post. Her right knee hits the floor hard, followed by her right arm, shoulder, and side of her head. She twists her dust-covered torso to look at her captor.

He moves the chair to the side, walks out of the room, and closes the door.

She raises herself onto her knees and dusts herself off. Is Arizona really free? If so, where is she? *How* is she? How is she coping on her own? The questions bring to mind their last exchange. *Differences, not disorders.* And Arizona's reply. *I don't need to be protected. I'm not your sister. I'm not going to kill myself.* The words weren't meant to hurt, but they did. They hurt even in recollection. But maybe Arizona is right. After not being able to protect her sister—who would have been Arizona's aunt—from their father, she needed to protect everyone else. Maybe she's been even more overprotective since her husband's death, in the absence of his counterbalance? Then again, since people have been stalking the family, maybe not. But how could she have protected Arizona from them anyway?

"Fuck," she says under her breath.

8.

Active Voice and the King-fisher Song

ARIZONA NEEDS SOME FRESH AIR, SOME ACTIVITY TO CLEAR her mind. Dad always said that his best thoughts came when his mind was relaxed by physical activity. In a nod to the career path left untraveled, as a writer, he called it his *active voice*. Arizona inherited that from him, too. Dad. Mom. She touches her cheek and finds it wet. Mom, *where* are you?

She walks Mojo over the low dunes that separate the campground from the lake, which, while not full, does have water this time. She wonders how deep it is, tries to distract herself by doing the math based on estimates of shoreline angle and distance, but she can't focus. Mojo's ears (which stand up halfway before falling down on the job) flap in a steady breeze that carries the sounds of seagulls and the smells of lakeshore.

Her senses carry her to a memory. She is paddling her kayak through Drakes Estero in Point Reyes National Seashore. Sun on her arms, salt on her lips. The wingtips of bat rays break the surface ahead of her. Leopard sharks forage in the shallow tidal waters as she glides over them. California brown pelicans dive into the water near the oyster farm.

The oysters bring her back to the present.

"Oysters have beards, said Lady Bird," she says under her breath. *"Sing flies, sing frogs, sing fiddle strings."*

"Lewis Carroll," a voice says from behind her.

Arizona starts. "What the frick?" She turns around to face a young woman with a freckled face and strawberry-blond hair partly hidden beneath a kerchief.

"Sorry, didn't mean to startle you," she says. "Personally, I find *fuck* much more satisfying than any of the toned-down variants, but maybe that's just me." She smiles.

Arizona nods for lack of a better response.

"I'm Lily and that's Gus." She points to her French bulldog, who is busy giving Mojo a sniff-over. "We're in the yellow VW camper. I saw you pull in right ahead of us. You're in the Airstream, right?"

"Yes," Arizona says. "Like the flower?"

"I'm sorry?"

"Lily, like the flower."

"Oh, yes, exactly." Lily smiles again.

Arizona finds her eyes on Lily's freckles, forces them down. One breath. In and out. "I'm Arizona and that's Mojo."

"Like the state?"

"Yes, exactly."

"Well, it's nice to meet you, Arizona-like-the-state."

"It's just Arizona."

"Sorry, I was trying to be funny. That was Lewis Carroll you were reciting, right? *Oysters have beards, said Lady Bird*?"

"Uh, yeah. I guess it was." *Lewis Carroll?* Of course. She feels so stupid. "I . . . have to go." Another lie. Or is it? The throat bramble is back regardless.

"Oh, okay. See you around camp, I guess." Lily waves, a hand raised halfway.

Arizona mimics the gesture, then rushes back to the Airstream with Mojo in tow. Racing over the low dune, they startle a deer as it browses on golden blooms of rubber rabbitbrush, then scurry past the VW camper van. The curtains are still closed, but they no longer menace—Lily doesn't look like a kidnapper. But then again, you can't judge a book by its cover.

Arizona locks the Airstream door behind them, opens Lewis Carroll's complete works, and searches for *oysters*. She is surprised by the number of matches, then nods as she remembers the oysters in Twee-dledum and Tweedledee. She scrolls through the search results and there it is:

> Chapter I. Bruno's Lessons.
> "Oysters have beards," said Lady Bird—

She taps the search entry and reads the four verses of "The King-fisher Song." The borrowed lines are from Carroll's third verse:

> "Oysters have beards," said Lady Bird—
> Sing Flies, sing Frogs, sing Fiddle-strings!
> "I love them, for I know
> They never chatter so:
> They would not say one single word—
> Not if you crowned them Kings!"

Arizona squeezes her left earlobe between thumb and forefinger, hanging the entire weight of her arm there while she thinks. She looks at her cipher disk.

The G-to-E mapping worked for two lines of the poem, then broke, which means that the cipher isn't strictly monoalphabetic. But if it was truly polyalphabetic, with a different shift for every letter, the cipher disk wouldn't have worked at all. What if it's something in be-tween? Rather than changing the shift for every letter, maybe they changed it every two lines? Pretty clever, actually. Kind of a poor man's polyalphabetic cipher. That would explain why the frequency analysis didn't work over the whole cipher text. But it probably would have worked over just the first two lines. So maybe it'll work for the next two lines. She repeats the letter-counting process for lines three and four. H is the most common letter. She rotates the inner disk until H lines up with E and decodes again.

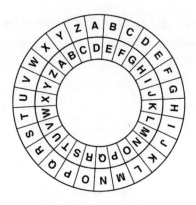

L O R Y H W K H P I R U L N Q R Z
I L O V E T H E M F O R I K N O W

I love them, for I know.

That's how frequency analysis is supposed to work. She smiles and decodes the fourth line, using the same H-to-E mapping.

W K H B Q H Y H U F K D W W H U V R
T H E Y N E V E R C H A T T E R S O

They never chatter so.

She tries line five but it doesn't work, which seems to confirm that they changed the shift every two lines. Arizona repeats the letter-counting process for lines five and six. T is the most common letter, so she rotates the inner disk until T lines up with E and tries to decode again, but it just produces gibberish. So she moves on to the next most common letter, S, but the output is still garbage. The third most common letter is J, which finally works.

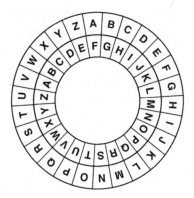

YMJDBTZQISTYXFDTSJXNSLQJBTWI
THEYWOULDNOTSAYONESINGLEWORD

STYNKDTZHWTBSJIYMJRPNSLX
NOTIFYOUCROWNEDTHEMKINGS

They would not say one single word.
Not if you crowned them kings.

So far it's all from Carroll's poem. But why encrypt a published poem? And why start with the third verse? Weird.

She counts letters in lines seven and eight and tries to decode. The most common letter is Z, but equating that with E produces garbage. Unfortunately, the next several most common letters also don't work, so she keeps going, until she equates L with E.

DVYKZOHCLWVDLYZHPKSHKFIPYK
WORDSHAVEPOWERSAIDLADYBIRD

ZPUNZSHNZZPUNZSBNZZPUNZPUALYLKJSHF
SINGSLAGSSINGSLUGSSINGSINTEREDCLAY

Words have power, said Lady Bird.
Sing slags, sing slugs, sing sintered clay.

Those words aren't from Carroll's poem. Arizona stares at the cipher disk. The first two lines are shifted by only two letters—E becomes G. Then three letters—E becomes H—for the next two lines. Then five letters—E becomes J. Then seven—E becomes L. Interesting. Each shift has been greater than the previous one. She tilts her head, like Mojo trying to better hear a sound, and it works. Perspective is everything.

Shifts of two, three, five, and seven. Prime numbers. The next prime number is eleven, four more than seven. She rotates the inner disk by four more letters, so P lines up with E.

Q Z C E S P T C C T R S E D E Z L X P Y O
F O R T H E I R R I G H T S T O A M E N D

For their rights to amend.

She has cracked the code. Now that she knows the pattern, she doesn't have to do any more frequency analysis. She knows that lines eleven and twelve will be shifted by thirteen letters, lines thirteen and fourteen by seventeen letters, and so on. The rest is easy, mechanical. Once she has finished, she types it into her computer and adds punctuation.

> "Oysters have beards," said Lady Bird—
> Sing Flies, sing Frogs, sing Fiddle-strings!
> "I love them, for I know
> They never chatter so:
> They would not say one single word—
> Not if you crowned them Kings!"

> "Words have power," said Lady Bird—
> Sing Slags, sing Slugs, sing Sintered-clay!
> "For their rights to amend,
> Magnum opus he penned.
> Yet two score and part of a third
> Passed 'fore birds had their say!"

> "Fire has life," said Lady Bird—
> Sing Jiggery-pokery, Jeering-jibe!
> "Fused with water it blooms

Among pioneer tombs.
A token on stone so averred
For messenger and scribe!"

She reads the borrowed verse again and sees a theme this time. *I love them, for I know they never chatter so. They would not say one single word.* Silence is a good thing? Silence as in keeping secrets?

Do the other verses have themes, too? She scans for patterns, seeing both words and pictures in her mind.

Three references to writing—*words, penned,* and *scribe.* The latter reminds her of Dad again. But there is work to do. No time to feel, to hurt.

Two mentions of birds—*Lady Bird* and *'fore birds had their say.* But how the hell can birds have say?

She sighs and places her palms over her eyes. Sometimes she can see better in the dark.

'Fore birds had their say.
For their rights to amend.

Her hands fly open, thumbs still on temples, fingers splayed like wings. *Bird* is also old slang for *woman.* Before women had their say? It wasn't long ago that Arizona studied the women's suffrage movement. The nineteenth amendment to the U.S. Constitution gave women the right to vote.

She removes her thumbs from her temples, opens a web browser, types *19th amendment* in the search box, and hits RETURN. To the right of the DuckDuckGo results (she doesn't like to have her searches tracked) is a box summarizing a Wikipedia entry. Wikipedia, the low-hanging fruit on the tree of research. But it's not like Mom is grading her on this, making her cite her sources. She clicks on the Wikipedia link.

A federal amendment intended to grant women the right to vote was introduced in the U.S. Senate for the first time in 1878 by Senator Aaron A. Sargent.

Magnum opus he penned?

> Congress proposed the Nineteenth Amendment on June 4,
> 1919, and the following states ratified the amendment.

1878 to 1919. Forty-one years. *Two score and part of a third.* She clicks on the link for Senator Sargent.

> Sargent's wife, Ellen Clark Sargent, was a leading voting rights
> advocate and a friend of such suffrage leaders as Susan B.
> Anthony . . .

Cool. Arizona dons her tight-lipped Mona Lisa smile.

> The bill calling for the amendment would be introduced un-
> successfully each year for the next forty years.

Buttholes.

> He died in San Francisco in 1887. A monument to him may be
> found in the old Pioneer Cemetery in Nevada City, California.

Pioneer Cemetery in Nevada City. *Among pioneer tombs.*

Arizona's brow furrows. When the family isn't living in the Airstream, home is in the small town of Grass Valley, right next to Nevada City.

"Home?" she says with a whimper. The family—or what was left of it—had just been home. She recalls her dad's memorial service, and a tear rolls down her cheek.

9

Libraries and Cemeteries

ARIZONA WIPES THE TEARS AWAY AND GOES OUTSIDE WITH Mojo on her heels. She looks west and thinks about the route to Nevada City, on the other side of the mountains. The terrain cries out for a motorcycle. She looks at her Ural and nods.

The Ural sidecar motorcycle is a relic of the past, a decades-old Russian design that was purportedly stolen from BMW before World War II and has gone virtually unchanged since. It has all the styling of a platypus, albeit a shiny red platypus in Arizona's case. It even has the classic two-cylinder four-stroke air-cooled boxer engine. The boxer part always makes her smile. Perhaps most important, with its two-wheel drive (rear wheel and sidecar wheel), the Ural can handle terrain that most motorcycles can't—deep sand, loose rock, snow, and even hair-raising creek crossings.

Arizona unhitches the Airstream and moves the truck forward. She opens the truck's tailgate and pulls out the ramps from beneath the rack that Dad had built for his own Ural (with its sidecar, the bike is too wide to fit in the pickup's bed). She winches her bike down, packs snacks and water into the sidecar's trunk for the two-hour ride, and slips the shotgun under Mojo's blanket.

She beckons Mojo into the sidecar, straps on his goggles, and they head out of camp. As they ride by, Lily gives them a thumbs-up and smiles (Mojo's goggles make everyone smile). Arizona acknowledges with a nod. She doesn't like to take her hand off the handlebars, even for a brief wave. They ride north on 395. Half an hour later, just after 3:00 P.M., they are motoring through Reno, a miniature Las Vegas, past the half dozen high-rise buildings—all casino hotels, and not really all that high. Mojo's ears and jowls flap in the wind.

They turn west on Interstate 80 and climb into the foothills. The eastern escarpment—the exposed edge of a massive granite slab that had been tilted and sheared off—is so steep that the microclimate changes every few miles. Leaving the sagebrush behind, they ascend a twisting canyon stippled with Jeffrey pine astride the Truckee River, whose waters flow from Lake Tahoe into the terminal sink of Pyramid Lake, the largest remnant of the ancient inland sea that once covered most of Nevada. They cross back into California, through the boreal forest that dominates middle elevations of the entire range, and pass the town of Truckee, famous for its record-setting snowfalls. Above the sapphire blue of Donner Lake, they wind past exposed granite blocks that comprise the massive Sierra Nevada batholith. Her dad taught her that the blocks are called plutons—after Pluto, Roman god of the underworld. She wonders how thoughts of her parents can make her feel warm and cold at the same time.

As they crest Donner Summit, her thoughts turn to the infamous Donner party, dozens of whom perished during the winter of 1846–47. Gooseflesh ripples across her skin as she recalls the tales of cannibalism. Or are the goosebumps from the parental memories? Or the riding wind?

They cruise down the gentle western slope until they reach Highway 20, the meandering two-lane road that will lead them to the quaint town of Nevada City. Arizona steers the motorcycle down the off-ramp and pulls over to the side of the road for a brief rest. She removes Mojo's goggles, gets him out to pee, and fetches him a biscuit and some water.

Perhaps if she wasn't so distracted she would have picked a more scenic place to rest. The burn scar of a wildfire stretches right up to the road, from the shores of an alpine lake a half mile below. The forest slope has been obliterated—only a few trees remain, most of them dead and black. So much death.

Yet even though the fire was less than a year ago, there are signs of recovery. Fire annuals, plants that grow in the wake of a fire, are thriving. First she notices goldenrod, a member of the sunflower family, and the brilliant orange petals of the state flower, the California poppy. She looks more closely and sees ruby-red Indian paintbrush, California fuchsia, and the delicate purple of Anderson's thistle. Arizona hopes that she—and Mom, if she can find her and free her—will recover like the flora.

She turns away from the burn scar and the associated feelings and looks back toward the freeway. Someone is standing on the overpass, facing her direction, with hands near their face—as if using binoculars. *We'll be watching.* Is it one of the kidnappers? Had they followed her? She watches them watching her. Or is she just being paranoid? She isn't going to stick around to find out. Maybe she can lose them in the final forty minutes of the ride, where opportunities to pass are limited. She gets Mojo back in, mounts up, and motors on as fast as she can.

SHE PULLS INTO THE parking lot at the main library, a short walk to Pioneer Cemetery if they take the path through the adjacent St. Canice Cemetery. It's a perfect fall afternoon—white clouds parting for blue sky, leaves going to color, and warm. She parks the Ural, takes off her helmet and jacket, and places them on the pillion. Mojo jumps out and she puts him on leash. They walk down the driveway. It feels good to be home but strange to be here without her parents. *Bittersweet* doesn't quite suffice, but she isn't sure what would. Her mind has barely lighted on that thought before it buzzes on—a bumblebee off to pollinate another notion.

Libraries and cemeteries again, she thinks. Places she is comfortable.

10

Among Pioneer Tombs

ARIZONA AND MOJO EXIT THE LIBRARY DRIVEWAY, CROSS the street, and walk down Orchard Street toward Pioneer Cemetery and the adjacent St. Canice Cemetery. A canopy of oak trees, still glistening from midday rain, sways in the breeze, shaking off water like a wet dog. Mojo, a big baby when it comes to rain, demonstrates the proper shaking technique every time a drop lands on him.

Pioneer Cemetery can be accessed only from West Broad Street, so they take a gated path through St. Canice Cemetery. Arizona follows Mojo in, closes the creaky gate behind them, and walks briskly, keeping Mojo on a short leash so he won't stop and pee on a grave. One eye on Mojo, she looks through the chain-link fence to her left. They are more than halfway through St. Canice when she spots old headstones on the other side—Pioneer Cemetery. They exit onto West Broad Street and, after a dozen paces to the corner of the fence, stop at a small stone monument on an unmaintained path.

PIONEER CEMETERY

· · ·

THIS CEMETERY WAS ESTABLISHED
IN 1851 ON A KNOLL, BACK OF
THE FIRST METHODIST CHURCH.
MANY NOTED CITIZENS REST HERE.

Arizona and Mojo walk past the monument into Pioneer Cemetery. They pass decrepit headstones, some broken and lying on the ground. Dead leaves, pine needles, and weeds obscure the names. Two crows caw a greeting, or a warning. Lone sentinels of a graveyard long forgotten.

Arizona brushes leaves away from a broken headstone while Mojo pees on a grave. "Sorry about that," she says on his behalf.

She scans the surroundings and notices larger monuments on the apex of the small hill. Leading Mojo (off leash now), she finds what she's looking for—a large stone monument shaped like a sarcophagus, with Doric columns on the corners.

AARON AUGUSTUS SARGENT

BORN AT

NEWBURYPORT MASS. SEPTEMBER 28TH, 1827

DIED AT

SAN FRANCISCO CAL. AUGUST 14TH, 1887

"Hello, Senator," Arizona says. "Thanks for the nineteenth amendment, even if it didn't pass for forty friggin' years."

She walks around the monument to see if there is anything else. On the back it reads:

PRINTER, LAWYER, SENATOR,

MINISTER PLENIPOTENTIARY.

But that doesn't help. Are they looking for something or someone else? Mojo mills about, short boxer nose to the ground, while Arizona sits down with her back against the cool monument and thinks about the poem. The first verse—Carroll's—is presumably about secrets. The second verse is about Senator Sargent. But she has solved only one line of the third verse—*among pioneer tombs*.

"Fire has life," said Lady Bird—
Sing Jiggery-pokery, Jeering-jibe!

"Fused with water it blooms
Among pioneer tombs.
A token on stone so averred
For messenger and scribe!"

Her mind races.

Fire has life. Fire has long been described as alive, but why here?

Fused with water it blooms? Does *it* refer to the *fire* from the first line? But how can you fuse fire and water?

Mojo growls behind her. Arizona spins around and looks but sees no movement between the moss-bearded redwoods that tower over blanched headstones. "What is it, buddy?" she whispers. Was she so focused on the poem that she didn't hear something? She listens. The wind, cool in the shade of the giant trees, rustles fallen twigs and leaves. Just the wind. She returns to the poem.

A token on stone. That must mean a tombstone, considering their location.

Aver. To assert. Does *so averred* imply that what is on the tombstone is referenced within the poem?

For messenger and scribe. If someone buried here was a scribe, how the hell is she supposed to know? Senator Sargent's monument says he was a printer. Is *scribe* another reference to him?

She looks around again, listens. Still nothing but the wind.

She returns to the poem, wanders down a winding stream of consciousness, keeping to the shallows, looking for answers, for connections—but comes up empty. She is stuck. She'll have to look at every tombstone and hope she recognizes whatever it is she's looking for.

She walks to a nearby headstone, reads it, goes to the next, and so on. Mojo sniffs the rich ground as he follows. And so it goes, grave after grave. But the headstones don't mean anything. Arizona scuffs to another tombstone and stops, listens. Was that another sound or just her own shuffling? She looks to see if Mojo heard it, too, but he isn't there.

"Mojo!" she says, almost in a whisper.

Behind her, a dog barks in the distance, and Arizona takes off at a run toward the sound.

"Mojo?" she calls. He almost never barks.

Where the hell is he? Another bark, but from off to the right. She pivots and runs that way. Is he chasing something? Or someone?

"Mojo?" she calls again.

Seconds later he comes bounding toward her. As she watches him, she recalls how his frolicking jackrabbit gait always made the whole family laugh—when there was a whole family. Yet another happy memory blackened.

"Where have you been?" she says, as she puts him back on leash. "Did you see something?"

Her run through the cemetery reminds her of another famous cemetery run, in the classic western *The Good, the Bad and the Ugly.* Dad loved that movie. Never enough degrees of separation.

She turns around to resume her search but freezes in front of a grave.

OUR LITTLE ANGEL HAS
GONE HOME TO GOD

...

MALACHI SOFER

BORN NOVEMBER 7, 1850

DIED FEBRUARY 29, 1853

AGED TWENTY-SEVEN MONTHS

She wonders why she stopped. Brow knitted, she reads over the inscription several times, until her eyes lock on the date of death. Arizona kneels down and examines the weathered engraving. She scratches at the date and then traces a number with her forefinger. It is definitely a nine, but that doesn't make sense. February 29 occurs only during leap years, and all leap years are even. So, is it just . . . a typo? *On stone so averred?*

Her eyes shift to the small Star of David on the tombstone, then back to the child's name. A knowing smile forms on her lips. Malachi Sofer. Malachi is Hebrew for *messenger*. She looked up the name once, after reading Stephen King's *Children of the Corn*. Maybe Sofer means something, too? She pulls out her phone and does a web search. Sure enough, a sofer is a Jewish scribe. Malachi Sofer. *For messenger and scribe.*

Okay. That can't be coincidence. Malachi's tombstone is the one she was meant to find. But now what? She looks at the back of the tombstone, but it is smooth and blank. She is stuck again.

She walks to a nearby redwood tree and sits down to think, her back against the bole. Mojo curls up next to her. It reminds her of a time a few years earlier, before the family traveled full-time, when she sat against a different tree with Mojo at her side. The family had come to know that day as *the adventure gone a little long*.

ARIZONA AND MOJO HAD explored farther by foot that day than ever before, but as twilight gave way to nightfall, they were only halfway home. She tried to press on as the fading light slanted through the dense stands of oak and pine, but she could no longer find the path among the black. She had removed her pack, pulled out her headlamp, and pushed the button. Nothing happened. *Click.* Nothing. She hadn't thought to bring extra batteries.

She had known that day was a new moon, so there would be no moonlight, but understanding the lack of light had been little solace in the dark. She found a large tree, sat on the ground with her back to the rough bark. Mojo lay down beside her, but without long hair to keep him warm, he began to shiver. Arizona took off her denim jacket and put it over both of them. Above but close by, a great horned owl loosed a solemn *whoo-hoo-hoo-hoo,* and a distant neighbor hooted back. Arizona offered a faint smile. "Do you hear the hooty-hoos, buddy?"

She had wondered if they were lost, had pondered the definition. But her dad used to say that you're lost only if you don't know where you are. Otherwise, you're just stuck. After a cold hour, Dad had come to the rescue on his sidecar motorcycle—and possibly just in time. As he rolled to a stop, a mountain lion stood in the yellow cone of the motorcycle's headlight. They watched the cat slip into the brush, its three-foot-long tail trailing behind it like the exclamation point on a warning sign. Arizona called Mojo into the sidecar, put her jacket and pack back on, hopped on the motorcycle's pillion, and wrapped her arms around her warm father.

AS HER MIND RETURNS to the present, to the unsolved riddle of fire and water, she feels lost again. But since she knows where she is, is she just stuck? What would Dad do now? The memory still fresh in her mind, she can see the tattoo on the back of Dad's hand as he grips the motorcycle handlebars. The overlapping circles were an homage to the great mathematicians who had inspired him to follow in their footsteps—Pythagoras, Euclid, Aristotle.

Overlapping circles.

Overlapping shapes.

Fire and water.

Air and earth? The classical elements?

Magnum opus he penned. Magnum opus. Great Work.

Arizona's first tastes of alchemy—in *Journey to the Center of the Earth, Frankenstein,* and the *Harry Potter* books—had only whetted her appetite, left her curious mind wanting more, so she had poured herself into the spellbinding subject. The alchemists had used triangles to represent the four classical elements for their Great Work, as had Aristotle before them.

When you combine, or *fuse,* the symbols for fire and water, it creates a six-pointed star, a hexagram. Star of David.

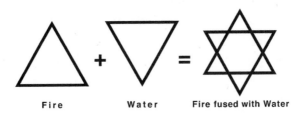

Fire   Water   Fire fused with Water

She sighs. Okay, great. More evidence that Malachi's grave is the one she is meant to find. But what now? Is something buried with him? She isn't up for grave-robbing. *This feels like a dead end,* she thinks. *No pun intended.*

She takes pictures of the front of the tombstone, wonders what secrets Malachi keeps, and shakes her head. Leaving without understanding feels like abandoning Mom again. But staying here isn't accomplishing anything. Hopefully what she needs is on the tombstone, and she has pictures of that.

"Come on, buddy," she says. "Let's go back to the library, then we'll visit home." Mojo doesn't wag just his tail but his whole wiggly boxer butt. He knows the word *home.*

11

Home

THE FAMILY HOME IN GRASS VALLEY SITS ATOP A SMALL HILL that, despite being no more than two hundred feet above its surroundings, affords phenomenal views to the east—successively higher tree-covered ridges (first oak, then pine), culminating in the snow-covered crest of the Tahoe Sierra, some forty miles distant.

As they get close, Arizona parks the motorcycle in a discreet spot nearby and they approach quietly on foot. The quarter-mile driveway is gated and the five-acre parcel fenced to keep coyotes out, making a clandestine entrance difficult for Mojo. But she knows where there's a hole in the fence, courtesy of a fallen tree. Dad never got around to fixing it. In hindsight, she should have brought the truck and left Mojo in it, but it's too late for that.

Mojo's leash in left hand, shotgun in right, she follows a deer trail up the steep roadside berm and walks to the corner of the fence. The hole is set back from the road a ways. To get to it, she'll have to parallel the fence from the outside, on their neighbors' property. But trespassing is the least of her worries. Far more annoying is the hundred or more feet of wild chaparral ahead of them, an unyielding tangle of shrubs and thorny bushes passable only at ground level. The scruff is in stark contrast to their property, where her dad worked hard to make it more resistant to wildfires—removing brush and all tree branches within six feet of the ground, creating so-called defensible space. Too bad the neighbors hadn't reciprocated.

Yeah, she definitely should have brought the truck and left Mojo in it.

She sighs, pushes the loop of Mojo's leash up to her elbow, stoops down, and crawls as quietly as she can. As she slides the shotgun beneath the briar ahead of her, she smirks at the double meaning that the gun brings to the phrase *defensible space*. Sharp serrated leaves of canyon live oaks dig into her hands, and she pauses every ten feet or so, pulls them out, and listens for activity on the other side of the fence.

Wild turkeys gobble in the distance. Closer, something stirs the leaf litter. She listens, hears it again over the drumbeat of her pulse in her temples. But it's not the clumsy sound of a person. She turns her head. Twenty feet away, a large California thrasher uses its deeply down-curved bill as a pick, then switches to a side-to-side motion to clear away the debris, like a miner digging for gold. She nods to the bird and crawls on.

Through the fence and free of the chaparral, Arizona and Mojo sneak uphill. Keeping to the shade of the oaks and pines, she pauses behind their trunks to watch and listen. She passes the small pump house that covers the well head, steps over the fresh dirt of mole hills, and dodges the poison oak, which is thankfully easy to spot in the fall with its leaves turned crimson. She can barely control Mojo, who wants to run up to the house and crash through his dog door.

"Come on, Mojo," she whispers. She heads up the hill slaunchwise— the family's neologism for diagonally—maintaining distance from the house until she can see more—the barn that had been converted into Mom's art studio, the detached garage, the driveway. There are no strange cars in the driveway. Of course not. They'd approach on foot, too. Duh.

She stops and watches. If anyone is here, they are either inside or out of view. She listens. No voices. Nothing but eerie silence. She takes Mojo off leash but tells him to stay. Both hands free now, she pumps the shotgun, then admonishes herself for the noise. So much for the element of surprise.

She creeps up onto the deck, swings the Mondrian-styled French doors open (nobody locks their doors in the country), and steps inside with the gun raised. It is even worse than the Airstream was. Every chair cushion torn open, stuffing on every surface. She lowers the shotgun, not because it is safe to do so but because she is stunned by the level of destruction.

She takes five slow breaths, then raises the gun and scouts out the rest of the house. Every room is trashed, but, as she'd expected, nobody is here. She checks her own room last. Her books are on the floor, along with her entire collection of Airstreams, some of which are broken. The closet and dresser have been emptied onto the floor, the drawers left pulled out and the dresser itself toppled over. The only thing that remains untouched is the Einstein marionette, which still hangs by the door. She ruffles his mop of white hair as she leaves the room, her eyes wet. She feels . . . what? She searches for the word. *Violated.*

She checks the studio. Clear. And the garage. Nobody. As she and Mojo enter the house again, Arizona shakes her head. She can't deal with the mess, but they should at least gather some supplies for the Airstream while they're here. Mojo is already busy gathering his own supplies, eating dry dog food off the kitchen floor from a bag that has been ripped open. She lets him eat while she scrounges.

She finds a canvas shopping bag, picks up several cans of food, for her and for Mojo, and puts the bag on the counter, which is uncluttered since everything is on the floor. The fridge and freezer doors have been left open, the contents dumped out. As her nerves calm down, she groks to the stench of rotting food and pulls her T-shirt up over her nose.

She adds more cans to the bag, along with a few boxes of mac and cheese, then picks up the bag and turns to leave the kitchen, largely to escape the smell. Wait. Rotting food? Hadn't Mom cleaned out the fridge when they left? She almost never forgot. Arizona scans the kitchen floor and immediately regrets looking.

Leftovers from Dad's memorial service. When she and Mom left home, they simply walked out the door. They'd both been broken. Arizona is used to being somewhat dysfunctional, but Mom isn't. Mom. How is she? *Where* is she? Arizona puts down the bag and gun, pushes her palms into her eyes. Pushes back the tears and pain.

Ten seconds later she picks up the bag and shotgun. She wanders through the house, finishes her shopping spree, and finds Mojo curled up in a corner of the family room.

"Okay, buddy, it's time to go."

Mojo whines. He misses home even in its current state, which isn't surprising. He has more freedom at home. The Airstream doesn't have a dog door.

"I know, buddy," she says. "Me too, but we can't stay here. Come on."

Mojo stands up slowly, complying but in protest, and they make their way back to the motorcycle.

TWO HOURS LATER, a little after 8:00 P.M., Arizona pulls the motorcycle into their campsite near Carson City. Lily waves as they drive in, and Arizona waves back once the bike has come to a complete stop.

Arizona locks the trailer door behind them. Everything appears to be as they left it. Mojo jumps up on the daybed and strikes a plaintive pose, chin on top edge of cushion, looking out the window. Probably at Lily and Gus.

They've barely settled when Arizona's cell phone rings. It's from a blocked number. She hesitates but then answers, figuring it might be Sam again.

"Hello?"

"Hello, Arizona," says the male voice.

"Who is this?"

"I'm the one who left you the note."

She recognizes the voice. "Stephen Gordon, I presume?"

"You can call me that if you like."

A rope tightens around her head, ties her neck in cords, binds around her chest. *You kidnapped my mom, desecrated my trailer, my house, my room.* "What do you want?" she says through clenched jaws.

"I want to know what you've discovered so far," he says.

"I'm not going to tell you anything until you let me speak with my mom."

"You're not calling the shots, Arizona. You're in no position to make any demands whatsoever."

She doesn't respond, because she knows he's right and it pisses her off.

"Let's start with the cipher," he says after three seconds of silence.

"Fine. It's a poem. Why don't you give me your phone number and I'll text it to you."

"Funny girl," he says. "Read it to me."

She reads the poem.

"Very good. So it's true that you're good with codes."

"With all due respect, which is to say *none* in your case, you don't have to be born at Bletchley Park to solve a simple Caesar shift. I could have done it when I was five using a decoder ring from a box of Cracker Jack. In other words, maybe I'm just normal and you're an idiot."

She thinks she hears a slight titter. Was it Gordon or Mom? Is Mom there with him? Where are they?

"And what did you find at the cemetery?"

We'll be watching. The man on the overpass. The sounds in the cemetery.

"The usual," she says. "Dead people."

"One in particular I assume, other than the senator?"

"Yes."

"And the name please?"

"Malachi Sofer."

"Very good," he says.

"If you already knew these things, what's the point? Why make me jump through all of these hoops?"

"Let's just say we believe in a process of initiation. And the hoops are about to get harder, so let's hope you continue to rise to the occasion, for your mother's sake. Check your email. You'll need Malachi's full name."

Click, and he is gone.

"Frick, frick, frick!"
She opens her notebook and writes.

>Gordon said *we* believe in a process of initiation.
>He's not working alone.
>
>I can see him.
>Eyebrows
>I browse
>I graze
>Grays
>Shades of gray
>Eyeshades
>Eyebrows
>Circular thinking
>Thoughts circling my brain
>Like water down the drain
>Stupid poems remind me of Dad
>The strangest things make me cry.

HIJKLMNOPQRSTUVWXY
L   KMN   WXY

NLHTHDTQGKHRHKCGKH
THE   E   RE ER   RE

GTNLHBDMNNLHEHMNGQ
    THE   STTHE   EST

NLUMCGKNDBSGOKFHYH
TH S   RT   R   EYE

VHDLGMNAGCHMMCUBUF
  E   H ST   ESS

LHPKHHNMOMGFNLDNNK
HEGREETS S   TH   TTR

JKLMNOPQRSTUVWXYZ
        KMN   WXYZ

PART TWO

A man is crazy who writes
a secret in any other way than
one which will conceal it
from the vulgar.

—ROGER BACON,
"EPISTLE ON THE SECRET WORKS
OF ART AND
THE NULLITY OF MAGIC"

HTHDTQGKHRHKCGKH
E E   RE ER   RE

NLHBDMNNLHEHMNGQQKUH
THE   STTHE EST   R E

UMCGKNDBSGOKFHYHFTM
  S   RT   R   EYE   S

DLGMNAGCHMMCUBUFRNGNE
  H   ST   ESS

PKHHNMOMGFNLDNNKDFJOL
GREETS   S   TH   TTR

LHKIUIUFPEUKTFGKTHHJL
HER   G   R   EE

HIJKLMNOPQRSTUVWXY
_   KMN   WXY

NLHTHDTQGKHRHKCGKF
THE   E   RE ER   RE

GTNLHBDMNNLHEHMNGC
    THE   STTHE   EST

NLUMCGKNDBSGOKFHYH
TH S   RT   R   EYE

VHDLGMNAGCHMMCUBUF
  E   H ST   ESS

LHPKHHNMOMGFNLDNNK
HEGREETS S   TH   TTR

JNLHKIUIUFPEUKTFGK

12

Dry Rot

S HE IS LYING ON THE FLOOR, STILL THINKING OF HER DAUGH-
ter. What would Arizona do in this situation? That's easy. Whatever her dad taught her. *Start by taking inventory,* he would have said.

She surveys the small room again. There isn't much to work with—
cot, chair, a couple of hooks in the wall by the door—and she can't
reach any of it. But her husband also said that there is always more
than meets the eye. But what? All she can reach is wood.

She nods. Where there is wood, there are nails. She runs her hands
along the floor, feeling for a nail that sticks up. She finds one, but it
won't budge. She finds another, but same problem. *Arrested decay, my
ass,* she thinks. *There's no fucking decay here at all.*

As she searches for loose nails, she recalls all the rotten wood they
had to replace on their old house. Every minor project turned into a
major one because of dry rot. Go to replace a deck board and the entire
ledger board is rotten. Have to pull up all the decking to replace that.
Then go to replace the ledger board and the siding is rotten. She's not
just reminiscing. She is working the problem, *doing the math,* as her
husband used to say. Trying to think like him, like her daughter.

Dry rot is a misnomer. It is fungal and requires moisture. Moisture
collects where two pieces of wood meet, especially where one is vertical and the other horizontal. Like where the floor meets the walls. Or
the post.

She pushes herself up onto her knees, reaches between her legs, and drags her fingernails across the seam where the post rises from the floor. The old wood yields. She rakes again, and again, and feels toothpick-sized fragments come loose. She looks at the splinters, rolls them between her fingertips, holds them to her nose, and sniffs the musty wood. There should be at least two nails where the floorboard ends against the post.

She gets to work. She can reach the post only from the kneeling position, and her knees start to ache. She lowers herself onto her elbows to give them a break, but half a minute is all the rest she'll allow them. Her right hand cramps after a couple of minutes of digging, so she switches hands. After changing hands a few times, she needs to give her knees another break. But by then she's found two nails. Neither is anywhere near loose yet, but she thinks she has exposed about half an inch of one and a quarter inch of the other. Progress. She rakes fingernails across the wood three times, wiggles one nail, then the other. Rake, rake, rake, wiggle, wiggle.

HALF AN HOUR LATER, she looks at the nail in her hand. Two and a half inches long. No wonder it was hard to get out. It will be an excellent digging tool in the moldering wood, give her raw fingers a break. Within minutes she has the second nail out. She places one nail in the palm of her left hand and curls her fingers to make a fist. The nail sticks out between her forefinger and middle finger. It will easily penetrate flesh.

Holding the other nail close to its point, between her right thumb and forefinger, she guides the tip of the nail against one of the zip ties, pushes it into the plastic as hard as she can and then snaps it to the side. She runs her fingernail along the zip tie but can't feel a scratch. She tries again. Still nothing. On the third try she angles the nail before snapping it to the side, then feels again. Her fingernail catches in a small groove. Proof of concept. One corner of her mouth turns upward. It is a crooked smile of determination, not unlike her daughter's. Guide, push, snap, scratch.

Within ten minutes the nail has worked through the zip tie, but there are three zip ties in all. When she hears footfalls approaching, she tucks the ends of the cut zip tie under the others so it won't be obvious. She crosses her arms. Each fist conceals a nail.

"I brought you some food," he says through the balaclava. "You want to sit in the chair to eat?"

She hesitates. The chair would be more comfortable than kneeling, but she can't risk him seeing the cut zip tie. "No, I'm fine on the floor."

"Suit yourself. It's nothing much. Peanut butter sandwich and water."

She thinks of her daughter and channels her fear into anger, into the type of scorn that only a teenager can wield. "I'm allergic to peanuts," she lies. "I'll go into anaphylactic shock and die."

"For real? We've got baloney, too."

"Kosher?"

"You're just bustin' my balls, huh?"

"Yeah." She smirks. "Peanut butter is fine, as long as it's chunky." She visualizes stabbing a nail into his neck as he bends down to deliver the food. It might be satisfying, but it won't lead to freedom. He'd scream and someone else would come.

He places the plate and a jug of water within her reach and leaves the room.

She drinks half the water, inhales the sandwich, and gets back to work on the zip ties.

THE MAN WHO CALLS himself Stephen Gordon closes the hasp on the door, slips the padlock through, and pulls off the balaclava. "Bitch," he says under his breath. He rounds the outside corner of the building and walks toward the stamp mill, where a man is standing guard.

"Report," Gordon says.

"All quiet, sir. Everyone checked in within the last ten minutes."

"Very good. Carry on." He gives the guard a friendly slap on the shoulder.

He closes his office door, sits down behind the old desk, and opens a drawer. Grabs the satellite phone and waits for it to power up. He dials the number stored in the phone's memory and puts the phone to his ear.

"Did you make contact with the girl?" says the man on the other end.

"Yes, it went fine. I told her to check her email and that she'd need the name from the cemetery, just as you instructed."

"Good. And how is our new guest?"

"Uncooperative and sarcastic but otherwise fine." Gordon hesitates. "Do you believe her, sir? That she really doesn't know the secret?"

"She had to be following her husband's trail. It can't be coincidence that he went to Titus Canyon and then she came to Bodie. But either way, it doesn't matter. This way we let the daughter do the work for us. And meanwhile, we don't risk the mother finding clues that rightfully belong to . . ." He almost says *me* but catches himself. ". . . to the Golden Dawn."

"I understand, sir."

"Keep me posted."

"Of course, sir."

13.

The Adept and
the Journal — Part One

- - - - - - - -

Bridgeport, California

THE ADEPT HANGS UP THE PHONE, SIGHS AT THE INTERRUP-
tion, and returns his mind to the solitude of his simple rented
room. Far enough from Bodie to remain hidden, but close enough to
get there quickly should Gordon find what they seek.

Uncooperative and sarcastic, Gordon said about the woman. Just like
his own old crow was, before she got what was coming to her. Always
focused on her precious work, never on him. And this work, most precious of all, she had kept from him, kept hidden.

He holds the small leather-bound book with tentative fingertips,
trying not to let it touch his sweaty palms. The lack of gloves does not
reflect a lack of reverence. He considered them, but the truth is that he
doesn't want anything between himself and the pages that will unlock
secrets beyond imagination. Beyond the imagination of others, that is.

He holds his Rosetta stone. Yet it is so much more than that. He
snickers at the languages on the worthless slab of rock. Hieroglyphs.
Demotic script. Ancient Greek. They are nothing, jokes compared to
the divine language of the Masters.

His chair creaks as he leans toward the lamplight. He strains his
eyes and the journal's binding in an effort to count the torn pages, to
know the breadth of the rift in his knowledge. The spine of the journal
resists, like the spine of the old woman did when he twisted her neck.
But unlike then, he will push no further. He leans back and remembers.

———

HE HAD FOUND THE journal and confronted her about why she'd kept it from him.

"What on earth are you talking about?" she said, already seated at the table set for two. "I don't have time for your games."

She never had time. She only had time for her job and for her government colleagues. Government sycophants was more like it.

He pulled out the journal and slammed it on the table, upside down. He stood there, hovering over her, a statue with arm outstretched, pointing at the journal and the symbol branded onto its back cover.

"Oh, my God, is that what you're talking about, you silly boy?" She laughed. She had laughed at him.

It was her laughter that sent him over the edge. But only on the inside. Outside, he remained calm.

"We can talk about that after dinner," she said. "Come, sit down. The food is getting cold."

"Okay, Mother. You're right, as always." He stepped behind her chair, rested his hands lightly on her shoulders, and kissed the crown of her head. "I'm sorry," he said, as he wrenched her head to the side, heard her neck snap.

It's okay, sweetheart, said her voice inside his head.

Like a good son, he sat down across from his mother, ate his dinner, and thought about his future.

IT WAS HIS MOMENT of emancipation, a red-letter day.

He turns to the first page of the journal that wasn't destroyed and reads, as he has done countless times before.

[missing text]

in all my time working for the National Security Agency. Perhaps if things had gone differently, this could have been just

another report to my superiors rather than what it is now, a desperate attempt to tell my story while I still can. But I'm getting ahead of myself.

One of the realities of the U.S. intelligence community is that virtually all published government documents are routinely reviewed by the NSA for hidden messages. It's one of many ways that spies are found. Reviewing government documents was my job. It was dull, but I was good at it and proud to be of service to my country.

Among the many pieces of paper that crossed my desk in recent weeks were what appeared to be some unremarkable old documents from the U.S. Department of the Interior, Bureau of Reclamation. They included a booklet and a set of drawings, both relating to public artwork at a well-known landmark.

As is standard practice, I queried the system to see if the documents had previously been cataloged. They had, which is not unusual, so before closing the file and moving on to the next set of documents on my desk, I compared them with the ones previously cataloged to ensure they were in fact the same.

They appeared identical but for two resounding differences. The previously cataloged versions had been redacted and also marked as classified. But how could that be? Why would the unredacted version of the documents be unclassified, still available to the public, while the redacted set was marked secret? Why make redactions to a totally innocuous set of documents? And how could redactions turn documents from harmless to dangerous?

Thus began my journey down the rabbit hole.

He hadn't thought anything of it the first time he read the journal. It had become such a common expression. But now he knows its true significance. *Down the rabbit hole.* Clever. He wears an approving smile as he turns the page.

14

Death, to the Dead
for Evermore

AFTER THE PHONE CALL FROM GORDON, DOUBTS BUZZ AROUND Arizona's mind like blowflies. Is cooperating the right thing to do? Is going it alone? She swats them away for the moment but knows they'll come back. Such is the nature of flies.

She checks her email and finds a message without a subject. It was sent from Proton Mail, the world's largest secure email provider, and contains just two words—*Drafts folder*. She understands. If two or more people have the password to a web-based email account, they can avoid transmitting sensitive messages by leaving them in the drafts folder. And doing it through Proton Mail means everything is encrypted, too.

She opens her web browser, logs in to the Proton Mail account using *MalachiSofer* as the password, and clicks on the drafts folder. There is only one message, another cipher.

```
THDNLNGNLHTHDTQGKHRHKCGKH
DVUFPDPGTNLHBDMNNLHEHMNGQQKUHFTM
WLHFHHKNLUMCGKNDBSGOKFHYHFTM
THDNLBUVHDLGMNAGCHMMCUBUFPNGNLHTGGK
MCUBUFPLHPKHHNMOMGFNLDNNKDFJOUBMLGKH
WLHKHFHUNLHKIUIUFPEUKTFGKIHHIUFPTDWF
RTLPQKELPNZZPZKDYBLBZZG
```

```
EQPTDPNZLPTBBDZLLMYKUTPNRKYUD
FQKRKZYCBZLLKZLPMFKZSZKCFKZUZJZZG
BTMZPFPNZBTSTDOMFKZSZKCFKZ
MTLNZKJTDOYOFRYPZLPFMMKTZDRL
CQLPPNTLCFKPYBHFQKDZWZDR
WHOHHCBFBNCJXDHJTHOW
UAHGRHIHDBGKQBGBFBNYBOJTWOOHW
YGOAYXPYGDOBGTOKQOPOJQPAJXOAJNH
OJFHPUHGPWEHBDQHOJHNPAHTHHL
BOPBFLJGBFBNCHNTHFBNYRJQNP
EHOPXEHTDEYGDOHRNHPOGHSHNOABEEWHNHBL
```

She fetches a bacon-flavored treat for Mojo (who is bored by word puzzles), then counts the lines of cipher text. Eighteen, just like the first cipher. Is that significant? She considers the number and then, because it's her nature, breaks it into its integer divisors (2, 3, 6, 9) and considers those. The first cipher was three verses of six lines and encrypted as nine pairs of two lines. Will this be the same? That seems unlikely. Still, a frequency analysis is as good a place as any to start.

Last time, though, the encryption evaded her first attempts at frequency analysis because the encryption changed from one couplet to the next. The patterns held line by line but not for the cipher as a whole. So this time, she decides, she'll look for individual patterns in each line. She makes a new frequency-analysis spreadsheet, with eighteen count-columns for the eighteen lines.

Mojo finishes his treat and begins nesting on the daybed. He paws at the fleece blanket, then claws at the cushion as if intent on its destruction. He turns two circles in one direction, then the other, then back again, and finally settles down. Arizona watches and wonders if he is satisfied with his nest or if he just gave up. Some things are unknowable, but still she wonders.

She counts letters in the cipher and fills in her table.

	1	2	3	4	5	6	7	8	9	10	11	12	13	14	15	16	17	18
a				1										1	3	1		1
b		1	1	2	2		2	2	1	2		1	2	5	1	1	5	2
c	1		1	2	1				2	1		2	2			1		
d	2	3	1	2	2	1	1	3		1	2	2	1	1	1	1		2
e		1				1	1	1								1		5
f		2	3	1	3	5			3	3	2	2	1	1			1	3
g	3	2	2	5	2	1	1		1					3	3	1	1	2
h	6	4	5	4	4	6						1	5	4	1	8	2	8
i				4									1					
j				1					1		1		2	1	3	2	2	
k	3	1	3	1	3	4	2	2	6	3	2	2		1	1			
l	2	2	2	3	3	2	3	3	3		3	2				1	1	1
m		3	2	3	4			1	1	2	3							
n	3	4	2	4	4	1	1	2		1	1	1	1	1	1	1	4	3
o			1		2				1	2		2	3	6	2	1		4
p		2		1	2	2	3	4	1	2	2	3			3	3	2	2
q	1	2					1	1	1			2		1	2	1	1	
r	1						1	1	1		2	1		1			1	1
s			1					1	2									1
t	3	2	1	2		2	1	3		3	3	1	1	1	1	1	1	1
u		2	1	3	3	5		2	1					1		1		
v		1		1														
w			1			2						1	2	2		1		1
x													1		2			1
y			1				1	2	1		2	1		1	3		1	1
z							5	2	9	5	3	2						

She scans for patterns. The letter H is most common in both the first six lines and the last six, but only occurs once in the middle six. The opposite is true for Z. Three different codes, each on six lines? She grabs her dog-food-box cipher disk and rotates the inner disk until H lines up with E. She writes out the first line of the cipher text and starts decoding.

T H D N L N G N L H T H D T Q G K H R H K C G K H
Q E A K

Rubbish. Dreck. She tries equating G, K, L, and N to E, but none of them work. She tries D, F, M, U, and T, but nothing. She tries the rest of the twenty-five possibilities. Still no-go. It isn't a Caesar cipher this time. Crap. No surprise, really—she was lucky last time—but crap.

But it can't be a polyalphabetic cipher, either, can it? If it was, she wouldn't see the frequency patterns.

She raises both hands and pinches her brows, thumbs down, eyes open. Sometimes memory needs a little coaxing. As her focus wanes, she hears noises outside. She checks the time—9:20 P.M.—then looks out the window. Lily is splitting logs, feeding them into a rusted metal fire ring, a tongue of flame lapping from the iron maw. Arizona watches for a breath. Two. Three. Ten. There's something fascinating about extroverts, as if they're an alien species. To be so free, so unrestrained. It's maddening. And beguiling.

She thinks about the many ways that her parents explained to her that she is different. About one in particular. Gears. Square gears. She can see them.

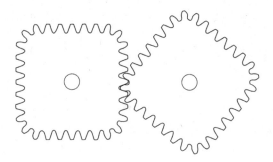

She opens her notebook and writes.

Square gears can work, but they don't work well with most others. That's me. But I found other gears I could mesh with. Things I could do alone or with Mojo—reading, writing, math, puzzles, exploring. So I built a machine, a frame of reference, that didn't require other people. Or so I thought. But I had my parents.

She closes her notebook and gazes out the window with watery eyes. Lily glances in the direction of the Airstream, so Arizona looks away, back to the screen of her laptop. Words she just wrote settle in her head like lead fishing weights. *Frame of reference.*

Context. She's already determined that this cipher isn't a Caesar shift. But there are many kinds of substitution ciphers. If it's one of those, ETAOIN SHRDLU will still apply. The letter E will probably still be the most common. Since H is the most common letter in the first six lines of the cipher text, there's a good chance that H represents E. She writes out the first six lines of cipher text and puts an E below each H.

```
T H D N L N G N L H T H D T Q G K H R H K C G K H
  E           E   E           E   E           E

D V U F P D P G T N L H B D M N N L H E H M N G Q Q K U H F T M
                    E           E   E                       E

W L H F H H K N L U M C G K N D B S G O K F H Y H F T M
    E   E E                               E   E

T H D N L B U V H D L G M N A G C H M M C U B U F P N G N L H T G G K
  E           E             E                           E

M C U B U F P L H P K H H N M O M G F N L D N N K D F J O U B M L G K H
            E       E E                                             E

W L H K H F H U N L H K I U I U F P E U K T F G K I H H I U F P T D W F
    E   E   E       E                           E E
```

She pulls the collar of her T-shirt up over her mouth and holds it there with both hands. She likes the way the ribbing feels on her lips.

She scans for patterns. The trigrams NLH and UFP both occur five times in the first six lines. The most common trigram in English is also the most common word—THE.

If H represents E, then the NLH trigram is probably THE, in which case N represents T and L represents H. She looks at her table of letter counts and, sure enough, N and L are common enough in the first six lines to represent T and H. She lets go of her shirt and creates a substitution alphabet to keep track of her letter assignments.

```
A B C D E F G H I J K L M N O P Q R S T U V W X Y Z
      H     L               N
```

She adds the new letters to her decryption, a T below each N and an H below each L.

```
T H D N L N G N L H T H D T Q G K H R H K C G K H
  E   T H T   T H E   E           E   E           E

D V U F P D P G T N L H B D M N N L H E H M N G Q Q K U H F T M
              T H E         T T H E   E   T               E

W L H F H H K N L U M C G K N D B S G O K F H Y H F T M
  H E   E E   T H         T             E   E

T H D N L B U V H D L G M N A G C H M M C U B U F P N G N L H T G G K
  E   T H       E   H   T       E               T   T H E

M C U B U F P L H P K H H N M O M G F N L D N N K D F J O U B M L G K H
            H E       E E T       T H   T T               H       E

W L H K H F H U N L H K I U I U F P E U K T F G K I H H I U F P T D W F
  H E   E   E   T H E                       E E
```

She scans the letters again. Just as she's starting to feel stuck, the beginning of the sixth line of cipher catches her eye. WLH, with the last two letters assigned as HE. If she hadn't already assigned N to represent T, she'd wonder if W represents T, so that the line would start with THE. But it can't if she's right about N representing T. So that also rules out THEME and THERE for the first five letters. So what else has the pattern _HE_E? The only thing she can come up with is WHERE. She checks her letter counts. K is common in the cipher text, so it could certainly represent R. But that would mean that W represents W, which doesn't make much sense. Or does it?

Arizona smiles. There's one kind of cipher where a W very likely would represent a W, and it's also the second most common monoalphabetic cipher after the Caesar. A keyword cipher.

To create a substitution alphabet for a keyword cipher, you write down the alphabet and then the keyword below that. Then you take the letters *not* used in the keyword and lay them out in order from A to Z, after the keyword. The nice thing about this technique is that even a relatively short keyword ends up shifting the letters after it. For example, if the keyword is CIPHERS, the first letter not used in the keyword itself is A, so A ends up representing H in the substitution alphabet:

A B C D E F G H I J K L M N O P Q R S T U V W X Y Z

C I P H E R S A B D F G J K L M N O Q T U V W X Y Z

But there's a weird side effect of this technique. Because the last letters of the alphabet are less common in English, they're also less likely to occur within a keyword. The letters in the bottom line start "catching up" with the ones in the top line, because you have to skip letters already used in the keyword. The Caesar shifts get shorter. So by the time you get to the end of the alphabet, the last letters often end up being represented by themselves, essentially unencrypted.

W is W, in other words.

And if this is a keyword cipher, then the letters after it—X, Y, and Z—represent themselves, too.

She adds the five new letters (K to represent R, plus W, X, Y, and Z) to her substitution alphabet.

```
A B C D E F G H I J K L M N O P Q R S T U V W X Y Z
    H     L                   K   N       W X Y Z
```

Then she fills in the new letters in her decryption. The X's and Z's don't actually help, but whatever.

```
T H D N L N G N L H T H D T Q G K H R H K C G K H
  E   T H T   T H E   E       R E   E R     R E

D V U F P D P G T N L H B D M N N L H E H M N G Q Q K U H F T M
          T H E       T T H E   E   T       R   E

W L H F H H K N L U M C G K N D B S G O K F H Y H F T M
W H E   E E R T H       R T       R   E Y E

T H D N L B U V H D L G M N A G C H M M C U B U F P N G N L H T G G K
  E   T H     E H     T       E               T   T H E       R

M C U B U F P L H P K H H N M O M G F N L D N N K D F J O U B M L G K H
          H E   R E E T       T H   T T R           H   R E

W L H K H F H U N L H K I U I U F P E U K T F G K I H H I U F P T D W F
W H E R E   E   T H E R           R       R   E E           W
```

Ugh. She scans for more patterns and latches on to HE REET in the fifth line. She runs through the alphabet, substituting each letter for the blank. HEAREET, HEBREET, HECREET . . .

The only letter that works is G. HEGREET isn't a word, but it could be *he greets* or *he greeted*. Actually, it can't be *he greeted*, because the next letter after *greet* isn't an E, so she assumes it's *he greets*. In that case, P represents G and M represents S.

She updates her substitution alphabet and decryption.

```
A B C D E F G H I J K L M N O P Q R S T U V W X Y Z
      H     P L                   K M N     W X Y Z
_____

T H D N L N G N L H T H D T Q G K H R H K C G K H
  E     T H T     T H E     E         R E     E R       R E

D V U F P D P G T N L H B D M N N L H E H M N G Q Q K U H F T M
      G     G         T H E       S T T H E     E S T       R   E       S

W L H F H H K N L U M C G K N D B S G O K F H Y H F T M
W H E     E E R T H   S     R T         R   E Y E       S

T H D N L B U V H D L G M N A G C H M M C U B U F P N G N L H T G G K
  E     T H       E   H   S T       E S S       G T     T H E             R

M C U B U F P L H P K H H N M O M G F N L D N N K D F J O U B M L G K H
S           G H E G R E E T S     S       T H     T T R                 S H     R E

W L H K H F H U N L H K I U I U F P E U K T F G K I H H I U F P T D W F
W H E R E     E     T H E R           G         R         R   E E       G       W
```

She stares at the results for several seconds, then grins in triumph. One of the common trigrams she identified was UFP. And if P represents G, that's most likely ING. She checks the letter count table, and indeed U and F are both pretty common, as they should be if they represent I and N respectively.

She adds the new letters.

```
A B C D E F G H I J K L M N O P Q R S T U V W X Y Z
      H     P L U               F     K M N     W X Y Z
_____

T H D N L N G N L H T H D T Q G K H R H K C G K H
  E     T H T     T H E     E         R E     E R       R E

D V U F P D P G T N L H B D M N N L H E H M N G Q Q K U H F T M
    I N G     G         T H E       S T T H E     E S T       R I E N       S

W L H F H H K N L U M C G K N D B S G O K F H Y H F T M
W H E N E E R T H I S     R T           R N E Y E N       S

T H D N L B U V H D L G M N A G C H M M C U B U F P N G N L H T G G K
  E     T H   I     E   H   S T       E S S     I   I N G T     T H E             R

M C U B U F P L H P K H H N M O M G F N L D N N K D F J O U B M L G K H
S     I     I N G H E G R E E T S     S     N T H     T T R       N       I   S H     R E

W L H K H F H U N L H K I U I U F P E U K T F G K I H H I U F P T D W F
W H E R E N E I T H E R     I     I N G     I R     N     R   E E     I N G         W N
```

She looks at the fifth line again, and the sequence NTH _TTR in particular. Given what she's already filled in, the only way she can make sense of that sequence is if the N is the end of a word and the

TR is the beginning of another word. In which case, it seems like the middle word is probably *that* and, therefore, D represents A.

```
A B C D E F G H I J K L M N O P Q R S T U V W X Y Z
D       H   P L U           F       K M N     W X Y Z
```
_____

```
T H D N L N G N L H T H D T Q G K H R H K C G K H
  E A T H T   T H E   E A     R E   E R     R E

D V U F P D P G T N L H B D M N N L H E H M N G Q Q K U H F T M
A   I N G A G     T H E   A S T T H E   E S T       R I E N   S

W L H F H H K N L U M C G K N D B S G O K F H Y H F T M
W H E N E E R T H I S     R T A       R N E Y E N   S

T H D N L B U V H D L G M N A G C H M M C U B U F P N G N L H T G G K
  E A T H   I   E A H   S T       E S S   I   I N G T   T H E       R

M C U B U F P L H P K H H N M O M G F N L D N N K D F J O U B M L G K H
S   I   I N G H E G R E E T S   S   N T H A T T R A N     I   S H   R E

W L H K H F H U N L H K I U I U F P E U K T F G K I H H I U F P T D W F
W H E R E N E I T H E R   I   I N G   I R   N   R   E E   I N G   A W N
```

Death? The first word has to be *death,* doesn't it? And if T represents D, then the first line begins DEATHT_THEDEAD, which has to be *death to the dead,* and G has to represent O. Hah. G occurs fifteen times in the cipher text, and having O identified gives her four out of five vowels, so it's a huge win. She's got this thing beaten now.

```
A B C D E F G H I J K L M N O P Q R S T U V W X Y Z
D     T H   P L U           F G     K M N     W X Y Z
```
_____

```
T H D N L N G N L H T H D T Q G K H R H K C G K H
D E A T H T O T H E D E A D   O R E   E R   O R E

D V U F P D P G T N L H B D M N N L H E H M N G Q Q K U H F T M
A   I N G A G O D T H E   A S T T H E   E S T O     R I E N D S

W L H F H H K N L U M C G K N D B S G O K F H Y H F T M
W H E N E E R T H I S   O R T A     O   R N E Y E N D S

T H D N L B U V H D L G M N A G C H M M C U B U F P N G N L H T G G K
D E A T H   I   E A H O S T   O   E S S   I   I N G T O T H E D O O R

M C U B U F P L H P K H H N M O M G F N L D N N K D F J O U B M L G K H
S   I   I N G H E G R E E T S   S O N T H A T T R A N       I   S H O R E

W L H K H F H U N L H K I U I U F P E U K T F G K I H H I U F P T D W F
W H E R E N E I T H E R   I   I N G   I R D N O R   E E   I N G D A W N
```

Distracting reflections of light and shadow dance across the aluminum walls of the trailer. Lily and her fire. Arizona visualizes Lily dancing around the circle, spinning as she does. A rain dance perhaps. But she gets back to work, plugs away.

Ahh. Given the letters around it, the blank in S_S in line five has got to be a vowel, and U is the only one left. And that gives her _OURNEY in line three, which has got to be *journey*, right? The dominoes fall from there, and suddenly she finds that she's done with the first six lines.

```
A B C D E F G H I J K L M N O P Q R S T U V W X Y Z
D E A T H Q P L U S V B C F G I J K M N O R W X Y Z
```

```
T H D N L N G N L H T H D T Q G K H R H K C G K H
D E A T H T O T H E D E A D F O R E V E R M O R E

D V U F P D P G T N L H B D M N N L H E H M N G Q Q K U H F T M
A K I N G A G O D T H E L A S T T H E B E S T O F F R I E N D S

W L H F H H K N L U M C G K N D B S G O K F H Y H F T M
W H E N E E R T H I S M O R T A L J O U R N E Y E N D S

T H D N L B U V H D L G M N A G C H M M C U B U F P N G N L H T G G K
D E A T H L I K E A H O S T C O M E S S M I L I N G T O T H E D O O R

M C U B U F P L H P K H H N M O M G F N L D N N K D F J O U B M L G K H
S M I L I N G H E G R E E T S U S O N T H A T T R A N Q U I L S H O R E

W L H K H F H U N L H K I U I U F P E U K T F G K I H H I U F P T D W F
W H E R E N E I T H E R P I P I N G B I R D N O R P E E P I N G D A W N
```

The first part of the substitution alphabet is the keyword—*death Q plus*, whatever the hell that means. She does a web search for the first line and clicks on the most promising link. She reads the source poem, "Death, To the Dead For Evermore," by Robert Louis Stevenson. Whoever picked the poems had pretty good taste, at least in what they plagiarized.

Based on the results of her frequency analysis, she's expecting that the cipher changes after the first six lines. Encrypted by a different keyword, most likely. But just in case, she tests the seventh line with her substitution alphabet.

R T L P Q K E L P N Z Z P Z K D Y B L B Z Z G

V D H G F R

Nonsense, just as she expected. Hmm. She looks at Stevenson's poem again. The first verse is nine lines in all:

Death, to the dead for evermore
A King, a God, the last, the best of friends—
Whene'er this mortal journey ends
Death, like a host, comes smiling to the door;
Smiling, he greets us, on that tranquil shore
Where neither piping bird nor peeping dawn
Disturbs the eternal sleep,
But in the stillness far withdrawn
Our dreamless rest for evermore we keep.

She looks at lines seven through nine of both Stevenson's poem and the cipher text.

```
RTLPQKELPNZZPZKDYBLBZZG
EQPTDPNZLPTBBDZLLMYKUTPNRKYUD
FQKRKZYCBZLLKZLPMFKZSZKCFKZUZJZZG
```

In both places the lines go from short to medium to long. Is it possible that the cipher is continuing with Stevenson's poem, just with a different keyword? She writes out lines seven through nine of cipher text and the corresponding lines of the poem beneath. Indeed, they're all the same length.

```
R T L P Q K E L P N Z Z P Z K D Y B L B Z Z G

D I S T U R B S T H E E T E R N A L S L E E P
```

Arizona creates another substitution alphabet, fills in the letters used in lines seven to nine, and double-checks that each letter is translated consistently throughout the three lines. They are.

```
A B C D E F G H I J K L M N O P Q R S T U V W X Y Z
Y E   R Z M   N T   J B C D F G   K L P Q   U
```

She stares at the first part of the substitution alphabet, the keyword portion—*year Z month*? The first keyword was *death Q plus,* also two words separated by a seemingly random letter, so that's consistent. She fills in the rest of the keyword followed by the rest of the alphabet, then uses the result to decipher the next three lines, ten through twelve.

Life, to the living for evermore.
Fisher King, a God, a test of friends.
Must this mortal journey end?

Those lines aren't in Stevenson's poem, which means that when the code changes to its third and final cipher for the last six lines, she'll have no clues about their content and will have to resort to frequency analysis and context again. That sucks, but whatever. She plods through the remaining six lines as she did the first six. This time the keyword is *birth X day.* When she is done, she adds the deciphered text to the rest and formats it to match the original poem.

> Death, to the dead for evermore
> A King, a God, the last, the best of friends—
> Whene'er this mortal journey ends
> Death, like a host, comes smiling to the door;
> Smiling, he greets us, on that tranquil shore
> Where neither piping bird nor peeping dawn
> Disturbs the eternal sleep,
> But in the stillness far withdrawn
> Our dreamless rest for evermore we keep.

> Life, to the living for evermore
> Fisher King, a God, a test of friends—
> Must this mortal journey end?
> Ye seek a mark of geodesy,
> Whence began Juana Maria's odyssey,
> In shifting sands just south of shore,
> Some twenty leagues o'er the deep,
> A stamp on a marker de Maricourt,
> Lest fledgling secrets never shall ye reap.

The windows are open and the night air is cool, yet sweat gathers on her shirt. It smells tart.

The first verse by Robert Louis Stevenson is all about death, as is his entire poem. She rereads the first three lines of the second verse.

Life, to the living for evermore . . . Must this mortal journey end? Death's opposite, immortality? She pictures the first poem and Malachi's headstone, where the symbols for fire and water had been fused. *Magnum opus.* Great Work. *Slags and slugs.* References to metals. Alchemy? Immortality had been one of its aims—the elixir of life. It sounds crazy, but she isn't a big believer in coincidence.

Fisher King, a God, a test of friends. In Arthurian legend, the Fisher King was the last in a long line charged with keeping the Holy Grail. And she does seem to be on some type of quest, even if she doesn't know what she's seeking yet. *Fisher King* could also be another allusion to immortality, since in many versions of the Holy Grail story, the Fisher King was aged well beyond normal life expectancy. Lastly, it's a rearrangement of *King-fisher*, from the first cipher poem. Does *a test of friends* mean that this entire thing is a test? What was it that Gordon had said? They believe in a process of initiation. Initiation into what?

Ye seek a mark of geodesy. She twists her lips into a lopsided pout. Geodesy, the branch of mathematics that deals with the shape and area of the earth. As in United States Geological Survey, where Dad had worked as a cartographer before he took an online teaching job so the family could travel full-time. Geodesy. Arizona's hands form a sphere, her fingers meridians on an invisible globe. She rotates the finger-globe back and forth, as if searching the world for her mother.

Her brain has always wandered off on tangents (or cotangents, as Dad had joked). Such is the nature of a polymath, more blessing than curse until now. But now the tangents hurt. Geodesy, cartography, USGS, Dad, Mom, tangents, circles, Dad's tattoo. Crap. The doubt flies are back, and they're biting her eyes.

15

Twenty Leagues O'er
the Deep

S HE CLOSES HER EYELIDS AS IF THEY ARE FLOODGATES THAT will keep the feelings at bay, but tears sneak through. Slow, deep breaths. One. Two. Three. Four. She plucks a tissue from the box, dries her eyes, and returns to the poem.

She rereads the rest of the verse. Her eyes lock on to the last line. *Lest fledgling secrets never shall ye reap.* Fledgling. Something not fully developed, including a young bird that has just fledged. But *underdeveloped secrets* doesn't make sense.

Maybe working backward will help. She shifts her focus to the second-to-last line.

A stamp on a marker de Maricourt. Combined with *a mark of geodesy* a few lines earlier, does *marker* refer to a geodetic survey marker? Her dad's work as a cartographer made her very familiar with survey markers—objects, usually metal disks, placed to mark key points on the earth's surface. Geodetic surveys are at the heart of all mapmaking, and survey markers are the cornerstones of surveys, literally.

But who, what, or where is Maricourt? She looks up *Maricourt* in the Dictionary app:

Commune in Somme, France.

Not helpful. She switches back to her web browser and searches for *de Maricourt.*

> Petrus Peregrinus de Maricourt was a 13th-century French
> scholar who conducted experiments on magnetism and wrote
> the first extant treatise describing the properties of magnets.

Scholar. The word reminds her of school again. Her shoulders slouch and her chin drops, assuming the familiar posture of ostracism. Intellectually gifted, her teachers had said, but socially challenged and hypersensitive to certain auditory stimuli. Unlikely to thrive in a traditional school environment. Both of her parents had challenged the assertion, but it was Mom who was most vehement in her criticism of the school system for failing to accommodate Arizona's needs. *Mom,* she thinks. *Where are you?* She straightens up, tries to shake off the thoughts of school and Mom, as if the shame and sorrow will go with.

She clicks on the link for Petrus Peregrinus de Maricourt and continues reading.

> His work is particularly noted for containing the earliest
> detailed discussion of freely pivoting compass needles,
> a fundamental component of the dry compass soon to
> appear in medieval navigation.

Wait, this guy wrote the first treatise on magnetism and basically invented the compass? Why hasn't she heard of him?

> Peregrinus' text on the magnet is . . . commonly known by
> its short title, *Epistola de magnete* ("Letter on the Mag-
> net"). . . .
> "You must realize, dearest friend," Peregrinus writes, "that
> while the investigator in this subject must understand nature
> and not be ignorant of the celestial motions, he must also be
> very diligent in the use of his own hands, so that through the
> operation of this stone he may show wonderful effects."

She reads the quote a second time, then a third. Reads between the lines, connects things that aren't connected. Or are they?

Through the operation of this stone he may show wonderful effects. Does *this stone* refer to a lodestone? Or the philosopher's stone of the alchemists? She shakes her head at the very question, one that borders on absurdity. Moves her hands to the crown of her head, fingers interlaced, and stares at the screen.

Her thoughts are interrupted by Mojo, who is wheezing, his short boxer nose jammed against the daybed cushion. She smiles at his version of a thinking pose, then returns her attention to her computer.

Magnetism seems to be the takeaway. *A marker de Maricourt.* A magnetic survey marker? What does that even mean? A survey marker that has been magnetized? Where?

Ye seek a mark of geodesy, Whence began Juana Maria's odyssey. She searches for *Juana Maria*:

> Juana Maria, better known to history as the Lone Woman of San Nicolas Island, was a Native American woman who was the last surviving member of her tribe, the Nicoleño. . . .
> Scott O'Dell's award-winning children's novel *Island of the Blue Dolphins* (1960) was inspired by her story. . . . autumn of 1853 . . . discovery of Juana Maria . . . dressed in a skirt made of greenish cormorant feathers . . .

Greenish feathers, Arizona thinks. *Probably from pelagic cormorants.* When she has finished scanning the dark story of Juana Maria—massacre, abandonment, eighteen years of isolation, death just weeks after her discovery—she wonders how it was ever made into a story for children. Yikes.

Outside, faint shadows cross the campground as slate-gray clouds roll past the moon.

She changes her search to *San Nicolas Island*:

> San Nicolas Island is the most remote of California's Channel Islands, located 61 miles from the nearest point on the mainland coast.

Sixty-one miles. *Some twenty leagues o'er the deep.*

> The 22-square-mile island is currently controlled by the
> United States Navy and is used as a weapons testing and
> training facility.

She reads it a second time before she explodes.

"Sixty miles of open ocean! To an island controlled by the U.S. Navy? Come on. What am I, G.I. friggin' Jane going through SEAL training?" She looks at Mojo, whose eyes are so wide he must think he's being yelled at. "Sorry, buddy. I'm not mad at you," she says as she scratches his head and elicits a tail wag. "But I think we're sunk. I don't see how it's possible."

Tears well up. She sits still, watery eyes unfocused on the nothingness of the middle distance. Gordon, and whoever he's working with, already had the first cipher decoded. Maybe they had the second cipher decoded, too, and figured out the San Nicolas Island part. That could explain why they recruited her—so they don't have to go to the island themselves. Friggin' cowards. Talk about jumping through hoops. Gordon said the hoops were going to get harder, and apparently he wasn't kidding.

How can she go to an island that is used as a weapons testing and training facility? She'll get caught and thrown in jail—or the brig, in this case. How can she sneak onto and off of a Navy island without being seen?

"When I see the sea once more, will the sea have seen or not seen me?" She winks at Mojo but is pretty sure he doesn't get the *G.I. Jane* reference.

One thing is for sure. If it can be done at all, it will have to be done quickly. She can't just amble around. She'll have to know what she's looking for and right where to find it. She opens a new web browser tab, types *survey markers* in the search box, and scans the results but doesn't see what she is looking for. She changes the search text to *survey marks* and tries again. In the middle of the page, she sees something promising.

National Geodetic Survey—Survey Marks and Datasheets
https://www.ngs.noaa.gov/datasheets/

She clicks on the link, then on the interactive map on the right side of the page. A new tab opens with a large map and a control pane on the left. She types *San Nicolas Island* in the text box and clicks *Go*.

Within a second, the map shows San Nicolas Island with a red circle around it. Five colored squares with numbers inside are scattered about the island. She zooms out for context, to make sure she has the right San Nicolas Island. The island and red circle get smaller, and the colored squares merge into two, containing the numbers 150 and 90. She zooms out again, and two of the other Channel Islands appear as well as Long Beach, barely visible in the upper right. There is only one red square on the island now, containing the number 240. She zooms out again and Channel Islands National Park comes into view, as well as Los Angeles, San Diego, and Tijuana, Mexico.

It's the correct island, all right. But, holy crap, is it way out to sea. And two hundred forty survey markers? Double crap. She sighs, then mindlessly zooms out until she can see the entire contiguous United States and Hawaii. The red square with the number 240 still hangs annoyingly far off the southern California coast. She zooms back in, all the way to where she started and a little more. As the island fills the map, the colored squares disappear, replaced by icons that represent individual survey marks. The island is peppered with them. Arizona puts the fingers of her left hand on her forehead. How the hell is she supposed to find the right needle in this haystack of survey markers?

She switches back to the poem and looks for clues to help narrow the search. One line jumps out.

In shifting sands just south of shore

She scrolls the map up so she can see all of the southern shore. There are only two markers. She moves the cursor to one of them. It has an ID of DY3091 and is named SURF. The other one is DY3078, FENCE.

She stares at the screen. Left forefinger on bridge of nose, thumb under nose, other fingers curled. She reads the deciphered text again and realizes she is looking in the wrong place. The poem said south *of* shore, not south shore. To be on the island, it would be south of the *north* shore. Duh. Being brilliant doesn't stop her from feeling stupid sometimes.

Unfortunately, the north of the island has many more markers. Starting at the eastern end of the island, she hovers the cursor over each survey mark on the north shore so she can see its information. She hopes something will stand out.

DY3090, KNOB ...
DY3081, ISLE 1932 ...
DY3094, CONEY ...
DY2153, TIDAL 1 ...
DY2256, HAWK RM 1 ...
DY3107, MAGNETIC 1908 ...
DY2254, Q 1000 ...

Magnetic. She moves the cursor back to the previous marker and clicks on it. A small window pops up containing the same information as the pane on the left. She clicks on the *Datasheet* link, and a new tab opens containing the detailed information for the marker, which is also known as a station.

STATION DESCRIPTION (1908)

Station is located on the north shore of San Nicolas Island, 9 paces back from the edge of the bluff overlooking the east end of the rocky reef extending eastward from Corral Harbor. It is about 15 feet above mean tide. On a flat shelf dotted with sand dunes covered with grass. It is also 16 paces from the point of shore bluff to the eastward. Between the shore bluff to the north and the outlying reef is a small cove with sandy beach which affords a good boat landing and the station is

south of that part of the sandy beach which is about 50 feet
west of water at low tide.

This is perfect. She might actually be able to find it. She hears
waves crashing and wind whistling. Tastes salt on her lips, as if she had
kissed Mojo's nose. She sees snowy plovers foraging, running a few
steps across the wet sand before pausing like distracted toddlers. Sea
air in her lungs, she continues reading.

STATION RECOVERY (1932)

Station was not recovered. A very thorough search was made
of the locality but no evidence of the station was found. An
abandoned ranch house was found near the station site and
it is believed that the station was disturbed when the ranch
was occupied. The shifting sands in this locality made it necessary to dig for the station, and two days were spent in at-
tempting to recover same.

Her heart sinks. Recovery just means looking for a marker again,
and they couldn't find this one. She rereads the paragraph and two
words pop.

shifting sands

In shifting sands just south of shore. But her eyes go back to the words
no evidence of the station was found.
"It looks like the trail ends here, buddy."
Mojo's big brown eyes seem to reflect her own despair.

16.

Recovery

ARIZONA TAKES MOJO OUTSIDE. LILY IS SITTING BY HER CAMP-fire. Gus raises his flat French bulldog nose, jumps up, and runs to Mojo, who greets him with a playful downward-dog pose.

"You can't sleep, either?" Lily says.

Arizona shakes her head.

"You want to join us, then?"

Arizona waits to feel her stomach roil, the pulse throb in her temples. But what comes is just a few butterflies and more of a mild thrum than a throb. Huh. She ponders. With Dad and Mom gone, she does miss having someone to talk to. Lily is only one person and seems harmless enough. And Arizona is still curious about the extrovert thing. "Sure," she says. She grabs her own camp chair, carries it across the tarmac, and sets it across the fire from Lily.

"Smoke's blowing that way," Lily says, "so you'll probably want to come over here. I don't bite."

Arizona moves her chair next to Lily and sits down. Mojo and Gus settle at their feet.

Gus whistle-wheezes through his short nose. Arizona struggles to tune out the sound, but fortunately it's only annoying, not triggering.

"So what's keeping you up till one in the morning?" Lily says.

Arizona pauses. "Family, I guess."

Lily titters. "Yeah, that'll do it, all right. Yours is messed up, too, huh?"

Arizona nods.

"You pissed at them, worried about them, or both?"

"Both."

Lily nods. "So, did you have to sneak out?"

"I don't know what you mean."

"Did you have to sneak out of the trailer? To get some alone time?"

"Oh," says Arizona. "No. I was traveling with my mom, but . . . something came up. So it's just me now."

"Seriously? Holy shit. My parents would never trust me with a rig like that."

"Yeah?"

"Uh, *yeah*. I mean, how old are you?"

"Seventeen. They made me practice towing in a parking lot. I killed some cones."

Lily laughs.

"How about you?" Arizona says. "You traveling alone?"

"Yup. Taking a gap year, a year off from college. Or at least a semester, anyway."

"Between undergrad and grad school?"

"In the middle of undergrad in my case. I finished my sophomore year in May. I was gonna go back at the end of summer, but, well, family shit happened. And now I don't think I can focus enough for school."

"I know what you mean," Arizona says. "I had some family stuff, crap, happen, too." She hesitates. "My dad just died. Motorcycle accident."

"Was he a good dad?"

Arizona nods.

"Then I'm sorry for you," Lily says. "My mom died, too. She was driving drunk and hit an oak tree. At least she didn't hurt anyone else, so I guess that's good."

"Sorry," Arizona says. "How is your dad doing?"

"Not good." Lily hesitates. "It's complicated."

"Oh. You don't have to talk about it if you don't want. I totally understand."

"Thanks. I don't mind talking about it. It's nice to have someone to talk to, actually."

"Can I ask a related question?" Arizona says.

"Sure."

"How do you do it? Talk to strangers, like you did to me? I could never do that."

Lily smiles. "Yeah? I don't know. I just do it. Always have. Why couldn't you?"

Crap. She hadn't thought that through. Of course Lily would want to know why. See, it's better not to engage. She sighs, pauses for a breath. "Fear, I guess."

"Of what?"

"Being teased, laughed at, for being different."

"Has that happened before?" Lily says.

Arizona nods.

"At school?"

"Yeah."

"Sorry to hear that. Is it still happening?"

"I don't go to school anymore. I'm homeschooled now."

"Kids can be really cruel."

Arizona nods. "It sucks that people can be good, or at least okay, by themselves but so horrific as part of a group."

"Yeah, mob psychology is a pretty ugly part of human nature. But if people prejudge you, that's their problem, not yours. And not everyone is an asshole. Take me, for example. I'm pretty awesome, wouldn't you say?" Lily winks.

Arizona laughs, then nods.

"So, want to hear the rest of my messed-up family history?"

Listening seems safe enough, much safer than talking. "Okay."

"After my mom starting drinking, my dad and I talked her into a short-term rehab program. It seemed to work and she was going to AA meetings, staying sober, and everything was good for a while. But then she relapsed and hit the oak tree, and my dad kind of lost it. He became really volatile, switching from sad to angry in an instant. Anyway, I stuck around for a few months, but then I couldn't deal with it anymore. So about two months ago I just took his van and left."

"Wow. I'm sorry. You took his van? As in stole it?"

"Technically, yes. I didn't ask his permission, but I don't think he'll report it stolen."

"Have you talked to him since you left? Will you go back?"

"I call him occasionally, but he's hard to talk to. I'll go back eventually. I just need some time away. Meanwhile, his brother, my uncle, is looking in on him." Lily sighs. "So, is your mom doing okay or is she messed up like my dad?"

"I'm not sure."

"Yeah, I hear ya. But what can you do? You can't give up on family." Arizona nods.

They watch the fire silently for several minutes, as if contemplating its eternal mysteries. Fire really does have life. Lily's words ring in Arizona's ears. *You can't give up on family.* She thinks of the survey-marker description—*no evidence of the station was found.* Did she give up too quickly?

No, she hasn't given up. Not at all. She just needed a break.

"I think I'll go back inside," Arizona says as she stands. "Come on, Mojo."

"Okay. Goodnight, Arizona. Thanks for the company."

Arizona goes into the Airstream, sits down at her computer, and continues scanning the markers on the north shore. There are quite a few overlapping marker icons, so she zooms in to separate them.

She is about to scroll farther west when she notices that the previous marker, DY3104, SPRING 1932, has a faint shadow, as if there is another triangular marker icon barely visible behind it. She zooms in until the two triangles are separate and hovers over the one that had been partly hidden. DY3109, SPRING 1879.

Could there be others so close that she missed them? Without zooming out, she drags the map across the screen, keeping the north shore in the map window. Hiding behind DY3107, MAGNETIC, is another marker. She hovers over it. DY3105, MAGNETIC 2 1932. She clicks on the *Datasheet* link and scrolls down to the description.

STATION DESCRIPTION (1932)

The station is on San Nicolas Island, about 25 meters west of the next bight east of Corral Harbor and about 15 feet above high water. The station is near a line of fence posts near the site of an abandoned ranch house. . . . All marks were stamped.

STATION RECOVERY (1940)

Station is located on the north side of San Nicolas Island, on the west side of the first bight east of Corral Harbor and it is also about 1 mile northwest of the U.S. Navy radio station and ranch buildings. . . . A narrow rock point about 40 meters long extends in an east–west direction at the station. . . .

All marks are disks set in concrete posts. The shifting sands may cover all marks. Land at Corral Harbor, or at Navy radio station. No sub-surface mark listed on original description.

Shifting sands again, but this one was successfully found in 1940. That was a long time ago, but maybe all hope isn't lost. Arizona wants to have hope, so she reads it again. This time another phrase jumps out.

All marks were stamped.

A stamp on a marker de Maricourt. She opens the datasheet for the other magnetic marker and reads it again. No mention of stamps. This has to be the one. Now that she knows what she is looking for (she hopes), she switches back to the San Nicolas Island browser tab and continues reading.

. . . at least 200 military and civilian personnel live on the is-land at any given time. The island has a small airport and sev-eral buildings, including telemetry reception antennas.

She scrolls down, sees a map with the caption U.S. NAVY FACILITIES ON SAN NICOLAS ISLAND, and clicks on the map to enlarge it. What she sees brings her fingertips to her temples as if she needs to hold her head up.

> Cruise Missile Soft Landing Area . . .
>
> Aerial Target Launch Site . . .
>
> Inert Missile Impact Area . . .
>
> Weapons Test Area . . .
>
> Precision Radar Systems . . .

The only potential saving grace is that the map shows no buildings or active sites near the survey marker, but she needs more detail. Finding the topographic map is easy. She already has USGS topoView bookmarked, and within two minutes she has downloaded the most recent topo map for San Nicolas Island. It shows the primary roads, airstrip, and detailed terrain information. In conjunction with the map of military facilities, it gives her a pretty good picture of the island.

But she will have to approach by water, so there is one more map to find—the nautical chart. *Here Be Monsters,* she thinks as she pictures a vintage nautical map, hand-drawn on yellowed parchment, serpents and kraken in the margins, beyond the realm of the known. It is how all maps appear in her head. And yet the most horrific monsters inhabit not the margins of maps but the margins of society. Walk among us, wear human skin. Monsters like Stephen Gordon. Her face has transformed, lips twisted, neck tight, cheeks flushed. She hates the sensation, whatever it is. She forces her thoughts to Mom instead, takes three slow, steady breaths, and regains her focus.

She goes to the website for the National Oceanic and Atmospheric Administration (NOAA) and clicks on *Chart Locator.* She zooms the global map in on southern California and within a minute has downloaded the detailed marine chart for San Nicolas Island. She opens it and zooms in. The chart shows water depths, locations of rocks and reefs, even the location of underwater cables—all the information she'd need to approach the island. But it also shows three Naval restricted areas that circle the entire island.

Restricted Area A is the one near the survey marker. Maybe a commercial fishing charter could get her close? But what good is close? The restricted areas appear to be two or three miles wide. What about a commercial *diving* charter? She's done a little diving with her parents, and at least that way she'd have a reason to be in the water and with the right gear.

She does an internet search for *San Nicolas Island diving,* clicks the first link, and scans the page. It doesn't have much information beyond a bullet list of dive characteristics—average depth, visibility, site quality, et cetera—but it does show the dive site on a zoomable map. Arizona zooms out and is surprised to see that the dive site is relatively close to the island, within the restricted area.

It's probably not an accurate map, she tells herself. She goes back to the search results and on to the next one.

DIVE SITES NEAR SAN NICOLAS ISLAND

Begg Rock . . .
Three Mile Reef . . .
The Boilers . . .
Alpha Area . . .

Alpha Area? Could that be Restricted Area A? She reads the description of the dive site and, sure enough, it says, *when access is allowed by the Navy.*

Eyes wide, Arizona scrolls back to the top of the page and clicks on the *Dive Calendar* tab. Many of the trips have been booked up. She finds a trip labeled *Begg Rock/San Nick* that is only a few days away and isn't marked as sold out. She clicks the *Book Now* button and finds out why. It's for advanced divers only. She hasn't done enough diving to sign up for an advanced trip.

She hesitates, then embellishes her diving experience and books a spot. She still isn't comfortable telling lies, but written lies are easier since nobody can hear them catch in your throat. Besides, what choice does she have? Mom's life is at stake.

She wants to scream, or punch something. She imagines the release, the brief moment of satisfaction it would provide, like popping a balloon. But she looks at Mojo, asleep on the daybed, and doesn't want to scare him. When he was just a puppy, her parents told her that animal companions should never be asked to carry our burdens but should lead lives of unfettered freedom. She desperately wants to live up to that ideal, to insulate Mojo—all that is left of her family—from this madness.

She's trying to hold it together but feels like she's coming apart at the seams. It's all just . . . impossible. Not only her mom and this insane task, but the thought that her dad—her dorky, sweet, pun-loving dad—was really hiding some gigantic secret. The kidnappers certainly seem convinced of it, and now, with the connection to surveying, it's feeling harder for her to deny.

And what does any of this have to do with alchemy, or Senator Sargent, or Malachi Sofer's grave?

She watches Mojo breathe, matches her breath to his, counts to ten. Right now, she reminds herself, none of the questions matter. All she has to do is take it one step at a time, put one foot in front of the other. For now, she has to make it to San Nicolas Island, find the survey marker, and bring back whatever clues are there with it.

Hope is a log on a raging river, and she clings to it.

17.

Searching

ARIZONA OPENS THE MAP APP AND SURVEYS THE ROUTE TO Ventura, from where the dive boat will sail in less than forty-eight hours. It's a nearly eight-hour drive from Carson City, and that doesn't include stops for gas, food, and bathroom breaks or account for the 55-mph towing speed limit. So at least ten hours realistically. The quickest route is along the east side of the Sierras, so she changes the destination from Ventura to Lone Pine and is pleased to see that it splits the trip in half. They're going back to the Alabama Hills after all. She can leave the Airstream there and take the truck to Ventura, where Mojo can spend a couple of days at a high-end dog kennel. She'll tell him it's a dog spa.

She looks at the time. One-thirty in the morning. It's been only twelve hours since they pulled into this campsite, fifteen hours since she found the note. But there is no time like the present. She can't sleep anyway, and traffic will be lighter in the middle of the night.

She goes outside and starts hitching up. Lily isn't out but there's a light on in her van, and Arizona thinks she sees the curtains move. As Arizona is finishing, the door of Lily's van slides open and she steps out.

"Looks like you're prepping to leave first thing in the morning."

"Not so much morning as now," Arizona says.

"That's pretty dramatic, the whole middle-of-the-night-getaway thing. Did something happen?"

"No," Arizona says, "but it's like you said. You can't give up on family."

Lily smiles. "Good for you. So are you going home to see your mom?"

"No, she's not home . . ." Arizona searches for words and adds, ". . . at the moment."

"Oh. Where is she? Where are you going?"

Where is she, indeed? Arizona skips that question. "My next stop is the Alabama Hills, down by Lone Pine."

"Never been there," Lily says.

"It's cool. They've shot a lot of movies there."

"I'll have to check it out. Well, be careful. Don't fall asleep at the wheel."

"I've got plenty of Coke."

Lily nods. "So you weren't planning on saying goodbye?"

"I, uh . . ."

"I'm just teasing."

Arizona looks at Lily's freckles and wide smile. It's been nice to have someone to talk to. She's a little sad to be saying goodbye, but she could never say so.

"Take care of yourself, Arizona-like-the-state."

"You, too, Lily-like-the-flower."

Lily smiles, steps back into her van, and slides the door closed.

Arizona puts Mojo in the truck, climbs in, and turns the key. She looks at Lily's van one last time, all its lights off now, and pulls out of camp.

THE FIRST TWO HOURS take them right back the way they came. She holds her breath as they pass Bodie Road, a rictus of pain across her face. As they pass their previous camp, where the Airstream was ransacked, her eyes dart around in search of suspicious vehicles. Are they still there? Watching her drive by?

With no bad memories associated with the area south of Bodie, a wave of relief washes over her. She turns on the radio to tune out the drone of the tires, sets the digital volume control to twenty-nine, a prime number. That and thirty-one are her favorites—twenty-three is too quiet and thirty-seven too loud. But she can't settle on anything and turns the radio off.

Another hour brings them to Bishop, where she stops for gas and snacks and takes Mojo for a pee walk. One hand holds Mojo's leash and the other a gas-station corn dog. She mulls over the thought that if the stick wasn't so pointy and frangible, corn dogs would be the perfect dog food. There are few things Mojo loves more than hot dogs and sticks.

She finishes her corn dog, puts Mojo in the truck, and walks around to the driver's side. But before getting in, she looks east. Barely visible beyond the glare of the gas station lights, the moon—waxing gibbous—reflects off the snow-clad peaks of the White Mountains. There, two vertical miles above the sea, grow the ancient bristlecone pines, the oldest living things in the world.

On the verge of mountain and desert, she stands and stares. To her west looms the great eastern escarpment of the Sierra Nevada, on the other side of which the manic search for gold altered the course of American history. To her east, in the rain shadow of the Sierra, lies the mammoth and aptly named Great Basin Desert, whose rivers, ever searching, never find the sea. Searching. It feels like she is always searching—in this moment, for the respite that nature provides her from the world of people, pressure, and pain. In the short term, in lieu of respite, perhaps resolve will do.

Back in the truck, Arizona notices she has a voicemail. Her heart races. Is it from Stephen Gordon? No, it's not a blocked number. She taps the PLAY button.

"Hi, Arizona. Sam Yeats here. Sorry to be calling so early, but I wanted to try to reach you before I left for home. We completed the search and didn't find anything. I'm sorry. I wish I had better news. I'm leaving the park now, so call me on my cell when you can."

Arizona calls Sam's cell and it goes straight to voicemail.

"Hey, Sam. Arizona here." She thinks about saying, *Sorry I missed*

THE LANGUAGE OF THE BIRDS

your call, but it wouldn't be true. She prefers the asynchronous nature of voicemail. "I got your message, thank you." She briefly wonders if she should share everything. The note, the ciphers, Pioneer Cemetery, the survey marker—but maybe not its location. But she needs to think about that some more, and it's way too much for voicemail anyway. "Maybe I'll try you again later." Or maybe not.

They motor on. The moon drops behind the mountains, silhouettes them against the predawn sky—charcoal strokes on a gunmetal canvas. During the rest of the drive, Arizona's mind wanders. She daydreams about Lily and Gus, wonders whether she should have told Lily that she was sad to say goodbye. What would Lily have said? Would she have given her their contact info? She thinks about Sam's search. If she had shared more with Sam, would it have helped or just put Mom in more danger? Then, despite her best efforts, her thoughts turn to another search, a few weeks earlier.

THE FAMILY HAD BEEN camping in Death Valley after the oppressive heat of summer had passed, and Dad had planned a day trip to two ghost towns—Rhyolite, Nevada, and Leadfield, California. However, after two days of hiking, Mom and Arizona were more interested in relaxing around camp.

"Come on," he said, "not just one but two ghost towns. And Titus Canyon, an epic canyon drive, to boot."

"I'm just going to take it easy today. But maybe Arizona will go with you."

"Sorry, Dad," Arizona said. "Me, neither. Just gonna hang out and read. Do you want to take Mojo?"

"No, he seems pretty content," he said with a smile as he looked at Mojo, who was snoring on his blanket. "All righty then, I guess I'll fly solo."

He leisurely packed lunch, snacks, water, and extra clothes into his Ural sidecar motorcycle, as if giving them time to change their minds before one last nudge. "You sure you won't join me?"

"Yes, go!" said Mom.

"Okay." He hopped on his bike and began to sing "Bohemian Rhapsody."

"If I'm not back again this time tomorrow, carry on, carry on, as if nothing really matters." He winked, pulled out of camp, and twisted the throttle more than necessary. His last words to his family would prove to be a prophetic choice.

When the sun dropped behind the mountains and the shadows stretched to draw the curtain of night, Dad had been gone longer than was needed to ride the loop. But Arizona told herself that wasn't completely out of the ordinary. He liked to stop and explore on foot, in ghost towns, on hiking trails, and even off trail. Nor was it unusual that he hadn't checked in by phone. Cell phones didn't work well in remote areas, especially in canyons.

"He's an experienced adventurer," said Mom. "He'll be fine. He probably had some minor mechanical issue, like a broken chain or spokes, and knew he didn't have enough daylight to walk out, so he settled in for the night. He'll walk or hitchhike out when the sun comes up. Titus Canyon Road is so popular he probably won't even have to wait that long to get a ride." Arizona wondered who her mom was trying to convince.

Dawn came. Mom and Arizona packed first-aid supplies, snacks, and water and hopped into the F-150 with Mojo in the back seat. An hour later they made the sharp left turn onto the dirt and gravel of Titus Canyon Road, raced across the dusty sagebrush flats, and began the climb into the red rocks of the Grapevine Mountains. The road became rough and steep. They passed the high point, Red Pass, at 5,213 feet, and began the vertical mile descent into Death Valley.

"You know that he probably already got a ride and he'll be waiting for us in camp with a beer in his hand, right?" Mom said.

"Yeah." As much as Arizona liked the image, she couldn't smile.

They descended the loose and winding road, keeping eyes peeled for anything that wasn't rock, dirt, or sagebrush.

"Mom, look," Arizona said, pointing to a gray wraith of smoke on the horizon.

"Probably just a campfire someone neglected to douse properly." Mom smiled, but her eyes betrayed her worry.

The truck bumped along the sawtooth spine of the serpent road, as the column of smoke grew wider and darker. Arizona feared what lay inside the dragon's flaming mouth. Mom would try to protect her, tell her to wait in the truck, but she had to see for herself. Mom pulled off at a wide spot in the road, but before the truck had even come to a stop, Arizona was out and plummeting down the steep slope toward the source of the smoke.

She scrambled as fast as her legs would carry her, slipping on the loose scree and rolling her ankles. She came to a stop halfway down so she could take her eyes off her feet. It looked like a vehicle wreck—too small for a car or truck, but too big for a motorcycle without a sidecar. She resumed her reckless descent and stopped about twenty feet from the smoking ruins. As she lifted her gaze from her feet again, her heart sank. Although it had been completely consumed by fire, she saw the clear outlines of a mangled sidecar motorcycle. But she didn't see a body.

She surveyed the scene and saw something thirty feet below the wreck, directly along the fall line. She continued down the incline until her worst fears were realized. Legs wobbly from the sight and smell of the grisly body, burned beyond recognition, Arizona collapsed onto the talus, catching herself with bare hands on shards of abrasive volcanic rock. She turned away from the corpse, emptied the contents of her stomach on the scree between her feet, and wiped the acrid-tasting drool from her mouth with a scraped hand. She put her elbows on her knees, head in hands, and summoned her courage. She had no right to hope that it wasn't her father, as sidecar motorcycles weren't exactly common, but she had to be sure.

She rose and continued toward the body until she was standing over it. She thought she could make out a wedding band but didn't have the stomach to remove it from the charred hand. So she turned her search to the figure-eight pendant that dated back to Dad's days as an amateur mountaineer. She was about to give up and go back to the ring when she spotted something, picked it up, rolled it in the palm of her hand, and blew the ash away. It was his pendant, its black nylon cord melted from the fire. As she stared at the pendant, she heard the sound of scree under Mom's boots. She turned and held out her open hand.

A WEEK LATER, ARIZONA had faithfully restrung the pendant, winding the cord around it the same way a climbing rope was wound around a figure-eight belay device.

She removes her right hand from the steering wheel, wipes tears away, caresses the pendant, and moves her hand back to the two o'clock position on the wheel. Safety first, after all.

18.

Dreams of
Forgotten Alchemists

D URING THE LONG DRIVE, WITH LITTLE TO DO BUT THINK, Arizona replays the conversation with Lily and wonders whether avoiding memories of Dad and Mom has been the right choice after all. It sidesteps some pain in the short term, sure, but is it akin to giving up on family? With Dad dead and Mom in danger, should she keep them closer instead of pushing them away?

She decides to conduct an experiment and camp in a specific site tied to good memories. A faint smile forms on her lips as she pictures the spot where the family parked the Airstream once before, only to find out later that it was the exact location of the bridge in the classic movie *Gunga Din*.

The surreal desert landscape of the Alabama Hills—curiously protruding rocks that stand up like the moai of Easter Island—and a dramatic mountain backdrop had made it a shooting location for hundreds of films and TV shows. On previous trips, the family visited the tiny Museum of Western Film History, did the self-guided tour of shooting locations, and reenacted many classic shots. With a lopsided smile, she recalls how excited Dad was when they found the residual boulder from *Tremors*, where Kevin Bacon, Fred Ward, and Finn Carter performed the pole-vaulting scene.

She pulls into the quaint downtown of Lone Pine, California, population 2,035. It's a few minutes after 6:00 A.M. and the truck windows are down, Mojo's head tilted back, nose twitching in the cool mountain air. They pass a diner, its exhaust fan pumping out the rich aromas of bacon grease and coffee. Arizona's stomach rumbles and Mojo whines, their snacks long since digested.

"I hear you, buddy. I'm hungry, too," she says as she turns right onto Whitney Portal Road. "I'll make breakfast as soon as we're parked—hopefully just fifteen minutes now."

In two and a half miles she takes another right onto Movie Road. *Movie*—short for *moving picture show*. She likes the longer term better. *Movie* somehow seems too informal. The pavement ends and she keeps driving, past the spot where Audie Murphy galloped by in *Showdown,* past *Lone Ranger* canyon, past the location of the graveside scene in *Rawhide,* past the *Tremors* residual boulder, and past the spot where Cesar Romero's Cisco Kid seemed to be out of luck in *The Gay Caballero.*

Her smile expands—albeit only slightly—when she sees that nobody is camped in *their* spot. She pulls in, makes sure the trailer is relatively level from side to side, shuts off the truck, and goes through the unhitching checklist.

With the driving done and the truck unhitched, she takes in the splendor of the mountains, the imposing east face of Mount Whitney aglow from the rising sun. A plume of white trails off the summit—snow chased off by withering winds. She stares at the facets and gullies, wrinkles on the weathered face of the mountain, and pictures the cartoonish illustrations from Dad's old edition of *Mountaineering: The Freedom of the Hills.*

Gradually, she becomes aware of the absence of uncomfortable feelings—no weight on her chest, no taut muscles, no queasiness. She wonders if it's the same as being happy. No, but maybe it's a start. Regardless, it doesn't matter now. Her phone is ringing and the feelings are back.

Blocked number. "What?" she says.

"Progress?"

"I decoded the second cipher, but—"

"Read it to me."

"Hang on," she says. "I don't have it memorized." She wakes up her MacBook and reads the poem.

"Very good."

"So, you knew that one, too? Doesn't really seem like you need me, or my mom."

"Why did you move?"

We'll be watching. Arizona looks out the windows but sees nobody.

"You don't know?" she says.

"Maybe I just want to hear it from you."

"I'm going somewhere, and this is on the way."

"Where are you going?"

"San Nicolas Island," she says after a breath.

"Very good. I'm going to let you talk to your mother, but only long enough so you know it's her."

Seconds pass, feeling like hours. Arizona's heart races.

"Hi, honey."

"Mom, is that really you? Are you okay? Where are you?"

"Yes, it's really me, and I'm all right. Don't—"

Mom—and it is definitely her—is cut off, and Gordon comes back on the line.

"When will you get to the island?"

"About forty-eight hours from now. That's the best I can do." What had Mom been trying to say? *Don't worry? Don't cooperate? Don't what?*

"Why the delay?"

She exhales a sigh of exasperation. "Seriously? You obviously had the solution to both ciphers, and you didn't sound at all surprised when I said where I was going. So you must know what I'm up against, right? I can't just stroll onto that island like some wayward beachcomber."

"Then what's the plan?"

"I booked a diving trip to that area, and I was lucky they had an opening so soon. It leaves Ventura tomorrow night and returns forty-eight hours later. If my luck continues, I'll be able to sneak onto the island and find what I'm looking for. Or, more accurately, what you're looking for."

"Smart," he says. "And what happens if your luck doesn't continue?"

"It seems like I should be the one asking that question."

"True enough, and I expect you know the answer."

She expects she does, too, but can't say it out loud. Can't even think about it without getting sick. She swallows to get the acrid bile back down.

"I'll take your silence as confirmation that you understand," he says. "Good luck. Your mother is counting on you."

Click. Disconnected.

Veins stand out on her neck and her pulse pounds. His last words ring in her ears. *Your mother is counting on you.* So much for the peace of Alabama Hills. She looks toward Mount Whitney again, but the summit is enveloped by threatening clouds.

AFTER SHE CALMS DOWN, eats breakfast, and has a brief nap, she has thirty hours to kill before leaving for Ventura. She throws herself headlong into alchemy research. Any day is a good day to read, but rainy days even more so. She was both lucky and negligent in that regard—negligent in not checking the weather forecast before towing the trailer, and lucky that the storm hadn't arrived earlier. When it does, it arrives with fury. Fog enshrouds mountain and foothills. Wind and rain hammer the Airstream, corrugate the dry earth into a series of rills that terminate in the small canyon adjacent to the campsite. Arizona loves the sound of rain on the trailer, the soothing plinks of raindrops on its thin aluminum skin.

As she begins her research within the warm and dry confines of the trailer, she recalls another of her introductions to alchemy, looks up a quote, and copies it into her notebook.

As a child I had not been content with the results promised by the modern professors of natural science. With a confusion of ideas only to be accounted for by my extreme youth and my want of a guide on such matters, I had retrod the steps of knowledge along the paths of time and exchanged the discoveries of recent inquirers for the dreams of forgotten alchemists.

—MARY SHELLEY,
Frankenstein

Reading about alchemists had been fascinating, but when she tried to read the writings of the alchemists themselves, she had become disenchanted by their abstruse nature.

But now she needs to know more about alchemy, much more. She makes a list of books to read, prioritizes it, finds free digitized versions of many of the classics written by the alchemists, and buys ebook versions of the rest.

> *The Triumphal Chariot of Antimony*, by Basil Valentine,
>   and his *Last Will and Testament*
> *The Mirror of Alchimy*, by Roger Bacon
> *Of the Transmutation of Metals*, by Paracelsus
> *A New Light of Alchymie*, by Michael Sendivogius
> *Mutus Liber* and *Splendor Solis*, both comprised only
>   of elaborate illustrations
> *The Mystery of the Cathedrals* and *The Dwellings of the
>   Philosophers*, by twentieth-century alchemist Fulcanelli
> *Alchemy and its Mute Book*—a commentary on *Mutus
>   Liber*—by Eugène Canseliet, a disciple of Fulcanelli

Half reading and half scanning, she starts working her way through the bizarre texts, extracting what she can from the volumes of alchemical riddles. What she does glean, she absorbs just as the dry ground does the rain—until a knock at her door makes her jump and drop her iPad.

"What the fuck," she says. Lily was right—that's definitely more satisfying than *frick*.

Mojo concurs with a growl.

She looks at the deadbolt—locked, good—and then at the time.

4:05 P.M. She gets up and looks out the window over the sink. Someone is standing at the door, in a blue parka with the hood up. From this angle she can't see the face.

Knock, knock, knock again.

"Go away!" Arizona says, for lack of a better idea.

She thinks she hears a response, but it's hard to tell over the tumult of the rain.

Whoever it is, they're not leaving.

Fuck. Fuck. Fuck.

19

Awkward

ARIZONA RAPS ON THE WINDOW. "GO AWAY!"

The hood of the blue parka turns to the window, framing Lily's face.

"What the . . ." Arizona says under her breath.

Lily raises a hand, waves, and smiles. Water streams down her freckled face.

Arizona unlocks the door and opens it. "What are you doing here?"

"Nice to see you, too," Lily says. "Can I come in? It's kinda wet out here."

Arizona steps aside and closes the door behind Lily.

"Wow, nice rig," Lily says as she drops her hood and unzips her parka.

"Thanks. It's my parents'." *Parents*, plural. A fog swirls inside her head, then dissipates. "So, what are you doing here?"

"Here in Alabama Hills or here in your trailer?" Lily smiles, pulls the kerchief off her head, pats her face dry, and stuffs the kerchief in a pocket.

"Both."

"Here in Alabama Hills because you told me it's a cool place. Here in your trailer because I enjoyed hanging out with you and, since we're both traveling alone, I thought maybe we could keep each other company."

Arizona doesn't know what to say. She did like having someone to talk to, and Lily seems nice. But being followed here is a little weird. "I, uh, have a bunch of reading I have to do."

"Like studying? Schoolwork?"

"Where's Gus?"

"He's in the van, dry and warm. I'll go back and get him if you're cool with me hanging here."

"Yeah," Arizona says. She waits for more words to come out, but they don't.

"Is that yeah, you're studying, or yeah, I can hang out?"

"Both, I guess."

"What are you studying?"

"History."

"I like history. Well, some of it anyway. What era?"

"I'm studying alchemy."

"Alchemy, really?"

"Yeah, do you know much about it?"

"Well, I read *Harry Potter*. And I know that the first book was *Harry Potter and the Philosopher's Stone* in the UK, but here in the States it had to be *Harry Potter and the Sorcerer's Stone* because Americans are apparently too stupid to know what the philosopher's stone is."

Arizona titters and brings her eyes to Lily's. In the close quarters of the trailer, she can see flecks in Lily's eyes, like her eyes have freckles, too. Freckle fractals. She smiles, crooked and tight-lipped, for the first time since opening the door.

Lily smiles back.

One, two, three breaths, and Arizona looks away.

"Well, if you're sure it's cool, I'll go get Gus, and then you can tell me all about alchemy."

Arizona looks into Lily's eyes again and nods.

THEY SPEND TWO HOURS reading, talking, and walking the dogs when the rain lets up. Lily is kind of a chatterbox, so Arizona gets only half as much reading done as she would otherwise. But still, it's nice to have someone to talk to again.

"So," says Lily, "weren't the alchemists basically a bunch of bullshit artists? I mean the whole turning-lead-into-gold thing?"

"Some of them were con artists, sure. But many of them were also brilliant scientists. There's another quote from *Frankenstein*—hang on." Arizona pokes at her iPad.

"You're quite the nerd, aren't you?"

Arizona is whisked back to school, to the name-calling. Her smile melts into a grimace of betrayal. "So?" she says.

"No need to get defensive," Lily says. "I was just teasing. I like nerds."

She looks into Lily's eyes but sees no malice. "I hate it when people say you're being defensive. If you say yes, then you're copping to it, and if you say no, then they say *see, you're being defensive.* It's a trap. It's not fair."

"I see your point. I'll try to avoid that going forward."

"Do you want to hear the quote or not?"

"Yes."

"*These were men to whose indefatigable zeal modern philosophers were indebted for most of the foundations of their knowledge. They had left to us, as an easier task, to give new names and arrange in connected classifications the facts which they in a great degree had been the instruments of bringing to light. The labours of men of genius, however erroneously directed, scarcely ever fail in ultimately turning to the solid advantage of mankind.*"

"Cool." Lily smiles.

"The reason they thought they could transmute base metals into precious metals was that they believed all metals were made of the same basic ingredients but in different proportions. So, by separating a metal into its constituent parts, another metal could theoretically be produced by recombining those parts in different proportions. And they were right, of course, in that metals—and everything else, for that matter—are made of smaller things, the things we now know as molecules and atoms."

Lily nods. Her eyes stay on Arizona's.

"If you go back far enough, the great thinkers didn't confine themselves to a single field of study. They were true polymaths. The work of the alchemists even predates the term *science*. Back then the term *phi-losopher* just referred to a thinking person, regardless of field of study."

"As in the philosopher's stone," Lily says.

"Exactly." Their eyes meet for a breath, then Arizona returns to her reading. But she is smiling.

"I know I'm distracting you," Lily says, "so I'll give you a break and go feed Gus. But maybe we can hang out a little more later?"

"Oh, okay. Yeah."

Lily pries Gus away from Mojo and heads back to her van.

Arizona tries to read, but for some reason Lily is an even bigger distraction now that she's gone. Weird.

BY THE TIME SHE gives up on reading, the rain has stopped and the world has spun into darkness. Stars poke through parting clouds as she takes Mojo for a walk. She thinks about the diving trip and leaving him at the kennel. She has to leave in eighteen hours, and some of that should be sleep. The cold air wraps her chest and squeezes, makes it ache. But the air isn't that cold. It's the thought of leaving Mojo—and maybe, just a little, sneaking onto an island controlled by the Navy.

Mojo will be fine, she tells herself. The diving trip is only two nights, departing in the evening and returning less than forty-eight hours later. And she'll be fine, too. After all, she's accustomed to a lack of companionship. But it isn't true. She's accustomed to a lack of *human* companionship. For years now, time spent alone has been time spent with Mojo. He has been her constant companion. A great listener, al-ways up for exploring, and never judgmental. The perfect brother and best friend. And now he's the only family she has left. So how can she leave him, even for forty-eight hours? And with strangers. But what choice does she have?

"Hey," says a voice from nearby.

Arizona turns to see Lily and Gus. "Hey," she says.

"You need your hearing checked. I had to say *hey* three times."

"Sorry. Lots on my mind."

"No worries. Feel free to share the burden if you want."

Arizona doesn't respond.

"Or not," says Lily. "How goes the reading?"

"I think I'm done, for today at least. I'm kinda read out, which is rare for me."

"Well, in that case, do you want to do something more fun?"

"There's something more fun than reading?" Arizona grins.

"Oh, my God, did you make a joke? There may be hope for you yet, AZ."

The corners of Arizona's mouth twist downward.

"Sorry," says Lily. "Do you not like that? AZ is the abbreviation for Arizona, you know."

"Yeah, I know. It's just that my dad used to call me that."

"Oh, my bad. I'll refrain if you want. But Arizona is like a thousand syllables."

"It's okay, I guess. What do you want to do?"

"Well, it's still too wet to have a campfire, so something inside. Do you have any mindless games? Spin the bottle?" Lily winks.

Arizona blushes. "Does dominoes qualify? Just a little addition."

"I can probably do that, if you can teach me."

"Dominoes or addition?"

Lily laughs. "You go, girl."

They turn and head for the Airstream, Mojo and Gus leading the way.

THEY'VE BEEN PLAYING DOMINOES for an hour when Lily asks a question.

"Do you want to do something tomorrow? Maybe go into Lone Pine or go hiking up at Whitney Portal?"

"Both of those sound fun, but I have to leave tomorrow afternoon."

"Oh?" Lily's smile flattens. "Connecting with your mom?"

"Uh, no, not yet. I'm going on a diving trip."

"Like scuba diving? Cool. I've always wanted to try that. Where?"

"Out of Ventura. I'll be back in two days, plus driving time."

"You're coming back here?"

Arizona nods. "Yeah, I'm going to leave the trailer and just take the truck."

"You want me to keep an eye on it for you? Scare off any big baddies? I can be pretty intimidating, you know."

Arizona smiles. "I have no doubt. Sure, but if the baddies are particularly big, maybe you should, you know, take it easy on them."

"Sage advice, young one. What about Mojo?"

Mojo's ears perk up.

"Well, I booked a kennel for him. It looks really nice."

Lily nods, mouth flat again.

"But," Arizona says, "would you be willing to take care of him instead?"

"I'd love to." Lily touches Arizona's hand. "So, Mojo would be like my ward for two days. What if he goes off looking for you and doesn't come back?"

"Then I'll have to hunt you down and kill you."

"Something tells me you're not kidding," Lily says. "Well, that's a little awkward. OMG, Mojo will be my awk-ward!" She laughs.

Arizona smiles without thinking, as if her mouth has a mind of its own.

20

The Adept and the
Journal — Part Two

A SPIDER WALKS ACROSS THE DESK, CATCHES HIS ATTENTION. He thinks back to his youth, to the spider he caught as a boy. He had pulled off one of its legs to see how it would get along, then another. Three. Four. Not all on the same side, of course—he was curious, not cruel. Once it had only four legs left, he wondered if he had transformed it into a mammal. Spiders had eight legs, so it certainly wasn't a spider anymore.

He returns his attention to the journal, tilts it into the cone of yellow light from the table lamp, and runs his forefinger along the ragged edges of the missing pages. Wonders what has been forever lost. A hangnail catches, so he peels it back beyond the quick, like plucking off the leg of a spider. Blood collects in the well of his fingernail.

He flips to the bookmark, taking care to not get blood on the precious pages, and once again reads about what the NSA analyst found hidden within the inexplicably redacted documents.

[missing text]

> within the redacted set of drawings I found three sets of numbers. Two of these sets were composed only of numbers ranging from one to twenty-six, and a straightforward substitution of letters for numbers yielded two alphabetic ciphers,

which I will discuss in detail later. The purpose of the third set of numbers eluded me until I realized that its range corresponded to the number of redactions in the booklet. Stringing together the redacted words and phrases from the booklet, but in the order specified by that third set of numbers, resulted in the following twelve coherent yet inconceivable sentences and a signature of sorts (punctuation added):

Man's control over natural forces has grown, but we were forever held back by the limited knowledge bred down to us through the past experience of the whole race of men.

Just the few prodigies were able to navigate through the darkness and cast off the apparel, disguises, or trappings which the weak wear in order to seem great.

Before the collective genius of the masters, the potent powers of evolution were forever held in the guardianship of the Creator.

The potential nobility of the race of men is an achievement within the reach of the art.

Within the reach of the art. He dons a knowing smile. Twelve sentences. Twelve signs of the zodiac. Twelve steps in the Great Work, from Calcination through Projection. He has come so far in his knowledge. Soon he will make the final transition, from Adept to Master.

Time, the intangible governor of all our acts, is the nemesis of the human race.

The exhilaration of a journey far flung, the enormous power to live for thousands of years, nearly imperishable against the oblivion imposed by time.

Thousands of years, he thinks. *Nearly imperishable.* So many great minds had their lives cut short by disease. So many lost before they even scratched the surface of their potential. All that can change.

The practice of the masters was to speak in the lexicon of complex code—vessel of quicksilver, signs of the zodiac; even the spoken word may not state the truth.

But the ancient key to interpreting and understanding the great work was inadvertently found.

The ancient key. He wonders about its form, pictures the possibilities. A key of solid gold to unlock an ageless door? Or is it merely figurative? Diagrams and symbols on a long-lost manuscript? He will know soon. But still not soon enough.

But the result was unprecedented strife among the members of the inner circle.

Therefore, with withered hopes and the knowledge that humanity is treading with uncertain, emotional steps the paths of youth in springtime, the Secret was put away for future generations.

Just after the Apex of the Sun's way in space, the fire was set in bodies to burn the Secret, but the fire was not successful.

The Secret remains and lies within.

Kingfisher

The name echoes in his mind. *Kingfisher.* Fisher King. Who had he been? Someone of great power, to hide the secret within government documents. Perhaps a member of the original Golden Dawn?

He lowers the journal onto the table and daydreams about the power almost within his grasp. Power that his own mother—*dearest Maggie* to her government colleagues—had tried to keep from him. His right hand curls into a fist, fingernails plowing furrows in his palm.

21.

Kick, Jump, and Run

SHE IS FREE FROM THE POST BUT STILL STUCK IN THE SMALL room. The door opens in, so she jams the chair between the floor and the doorknob. It might buy her a few seconds, but no more. She walks over to the far wall, through which light is still streaming, and finds a crack that she can see through, at least a little. It is indeed an outside wall, as she had hoped. There is snow on the ground. But she can't see enough to tell where she is or if people are around.

Kick, jump, and run isn't much of a plan, but it's all she has. She examines the wall for loose or rotten boards. She pushes as hard as she can on the bottom of one, and it creaks loose. She turns sideways to see if she can fit through the opening. No, and the adjacent boards are solid. She lies down on her back with her feet to the wall and worms her torso closer, until her knees are bent. Rather than kicking, she uses the strength of her legs to push on the bottom of an adjacent board, hoping it will come loose quietly. Instead, it cracks in half, and she cringes at the noise. But the hole is big enough. She slips through and runs as fast as her legs and lungs will carry her.

She ducks around the corner of the nearest building, a shed so dilapidated that she worries it might fall down and give her away. She scans the horizon to get her bearings. Everything is familiar. Then she recognizes the unmistakable profile of the stamp mill. She is still in Bodie. Gordon was right about nothing being around for miles. She won't get far on foot, especially in the snow, but maybe she doesn't have to. If she can make it to the park office, a ranger could be there, or at least a phone. She needs to reach Arizona again, make sure she's okay. How much time has passed since they took her? At least one night, plus however long she was out after they drugged her. So maybe thirty-six hours? Forty-eight? Where would Arizona even be? Somewhere with cell reception, she hopes.

She sees the steeple of the Methodist Church, which is just past the park office. It's probably less than a quarter mile, but it looks so far away. The first few buildings are easy, close together. That gets her to the edge of the closed area, where she lifts one strand of the simple barbed-wire fence and ducks through. But now she has a decision to make—beeline it for the office across open terrain, or take a longer route and keep to the areas with more buildings, more cover.

She opts for the direct route and makes a mad dash for a barn less than a hundred yards away. She ducks behind it and stoops over with hands on knees, gasps for breath, and peeks around the corner to see if she is being pursued. Nobody yet.

The next stretch is another hundred yards, to the firehouse, she thinks. She takes off as fast as she can, but the thin air at eight thousand feet slows her down. If anything, the air feels thick, like trying to breathe syrup.

About halfway, she stops to give her lungs another break and ducks down against the shallow bank of Bodie Creek. She pokes her head up, like a soldier in a trench war, and looks back toward the barn and stamp mill. Still nobody.

A few seconds later, she is up out of the creek bed and running full tilt for the firehouse. She reaches the southeast corner and slows to a jog along the south wall to catch her breath. As she approaches the southwest corner, two men step out from behind the building and she runs right into them. One slams her into the old planked wall, while the other binds her arms behind her back with zip ties.

"Got her," one of them says into a two-way radio, while the other slides a hood over her head. Someone replies over the radio. She doesn't catch what they say, but it doesn't matter.

———

MINUTES LATER SHE IS back inside, standing with her hands still bound behind her back.

"I'm curious what you used to cut the zip ties," says the now-familiar voice.

She thinks of Arizona again, draws on her sarcasm. "My sharp wit," she says through the hood.

"Search her," he says to the men still holding her arms.

They pat her down, reach into one of her front pockets, and pull out a nail.

"Clever. Put her on the cot, face up, and bind her hands and feet to the cot. Then leave us."

The men do as they are told and leave without saying a word, closing the door behind them. He pulls the hood off her head. As her eyes adjust to the light, she sees the man with the balaclava standing over her. The wall behind him has already been patched with plywood from the outside.

"I'm sorry that you now have to have both your hands and feet bound," he says. "But it's your own doing."

She doesn't reply. He walks to the door, steps through, and turns back toward her.

"We'll talk more later," he says as he closes the door.

Are you sure? she thinks. *You only found one nail, didn't you, asshole?*

22

Serenity and Lack Thereof

DURING THE FOUR-HOUR DRIVE FROM THE ALABAMA HILLS to Ventura, Arizona tries not to think about Mojo. She pushes the thoughts away, but they keep pushing back. Her heart doesn't just ache, it keens. And yet she feels hollow, like an apple that has been cored. How can her insides hurt if they are no longer there? Tears flow, and not only for Mojo. What if she can't find the marker beneath the sand? What if it's not even the right marker? What if she gets caught by the Navy?

She drives past the Ventura Harbor shops and restaurants, finds the parking lot, and grabs her small duffel bag of clothes and a few personal items. She's arranged to rent the diving gear on board, explaining that she's on an extended vacation away from home. It's mostly true.

She follows the signs to G Dock and walks to the end, where the dive boat is moored. Small waves slap against hulls and splintered pilings. Ropes creak as they pull taut, slack, and taut again. Arizona looks up as western gulls circle and caw. As she approaches, a tanned young man in a sleeveless shirt says, "Not all who wander are lost."

"Excuse me?" Arizona says.

"Not all who wander are lost. That's what your T-shirt says. I like it."

"Oh, yeah. Me, too. I'm a dive client for the San Nick trip. Are you the captain?"

"Ha! That's a good one. The captain will get a laugh out of that, for sure. No, ma'am, I'm Ryan, just a crew member, but by all means, please come aboard." He motions to the gangplank with an open hand. "A couple of other folks already checked in, but they went to get a bite to eat since we won't be sailing for a while yet. Let me grab Captain Jack for you."

Ryan goes below and returns moments later, followed by a hand-some middle-aged man with broad shoulders, a broader waist, and a full head of light-brown hair that has been highlighted by years of sun and sea air and seems like it belongs on a younger man. Or maybe his wizened skin just belongs on an older man.

"Hello there, young lady," he booms in a baritone voice. "I'm Captain Jack. I know what you're thinking—I don't look anything like Captain Jack Sparrow from the movies. And it's a good thing, too, lest I scare off the customers. And who might you be?"

"I'm Arizona. I booked a couple of days ago."

"Yes, yes, excellent. Welcome aboard *Serenity,* the finest dive boat in southern California, to be sure."

Arizona smiles a genuine smile, albeit crooked and tight-lipped, and thinks it must be hard not to smile when you meet Captain Jack.

"Thank you, Captain. I'm looking forward to it."

"As you should be, young lady, as you should be." He turns to Ryan. "Please give our young guest a quick tour of the public areas and show her where she can stow her gear."

"Aye aye, sir," says Ryan with a comical salute.

Captain Jack chuckles, shakes his head, and goes back below.

"May I take your duffel?" Ryan says as he reaches for Arizona's bag.

"No thanks, I've got it," Arizona says, holding on tightly.

"Come on, I'll show you around." Ryan leads the way and recites the details of the boat from memory.

"*Serenity* is sixty-five feet stem to stern, with a twenty-two-foot beam. She sleeps up to thirty-two guests. All bunks have privacy curtains, lights, pillows, and blankets. There are two heads, both with showers, and an outdoor freshwater shower, too. When not diving, guests spend most of their time either up on deck or here in our large galley—mostly the latter, I'd say. You won't go hungry on this boat,

Arizona. Three squares a day, and damn good food if I do say so. Homemade desserts, too. There's a soda machine right there, along with ice and water. . . ."

Five minutes later they finish the introductory tour.

"And we sail at eleven o'clock tonight?" Arizona says.

"That's the goal, but it could be a little earlier or later depending on when everyone checks in. We'll sail all night while you folks sleep, and then you'll get up and do some of the best diving of your life."

"That sounds all right to me," she says, albeit with a notable lack of enthusiasm.

ONCE EVERYONE IS ON BOARD, they gather in the galley for introductions while the crew sets sail. The engines thrum and the lights flicker. The floor moves beneath their feet. Arizona's insides twist and swirl about, like the water behind the propellers.

The introductions start on the other side of the room, giving her a chance to brace herself for the onslaught of talking to a group. As the other divers speak, one by one or sometimes as couples—sharing names, hometowns, and diving experience—Arizona pictures them all as dominoes, falling inevitably in her direction. She hopes she doesn't fall face-first.

The oldest group comprises eight retirees, five men and three women, most of whom have decades of diving experience. They are followed in age and experience by two groups, a total of eight men and five women, who Arizona figures to be in their late thirties or early forties. They seem nice enough, but the level of chatter they generate is a bit overwhelming. It reminds her of school, of the cacophony of the playground. She hated the playground.

As the person before her speaks, Arizona takes a few deep breaths, just like her parents taught her. *Parents,* plural. Again. Dammit.

Her turn arrives, she opens her mouth, and the words flow out. "I'm Arizona. Home is in the small town of Grass Valley, up in Gold Country, but we've mostly been traveling with our Airstream for the last couple years." No stuttering, no stumbling, no big deal. Weird.

Last, there are two young men who Arizona thinks must have recently turned twenty-one, based on their inability to consume alcohol without acting like asses. Or maybe it's not the alcohol, but either way they won't leave her alone.

"Hey, what's your name again?" one of the young men asks.

"It's still Arizona."

"So, how long have you been diving?"

"Several years," Arizona says, stretching the truth.

"Cool. We've just been diving for a couple years now, but we're already into pretty advanced stuff."

"You do know that I'm not of the age of consent, right?" Arizona says.

"What?"

"Never mind." She shakes her head.

Before she can add anything else, one of the retired men, with gray hair and a warm smile, turns to the young man. "Hey, for the sake of a harmonious trip, can you give it a rest? She's clearly not interested."

"Sorry" is all the young man can muster, which he says more to the older man than to Arizona.

LATER THAT NIGHT, the older gentleman with the gray hair and warm smile approaches Arizona.

"Hi, Arizona. I'm Marty, in case you don't recall. Hey, I'm sorry if I stepped on your toes earlier. I'm sure you could have shut that down by yourself, but I have no tolerance for guys like that."

"I appreciated it. I just . . . well, I kind of have a lot on my mind and don't feel like confrontation, I guess."

Marty smiles and looks into Arizona's eyes while she looks past him.

"I understand," he says. "I've been there myself, although maybe not at so young an age. But I think things were simpler when I was growing up. Young folks seem to have so much on their minds these days. People so young shouldn't have to carry such weight."

The words catch her off guard. She wonders if she is that transparent. "That's a nice thought," she belatedly replies, "but it seems that life doesn't always work that way."

Marty nods slowly. "True enough. By the way, I loved your not-of-the-age-of-consent remark. Not many young folks speak like that."

Arizona looks away, embarrassed. "Too many old books, I guess."

Marty smiles again. "No such thing." His eyes flit up to the right, as if recalling something. "Did you ever hear that Arthur Conan Doyle quote? *The love of books in your heart is among the choicest gifts of the gods.*"

Arizona finds herself smiling in return. She doesn't know that line—*must be from one of his non–Sherlock Holmes writings,* she thinks—but she certainly likes the sentiment.

There is something very comforting about Marty, as if kindness and wisdom flow out of him. Arizona is grateful for his presence. Wait. What did she just think? She appreciates the company of someone who isn't family? And Marty isn't even the first, is he? It's as if Lily opened a door within her and left it open. And now people are coming and going as they please.

23.

Under Water

IN THE MORNING, EVERYONE GATHERS FOR BREAKFAST IN THE galley, where the crew reviews safety procedures, much to Arizona's relief.

"So," says Captain Jack, "which dive spots would you all like to visit first?"

"Begg Rock!" say numerous voices.

"We're already there," the captain says with a chuckle, "and conditions are surprisingly good. But keep in mind that Begg Rock is directly exposed to weather from all directions, which is why it's for experienced divers only. If the conditions deteriorate, we'll have to move on. Where else?"

"Alpha Area?" says Arizona.

"That's a good possibility, Arizona," says the captain. "As I think you all know, the Navy has given us permission for Alpha Area this time. If the swell gets too big for Begg Rock, which it often does, Alpha Area can be an excellent alternative. Lots of lobster there, for sure. Any other spots that folks are itchin' to see?"

"Three Mile Reef," suggests one of the thirty-somethings.

"Great diving to be sure but, like Begg Rock, Three Mile Reef is very exposed. I think a good plan would be to do one or more dives here at Begg Rock, then Three Mile Reef if the conditions remain calm enough, and then head into Alpha Area if, or more likely *when*, the swell picks up. How does that sound?"

Everyone cheers. They all know that trips often get rerouted due to conditions at Begg Rock or the Navy's presence on San Nick. A good forecast and permission from the Navy are more than they could hope for.

But Arizona can't stop thinking about all that has gone wrong already and all that could still go wrong.

Mom. *Your mother is counting on you.*

Mojo. Is he okay? Does he think she abandoned him?

Diving. She's no expert.

Landing in the brig or, worse, getting shot.

Fortunately, she doesn't have to worry about those last possibilities yet. This is just a dive, and the conditions are good. Even though her stomach is doing somersaults, she finishes her bagel and juice. She thought the stickiness of oatmeal might be less likely to come back up, but she's seen recent evidence to the contrary—when the oatmeal came galumphing back.

By 7:30 A.M., the most eager divers have already stepped off the stern dive platform of *Serenity*. Arizona finishes donning everything but her mask, steps to the back of the short line of waiting divers, pulls on and adjusts her mask, waits for the signal from the crew, and steps off into the mild swell.

Just deep enough to be free of the effects of the swell, she follows the group toward Begg Rock, an underwater pinnacle rising three hundred feet from the floor of the Pacific Ocean. As they arrive at the fringes of the submarine spire, the group drifts apart into yet smaller groups and pairs. Marty had offered to be her dive buddy, and she eagerly accepted. Better the devil you know.

While some of the other divers plan to descend to depths of one hundred feet or more, Marty and Arizona agree to keep this first dive to fifty feet. It's as deep as she's ever dived, but she can't admit that to anyone. Marty leads and she follows about twenty feet behind, close enough for them to easily see each other within the forty-foot visibility but not so close as to crowd him. He's an excellent dive buddy, turning around frequently and waiting for the thumbs-up from Arizona before continuing onward.

Even only thirty feet below the surface, Begg Rock is carpeted with life—green, brown, and red seaweed; urchins and anemones of every conceivable shape and size; starfish of every color; scallops, mussels, and myriad other mollusks—and surrounded by a plethora of fish small, medium, and large. It is another world down here, and she welcomes the escapism. Like the rays of the sun, her anxieties don't penetrate the depths below. She breathes calmly, perhaps even more so than above the surface, where paradoxically the pressures feel much greater.

They swim slowly, and sometimes not at all, and gaze at the underwater crag. As Marty is looking at Arizona and she back at him, a double-crested cormorant shoots down vertically between them like feathered lightning, diving for its breakfast. Arizona almost spits the regulator right out of her mouth. She pictures the unique adaptation of pelicans and cormorants—four webbed toes, versus three for ducks and geese—and thinks of a time when the family was kayaking on Drakes Estero. An entire flock of California brown pelicans, dozens if not hundreds, dove into the water on every side of them for what seemed like minutes on end.

Back on board, Marty raises his hand to Arizona for a high-five.

"That was awesome," she says as they smack palms.

"Indeed," Marty says.

But before she can even get her wetsuit off, her thoughts return to her family. She feels hollow again, as if her insides are falling out, stuck to the neoprene of the wetsuit. Is it wrong to feel happy, even if only briefly, when everything is so messed up? Is this what survivor's guilt feels like?

Marty notices the sudden shift in her mood and asks, "What's wrong?"

"Just all that stuff on my mind," she says.

To her relief, Marty nods and doesn't push further.

"Attention please," the captain bellows. "Conditions here at Begg Rock are so uncommonly good that we'll stay put for at least one more dive. So, get your tanks and bellies recharged and do it again."

"Well," Marty says, "we can't disobey a direct order, can we?"

Arizona smiles.

"Will you honor me by being my dive buddy again?" Marty asks.

"Of course," says Arizona.

THEIR SECOND DIVE IS no less spectacular than the first, and a little deeper. Octopus, bat rays, dozens of California spiny lobsters, and a few small sharks add to the excitement. The swell starts to pick up, but just slightly, and Captain Jack announces that he is going to steer the boat to Three Mile Reef while the conditions are still favorable.

With each dive and the time on board between dives, Marty and Arizona get to know each other better. Marty's wife passed a couple of years ago, after almost forty years together. He has a daughter and a son but no grandchildren. "Not yet, anyway."

Arizona finds herself telling him about Dad's death and admits to being worried about her mom. It's as close to the truth as she can get. Sharing her burdens lifts a small weight off her shoulders, at least in the short term.

The trip was advertised as having eight dives plus one night dive. However, they'll have to spend most of the next day getting back to Ventura, which only leaves time in the morning for two or three dives at most. While Arizona's confidence increases with each dive, so do two other things—the size of the swell and her anxiety that the chance to sneak onto San Nick is slipping away. After two dives at Three Mile Reef, she is freaking out on the inside. And maybe not just inside, as she thinks Marty is increasingly aware of her anxiety.

When Captain Jack announces that the swell has increased and it's time to move on to the next site, sounds of disappointment echo throughout the crowd.

"I know, I know, but you've had a pretty rare day of dives so far, right?"

Cheers replace the disappointment.

"That's more like it. Although the swell has gotten bigger, it's shifted from northwesterly to straight westerly, which means the part of Alpha Area closest to San Nick could provide some protection. So, before we retreat to one of the other islands, we're going to check out Alpha Area. To be clear, I'm not making any promises. But it's worth a short trip."

More cheers, albeit less boisterous.

Arizona's stomach does more somersaults. *Alpha Area*, she thinks. This is it. This is her chance. *Please.*

She stays topside for the short trip to Alpha Area and watches with eager eyes as San Nicolas Island gets closer and closer. The captain heads directly for the northernmost point of the island and then adjusts course to the southeast, following the shoreline. At first it seems that the swell hasn't decreased at all, but then, as they continue along the shore of San Nick, the wind lets up, and in two minutes the swell has been cut in half. *Please,* she thinks again.

A minute later the vibration of the engines ceases and the crew casts anchor. In the galley, the captain tells everyone that if the conditions don't deteriorate while they're having dinner, those interested can do a night dive here in Alpha Area.

The butterflies in Arizona's stomach feel more like vampire bats, and it isn't motion sickness. Thoughts race through her head as she tries to eat. But the thought that Mom's safety—her *life*—is dependent on the wind and waves is just killing her. She has no appetite and can't tune out the sounds of everyone chewing, anyway. She has four bites and goes up on deck to monitor the conditions. She exchanges looks with the ring-billed gull that surveys the view from the bridge, then looks toward the island.

"Not hungry?" the captain says.

Arizona shakes her head and says, "So, what do you think about a night dive here at San Nick?"

"I won't make a call until everyone has finished eating, but as of right now, it looks good."

Arizona nods, again without saying a word. She tastes stomach acid in her mouth and swallows repeatedly to get it back down.

24.

San Nicolas Island

MARTY HAS DECIDED TO SKIP THE NIGHT DIVE, ALONG WITH two other divers. She wonders if he somehow knows that she needs some space. It's strange. Sometimes being understood feels good, like a breath of fresh air, and other times it feels smothering, like a bag over her head. Regardless, it allows her to avoid the awkwardness of him asking to be dive buddies again.

On every dive there have been at least two groups of three divers. When the dive master asks Arizona who her buddy is as she prepares to step off the platform, she intentionally has her regulator and mask on already. She holds up two fingers and then points down at the water, indicating that she is with the two previous divers. Nonverbal lies still don't count, right? Since nobody is aware of being her dive buddy, nobody should question her whereabouts. Or so she hopes.

Audentes fortuna iuvat. Fortune favors the bold. With that thought, Arizona steps off the dive platform, her gear hugged to her chest. But rather than heading toward the rest of the group, she swims under the boat, keeping her dive light off so nobody can see her. She follows her wrist compass toward shore until she's gone far enough that the rest of the group won't be able to see her light. She points her dive light downward and switches it on. The kelp-covered bottom is only about thirty feet below her. She checks her compass again and swings the light in the direction of shore, but the light is blocked by something very large or very close.

Light shines on the shark's left side, behind the gills but with a wide enough beam to illuminate the entire business end. Arizona guesses that it is about twelve feet long and six feet away, but she is too scared to move—herself or the light. She stares into the shark's left eye but can't tell if it is staring back. Wonders if it is just as startled as she is. She directs her thoughts at the shark as if it were Mojo. *Leave it. Stay. Good fish.* In agonizingly slow and silent motion, the shark glides by and out of the beam of the dive light. Arizona is still frozen in place. Part of her wants to follow it with the light to see if it is going to turn and come back, but a larger part of her doesn't want to know.

She tries to resume a normal rate of breathing as she listens to her internal coxswain. *In, out. Pull, push. Probably just a mako shark,* she thinks. *Just a mako—only the fastest shark in the world and a top predator. No big deal.* She rolls her eyes inside her dive mask.

She keeps one eye on her compass and heads for shore. After a few tense minutes, her dive light is illuminating both the seabed and the troughs of the swell above. Close now, she scans the bottom. A ribbon of sand winds through the rocks. She follows it for a dozen yards, turns off her dive light, spins into a crouched vertical position, and pokes her head up through the waves. Enough moonlight filters through the patchy clouds that she can just make out the empty beach ahead of her. *The coast is clear,* she thinks, and would smirk at the unintended pun but for the regulator in her mouth. She stands and begins walking toward shore.

She manages two steps before she is slammed down and forward. Underwater again, she tumbles in the surf zone, bounces off rocks, thrashes around and around. As the wave subsides, she finds herself prone on the wet sand. She turns her head toward the sea but doesn't see any other large combers. She stands, wobbles, removes the regulator from her mouth, and sweeps the skeins of wet hair from her face.

"Maytagged," she mumbles. It's not her first time. The kayaking term was aptly named after the venerable washing-machine brand, but when kayaking one generally wears a helmet. She raises her fingers to her head and searches for tenderness. There are a couple of sore spots but no sign of blood on her hands. She scans the rest of her body and finds more of the same. She will be sore, bruised, but otherwise fine.

She looks to the water again. Still no large waves. Maybe it was wake from a passing ship and it lined up with the swell so their amplitudes added together. *Constructive interference,* she thinks, *lucky me.* She shakes her head and walks ashore into a light wind. She removes her tank, mask, and fins, licks the salt from her lips, and stows her gear against a kelp-covered rock twenty feet from the water. With her mask off, she can smell the rich aroma of the seaweed, still wet from high tide.

In this remote place, separated by both time and space from Dad and Mom and Mojo and home and the Airstream, the small dry bag in her hand feels like it contains all that is left of her world. She swallows, unclips the buckle of the bag, unrolls the lip, and pulls out the yellow Garmin GPS device that her parents gave her when the family started geocaching. While the GPS is acquiring satellite signals, she reaches into her dry bag again and removes the handheld metal detector that she purchased online. It's just like the ones used by airport security, not much range but lightweight and portable. She retrieves her phone, wakes it up, and reads the marker description to refresh her memory.

STATION DESCRIPTION (1932)

. . . Center was marked by a standard disk cemented in a pillar of concrete 6 by 6 by 30 inches. Two reference marks were established in the same size pillars. All marks were stamped.

STATION RECOVERY (1940)

. . . A narrow rock point about 40 meters long extends in an east–west direction at the station. The mark is about 15 feet above high water, 5 meters south of bluff, 12 meters west of bluff, 3.6 meters north-northwest of concrete foundation for building, and 23 meters north of northwest corner of ruins of building.

. . . The shifting sands may cover all marks.

She heads for the easiest way up and over the short bluff. Once on top, she scans inland for anything mentioned in the description but can't see far in the dim light. She looks back out over the bluff and thinks she can make out the outline of the narrow rock point mentioned in the description. To the east she can see the lighthouse, two or three miles away.

She walks in the direction her GPS indicates, slowly, to let it update. Since the station is only twelve meters west of the bluff and five meters south, she has to go only a few dozen paces. She stops at the waypoint coordinates. Nothing but sand. Kneeling, she turns on the metal detector and waves it back and forth above the sand. Nothing. While she digs with her hands, she wonders what she is going to say when they notice she used much less oxygen than everyone else. *Well, you see, I have very shallow breathing. Yeah, that's it.* One thing at a time.

Within thirty seconds she is more than a foot deep but finds nothing. She expands the diameter of her hole, but it's still just sand, so she makes another sweep with the metal detector. Nothing, so she digs deeper.

She makes another pass with the detector. There is a faint signal in one spot, so she focuses her digging there and goes down another foot. She scans again, and the signal is stronger. She digs, hits something solid, and scoops sand away as the object takes shape. Bingo. She brushes and then blows sand from the metal disk.

"What the . . ." she says under her breath.

At the center is a six-pointed star. *Fire . . . fused with water.*

She brushes the remaining sand off the convex surface. In the space

around the hexagram, more text slowly appears, like thinning fog reveals the world anew.

So much effort, so much risk, for a few stupid numbers and letters.
Arizona takes pictures and then, having a sudden epiphany, tries to use
her dive knife to pry up the disk. She works at it from four different
points, but it doesn't budge. If it turns out to be two-sided, like the
headpiece to the staff of Ra in *Raiders of the Lost Ark,* that is really
going to piss her off.

She puts everything back in the dry bag, folds its edge three times,
and clips it closed. Briefly wonders if she should try to cover her tracks.
Screw it. Let the shifting sands take care of that.

She follows her footprints back over the bluff, scattering a riot of
birds that have gathered around her equipment. The Channel Islands
have some of the largest colonies of shorebirds on the entire West
Coast, so her head pivots to identify some—plump Cassin's auklets
with pale eyes, ashy storm petrels, and black oystercatchers with long
orange bills like slender carrots. Part of her wants to stay, but she can't.

She puts on her fins and tank and looks at her dive watch. Not bad,
all things considered. She dons her regulator and mask and wades back
into the Pacific Ocean.

H I J K L M N O P Q R S T U V W X Y
L   K M N   W X Y

N L H T H D T Q G K H R H K C G K H
T H E   E   R E   E R   R E

G T N L H B D M N N L H E H M N G Q
      T H E   S T T H E   E S T

N L U M C G K N D B S G O K F H Y H
T H   S   R T   R   E Y E

V H D L G M N A G C H M M C U B U
    E   H   S T   E S S

L H P K H H N M O M G F N L D N N K
H E G R E E T S   S   T H   T T R

J K L M N O P Q R S T U V W X Y
                  K M N   W X Y

PART THREE

Let no man trouble to explore the art
If he can't understand the aims and jargon
Of alchemists—and if he does, then
He is a pretty foolish sort of man
Because this art and science is, said he,
Indeed a mystery in a mystery.

—GEOFFREY CHAUCER,
The Canon's Yeoman's Tale

H T H D T Q G K H R H   K C G K H
E   E   R E   E R   R E

N L H B D M N N L H E   H M N G Q
T H E   S T T H E   E S T   R E

U M C G K N D B S G O   K F H Y
  S   R T   R   E Y E

D L G M N A G C H M M   C U B U F P N G N
  H   S T   E S S   G T   T

P K H H N M O M G F N L D N N K D F J O L
G R E E T S   S   T H   T T R

L H K I U I U F P E U K T F G K H H
H E R   G   R   R   E E

H I J K L M N O P Q R S T U V W X Y
                    K M N   W X Y

N L H T H D T Q G K H R H K C G K H
T H E   E   R E   E R   R E

G T N L H B D M N N L H E H M N G C
      T H E   S T T H E   E S T

N L U M C G K N D B S G O K F H Y H
T H   S   R T   R   E Y E

V H D L G M N A G C H M M C U B U F
    E   H   S T   E S S

L H P K H H N M O M G F N L D N N K
H E G R E E T S   S   T H   T T R

J N L H K I U I U F P E U K T F G K

25

Fish Stories, Focus, and Fare-Thee-Wells

To Arizona's relief, she arrives back at the dive site shortly before the other divers start heading up. She finds the pair who are supposed to be her buddies and follows behind, close enough to be with them, far enough to be discreet.

After the divers stow their gear and shower off the sweat and salt, everyone gathers for the usual post-dive ritual. Despite their best efforts to clean up, Arizona notices a faint fog of body odor as she enters the galley. She takes a clandestine sniff as she raises each T-shirt sleeve to pat her temples dry. Not too bad.

Lounged as comfortably as possible on the cheap cafeteria furniture, they take turns sharing their most memorable moments. As Arizona waits for her turn, she braces against the tsunami of unpleasant but familiar sensations—tight throat, drumming pulse, gymnastic stomach—while trying to hide her discomfort. Common highlights from other divers include fauna more active at night, such as lobster, octopus, squid, and angel sharks. One diver saw a six-foot Humboldt squid and claims top bragging rights for spotting the formidable predator, until they get to Arizona.

"So, Arizona, did you have any particularly exciting sightings tonight?"

"Uh, well, yeah. I almost ran right into a pretty big shark," she says.

The galley is silent. Eyebrows arch.

"What do you mean by almost ran right into?" Captain Jack says with a smile. "And how big is pretty big?"

"Well, I think it was about twelve feet long. I had my light pointing down, and when I lifted it up the shark was right in front of me. I felt like I could reach out and touch it, but I think it was really about six feet away. It wasn't coming toward me but was going to my left. I froze and it eventually glided by."

"Any idea what type of shark it was?" Marty says.

"My first thought was shortfin mako, but it could have been a blue. I'd have to look at pictures or drawings to be sure."

"Speaking of pictures, did you get any?"

"Unfortunately not. I just froze until it was gone." Arizona hesitates, not sure that she should continue, but in a rare moment of social bravery, she does. "And then Jules Verne spoke to me . . ."

"When we return to shore, jaded from all these natural wonders, think how we'll look down on those pitiful land masses, those puny works of man! No, the civilized world won't be good enough for us!"

One of the twenty-somethings snickers, and Arizona wants to melt into the floor. But Marty says, "Bravo!" and applauds, and many of the other divers join in. Her embarrassment is lost among the praise. Maybe social bravery has its own reward. She smiles.

"Well, I'd say that being just six feet away from a twelve-foot shark gives Arizona the prize for tonight," Captain Jack says. "And a bonus for quoting *Twenty Thousand Leagues Under the Sea*."

After the night dive, *Serenity* has to leave Alpha Area. Captain Jack heads to the one-square-mile Santa Barbara Island, the smallest of the five islands in Channel Islands National Park, and shelters on its lee side while everyone sleeps. Before turning in, Arizona writes in her notebook.

I did it, but I almost ran into a shark.

Farewell and adieu to you, fair Spanish ladies,
Farewell and adieu, you ladies of Spain,
For we've received orders for to sail back to Boston,
And so nevermore shall we see you again.

In the morning the group manages three more dives off Santa Barbara Island, with Arizona and Marty buddied up for each. With her business concluded for now, Arizona is at ease again, at least while underwater. During the first dive, at the Rookery, sea lions twirl like acrobats and play with the divers, charging straight at them only to dart away at the last second. Arizona doesn't think playing with seals and sea lions could ever get old. The second dive is at Drop Off Reef and the final one at Black Cavern, an advanced dive site between sixty and one hundred feet deep and named for its roomy caves and caverns.

THAT AFTERNOON, WHILE THE captain and crew are occupied with the sixty-mile trip back to Ventura, other divers socialize, but Arizona is lost in thought. She tries to regain her focus, to get her mind back to the survey marker's cryptic numbers and letters, but the path is blocked by images of Dad, Mom, and Mojo—ghosts of a family now dead, kidnapped, and abandoned.

"You okay?" says Marty. "You're awfully quiet."

"Yeah, I'm okay." She sighs.

"That's not very convincing."

Arizona forces a smile.

"Okay," Marty says, "I'll leave you with your thoughts, then."

"You don't have to do *that*," Arizona says, surprising herself. "But maybe we can talk about other stuff?"

Marty smiles and takes a seat beside her.

THEY TALK FOR A couple of hours.

About the people and animals in their lives. Arizona had already mentioned the recent death of her dad, but she shares a few particu-larly good memories, conveys how much she misses him without say-ing so. And she upgrades her comments about Mom from *worried about her* to *might be in some kind of trouble* but can say no more.

Places they've lived and visited. Marty currently lives just outside Las Vegas but has traveled widely. Arizona has only lived in their house in Gold Country, unless you count all the places they've been with the Airstream.

Things they like to do. For Arizona, reading, exploring, maps, math, and puzzles—"but to me they're all just different ways of exploring." For Marty, mostly reading, traveling, and diving.

"So," Marty says. "You obviously love to dive, but I got the impres-sion you haven't been diving much recently. Why not?"

"Mostly because of Mojo. Diving isn't particularly dog-friendly, with the exception of Scooby-Doo, of course."

Marty laughs. "I can picture Scooby with his diving mask on. *Ruh Roh!*"

Arizona is grateful for the distraction.

THEY ARRIVE IN VENTURA in the early evening and everyone starts gathering their gear, saying their goodbyes, and disembarking. To Ari-zona's surprise, the twenty-somethings even apologize as they say goodbye, redeeming themselves slightly.

As they are filing toward the gangplank, Marty says, "So, what's next for you?"

"Well, I've got to go meet up with my mom and Mojo. Not sure after that." The Mojo part is true, as is the not-sure part. But she senses that Marty can somehow tell that her statement isn't entirely truthful.

"Give Mojo a pat on the head for me. It was a pleasure to meet you, Arizona," Marty says as he extends his arms for a hug. "Fare thee well, young lady."

Arizona smiles at his insightful use of Old English and, after her standard pre-hug hesitation, embraces him.

"This is me," Marty says as he hands Arizona a small scrap of paper with his name, address, and phone number. "You remind me of my daughter when she was young. If there's any way I can help, please don't hesitate."

For a moment she feels vulnerable, transparent again. But in the grandfatherly warmth of Marty's smile, the sense of vulnerability passes, like a word on the tip of her tongue. She simply says, "Thank you," smiles, and turns toward the captain.

"Goodbye, Captain," she says as she gives him a casual salute. "Thank you for a wonderful trip."

He smiles and says, "Goodbye, Arizona. You take care."

Arizona doesn't reply as she bounces down the gangplank, her mind refocused on the cryptic numbers and letters.

"Curious girl," Captain Jack says to himself as he turns to go back below.

ARIZONA TOSSES HER GEAR into the back of the truck and checks her phone. She has voicemail from Sam.

"Hi, Arizona. Sam Yeats here. Just checking in. Call me when you can. Thanks."

Her finger hovers over the CALL BACK button but never lands. She puts her phone to sleep and starts the long drive back to Alabama Hills.

26.

Puzzle Pieces

A S ARIZONA DRIVES BACK TO ALABAMA HILLS, SHE WISHES she'd taken Mojo to the kennel in Ventura, just so she wouldn't have to wait four more hours to see him. But he's probably been happier with Lily and Gus, so she dismisses the selfish thought and focuses on the road.

It's a bit after 11:00 P.M. when the sight of the truck's headlights reflecting off the silver Airstream brings a sigh of contentment. It's been a long day. Twenty leagues o'er the deep, then two hundred miles over land. But it's good to be home, and it will be even better to be with Mojo again. She parks the truck and hops out. At the sight of Arizona, Mojo sings his best boxer woo (somewhere between a bay and a howl) and bends his body into a kidney bean. *You're back!* that woo says. *You've been gone for weeks in dog time.* She cradles his soft black jowls and brings their noses together, his rough and wet, hers smooth and dry—until he licks it.

"He is such a doll," Lily says with a smile. "It's good to see you, AZ."

"Thank you," Arizona says. "How about we all go for a brief walk? But after that I think I'll turn in. I'm pooped, and peopled out."

Lily chuckles. "Okay, a talk-free walk sounds good. Come on, Gus."

They walk through the small canyon next to camp, then up an unmarked trail that winds through the rock formations. The sky is clear and Arizona's headlamp necessary only in the moon shadows of the large rocks that jut upward, as if paying homage to their gods. As she looks at the moon—almost full—it's hard to believe that she was on San Nicolas Island just thirty hours earlier. It seems a world away from where she stands now. From verge of land and sea back to verge of mountain and desert.

Verge, she thinks. *The edge.* California isn't merely the edge of the continent. It's also the edge of the continental plate, the front line in a never-ending war between inconceivable masses that crash and grind against each other over incomprehensible time frames. Those immortal forces created the mountains and deserts that she had spent much of her life exploring—the same mountains and deserts that one hundred fifty years earlier had been the most formidable barriers to exploration of the West. She notes the paradox with a faint smile.

Life on the edge—of a continent, of mountains and desert, of society. Immortal forces. Paradox. Immortality. Alchemy. As they amble, so does her tired mind.

They find their way back, say goodnight, and Arizona and Mojo retire to the trailer. Despite her fatigue, she can't get the latest puzzle out of her head. She grabs some snacks for both of them, imports her pictures from San Nicolas Island onto her MacBook, and begins to study the survey marker.

She stares at the text stamped above and below the hexagram, then types it into a new document, spacing out the parts separated by the colons.

$$36 : XZ\text{-}18 : XJ$$

$$XJVK : QJ : 34$$

She sighs. Normally she likes puzzles, but this is different, stressful. Being forced to do something takes the fucking fun out of it. When this is all over, will she even want to do puzzles again?

The new cryptogram—if that's what it is—seems far too short for frequency analysis, but she does an inventory of the numbers and letters anyway.

Numbers	Count
1	1
3	2
4	1
6	1
8	1
Letters	Count
J	3
K	1
Q	1
V	1
X	3
Z	1

Just five numbers and six letters? She counts again as she passes her hand from her brow over the crown of her head and down to her neck in slow motion. The other two ciphers were substitution ciphers, so maybe this is, too? If so, do the numbers represent letters, or do the letters represent numbers, or both?

She looks at the first line, at XZ-18 in particular. Mathematical equations? If the six letters are variables, she'd need six equations to solve for them. But she doesn't have six equations. She isn't even sure she has one.

Alternatively, if the dash is a minus sign, then the letters would have to represent numbers. The letters are all among the least commonly used letters in English. Is that meaningful?

She stares at the cryptic stamps, but nothing else comes to her. Her eyelids are anvils. She looks at the clock in the Mac's menu bar. One o'clock in the morning. She jots down some thoughts in her notebook, then her phone rings. Blocked number.

"Yeah," she says with attitude.

"Did you find what you were looking for?" says Stephen Gordon.

"I did."

"And?"

"It had some cryptic numbers and letters on it."

"Read them to me."

She reads the numbers and letters, including the colons. It doesn't feel right sharing information with her mom's kidnappers, but she isn't sure what else to do. Yet.

"Do you know what it means?" he says.

"Not yet," she says, glad it's the truth.

"I'll be in touch." *Click.*

"I'm sure you will," Arizona says. "I wasn't really in a palavering mood anyway."

She puts the phone down and decides to turn in for the night, hoping to tackle the puzzle with a fresh mind tomorrow. Mojo is already busy refreshing his mind, snoring as he does so. She goes to bed, and Mojo wakes up just long enough to follow her.

SHE SLEEPS SOUNDLY. IT'S a welcome change. Sleeping on the boat was a novelty, but, all things being equal, she prefers a bed that doesn't move beneath her. She wakes with much of Mojo's weight across her legs and her hands holding his front paws, as if they'd been dancing in their dreams. Lying there, she thinks about the cryptic stamps on the survey marker, before her thoughts drift to the previous unsolved quandary—the meaning of Malachi's tombstone. Two dead ends. She is failing. She is failing Mom.

She eases Mojo off her legs, takes him outside. Lily is sitting in the shade of her van. Gus meets Mojo halfway.

"Morning, sunshine," Lily says. Her hair looks wet, as if she washed it in the creek.

"Good morning."

"Feeling better after sleep?"

"Yes, thank you."

"Wanna hang out today?"

"Uh, not sure yet. I've gotta do some stuff."

"No worries. Not sure what time the fun train will leave the station, though, and you know what they say. She who hesitates is lost. So all aboard who's coming aboard."

Arizona smiles. "Understood. I would like to catch the fun train for sure. I could use some fun."

"Was the diving not fun?"

"It was pretty great, actually. I just have so much on my mind."

Lily nods. "Okay, get that stuff done and we'll go from there."

It's Arizona's turn to nod.

She takes Mojo back in and makes breakfast for both of them. Gives him a piece of bacon, since her parents aren't there to stop her, although she would give almost anything for some parental disapproval.

She piles the dishes in the sink, wakes her laptop, and looks at the inventory of numbers and letters from the survey marker again.

Numbers	Count
1	1
3	2
4	1
6	1
8	1
Letters	Count
J	3
K	1
Q	1
V	1
X	3
Z	1

She opens pictures of the tombstone and survey marker. Her eyes flit back and forth between the images. Two dead ends. Or are they?

Both have a hexagram. Two different pieces of the same puzzle? She scans the tombstone for the six letters from the survey marker, but only V is there.

OUR LITTLE ANGEL HAS

GONE HOME TO GOD

...

MALACHI SOFER

BORN NOVEMBER 7, 1850

DIED FEBRUARY 29, 1853

AGED TWENTY-SEVEN MONTHS

Her thoughts fly about with no apparent purpose, like small birds inside a hedge. No apparent purpose to the observer, that is, but the thoughts, like the birds, know better. She pages back in her notebook, to the cipher that sent her to the island in the first place. Surely there's a connection? She looks again at the keywords:

D E A T H Q P L U S

Y E A R Z M O N T H

B I R T H X D A Y

Pairs of words separated by seemingly random letters—Q, Z, and X. Three of the six letters on the survey marker. And five of the six words—*death, year, month, birth,* and *day*—could be references to the tombstone. She isn't sure about *plus,* though. And that still leaves three other letters from the survey marker that aren't in the keywords—J, K, and V.

She wraps her left arm around her head, fingers on the back of her neck, biceps against her temple. She thinks for four breaths, then goes back to her solution to the second cipher. She is such a dumbass. The keywords she copied into her notebook aren't complete. Each keyword has one more letter—the missing J, K, and V.

DEATHQPLUSV

YEARZMONTHJ

BIRTHXDAYK

Each letter follows a word—the word it represents? She breaks the keywords into six parts and spaces out the letters at the end of each line.

D E A T H	Q
P L U S	V
Y E A R	Z
M O N T H	J
B I R T H	X
D A Y	K

She copies the stamped text from the survey marker.

36 : XZ-18 : XJ

XJVK : QJ : 34

Converts the letters into words and then, using the tombstone, into numbers.

> XZ = birth year = 1850
> XZ − 18 = 1850 − 18 = 1832
> XJ = birth month = November = 11
> Q J = death month = February = 2
> XJVK = birth month plus day = 11 + 7 = 18

Finally, she substitutes the numbers into the text from the survey marker.

$$36 : 1832 : 11$$
$$18 : 2 : 34$$

Arizona tilts her head and stares at the sets of numbers. Her thoughts turn to *Close Encounters of the Third Kind,* when the scientists are trying to interpret the sets of numbers sent by the aliens. They were coordinates. Latitude and longitude in degrees, minutes, and seconds. But these numbers can't be coordinates, because 1832 is too large. Values for minutes have to be between 0 and 59.

Right thumb on eyebrow, index finger on center of her forehead, she pinches her brow, releases, pinches, releases. As if scratching an itch behind her eye. Mojo whines.

"I know, buddy. Puzzles are boring for you. But you want to see Mom soon, right?"

Mojo wags his tail.

"Okay, then let me do this. We'll take another walk soon."

Mojo puts his head back down on the daybed.

She double-checks the tombstone and her logic, but still comes up with 1850 minus 18 equals 1832. And interpreting the dash as a minus sign is consistent with one of the words being *plus.*

Consistent. Something isn't consistent. She's been treating XZ-18 as an arithmetical operation, but that doesn't make sense. If this were arithmetic, then XZ would be the product of X and Z, but it isn't. X means *birth* and Z means *year,* but *birth times year* makes no sense. It has to be *birth year.* So the operations aren't arithmetical after all. They're more like character strings in programming or words in a sentence, combining to form a phrase.

So if XZ-18 isn't 1850 *minus* 18, then what is it?

1850 *without* 18? So just . . . 50?

Arizona smiles. Is it really that simple? She changes the 1832 to 50.

$$36 : 50 : 11$$
$$18 : 2 : 34$$

Now they could be coordinates.

She grabs her iPad, opens her GPS app, and creates a waypoint with the coordinates 36° 50' 11" north, 18° 2' 34" west. But it's in the middle of the Mediterranean Sea and not near any obvious islands.

She tries all the other permutations of north and south latitude and east and west longitude, but none of them are on land. She double-checks her waypoints. They're all correct. Her left fingers rest lightly on her lips. She double-checks the letter-to-number conversions again.

Then it hits her. *Plus.* If you're doing arithmetic, 11 plus 7 is 18. But if you're combining character strings, 11 plus 7 is 117. She updates the decoded numbers and hopes it will be for the last time.

$$36 : 50 : 11$$
$$117 : 2 : 34$$

She creates a waypoint at 36° 50' 11" north and 117° 2' 34" west and zooms the map way out, expecting the location to be meaningless. It's on the eastern edge of California. She zooms in a little. Death Valley? She zooms in again.

It isn't possible. She squeezes her brow into deep furrows and double-checks the waypoint. It's correct. Trembling hands cradle her aching head as she stares. On the map, a road winds past the waypoint.

"How can that be?"

Nobody answers, but how she wishes someone would. She can't fit this puzzle piece into her reality. Her head throbs. Tsunamis of emotion pound the shores of her brain. Despair? Bewilderment? Rage? She can't tell, can't keep up. She is shutting down. Eyes that can no longer focus look away from the road on the map.

Titus Canyon Road.

The place where Dad died.

27.

The Adept and the
Journal — Part Three

H E BREATHES IN THE AROMA OF THE BRANDED LEATHER
cover. To him it smells of earth and fire. He opens to the bookmark and rereads the NSA agent's analysis of the twelve sentences
constructed from the booklet's redacted words.

> Some inferences within the twelve hidden sentences were as
> startlingly bizarre as they were obvious. There are references to
> the collective genius of the masters, an achievement within the
> reach of the art, a lexicon of complex code, vessel of quicksilver,
> signs of the zodiac, and the Great Work. These references leave
> little doubt that the author of the redactions was conveying a
> message about alchemy. I do not report that observation lightly.
> Including any mention of alchemy feels like it crosses into
> quackery. Yet the references are nonetheless obvious.

Quackery. The Adept bristles at the word in reference to the Masters. What could naysayers know, with minds so closed they see only
through pinholes? Yet the author of the journal had come around, for
a time at least.

> The eighth sentence clearly makes the case that someone,
> perhaps the author himself, stumbled on an ancient key to
> interpreting and understanding the Great Work. Sentences five

and six imply a momentous discovery, yielding the enormous
power to live for thousands of years, nearly imperishable against
the oblivion imposed by time. Although immortality was purportedly one of the primary pursuits of the alchemists, it is (or at
least had been) my understanding that the pursuit was allegorical
rather than literal.

He snickers. Allegorical, *please*. Even if the elixir of life is a process
rather than a potion, that doesn't make it any less real. The great thinkers knew. Plato's four arguments for the soul's immortality. Avicenna's
distinctness of body and soul, and the incorruptibility of the latter.
Thomas Aquinas's *Summa Theologica*. Descartes. Leibniz. The evidence
is indisputable.

Sentences nine and ten report that the discovery ultimately led
to unprecedented strife among the members of the inner circle
and that it was decided—by the author himself?—that it should
be put away for future generations, which presumably means
hidden.
    Sentences eleven and twelve imply that a fire was set to
destroy the Secret, presumably after it had been hidden, but that
it was not destroyed.
    It is worth reiterating that every word of these strange
spagyric sentences can be found in the original booklet. Considering the many obtuse words and phrases, I find it hard to believe
that all this language found its way into a government-printed
booklet by accident. Rather, I suspect the booklet's author placed
these words there specifically, to convey the hidden message.
    After uncovering these twelve hidden sentences, I set about
trying to decode the two ciphers that I had found hidden in the
redactions of the drawings. The following pages contain the
cipher text, decrypted plain text, and analysis.

As his eyes strain to read in the dim light, his mind races with possibilities. He wets his lips, thumbs past the cipher text and torn pages.

The two ciphers and their solutions that he had found in the journal had proven useful as a test for the girl. But otherwise they are, like the mother, just a means to an end. An end that justifies any means.

[missing text]

> six words (death, plus, year, month, birth, day) embedded
> within the keywords must relate to the grave of young Mala-
> chi. But how? I assume I'm still missing a piece of the puzzle.

The words echo in his head. *Missing a piece of the puzzle.* The author of the journal had obviously overcome that temporary setback, but then subsequently destroyed the corresponding pages of his work.

Nonetheless, the Adept is confident that the girl will do her job and deliver that missing piece. She has already proven herself to be competent, and she will continue to behave herself so long as she believes that her mother's life hangs in the balance.

He congratulates himself on the elegance of his solution to this problem, the cleverness of using her as his cat's paw to deliver what he needs, with no risk or effort of his own. Yet he wishes he could have made the discovery for himself, seen it with his own eyes. Despite how long he has worn the garb of jealousy, it still chafes.

28.

The Escape

HER HANDS ARE BOUND TOGETHER BEHIND HER HEAD, ZIP-tied to each other and to the cot. Two zip ties are around her ankles, as well. She runs her fingers along the parts of the cot that she can reach. All she can feel is fabric and wood, but it doesn't matter.

Should she wait for nightfall so they won't be able to see her? No, she wouldn't be able to see, either, and she needs someone to still be in the park office. Although she'll break in to use the phone if she has to.

She massages the scrunchie that holds her ponytail, pulls out the nail, and gets to work on the zip ties again.

THIRTY MINUTES LATER, CHAIR jammed under the doorknob again, she examines the patch to the wall through the cracks. It's a single sheet of plywood, placed horizontally. She can see the nails where they missed the studs. In the corner, past the end of the plywood, are two adjoining loose boards. She pushes them out, slowly and quietly this time, and is gone.

The direct route, through open terrain, had been a mistake. Better to use the cover of the buildings. But either way she's leaving tracks in the snow. She keeps left of her previous path, down to a leaning shed on the edge of the closed area. Under the fence again, and a twenty-yard dash puts her behind a small house. She stops long enough to scan for activity, then makes another twenty-yard dash to the next house. She listens but hears only her own breath and pulse.

The gap to the next house is a long one, about one hundred yards parallel to a street and across a side street. She ducks around the south side of the house and stops to look back for pursuers. Peeks around the corner, her face pressed against the rough gray wood that was a living tree sometime before her grandparents were born. No one is visible, but she didn't see anyone last time, either. She runs the next thirty yards to a house at the corner of the street—Green Street, she recalls from the park map—that will take her to the park office. Slips behind the southeast corner, pauses to look around and then bolts across Green Street and behind another house.

The air, thin and sharp like a razor, cuts her lungs. Each pause to catch her breath is longer than the previous. She is interval training at altitude, almost nine thousand feet above the sea. *Just like an Olympic athlete,* she thinks, *except for the actual fitness.*

The next three structures are pretty close, less than twenty yards between each. She stays on the south side so she can't be seen from the hill to the north, where the closed area is. Behind another small house, then two small buildings that might have been garages when the town was abandoned one hundred years ago. Three more forty-yard dashes get her across Bodie Creek to a house, the back of a hotel, and across the street to the alley between the morgue and the Miners Union Hall, where the museum and visitor center now reside.

From the southwest corner of a small shed just past the morgue, she can see the park office in the J. S. Cain Residence, diagonally (*slaunchwise,* she tells herself) across Green Street. But it is almost a hundred yards with little or no cover. She takes another look around.

Audentes fortuna iuvat. Fortune favors the bold. She leaves the relative security of the buildings and commits to the final hundred-yard dash through the snow. Thirty seconds later, breathless, she runs into the park office and slams the door behind her.

A male ranger sits behind a desk in the main room, and through an open office door she sees a female ranger. They both rise from their chairs, but neither has a chance to speak.

"Help!" she says, trying to catch her breath. "I was kidnapped . . . have been held hostage . . . in the closed area of the park."

The male ranger turns to look at the female ranger, who has emerged from the office.

"I'm the supervising ranger, Samantha Yeats. Did you say someone has been holding you hostage?"

"Yes."

"Were you here with your daughter, Arizona?"

She nods, with a watery smile. Of course Arizona would have raised the alarm. "Is she still here?"

"No, but we're very glad to see you. Please, come in and have a seat." Sam leads the way into her office and gestures to the chair in front of her desk. "You look exhausted. We'll call Arizona as soon as you've caught your breath."

"I'm all right," she says as she sits down. She has almost recovered from the strenuous sprint, still taking frequent deep breaths to overcome the thin air. "But we don't have much time. They'll be here any minute."

29

Into the Void

AS ARIZONA TRIES TO RECOVER FROM THE SHOCK OF THE coordinates, she thinks about the note. *Your father should have provided us with the information that we seek. His death could have been avoided.*

But those words were just a scare tactic. His death was an accident. Or was it? The location of the coordinates can't be a coincidence. Did they think he was looking for whatever is there, kill him, and make it look like an accident? Cooperating with kidnappers is one thing, but with killers? Would they kill Mom, too? Had they already? Or maybe they faked Dad's death and they're holding him captive, too?

She is spinning around the edge of a whirlpool, Dad already sucked under and Mom not far behind. Can she save Mom by herself? Or does she need someone to throw her a lifeline? But who? And asking for help requires trust, although she trusted Lily with Mojo and that was fine. Still, trust is a cactus—thorny and slow-growing.

The last words of the note pop into her head. *We'll be watching.* Watching from where? From where they have Mom? Where the hell is that? *We'll be watching.* Eyes wide, she races out of the Airstream with Mojo in tow and searches her motorcycle, as if she has misplaced a bomb that is about to explode. She moves beyond the interior of the sidecar and trunk and examines the motorcycle from every angle.

Two minutes later, running her hands along the underside of the sidecar's chassis, she feels something that shouldn't be there. She tugs hard and finds herself holding a small black box with a pair of magnets on its bottom. She opens the magnetic case. Inside is an anonymous square of black plastic, smaller than a deck of playing cards—a GPS tracking device. That's how they've been watching her. Why hadn't she thought of it sooner? Her saliva tastes metallic, like she has a mouthful of pennies.

She whirls around, ready to storm back into the Airstream, but Lily is standing there.

"What's that?" Lily asks, pointing to the GPS tracker in Arizona's hand.

Arizona's head is still spinning—from the coordinates, from the possibility that her dad was murdered, from her own stupidity. She opens her mouth, but no words come out. What can she possibly say?

"Are you okay, AZ?"

Arizona shakes her head side to side, wobbles on her feet.

"Come on," Lily says as she puts an arm around Arizona. "Let's sit before you fall over." Lily guides her to a flat boulder, eases her down, and sits beside her. "What's wrong?" She waits for Arizona to speak, but nothing comes out.

Arizona takes a breath, then another. Should she concoct an elaborate lie? Not telling the whole truth feels the same as lying, and she is so tired of lying to Lily. No, not just tired. Exhausted. The mere thought is a weight on her chest, makes it so hard to breathe. She takes another labored breath, then opens her hand.

"What is it?" Lily says.

"GPS tracker," Arizona says, her voice a whisper. "They've been tracking me."

"What? Who's been tracking you?"

"Come inside." She nods to the Airstream. "Bring Gus."

Lily's arm still around her, they make their way into the trailer. Arizona locks the door and sits down. Mojo jumps onto the daybed. Lily picks up Gus, puts him next to Mojo, and then sits next to Arizona.

The pressure has become too great to contain, and the truth spills out like magma. Unstoppable. Dad's death, Mom's disappearance, fake ranger Stephen Gordon, Sam Yeats, the note, the ciphers, Pioneer Cemetery, San Nicolas Island, the coordinates. Everything. Lily holds Arizona while it all comes out between sobs, gasps, chokes.

After an hour, Arizona is an empty shell. Void of secrets, void of sensation. As she surveys the emptiness, she realizes that there is one sensation after all, one feeling. It's familiar, but she can't quite place it. Vulnerability? No. Just as with Marty, a brief feeling of vulnerability was pushed aside by something warmer. By its opposite? Safety. Security. Connection.

Her eyes widen and her head tips to the side. It's as if vulnerability is the price of trust, and safety the reward. Maybe there is something to this trust thing after all.

Arizona looks into Lily's eyes. "Thank you, Lily."

"For what?"

"Listening. Being trustworthy."

"You're welcome, AZ. That's what friends are for. Thank you for trusting me with the truth. That's a hell of a weight you've been carrying. Do you feel better, at least a little?"

Arizona nods.

"And you're sure you don't want to go to the police? Or, I don't know, the FBI or something?"

Arizona's not sure, at all. But anytime she thinks about going to the authorities, she imagines what will happen to her mom if the kidnappers learn about it or things go wrong somehow, and her brain just . . . stops.

"For now, no. I don't want to risk it. And nobody is going to be more motivated than me."

"I can't argue with that," Lily says, "but this is all so crazy. Seems like a really good time to ask for help."

Arizona sighs. "I guess I am asking for help—*your* help."

"Of course," Lily says with a smile. "So what now?"

"I'll show you." Arizona fetches a hammer from the toolkit under the bed and takes the hammer and GPS tracker outside. Mojo, Gus, and Lily follow. She walks to the fire ring, places the tracker on one of the scorched rocks, and raises the hammer. She pauses. Thinks of magicians, sleight of hand, misdirection. She lowers the hammer slowly.

"No, let's go shopping instead."

"Shopping?" Lily says.

Back inside, Arizona sits down and motions Lily—with connected eyes and hand on the cushion—to sit next to her. She opens a new browser tab, finds the chamber of commerce for Beatty, Nevada, and scans the list of businesses. Her eyes lock on to a name. Two birds, one stone. She dials the phone and puts it on speaker.

"Beatty Nut and Candy Company," a woman says.

"Hi," Arizona says. "Would it be possible to speak to a manager?"

"Sure, hang on a sec."

"Hello?" says a different female voice a minute later.

"Hi. I'm going to be passing through Beatty and I'm wondering if I could have a package delivered to you folks. I'll definitely buy some nuts and candy, but I'd also be happy to pay a convenience fee."

The manager agrees, and Arizona takes down her name, confirms the address, and even remembers to thank her before she hangs up.

"What are we having delivered?" Lily says.

"You'll see."

Arizona finds the chamber of commerce for a larger Nevada town, Pahrump, and starts making phone calls. It takes several calls, but she finds what she needs and a service that can get it to Beatty in two hours.

"Death Valley road trip?" Lily says with a smile.

Arizona nods. "Can you watch Mojo for me?"

"What d'ya mean? I'm going with."

"I can't ask that of you. It might be dangerous."

"Well, duh. If it might be dangerous, then you need backup. Besides, you can't dump all this shit on me and then just expect me to sit here and twiddle my fucking thumbs until you get back. Now that you let me in on the truth, let me in on the action, too."

"Sorry. I didn't mean—"

"I'm not sorry. Honestly, the vagueness of your whole meeting-up-with-your-mother story was fishy anyway. But there's another way to look at it. I wasn't able to save my own mom. Let me help save yours. Please."

"Your mom's death wasn't your fault, Lily."

"I know, but still. Let me help."

Arizona looks at Lily and smiles. "I guess we're bringing the boys then, too."

"Gus likes geocaching. It's just another word for walkies."

Four ears perk up. Two tails wag.

"Okay," Arizona says, "but there's something we have to do first."

AFTER FIVE MINUTES OF searching, Lily finds another GPS tracker, this one inside the pickup's rear bumper. Arizona attaches it to one of the Airstream's propane tanks, right next to the tracker she found on the motorcycle. There's probably one hidden on the Airstream, too, but they can let that be for now. By leaving the Airstream and the trackers here, she'll make Gordon and company think she's still in the Alabama Hills, while she's actually off pursuing the next clue. *Misdirection*.

Because Lily was right about one thing. Arizona can't keep playing the kidnappers' game and hoping for the best. She needs to get ahead of them, get some leverage. If she can beat them to the endgame, find whatever it is they're seeking before they can, then she'll have something to trade for Mom.

They load food and water into daypacks and, in case, fill a duffel with headlamps, sleeping bags, and pads. They toss the daypacks, duffel, and a large jug of water in the bed of the truck.

"Let's go for a ride, Mojo." Arizona opens the rear door of the truck and Mojo jumps in. Lily lifts Gus in and climbs into the passenger seat. They pull out of the *Gunga Din* campsite and begin the two-hour drive to Beatty, leaving the GPS trackers safely behind.

Just south of Lone Pine, they turn left onto California 136 and twenty minutes later merge onto the Death Valley Scenic Byway, which will take them through some of the least hospitable terrain on earth. Despite the painful association with her dad's death, Arizona still thinks Death Valley is starkly beautiful. At its core, life in the desert is simple, binary. You live or you die. She has always felt at home in the desert. Perhaps it's her name. Perhaps it's her nature. Go where there is nothing but nothing, to get away from too much of everything. But there is no getting away from anything now.

They enter Death Valley National Park and descend the road as it twists around bajadas, the fan-shaped alluvial deposits that always remind Arizona of the term *angle of repose.* Her dad had taught her the term and then given her the book of the same name by Wallace Stegner, set in their hometown of Grass Valley.

The truck speeds across narrow Panamint Valley, where floodwaters from the recent storm reflect the cobalt sky and mountains through a brown lens. They climb up and over Towne Pass and then down into the heart of Death Valley itself, past Stovepipe Wells and the sand dunes of Mesquite Flat. She grimaces as she turns left on Scotty's Castle Road (where Dad would have come back from Titus Canyon if he had ever come back), turns right on Daylight Pass Road, and keeps driving toward Beatty.

Two dozen more miles and they enter Nevada and exit the park. With another grimace, this time accompanied by butterflies bordering on nausea, Arizona points out the sharp left turn of Titus Canyon Road. But first they have an errand to run in Beatty, only half a dozen miles up the road.

Arizona pulls the F-150 into the Beatty Nut and Candy Company and rolls down the windows. The girls tell Mojo and Gus to stay as they head inside. Arizona, still wearing sunglasses to mitigate the fluorescent lights, asks for the manager, Carol, and adds that she is picking up a package. The clerk picks up the phone, punches one button, speaks briefly, and hangs up.

"She'll be out in a few minutes," the clerk says.

"Thanks. Can you point me to the bathroom?" Arizona says.

The clerk, apparently taking her literally, points without saying a word.

"I'll be shopping," Lily says. "Is there anything you want?"

"Here, I made a list." She pulls it out of her pocket and hands it to Lily.

"Of course you did." Lily looks at the list. "*Pick up package. Atomic Fireballs. Unsalted nuts for Mojo.* Did you really need a list for that?" Lily winks.

"Writing helps me think. Oh, and not macadamia nuts. My parents told me they aren't good for dogs." *Parents,* plural again. A shiver runs up her spine. Her eyelids close for a breath.

"I still catch myself saying that, too," Lily says, then touches Arizona's shoulder. "Atomic Fireballs and unsalted nuts. You got it."

Arizona goes into the bathroom, past the sinks where a woman is washing her hands, and into a stall. Lost in her thoughts, she doesn't notice the hand dryers.

The sink faucet stops. Footsteps. A button press.

The hand dryer roars to life, like a fighter jet launching off an aircraft carrier. Arizona's hands move toward her ears in slow motion, even though she is pretty sure she told them to hurry. She feels herself fall forward, fold in half. Head between legs, she wants to scream out the words, drown out the noise. But nothing comes out, so she screams inside her head.

'TWAS BRILLIG, AND THE SLITHY TOVES DID GYRE AND GIMBLE IN THE WABE!

A FEW MINUTES LATER, she hears a voice.

"Arizona?"

" 'Twas brillig," Arizona mutters, still bent over, hands over ears.

She sees feet outside the stall. She removes her palms from her ears and straightens up.

"Arizona? Are you okay?"

The voice is vaguely familiar. "Mom?"

"No, this is Lily. The manager came to bring you your package. You've been gone for a while."

"Lily . . . like the flower," Arizona says.

"Are you okay?"

"I will be," Arizona says weakly.

"Okay, I'll wait right here."

"And the mome raths outgrabe," Arizona says under her breath.

She emerges from the stall and walks to the sinks. Splashes water on her face. Once, twice, three times. Doesn't look in the mirror.

"What happened?" says Lily.

"The hand dryers." She dries her hands on her T-shirt.

"I don't understand."

"The sound of the hand dryer," Arizona says. "It's like my kryptonite."

Lily smiles, nods. "My mom always said that we all have superpowers, but we have to figure out what they are and what our kryptonite is."

"I guess that means I'm halfway there."

"Exactly." Lily chuckles.

"I do have a super headache," Arizona says, fingertips on temples. "Does that count?"

"Sorry to hear that."

"Thanks. It's nothing a Coke or two won't fix. Let's get the package and get out of here."

They exit the bathroom. Across the hall is an open door labeled CAROL LEWIS, GENERAL MANAGER. Arizona knocks.

"Come in. Arizona, I presume?"

"Yes," Arizona says, as she hands Carol her ID.

"Are you sick?" Carol says, noting the wet hair as she hands the ID back.

Arizona scratches her temple, nods. Sometimes it's best to say nothing.

"Sorry. I have your package here." Carol points to a box in a shopping basket on the floor.

"Great" is all Arizona can muster as she picks up the shopping basket.

"Can I help you find something?"

"Find something?"

"Nuts, candy, souvenirs?"

"I think we're all set, thanks." Lily holds up her own shopping basket.

"You're welcome. Take care."

Arizona nods and they leave the office.

They pay for the candy, nuts, and several Cokes and go back to the truck.

Arizona pulls up to the gas pumps. While she tops off the truck, she downs a Coke and feeds Mojo seven unsalted peanuts, one at a time (five seems too few, eleven too many).

She looks around and wonders if it's the same gas station Dad stopped at—on his last morning. Only three weeks, but it seems so long ago. She closes her eyes and imagines him here, tries to feel his presence. She sees him pulling in on his sidecar motorcycle, to the same pump she's using. She smiles. But filling the Ural's tiny gas tank doesn't take even a minute, and he climbs back on the bike and rides away, deaf to her calls.

The gas pump clicks off. She opens her eyes. She's not ready to retrace the last few miles of Dad's life. Again. But there are some things you can never be ready for.

She climbs into the truck and they head out of town, to Titus Canyon.

30

Return to Titus Canyon

A RIZONA TURNS ONTO THE DIRT AND GRAVEL OF TITUS Canyon Road. Her headache has waned but, as she gets closer to the site of Dad's death, her nausea has waxed. The truck rockets up the eastern slope of the Grapevine Mountains, sliding around a couple of turns before she realizes she is driving far too fast. She looks at Lily, whose wide eyes are another giveaway. Arizona's heart and mind are racing, too, a cheetah chasing a gazelle. Is her mind the gazelle? Or the cheetah? She shakes her head, as if trying to shrug off the ill-fated metaphor.

She slows down, summits Red Pass, and begins the descent toward the coordinates and the ghost town of Leadfield, which even in its heyday was tiny compared to Bodie, and mostly tents. After two steep switchbacks, the road straightens briefly, and she brakes even more to keep an eye on her GPS. Shortly before the next set of tight turns, where her dad died, she pulls over at a wide spot in the road.

"The topographic map indicates old mine shafts in the area," Arizona says as she hops out, "so I'm putting Mojo on leash."

"Then you, too, Gustav." Lily clips a leash onto Gus's collar.

"Gus is short for Gustav?" Arizona says.

"Yeah, I named him after Gustav Freytag. He created Freytag's Pyramid, one of the first visual representations of story structure."

Arizona looks at Lily with a crooked smile as she dons her pack.

"What?" Lily says. "English major with an emphasis in creative writing."

Leash in one hand and GPS in the other, Arizona walks in the direction indicated. They pass rusted tin cans, so common near old mining camps that they wouldn't have caught her eye even if she wasn't focused on her GPS. Pebbles skitter beneath the long toes of a western whiptail lizard as it runs under a rock.

"I don't suppose that Mojo is short for anything?" Lily says.

"Kind of the opposite. His original name was just Mo, but I got tired of people asking me what it was short for, so I changed it to Mojo."

"Was it? Short for anything?"

Arizona shoots Lily with her eyes.

"Ouch. If looks could kill."

The six-foot-wide shadow of a turkey vulture soars across the ground. Arizona stops, looks up, then continues to follow her GPS.

"When we first brought Mojo home from the boxer rescue group, I told my parents that I wanted to name him Mo. My dad asked if it was short for Moriarty, since I liked Sir Arthur Conan Doyle. I said, 'Indubitably, my dear Watson.' My mom asked if it was short for Mowgli, since I liked Rudyard Kipling. I said, 'A man's cub. Look!'"

"So which is it?"

"Both. And neither."

"Hard to imagine why you weren't more popular in school."

Arizona adjusts course slightly to accommodate the steep terrain, turns around, and, without looking up from her GPS, backtracks two steps. "This is it."

"Sorry about the school comment, AZ. I was just trying to be funny and didn't think first."

Arizona nods. "It's okay. You're not wrong."

"Still, sorry."

"I think this looks safe enough for the boys," Arizona says. "Stay close," she says to Mojo as she takes him off leash. He immediately chases a lizard, and she rolls her eyes at his predictability.

"What are we looking for?" Lily says.

"I have no idea. Anything unusual, I guess." She stands on the designated spot, thinks of the survey marker buried under the sand, and scrapes a boot through the dirt. But there is just rock underneath.

Lily walks from rock to rock, turns them over, but finds nothing. Gus follows her.

Mojo wanders, nose to the ground.

Arizona drops her pack and walks around it. She examines the ground, increases the radius with each lap. A search spiral. Thoughts of sunflower florets. A conch shell. After five minutes she has found nothing. She is tired of searching—for Dad and then Mom, for solutions to cryptograms, for Senator Sargent, Malachi, a survey marker. For hope.

"When do we move on to the other waypoint?" Lily says.

She's referring to the conversation they had in the truck on the way over. Arizona—who is, after all, the daughter of a cartographer—explained that any given set of North American coordinates can refer to two different locations, depending on when the coordinates were recorded. The North American Datum (NAD), the geodetic reference system for the United States, goes through revisions. Recent topographic maps are based on the North American Datum of 1983, but older ones were based on the North American Datum of 1927. Using NAD 83 to find a location specified in NAD 27 can result in errors of one hundred yards or more.

Like most modern GPS devices, Arizona's Garmin doesn't support NAD 27, so before leaving camp she used online tools to convert the coordinates from NAD 27 to NAD 83 and added a waypoint there, as well. Given that the survey marker on San Nick was placed in 1932, the NAD 27 location is probably the right one, but the NAD 83 spot— where they stand now—was on the way, so she figured it was worth stopping here first.

"Let's go. It's probably the other one, anyway."

She puts Mojo back on leash, shoulders her pack, and navigates to the second waypoint, ninety yards to the west. Lily and Gus follow. They pass more rusted cans, some so large that Arizona wonders if they had contained kerosene or blasting powder rather than food.

Even larger pieces of rusted metal are strewn about, unidentifiable pieces of a camp or mining equipment ravaged by time and the elements. The elements—water, air, fire, earth.

Arizona approaches a slight depression that doesn't look natural. She stops, points. "I'm wondering if that's a mine shaft that was filled in." They go around it to be safe.

They walk down a concave slope toward the point where it steepens, becomes convex. An inflection point. The math term would bear fresh thoughts of Dad if she wasn't already shouldering that burden. Before they get to the inflection point, her GPS indicates they have arrived.

"We're here."

This time she marks the spot with a distinctive rock and keeps her pack on. She lets Mojo go, tells him to stay close, and searches again. There is nothing obvious or out of place. Lily looks at the largest pieces of rusted metal, but there is nothing under them or written on them. Nor is there anything under or behind any of the largish rocks.

Arizona begins spiraling outward again. With nowhere else to look now, the spiral gets bigger and bigger. But giving up is not an option. There has to be something here.

The treeless canyon is sheltered from the wind but directly exposed to the midday sun. Sweat beads on Arizona's skin, chills her whenever a momentary breeze sneaks its way in. She arrives at the inflection point, where the slope drops more precipitously to the west, looks down, and sighs. Continuing the search beyond this point will be even slower, not only because each loop of the spiral is bigger but because the steeper, looser terrain will hinder her.

She sits on a boulder near the edge, takes her pack off, gives Mojo a snack and water, and has some for herself. Lily settles next to her. On the other side of Arizona, small stones are scattered on the flat surface of the boulder. She picks up a handful and begins mindlessly throwing them sidearm down the slope, one at a time. She gives some to Lily, who joins in.

Skipping stones off an ancient sea, Arizona thinks. Much easier than on water. Rocks have excellent surface tension. Like her. She scans herself for tension, but to her surprise all her tension seems well below the surface.

The stones bounce off rocks, tolling one, two, sometimes three staccato tones. Throw, *clack*. Throw, *clack-clack*. Throw, *clack*. Throw, *clack, plink*.

The metallic sound catches Arizona by surprise, even though scrap metal is all over old mine sites. She stands and looks over the edge—sure enough, large pieces of rusted metal and some wooden beams. She sits, tosses a few more rocks. But she is no longer listening. She is thinking. She stands up and looks again, at the partly buried beams. One beam in particular has caught her eye—it lies perfectly horizontal on the rocky ground, as if placed rather than fallen.

She scrambles down the slope, past the horizontal beam, then turns back so she can look uphill at it from the other side. Sure enough, from here she can see a small hole in the ground just beneath the beam.

"It's a mine entrance, an adit!"

31

The Mine

A RIZONA SCALES THE SLOPE.

"Wait here. I'll be right back."

She runs to the truck. Mojo runs after her. To Mojo, running is play. She grabs her headlamp from the duffel bag, returns to the edge, grabs her pack, and scuttles down to the adit. Lily, Mojo, and Gus follow.

The mine entrance is mostly buried by rock, but below the horizontal cross beam there is a small opening, big enough to look into but not to crawl through. Arizona puts on the headlamp and looks in. How deep is it? How far does the beam travel? A fair distance, she thinks, but she isn't sure.

She sits on the talus slope that blocks the mine entrance, with her back to the hole, and thinks. She looks at the screen of her GPS, turns and looks up the slope toward her search spiral, then looks at the screen again.

"The GPS points in the same direction as the tunnel and says we're seventy feet from the waypoint."

They pull rocks away from the hole. After five minutes, the hole is big enough for her pack but not for her. Their T-shirts—Arizona's black *Vitruvian Man* and Lily's tie-dye—are soaked with sweat.

Arizona stuffs her pack through the hole. "I'm committed now, or I should be." It's a joke her mom has made too many times, and she wishes Mom was here to make it again.

They pry away more rocks, arms and shoulders feeling the strain, until the hole is big enough to crawl through.

"I'm going in alone," Arizona says. "This isn't a dog-friendly activity, so I need you to stay with them."

"We can put them in the truck," Lily says, "with water and the windows open."

Arizona shakes her head. "Please, Lily. But if I'm not back in half an hour, then okay, put them in the truck and come in after me."

"Fuck."

"Thank you."

Arizona squirms through and crawls down the back side of the rock pile, pushing her pack in front of her. The cool air, though stale and dusty, is refreshing, until she dons her pack, which pushes her wet shirt against her skin. A shiver cascades through her upper body and out through chattering teeth, loud enough that she thinks it echoes.

The headlamp beam doesn't penetrate far into the tunnel. She sees a support beam ahead, and another past that. Each support beam across the ceiling is held up by two vertical beams on the sides, like a wooden Stonehenge or the symbol for pi.

"Tunnel looks okay, so here goes nothing. See you in a bit," she calls out to Lily.

"Okay, be careful, AZ."

Arizona crouches under cobwebs, pushes others aside, and, when she doesn't see them, suffers through the trespass with closed eyes and more gooseflesh. She reaches the second support beam and looks at her GPS to see how much farther she has to go. Oh, right. GPS doesn't work underground. She'll have to guesstimate. She sees more support beams ahead, looks back, and guesses that the hole is about twenty-five feet behind her. If the beams are placed every twelve feet, just four more will get her to seventy feet.

She steps around a pile of rock and dirt from a small cave-in and walks to the fourth beam. A four-foot rattlesnake skin lies at her feet. She bends down and runs her fingers along its scales. It's beautiful but not what she is looking for. Then another thought occurs to her. If it was four feet long when it molted its skin, how big is it now? She ventures on, warily scanning the tunnel floor. Her boots scuff the uneven ground, kick loose stones, splash through pools of standing water. The rock walls echo everything, amplify her bated breath.

She arrives at the sixth beam and looks back, the light of her head-lamp reflecting off the puddles. The entrance hole is so small it makes her quail. She scans the floor, walls, and ceiling but sees only rock, pocked by drill marks and candle wax. She's come this far, so she con-tinues, scanning every surface as she goes. She passes the seventh set of beams, which is doubled up—two vertical beams on each side, sup-porting two ceiling beams rather than one—and reaches the eighth beam. If her estimate was right and the beams are a dozen feet apart, she is now almost one hundred feet underground and nearly thirty feet past the waypoint.

She sighs, tired of looking for things without knowing what they are. She thinks of her mom and of Gordon's words. *Your mother is counting on you.* No shit, Sherlock. But Mojo is counting on her, too. As she ponders what to do, staring at the distant dust mote that is the mine entrance, something skitters behind her. Or is it more of a flut-ter? She spins and catches it in the light of her headlamp. A silver-haired bat clings to the underside of the next beam, the furred membrane between its legs clearly visible just a dozen feet away. Then it is joined by another, and another.

Arizona loves bats, loves watching them fly. They are radar-guided, insect-seeking missiles. But being trapped in an enclosed space with them? And where there are a few (four now—no, five), there are un-doubtedly dozens, if not hundreds. She is already past the waypoint anyway, so she starts back toward the entrance. She will search again on the way out.

But she stops at the seventh beam, unsure why. It's different in that it's doubled up, but doubling up the beams periodically makes sense. That isn't it. She tilts her head to get a different perspective. Her eyes grow wide. One of the vertical support beams *is* different—not as rough as the other, as if newer.

She runs her fingers across both beams and could swear that the smooth one moves when she touches it. But that isn't possible, not if it's load-bearing. She pushes on it and it rotates. Pushes more forcefully. It spins and sticks, but the bottom of the beam has slid out an inch. She puts the fingers of both hands into the crack and pulls, eyes closed as if that will protect her when the ceiling comes down. The beam topples over, its impact like rolling thunder in the small space. As the dust settles, her headlamp reveals a square recess in the rock wall, four feet above the tunnel floor.

Arizona crouches so her headlamp shines inside. The hole looks empty. She thinks about all the scenes in movies where people reach into dark holes, only to have something grab their arm, bite it, or rip it clean off. But what choice does she have? She shuts her eyes, plunges her hand in. With her arm fully extended, she can barely feel the back of the hole, but she can't reach all the way in and see inside at the same time. She gropes along the back, floor, ceiling, and both sides of the hole. Other than a thin layer of rock dust that feels chalky on her fingers, it is empty. Another dead end. She pulls her hand out, dragging it along the floor of the hole.

"Ow!"

She examines her hand. A drop of blood forms on her fingertip. Seriously? Something actually *did* bite her? Her thoughts turn to the rattlesnake skin, but she didn't hear a rattle. Then again, baby rattlesnakes are purported to be particularly dangerous because their rattles haven't developed—hence no warning—and because they supposedly can't control the amount of venom they release—so they release all of it. She'd always meant to research the venom thing to see if it was true. Such knowledge might be handy now. Or maybe it was just a bat. Rabies, in that case. Given the choice, she prefers the snake. Rabies is a shitty way to die.

She adjusts her headlamp and raises her hand to get a better look. She thinks about sucking the venom out. Does that work for rabies? There seems to be only one puncture, so not a snake. She brings her finger closer to her eyes. Something is sticking out of it. She plucks out the sliver of metal and examines it. Tetanus, she thinks this time. Also a shitty way to die. She rolls the sliver between thumb and forefinger. It is a thin but stiff piece of wire, like one thread of a braided cable. She peers into the hole again but doesn't see anything like that. She reaches back in, slowly moving her fingertips across the floor of the hole.

"Ow," she says again. But at least she found it.

Her arm is about halfway in. She curls her fingers and scrapes across the rock, her fingernails the tines of a garden rake. Finds something smooth, a rod or dowel, but it won't move. She puts her fingers behind it and pulls, then pushes with her thumb. After half a dozen rounds of pulling and pushing, the rod breaks free and her fingers curl under it. She feels something like a cable between her fingers. A handle? She tugs on it, and the floor of the hole shifts. She lowers her hand and yanks harder. The object comes free, and her hand careens into the rock ceiling of the hole. Ouch.

Keeping her hand near the top of the hole, she pulls out her prize. It's a false bottom, she realizes. The handle is attached to a strip of wood about a foot long, its top covered in something that closely resembles rock. She recalls art projects with her mom when they had mixed things into glue—sawdust and powdered glass—and wonders if the surface is just glue and crushed rock. The handle fits in a recess obscured from view by a small ridge, which explains why she hadn't seen the wire. She places the false bottom on the floor of the tunnel and looks into the hole. In the space beneath is a small package sealed with twine. Arizona reaches in, wraps her fingers around the twine, and lifts it out.

She sits on the floor of the tunnel and stares at the package, not much bigger than a brick, then twists the twine off without breaking it. It is wrapped in waxed canvas. She unfolds the first layer of cloth, then a second, revealing a small box. With the canvas wrapping in her lap, she raises the box to see it better. It is made of dark-colored wood with brass hinges and two brass clasps.

She hears a flurry of fluttering behind her and pictures an army of bats—or would it be a squadron?—so she tamps down her curiosity for the moment, rewraps the box in the canvas, shoves it and the twine in her pack, and heads for the exit.

———

AS SHE APPROACHES THE mine opening, she hears what sounds like an impact sprinkler and freezes. Slowly, she shines her light toward the sound that she knows well. "Shit."

"Hey," Lily says as her face appears through the hole. "What's wrong?"

"Rattlesnake," Arizona says.

"Fuck," Lily says.

The large western rattlesnake is against the left wall, at the base of the rock pile, right between Arizona and the exit.

"Can you steer clear of it?" Lily says.

"Maybe, but it's going to be close."

Arizona reminds herself that rattlesnakes can strike only about half of their length and grow to only about six feet long, so she should be safe as long as she can stay four feet away from it. In theory, at least. Maybe she can avoid it if she goes up the right side of the rock pile, then traverses left on her belly toward the opening. It's not the first time she's come across a rattlesnake in the wild—hell, they have them at home—but this is the first time she'll be this close and in such a compromising position, on her stomach, unable to step away. Fuck indeed.

She moves cautiously up the right side of the slope, sweeping her headlamp back and forth between where she needs to go and the snake. Near the top, her backpack hits the ceiling of the tunnel, so she removes it, gets down on her belly, and starts moving left, nudging the pack along ahead of her.

As she approaches the hole, the snake is only about five feet from her, in classic viper stance, coiled with the business end erect and staring straight at her. Its forked tongue darts in and out. She suddenly understands the expression *snake eyes*—the worst possible outcome. Although clarity is never inopportune, sometimes life delivers epiphanies at the strangest times.

As she prepares to crawl through the opening, she pictures the snake lunging and biting her belly, which firms up at the thought. She passes her pack to Lily.

"Here I come. If I yell in pain, grab me and pull me out."

"Okay, but let's hope that's not necessary."

Arizona wriggles out into the daylight. Nothing bites her.

Lily'e eyes are wide. "I hope that was worth it. Did you find something?"

Arizona nods.

"Well, tell me."

"I'll do better than that. Give me my pack and I'll show you. Up at the flatter spot."

They clamber to the edge, where the dogs are waiting patiently.

"Good boys," Arizona says as she rubs Mojo's head.

The warm sun and fresh air feel good. She hadn't noticed just how stuffy the air in the mine was.

Arizona is relieved that she found *something*, even if she doesn't know what it is yet. But she is also anxious, glancing over her shoulder. She puts her pack on the flat boulder, pulls out the box, places it on top of her pack, and unwraps it again.

"Wow," Lily says.

"Yeah."

The box is even more impressive in daylight. The beautiful dark wood has a luster that is almost metallic. She looks around again. Just because she's paranoid doesn't mean they're not following her.

"Come on," says Lily, impatient.

Arizona nods, then realizes that she's holding her breath as if the box is Pandora's. She undoes the first clasp, the second. Exhales and slowly lifts the lid.

The interior of the box is lined with a luxurious black cloth, like watered silk. Nestled in a padded recess at its center is a single item—a small glass vial sealed with a cork. In the vial is what appears to be a piece of paper.

She looks at Lily. Lily nods.

She removes the vial and cork, slides the delicate scroll into her hand, and unfurls it carefully to avoid damaging it. At the top is a poem, handwritten in swooping faded script. She reads it aloud.

HALCYON DAYS

At the start we were but one and five;
Then three came and one did go.
Our replacements numbered four and six
'Til a brace came; six left, tho.
By all odds we tried, but many died,
So two and five were sent in our stead.
With our course all run through,
We had naught else to do.
Six and a leash was the count of the dead.

When the smoke had cleared, the victors cheered,
And the ships found their terminal berth,
Six fell from air to become odd fire
And water three from earth.
We were bereft when that vessel upturned,
Narrowly left with hope, but no mirth.
May you find more than hope here,
And in Carroll's letters,
As time flies, for whatever that's worth.

"*Carroll's letters?*" Arizona says. "As in Lewis Carroll, whose poem was used for the first cipher?"

"I don't know," Lily says, "but for the record, the title seems sardonic. The days described are anything but halcyon."

Below the poem, set off by a wavy-line flourish, is a forest of seemingly random letters. Hundreds of them. Another cipher, no doubt. Arizona unfurls the scroll fully to see if there is anything else, but it's just more cipher text. She shakes her head, returns to the poem.

"What are you thinking?" says Lily.

Still holding the scroll with both hands, Arizona raises one index finger.

"You need a minute?"

Arizona nods once, stares at the poem. The first verse is beyond convoluted. Almost every line contains numbers. The second verse has only a couple of numbers, so Arizona focuses on that. The first two lines seem straightforward enough, but the third and fourth lines are even more cryptic than the first verse. They do, however, reference all four classical elements—air, fire, water, and earth.

Lily leans away to give her space, but she's still peering at Arizona's face. Arizona pretends not to notice, but Lily's eyes betray her. Normally she hates being watched. But she doesn't mind this time. So does it depend on who is doing the watching?

She moves on to lines five and six of the second verse.

We were bereft when that vessel upturned,
Narrowly left with hope, but no mirth.

Is that a reference to Pandora's box? Or is she reading too much into it since she was just thinking about that? Pandora's box was also a *vessel,* and after all of the evils were released, only hope remained to assuage the lot of humankind. It does seem to fit. And does the use of the phrase *that vessel* reinforce the Pandora interpretation? Not *the* vessel? Not *our* vessel?

Arizona realizes her eyes are darting to and fro, as if seeing things that aren't there, and that Lily is still staring. Does Lily think she looks crazy? Does Arizona care what people think? Maybe some people?

Despite the distraction, a phrase from the poem reverberates. When that vessel *upturned*?

Arizona grabs the box so fast it startles Lily. She turns it over, but there is nothing on the bottom. She sighs at the failed epiphany. *Narrowly left with hope* is right.

But then she notices the slightest hint of something. She tilts the box back and forth to see if the angle of the light will make a difference. It does. At just the right angle, a subtle design stands out. It has been masterfully inlaid using the same wood but opposing grain.

A six-petal rosette formed from overlapping circles.

It can also be formed from a hexagram, with each circle centered on one of the hexagram's points and passing through the two adjacent points.

Fire . . . fused with water it blooms . . . into a flower.

It is a design she has seen a thousand times, known as the Flower of Life.

It was Dad's tattoo.

32

Hourglass

ARIZONA STARES AT THE BOTTOM OF THE BOX, UNABLE to assimilate it into her world. Her hands descend to her lap, as if the weight of the box is now too much to bear. "Daddy," she says under her breath.

"What's that, AZ?" Lily says.

Arizona doesn't respond. She hears a voice-like noise without meaning.

Lily waits several seconds, puts a hand on Arizona's shoulder. "Talk to me."

"Take this before I drop it. Look at the bottom."

Lily takes the box, examines the bottom. "What is it?"

"It's called the Flower of Life. It was my dad's tattoo."

"What? Your dad's tattoo? What does that mean?"

Arizona raises her fingertips to her temples. "When the coordinates turned out to be here, where my dad died, I knew it couldn't be a coincidence. But I still couldn't believe he was actually a part of all this."

"But now with his tattoo on the box," Lily says, "you think maybe he actually *was* looking for this? That this is what they killed him for?"

"I don't know." She shakes her head. "None of it makes any sense. That morning, he asked my mom and me if we wanted to come along on the ride. Why would he have done that if he wanted to be alone to retrieve this? It feels like I'm trying to create a picture out of pieces from completely different jigsaw puzzles."

Focus, she tells herself. *One thing at a time.* "Can I have the box back?"

Lily rights the box and hands it to her. Arizona sets it on her lap and reaches for the scroll. But there is something different about the box. The silken surface that holds the vial has moved upward.

"Lily, look."

Lily's eyes grow wide. "What are you waiting for?"

Arizona lifts out the insert, but there is nothing below it. She examines the underside of the insert itself, hoping for another clue. Still nothing.

"Nothing. But it gives me an idea. Come on, let's go to the truck."

"Are you thinking what I think you're thinking?" Lily smiles.

"Change of plan, if it fits."

They rush to the truck, load the dogs into the back, and climb in.

Lily grabs the parcel that they picked up in Beatty. She opens it, revealing the two items they purchased—a GPS tracker of their own, much like the ones they found on the motorcycle and truck, and a magnetic case. She sets aside the magnetic case, removes the GPS tracker from its box, and places it in Arizona's open hand, like a nurse handing a surgeon a scalpel.

Arizona puts the tracker in the bottom of the box and replaces the insert. It fits. She tilts the box back and forth but feels and hears the tracker sliding around.

"Batteries," she says, "and duct tape from the glove compartment."

Lily retrieves both and hands them over.

Arizona removes the insert again, installs the batteries in the tracker, turns it on, tapes the tracker inside the box, and reinstalls the insert. She tilts the box back and forth, then shakes it. Perfect.

"Honestly, AZ, this is so much better than the old plan. That was way too risky."

When Arizona ordered the tracker, her plan had been to give Gordon the coordinates, wait in hiding until the bad guys arrived, and somehow plant the tracker on their vehicle.

"Agreed. I didn't like that idea much myself. I just didn't have a better one until now. I only wish we could put a poisonous spider or scorpion inside." She pictures the red hourglass on the round black abdomen of the western black widow, fresh neurotoxin dripping from its fangs.

"I like the way you think, AZ."

"Thanks. But I guess the GPS tracker will have to do."

They take detailed pictures of the scroll, put it back in the vial, and place the vial in its recess. Arizona closes the box and wraps it up just as she found it, including the twine. She places it in her pack.

"Stay here with the boys," she says. "Please. I'll be as quick as I can."

"Okay, but be careful, Arizona-like-the-state."

"Thanks, I will," she says. But she thinks, *Lily-like-the-flower.*

IN LESS THAN FIVE MINUTES she is back in the cool stale air of the mine. The rattlesnake has moved to the other side of the tunnel. Good snake. She returns the box to its hiding spot and sprinkles it with rock dust. She picks up the false bottom, then thinks better of it. They need to find the box, so there's no reason to make this hard. She puts the false bottom in her pack and twists the beam into place.

SHORTLY AFTER THEY EMERGE from Titus Canyon, Arizona's phone rings. Blocked number. She pulls over (talking on the phone while driving is dangerous) and answers.

"Yeah."

"Why haven't you been answering your phone?"

"I went for a long walk with my dog and forgot to bring my phone." Lying to Gordon is so much easier than lying to Lily. Huh. Good to know.

"Keep it with you from now on. What have you learned about the stamps on the marker?"

"They represent coordinates, latitude and longitude."

"So the letters represent numbers?"

"Sort of—those same letters each appeared in the keywords for the second cipher, immediately after the words they represent."

"The *words* they represent? Don't they have to represent numbers?"

"They represent numbers indirectly. Directly, they represent words, and then those words have numerical equivalents on Malachi's tombstone."

"You continue to impress me, Arizona."

"Considering the source, that still means very little."

"So where do they lead? What are the coordinates?"

"Very close to where you killed my dad, in Titus Canyon."

He pauses. "Your father's death was tragic. I'm sincerely sorry for your loss."

"Bullshit," Arizona says without hesitation.

"What are the coordinates?"

"NAD 27, NAD 83, or both?"

"What are you talking about?"

She sighs, louder and longer than necessary, then explains.

"How do I do the conversion?" he says.

"There are web-based tools. Never mind, I'll just do it for you. Hang on . . ."

She mutes her phone. As she pretends to do the conversion, she rolls her eyes back and metronomes her head from side to side. The theme music from *Jeopardy!* plays in her head. After killing adequate time, she reads the coordinates from her notebook.

"Stay put," he says. *Click.*

"Stay put, my ass," says Arizona.

"It's a lot like fishing," Lily says. "Lots of waiting before the action, and they can't take the bait until they find it."

"Yeah, and they have to find the adit and figure out the beam that doesn't bear weight. Who knows how long that will take these clowns."

"Kinda bossy, isn't he?"

"Yes, and not much sense of humor, either. Probably standard for a sociopath."

Lily chuckles. "Garden variety."

Arizona is impatient but wears a crooked grin.

33

The Adept and
the Journal — Part Four

A LTHOUGH THE ADEPT KNOWS THE JOURNAL ALMOST by heart, he is no less frustrated each time he arrives at a section of missing pages. He sighs, flips past, and reads on.

[missing text]

> the specific location in Titus Canyon. I found a small wooden box that had been expertly hidden. The bottom was adorned with the Flower of Life, although I almost didn't see it because it was cleverly inlaid, with only opposing grain to give it away. The box contained an unencrypted poem and another cipher. I copied everything and put the box back, as if it had never been found.

He places the bookmark in the journal, closes it, and runs his fingertips across the symbol branded onto the back of the leather cover.

He thinks about the first time he saw the symbol outside of the journal. The man, Mother's colleague, had walked into the ornate living room of the Victorian house that Mother had so lovingly restored, the house that was now his.

"I'm so sorry for your loss, Peter," the man had said, hand extended. "Maggie was a remarkable person, a real force of nature."

He was momentarily speechless as he stared at the tattoo on the back of the man's extended hand. "Yes . . . thank you." He grasped the hand and shook, not taking his eyes off the symbol. "Mother certainly was a dedicated . . . civil servant."

He had struggled for the right words and immediately regretted his choice. Realized he was still shaking and let go. He felt sick, lightheaded. Worried about his expression, couldn't betray his thoughts. Sad for the loss? Grateful for the sympathy? As if one should ever be grateful for sympathy.

"That's an interesting tattoo," he said, still staring at it.

"Oh, that's a long story." The man chuckled. "The short version is it's just a simple flower. Please let me know if there's anything I can do . . ."

"I'm sorry?"

"In the wake of your loss."

"Oh, yes. Thank you."

The awkwardness was dispatched with slow and silent nods—like martial artists about to spar. The tattooed man turned and walked away.

THE RING OF HIS phone brings him back to the present. He puts the phone on speaker and folds his hands in his lap. "Yes?" His voice echoes through the phone and back into the small, bare room. He grimaces at the technology, necessary but so imperfect. Like so many things he will change once he has the power.

"She solved it, sir. Coordinates, latitude and longitude. In Titus Canyon, just as you suspected, sir."

"Smart girl. What are the coordinates?"

Gordon reads the coordinates, then adds, "She says it's extremely close to where her father died—or, as she puts it, to where we killed him."

"Fascinating," he says, responding only to the location, not the implied accusation. As if the latter hasn't registered or doesn't matter. "That supports my assertion that he was going to retrieve it, wouldn't you agree?"

"Yes, it does seem to fit, sir."

"I have an extremely important mission for you. If you succeed, it will represent a significant step forward for you within the Order."

"Thank you for your trust, sir. How may I be of service to the Golden Dawn?"

"Take the helicopter to the coordinates, immediately. You should find a small wooden box. Retrieve it. But under no circumstances are you to open it. Do you understand?"

"Perfectly, sir."

"Call me on the satellite phone as soon as you find it. Don't fail me."

He hangs up without waiting for a reply, opens the journal to the bookmark, and continues reading.

34

Carroll's Letters

BACK IN THE ALABAMA HILLS, ARIZONA LOGS IN TO THE website for the GPS tracker. It hasn't moved yet, but that's no surprise. It's been only a couple of hours since she gave the coordinates to Gordon. She'll keep checking it.

Meanwhile, she and Lily study the photos they took of the scroll—specifically, the cipher text that followed the "Halcyon Days" poem. Arizona tries to show Lily how to use frequency analysis, but to no avail—for either Lily or the cipher.

"Here, let's go through it again," Arizona says.

"No, that's okay, really. It's obviously just not my thing. And, more important, I'm slowing you down. How about if I take the boys for a walk, so you can focus? The three of us will just hang in my van after that, and you can come find us when you have a breakthrough or need a break."

"Okay."

"Come on, boys. Walkies."

Arizona returns to the cipher. Soon she's finished her frequency analysis. No obvious patterns emerge, but she plugs in some letters just to see. She double-checks her results and sighs. Nothing doing. Each cipher is harder than the previous one, it seems. Sure, one must prove oneself worthy to know the secrets of the Art. She rolls her eyes and rereads the unencrypted poem.

HALCYON DAYS

At the start we were but one and five;
Then three came and one did go.
Our replacements numbered four and six
'Til a brace came; six left, tho.
By all odds we tried, but many died,
So two and five were sent in our stead.
With our course all run through,
We had naught else to do.
Six and a leash was the count of the dead.

When the smoke had cleared, the victors cheered,
And the ships found their terminal berth,
Six fell from air to become odd fire
And water three from earth.
We were bereft when that vessel upturned,
Narrowly left with hope, but no mirth.
May you find more than hope here,
And in Carroll's letters,
As time flies, for whatever that's worth.

She had wondered if *Carroll's letters* was a reference to Lewis Carroll. In hindsight, of course it is. Lewis Carroll published "The Alphabet Cipher," which describes a polyalphabetic cipher. *Carroll's letters* is *Carroll's alphabet.* So this is a polyalphabetic cipher, which can't be cracked by frequency analysis and is very hard to beat without knowing the keyword or key phrase. She admonishes herself for not making the connection sooner. She could have avoided all that pointless frequency analysis. Whatever.

The unencrypted poem must lead to the keyword. She returns to the second verse:

When the smoke had cleared, the victors cheered,
And the ships found their terminal berth,

Six fell from air to become odd fire
And water three from earth.

The first two lines are clever. Not only do they strengthen the narrative of the battle but, in so doing, create an artful misdirection for later in the verse. An upturned *vessel* becomes a foundering ship rather than Pandora's box. Artful misdirection. An apt description of the writings of alchemists.

The third and fourth lines are so cryptic that they must have hidden meaning. And the references to all four classical elements can't be coincidence.

Since the poem seems to be all about numbers, she decides to take inventory, but first she has to look something up. She opens a book on her iPad and copies a quote into her notebook.

> The bushes were inky black, the ground a sombre grey, the sky colourless and cheerless. And up the hill I thought I could see ghosts. There several times, as I scanned the slope, I saw white figures. Twice I fancied I saw a solitary white, ape-like creature running rather quickly up the hill, and once near the ruins I saw a leash of them carrying some dark body.
>
> —H. G. WELLS,
> *The Time Machine*

It was where she had learned that *leash* also means three. A leash of Morlocks. But the mention of ghosts heats her mind, bubble-memories of family rising to the surface, popping before her eyes. To quench the flame at its source, before the simmer becomes a boil, she returns to the task at hand.

She closes her notebook and tallies the references to each number in the poem, counting *brace* as two and *leash* as three, of course.

Numbers	Count
1	2
2	2
3	3
4	1
5	2
6	4

Only one through six? She double-checks, but that is correct. The poem has no other numbers. She stares at the inventory of numbers and counts, but her mind is a chalkboard just erased. She prevails upon the chalky wraiths to rematerialize, but none do. Wraiths. Ghosts. How appropriate for another dead end.

Drawn by the four classical elements, she focuses on lines three and four of the second verse:

Six fell from air to become odd fire
And water three from earth.

The symbols for fire and water had fused to form the hexagram on Malachi's tombstone and on the survey marker on San Nick, and then the hexagram had bloomed into the Flower of Life. Maybe these references to the elements are references to the symbols again? She draws the symbols for the four classical elements and labels them.

Fire   Water   Air   Earth

She scratches her right temple with her thumb, leaves it there and lowers her fingers onto her forehead, pinky on left eyebrow. The only difference between air and fire is the line through the middle. Then it hits her.

Six fell from air to become odd fire.

Remove the line from air and it becomes fire.

So does *six* represent the line through air?

And water differs from earth by only one line.

And water three from earth.

So maybe *three* represents the line through earth?

Both hands are perched on her head, fingers barely laced.

But why the numbers? *Six* from air. *Three* from earth.

As she looks at the symbols for the elements, she has another epiphany. It's not just fire and water that can be fused. It's also air and earth. Or *all four* symbols.

In her mind's eye, she sees the four elements stack into a single symbol, the hexagram. Combine earth and fire, and the line cutting through earth—the one the poem calls line three—becomes the horizontal line in fire.

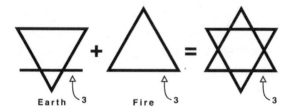

Earth   Fire

Then air and water, with the line through the center of air—line six—becoming the horizontal line in water.

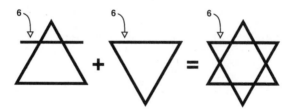

Then combined.

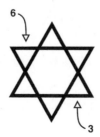

She stares for several seconds and realizes the obvious. A hexagram doesn't just have six points. It also has six *lines*.

She looks at the first verse again, which is packed with numbers. Do all those numbers refer to lines in the hexagram? But she has only two of the six lines identified. What are the numbers for the other four? She scans the second verse again.

Six fell from air to become odd fire. Odd fire. Does that mean the lines in fire are odd numbers? The horizontal line is three, so the two sloping lines would be one and five. But which is which?

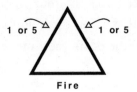

And then the other two lines in water would have to be two and four. But again, which is which?

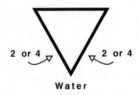

She double-checks her logic. Draws a diagram to keep track.

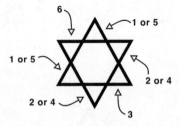

She scours the poem for clues to identify the last lines but, no matter how hard she scrubs the words, nothing lies beneath.

Her jaws clench and her middle finger drums the table. She looks at the time—a little after 5:00 P.M. Time for a break anyway. Find Lily and the boys, go for a walk. Fresh air might do her good, help get her head unstuck. Engage her active voice. Like Dad. Sigh.

Though it isn't twilight yet, the sun has dropped behind the mountains, and the colossal shadow of Mount Whitney has engulfed the Alabama Hills and most of Lone Pine. She ties the sleeves of a fleece jacket around her waist and grabs a Coke from the fridge. She finds Lily, Gus, and Mojo lounging in the van with the sliding door open.

"Walk?"

"Sure. Any progress?"

"A little maybe, but nothing significant yet."

"You'll get it," Lily says.

They amble into the small canyon, where Mojo and Gus play in the stream. Watching Mojo never gets old, always makes Arizona smile. Interestingly, she finds herself mostly watching Lily. The cool eventide air feels good on her skin, in her lungs. She breathes easily. But even with her eyes on her friend, she still can't keep her mind off the puzzle. How can the poem not contain clues to identify the other lines?

They climb out of the canyon and wander through the boulders. As they approach a boulder the size of a dump truck, Mojo and Gus go left around it. Arizona starts after them, changes her mind, and goes right with Lily. It doesn't matter—they'll all meet on the other side. The thought echoes in her head, comes out under her breath.

"It doesn't matter."

"What doesn't matter?" Lily says.

"Oh, sorry, just thinking out loud. I felt like I was missing a piece of the puzzle, but now I'm wondering if I don't need that piece after all. Maybe I can fill it in through trial and error. Or context, like I used for the second cipher."

"I told you."

"Told me what?"

Lily smiles. "That you'll get it."

"I haven't got it yet, but thanks."

Arizona leaves Lily and Gus at the van and goes back to the Airstream with Mojo.

Mojo noses his bowl, so she feeds him dinner and noshes on some snacks for herself.

Pistachios.

Dark chocolate.

English muffin with rhubarb jam.

She eats the latter without looking at it, then regrets it. What if there was a bug on it? Or mold? One should always pay attention to what one is putting in one's mouth.

Her phone rings. Not a blocked number but a familiar one. Sam Yeats. Arizona scans her memory for the last time they spoke. She had voicemail from Sam when she got off the boat yesterday but didn't call her back. Before that, they swapped voicemails when Arizona was driving from Carson City to the Alabama Hills. But that was . . . five days ago? Oops. Nobody likes being ghosted. She answers.

"Hey, Sam. Sorry I didn't call you back."

"That's okay. I just wanted to know how you're doing. Has your mom turned up yet?"

Arizona hesitates, but the question has boxed her in.

"No . . . she hasn't."

"Oh, Arizona, I'm so sorry. You must be going out of your mind. Is there anything I can do to help?"

The concern in Sam's voice almost cracks the dam for Arizona. The temptation to tell her everything is strong, but she pushes it down. Sam means well, but she'll want to get the authorities involved—sheriff's department, FBI, whatever—and Arizona's already decided that's not an option.

"Where did you and Mojo end up, anyway?" Sam asks, her tone casual. "I tried to look in on you at the campsite."

Arizona stumbles for an answer that isn't a lie. "We went home for a bit, and now we're in the Alabama Hills." She thinks about saying more, but what can she say?

They talk a little more—Sam asking if she can help with anything, chatting about the scenery in the Hills. It all feels . . . normal. Arizona is surprised to find herself comforted.

"Call me anytime," Sam says.

"Okay," Arizona says. "Thank you."

SAM HANGS UP THE phone and turns to the other person in her office.

"Well done, Sam," says Stephen Gordon. "She seems to trust you. That should come in handy."

Sam nods.

Less than half a mile away, in the area closed to the public, Arizona's mom is bound to the frame of the cot again. This time with handcuffs.

35

Halcyon Days

ARIZONA CHECKS THE GPS TRACKER AGAIN. IT'S FINALLY ON the move. But her devious cast fades to furrowed brow when she realizes that the blue dot isn't on Titus Canyon Road, or any road, for that matter. It's moving northwest, tracking the California–Nevada border almost perfectly. Three breaths, then she nods. They have a helicopter. In addition to tracking her location, have they been watching her from the sky, too? Do they have more than one helicopter? Are they watching her right now? She pictures a helicopter hovering above the trailer and looks skyward through the window, but it's dark outside. Listens for the thrum of rotors. Nothing. She'll need to start checking the tracker more frequently.

She returns her attention to the unencrypted poem, "Halcyon Days." If the second verse reveals—mostly at least—how to number the lines in the hexagram, and the numbers in the first verse refer to those lines, then . . . what?

She has no idea. She feels like she's getting mired in the details, can't see the forest for the trees. Time to take a step back.

The poem uses the phrase *Carroll's letters,* a reference to Lewis Carroll's "The Alphabet Cipher," which describes a polyalphabetic cipher.

And polyalphabetic ciphers require a keyword or even a key phrase.

And she had assumed that the unencrypted poem must lead to the keyword.

And the keyword has to be made up of *letters.*

So does the first verse indicate how to turn lines of the hexagram into letters?

There's only one way to find out.

She rereads the first verse.

At the start we were but one and five;
Then three came and one did go.
Our replacements numbered four and six
'Til a brace came; six left, tho.
By all odds we tried, but many died,
So two and five were sent in our stead.
With our course all run through,
We had naught else to do.
Six and a leash was the count of the dead.

At the start we were but one and five. Only lines one and five? She looks at her diagram again:

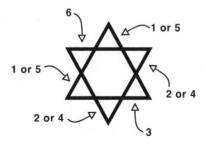

Interesting. So maybe she won't need to know line one from line five after all. Regardless of which is which, the two together will look like:

Then three came and one did go. Left pinky on upper lip, left thumb under chin. Add line three and remove line one, leaving lines three and five? Bummer. Two possibilities for that. Crap.

She looks at her diagram again, searches for patterns. Is there any order to the numbers? If the upper right line is 1, then going clockwise could be 1, 2, 3, 4, 5, 6. But if the upper left line is 1, going counterclockwise could be the same sequence. Not helpful.

The last line of the poem jumps into her mind:

As time flies, for whatever that's worth.

As time flies. Clockwise! There it is, the missing clue. She dons her crooked smile, scribbles out the alternate numbers on her diagram.

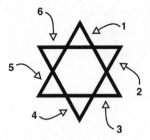

Then three came and one did go. Add line three. Remove line one. She draws the symbol for lines three and five.

Our replacements numbered four and six. Replacements? So, do we replace the previous set of lines with a new set containing just lines four and six? She draws the symbol for lines four and six.

'Til a brace came; six left, tho. Add line two and remove line six, leaving lines two and four.

By all odds we tried, but many died. No reference to adding or subtracting anything, but *all odds* has to refer to all of the odd-numbered lines—one, three, and five.

So two and five were sent in our stead. In our stead. Replacement again. Just lines two and five?

With our course all run through, we had naught else to do. All and naught. Representing infinity and zero respectively? But infinity and zero aren't in the one-through-six range. She massages the crown of her head. So are they red herrings?

Which brings her to the last line of the first verse.

Six and a leash was the count of the dead. Again, no references to adding or subtracting, so just lines six and three.

She puts them all together in sequence:

The first four symbols are essentially the same but with different orientations. Is that significant? Then the symbol for fire and two orientations of the parallel lines.

She rubs her chin as if she has whiskers there, her face a grimace of frustration. She's sure she's on the right track—that the poem is instructing her to draw these lines, in this sequence—but still, this feels like a dead end. She's looking for a *keyword* here, something she can use to decrypt the cipher text. For letters, not shapes.

Letters.

She looks again. That first symbol could be an A. The fourth could be a V.

Are these letters—or, rather, approximations of letters—derived from straight lines?

She fills in her guesses underneath the symbols.

Triangle. The only letters in English that have a single completely closed loop are D, O, P, Q, and R, sort of. Since the triangle is symmetrical, equilateral, O seems like the best choice.

Slanting parallel lines. No letters seem to fit there. H and N do have slanting lines if they're in italics, but that feels like a stretch. Or does it? Since the hexagram doesn't have any vertical lines, letters with vertical lines would have to be represented by slanting lines, as she had already assumed for L. Okay, H or N it is. But which one?

Next is horizontal parallel lines. Maybe E, F, or Z (or possibly I?).

If this is a word, E is more likely than F or Z, and N more likely than H. And together, NE is a far more likely ending than the other possibilities. So for now she assumes the last two letters are N and E.

She rechecks her work, tries the alternate letters, but ALCVONE is the closest she can get to a word.

Arizona stares at the symbols, at the word that isn't a word, and sighs. At once she is struck by an epiphany. Who said the keyword has to be a word? From a cryptography perspective, any known sequence of letters will work. So is ALCVONE the keyword after all? There is only one way to find out.

She stands and stretches, as if limbering up for a run. She isn't stiff or sore, just on edge. Ill at ease. Mojo rolls over to have his belly rubbed, so she complies.

"I love you, Mojo," she says. His eyes, ever expressive, return the sentiment.

She sits back down and thinks about the easiest way to test the keyword. If this is indeed the kind of cipher Carroll used, it's more complicated than anything she's cracked so far. In a monoalphabetic cipher, whether it's a simple Caesar shift like the first poem or a monoalphabetic keyword cipher like the second poem, the substitution alphabet doesn't change from one letter of cipher text to the next. A might become C, and B might become T, but A is always C, B is always T, and so on.

But in a polyalphabetic cipher, the substitution alphabet changes with every single letter of cipher text. The letter A might be represented by C the first time you encounter it but by F the second time, and V the third time, and so on. There are many ways of achieving this effect—including, Arizona recalls, the Enigma machine of World War II fame—but the simplest is to choose a keyword and use it as a sort of repeating template to assign different substitution alphabets.

And the simplest way to create those substitution alphabets is exactly the way Lewis Carroll did it in "The Alphabet Cipher." He used a tabula recta—a square table of alphabets with each row shifted by one additional letter—to represent all twenty-six Caesar shifts.

Arizona launches a spreadsheet program and creates one.

	A	B	C	D	E	F	G	H	I	J	K	L	M	N	O	P	Q	R	S	T	U	V	W	X	Y	Z
A	a	b	c	d	e	f	g	h	i	j	k	l	m	n	o	p	q	r	s	t	u	v	w	x	y	z
B	b	c	d	e	f	g	h	i	j	k	l	m	n	o	p	q	r	s	t	u	v	w	x	y	z	a
C	c	d	e	f	g	h	i	j	k	l	m	n	o	p	q	r	s	t	u	v	w	x	y	z	a	b
D	d	e	f	g	h	i	j	k	l	m	n	o	p	q	r	s	t	u	v	w	x	y	z	a	b	c
E	e	f	g	h	i	j	k	l	m	n	o	p	q	r	s	t	u	v	w	x	y	z	a	b	c	d
F	f	g	h	i	j	k	l	m	n	o	p	q	r	s	t	u	v	w	x	y	z	a	b	c	d	e
G	g	h	i	j	k	l	m	n	o	p	q	r	s	t	u	v	w	x	y	z	a	b	c	d	e	f
H	h	i	j	k	l	m	n	o	p	q	r	s	t	u	v	w	x	y	z	a	b	c	d	e	f	g
I	i	j	k	l	m	n	o	p	q	r	s	t	u	v	w	x	y	z	a	b	c	d	e	f	g	h
J	j	k	l	m	n	o	p	q	r	s	t	u	v	w	x	y	z	a	b	c	d	e	f	g	h	i
K	k	l	m	n	o	p	q	r	s	t	u	v	w	x	y	z	a	b	c	d	e	f	g	h	i	j
L	l	m	n	o	p	q	r	s	t	u	v	w	x	y	z	a	b	c	d	e	f	g	h	i	j	k
M	m	n	o	p	q	r	s	t	u	v	w	x	y	z	a	b	c	d	e	f	g	h	i	j	k	l
N	n	o	p	q	r	s	t	u	v	w	x	y	z	a	b	c	d	e	f	g	h	i	j	k	l	m
O	o	p	q	r	s	t	u	v	w	x	y	z	a	b	c	d	e	f	g	h	i	j	k	l	m	n
P	p	q	r	s	t	u	v	w	x	y	z	a	b	c	d	e	f	g	h	i	j	k	l	m	n	o
Q	q	r	s	t	u	v	w	x	y	z	a	b	c	d	e	f	g	h	i	j	k	l	m	n	o	p
R	r	s	t	u	v	w	x	y	z	a	b	c	d	e	f	g	h	i	j	k	l	m	n	o	p	q
S	s	t	u	v	w	x	y	z	a	b	c	d	e	f	g	h	i	j	k	l	m	n	o	p	q	r
T	t	u	v	w	x	y	z	a	b	c	d	e	f	g	h	i	j	k	l	m	n	o	p	q	r	s
U	u	v	w	x	y	z	a	b	c	d	e	f	g	h	i	j	k	l	m	n	o	p	q	r	s	t
V	v	w	x	y	z	a	b	c	d	e	f	g	h	i	j	k	l	m	n	o	p	q	r	s	t	u
W	w	x	y	z	a	b	c	d	e	f	g	h	i	j	k	l	m	n	o	p	q	r	s	t	u	v
X	x	y	z	a	b	c	d	e	f	g	h	i	j	k	l	m	n	o	p	q	r	s	t	u	v	w
Y	y	z	a	b	c	d	e	f	g	h	i	j	k	l	m	n	o	p	q	r	s	t	u	v	w	x
Z	z	a	b	c	d	e	f	g	h	i	j	k	l	m	n	o	p	q	r	s	t	u	v	w	x	y

The keyword is written repeatedly and then the cipher text beneath. So if the keyword is *Arizona* and the plain text is *good dog, Mojo,* she'd write:

A R I Z O N A A R I Z O N A

G O O D D O G M O J O

To encode, the keyword letter and corresponding plain-text letter indicate the row and column, respectively, to find the cipher-text letter. The first O in *good* lines up with R in the keyword and therefore gets encoded, using the R row and the O column, into an F. The second O in the plain text lines up with I in the keyword, becoming a W. And the third O lines up with N, becoming a B. Three different O's in the plain text, but three unique cipher-text letters.

To confirm that ALCVONE is the keyword, she'll need to decode enough text to ensure that the result is recognizable. Four repetitions of the keyword should do. She writes ALCVONE out four times in a row and writes the cipher text beneath.

A L C V O N E A L C V O N E A L C V O N E A L C V O N E

T H C Q W A V E O J M I F I O Y J M F A X O Y U R F R I

For each letter of cipher text, she highlights the row for the corresponding keyword letter and finds the cipher-text letter in that row. The letter at the top of that column is the plain-text letter.

The first keyword letter is A, which represents a Caesar shift of zero, essentially unencrypted, but she follows the process anyway. It's just how she rolls. She highlights the A row of her table and finds the corresponding letter of cipher text, T, in that row. Then the letter at the top of that column, also T, is the decoded plain-text letter. (If the corresponding keyword letter was B, the plain-text letter would shift over one, to S. If it was C, the plain text would shift two places, becoming R, and so on.)

She places a T below the first letter of cipher text.

```
A L C V O N E A L C V O N E A L C V O N E A L C V O N E
T H C Q W A V E O J M I F I O Y J M F A X O Y U R F R I
T
```

The next keyword letter is L, so she highlights the L row, finds the next letter of cipher text, H, in that row, then traces her finger to the top of that column—W.

```
A L C V O N E A L C V O N E A L C V O N E A L C V O N E
T H C Q W A V E O J M I F I O Y J M F A X O Y U R F R I
T W
```

She continues, writing the decrypted plain text under the other lines.

```
A L C V O N E A L C V O N E A L C V O N E A L C V O N E
T H C Q W A V E O J M I F I O Y J M F A X O Y U R F R I
T W A V I N R E D H R U S E O N H R R N T O N S W R E E
```

She tries to read it aloud. "Twav in red . . . ?"

It's almost English, but not quite.

She rubs the bridge of her nose and looks over at Mojo, who is on his back, four feet to the sky, muscles twitching in his sleep. Chasing a rabbit. Or maybe a squirrel.

She scans the decrypted text again, focuses on letters that don't seem to fit. The V sticks out, as does the W.

She smiles. Each of those letters is under a V in ALCVONE.

The V, the one obvious letter, isn't a V at all. She changes the V to a Y.

Alcyone. It was right there in the title the whole time. "Halcyon Days." A halcyon is a kingfisher. "The King-fisher Song," from the first cipher. *Fisher King* from the second cipher.

The very term *halcyon days,* as well as the bird of the same name, comes from the Greek mythology of Alcyone. If she remembers correctly, Alcyone somehow pissed off Zeus, who then killed her boyfriend, husband, lover, whatever, by sinking his ship. In her grief, Alcyone threw herself into the sea. But ultimately (out of compassion?) the gods changed them both into halcyon birds, which were named after her. And then Alcyone's father, who was god of the winds, calmed the winds and the waves so his bird-daughter could lay eggs in safety, and such a calm period was hence known as *halcyon days.*

What Arizona wouldn't give for halcyon days.

She changes each V to a Y and adjusts the decrypted text.

```
A L C Y O N E A L C Y O N E A L C Y O N E A L C Y O N E
T H C Q W A V E O J M I F I O Y J M F A X O Y U R F R I
T W A S I N R E D H O U S E O N H O R N T O N S T R E E
```

"'Twas in Red House on Hornton Street? Where the hell is Hornton Street? And what if they've painted the house since then?"

Regardless, it's enough to confirm the keyword. She writes a program to do the rest, the furious clicks and clacks of the keys sounding like a woodpecker thwarted by an artificial tree. Twenty minutes later she has the third cipher decrypted. It's yet another poem but much longer than the others.

She runs to Lily's van, with Mojo on her heels.

36

De Re Metallica

B ACK IN THE TRAILER, MOJO AND GUS NEST ON THE DAYBED
while Arizona reads the new poem to Lily.

'Twas in Red House on Hornton Street, in the library we adored,
We selected, sought, bought, collected, and exhaustively did pore
Over many a quaint and curious volume of forgotten lore.*
Yet from nigh a thousand volumes, the Agricola tome stood fore,
One dozen illustrated books—mining, smelting, refining ore.
Magnum opus of the metal corps.

He'd commissioned countless woodcuts, cross-referenced all the folklore,
And collated all the wisdom, but in a tongue we speak no more.
Lo and behold our work would yield an arcane portal long concealed
Behind the masters' vellum shield, their many manuscripts of yore.
To us the secrets now revealed; we had unlocked an ancient door.
The lost language of before.

A perfect language not of words, but more along the lines of birds,
A spagyric Rosetta stone, to stoke the long-cold athanor.
Deep into that darkness peering, long we stood there wondering, fearing,*
If from looking glass we would be leering, yet our likeness bear no more.
Doubting, dreaming dreams no mortal ever dared to dream before,*
We were riven to the core.

Counsel we sought but they just fought, like a lodestone cleft in two.
Use them to aid the sick and poor; lose them, destroy them forevermore.
Now both sides the secrets sought and in the middle we were caught;
In a standard stamp mill—fraught, crushed, and broken—we were the ore.
So we hid them, until the hour when man can wisely wield such power,
Where Tad and Mil had lived before.

The grandest theater of Rome, the Pharaoh's stately catacomb,
Athena's hilltop temple home, resplendent monuments of yore.
Like the brooding fervor of Chartres labyrinthian fleur,
Elements, but not those you think, delineate the contour;
Follow the arching corridor, through earth which wind and water bore.
So many petals on the floor.

Formed in Creator's loving hands, some say that when He made the lands
From shifting circles in the sands, He commanded who each was for:
Two for the angels aquiline, one for the beasts so anodyne,
With eagle as their king assigned, whence he was to rule and soar;
The closest two were made for man, our zealous penchant to explore;
The last His, for us to watch o'er.

The arc of the sky draws your gaze; one for repose in waning days,
One for the flare of summer's blaze, and one to guide you theretofore.
Worlds whip 'round concentric rings, summers fall and winters spring,
But always up extend the wings, a celestial semaphore.
By that Heaven that bends above us—by that God we both adore—*
The secrets are safe forevermore.

"Wow," Lily says.

"I know, right? More cryptic doggerel. But I recognize some of the lines and the structure. They're from a classic poem by Edgar Allan Poe."

"'The Raven'?" Lily says.

Arizona nods, opens Poe's complete works, and finds "The Raven." She marks the four borrowed lines with asterisks.

"Do you think those lines are significant?" Lily says.

"No idea, but if so, it's not obvious how. They changed the pronoun in one of the lines from *I* to *we*, but otherwise I don't see anything."

"At least the first two verses aren't *too* cryptic," Lily says.

"Yeah, that's true. The author, or authors, had a large collection of old books or manuscripts, including *the Agricola tome*, whatever that is. And they found some secrets hidden within, assuming that the references to *portal* and *door* are figurative."

Lily nods.

The wind blows outside. The particular pitch takes Arizona back to Pioneer Cemetery. The scent of pine. The cool shade of the giant redwood trees. The wind rustling through the leaves. She looks out the windows of the Airstream—mountains to the west, desert to the east—and listens. The hum of an evening breeze against the trailer. But no trees, no leaves.

Back from her reverie, she does an internet search for *Agricola*. She clicks a link for Gnaeus Julius Agricola, a Roman general responsible for the conquest of Britain. She searches the page for *metal*, but there are no hits, so she changes her web search to *Agricola metal*.

"Bingo." She clicks a link for *Georgius Agricola* and reads aloud.

> Lived 1494–1555, German mineralogist and metallurgist, known as "the father of mineralogy." Best known for his book *De Re Metallica,* published in 1556. Gifted with a precocious intellect . . . at the age of 24 he was appointed *Rector extraordinarius* of Greek at the Great School of Zwickau and made his appearance as a writer on philology. Then he went to study at Leipzig . . . medicine, physics, and chemistry. And to Italy, where he got his degree in medicine.

"*Rector extraordinarius,*" Arizona says. "Awesome title."

"Yeah, he sounds like your typical genius sixteenth-century polymath."

"Garden variety."

They look at each other, smile, and read on.

> De Re Metallica is a systematic, illustrated treatise on mining
> and metallurgy, describing how to extract ores from the
> ground, and metals from ore. It was published the year after
> his death . . . the delay is thought to be due to the book's
> many woodcuts.

"*He'd commissioned countless woodcuts,* the poem says. This has to be it. *The Agricola tome* must be a reference to *De Re Metallica.* Sounds like a pretty cool book."

Lily nods.

Arizona's eyes skim farther down the page.

> In 1912, *The Mining Magazine* published an English transla-
> tion of *De Re Metallica,* translated by the American mining
> engineer Herbert Hoover and his wife Lou Henry Hoover.

Her head shoots back two inches. "Herbert Hoover?"

But before she can even formulate the question, they both see the answer in the next sentence.

> Hoover was later elected President of the United States.

"Note to self—read a biography of Herbert Hoover."

Arizona scrolls back up to the link to the main article for *De Re Metallica,* clicks on it, and continues reading.

> The book remained the authoritative text on mining for 180
> years after its publication. It was also significant in the history
> of chemistry. Mining was typically left to professionals, crafts-
> men and experts who were not eager to share their knowl-
> edge. . . . knowledge was handed down orally within a small

group . . . these people held the same leading role as the
master builders of the great cathedrals, or perhaps also alchemists.

The word strikes her like a bolt of lightning. "*Alchemists.*"
She sits back, leans forward again, rereads the words.

She types *alchem* into the search box on the *De Re Metallica* webpage and hits RETURN. Just four other instances, all in one paragraph
about the book's preface.

> The works of alchemists are then described. Agricola does not
> reject the idea of alchemy, but notes that alchemical writings
> are obscure and that we do not read of any of the masters
> who became rich. He then describes fraudulent alchemists,
> who deserve the death penalty.

Arizona pauses to think, but her thoughts are splintered by Mojo's
snoring. She gathers thought fragments like kindling and scrolls down
to the bottom of the page. Finds a link to the full searchable text of *De
Re Metallica* with illustrations. Smiles. Clicks. A new browser tab
opens, showing the title page.

GEORGIUS AGRICOLA

DE RE METALLICA

TRANSLATED FROM THE FIRST LATIN EDITION OF 1556
with
Biographical Introduction, Annotations and Appendices upon
the Development of Mining Methods, Metallurgical
Processes, Geology, Mineralogy & Mining Law
from the earliest times to the 16th Century

BY

HERBERT CLARK HOOVER

A. B. Stanford University, Member American Institute of Mining Engineers,
Mining and Metallurgical Society of America, Société des Ingénieurs
Civils de France, American Institute of Civil Engineers,
Fellow Royal Geographical Society, etc., etc.

AND

LOU HENRY HOOVER

A. B. Stanford University, Member American Association for the
Advancement of Science, The National Geographical Society,
Royal Scottish Geographical Society, etc., etc.

Published for the Translators by
THE MINING MAGAZINE
SALISBURY HOUSE, LONDON, E.C.
1912

But then her eyes catch on something and her heart falls into her stomach.

Page 1 of 674

"Six hundred seventy-four pages. Another fucking haystack, and we don't even know what the needle is."

ARIZONA, MOJO, LILY, AND Gus walk along the Mobius Arch trail, near camp. The moon is so full and bright they don't need headlamps. There is nobody else around, just the way Arizona likes it. The wind that so often blows through the Alabama Hills has taken the night off. There are no sounds but their own breath and footfalls, and she notes that her breath is quicker than is warranted by the easy hike.

As they turn back toward the trailer, Arizona's thoughts turn back to *De Re Metallica*.

"I feel lost, Lily. Like I don't even know where to start. I feel like it's another dead end. I feel fucking hopeless again."

Lily takes Arizona's hand. "We'll figure it out, together."

As they walk in silence, warmth spreads throughout Arizona's body. She traces the source to Lily's hand. Curious.

BACK IN THE AIRSTREAM, Arizona wakes up her MacBook. The web browser still displays the title page of *De Re Metallica*. Just to the right of the page number is a search box.

"Do you suppose it has an index?" Arizona twists her lips.

"Worth a shot," says Lily.

Arizona types *index* in the search box and hits RETURN. Her left thumb is under her cheekbone, fingers over brow, pinky dangled in front of eye.

There are numerous matches, but one stands out—*General index*. She clicks on it and the display changes to the first page of the general index, two columns per page.

Lily points at the screen, halfway down the lefthand column.

Alchemists.. . . . . XXVII–XXX; 44; 608

Arizona clicks the Roman numerals and the display changes to part of the Preface, written by Agricola and footnoted by Hoover. She reads aloud from the beginning of the paragraph.

> Seeing that there have been so few who have written on the subject of the metals, it appears to me all the more wonderful that so many alchemists have arisen who would compound metals artificially, and who would change one into another. . . . there are Hermes; Chanes; Zosimus, the Alexandrian, to his sister Theosebia . . . Africanus, Theophilus . . . Geber . . . Merlin, Raymond Lully, Arnold de Villa Nova . . . and three women, Cleopatra, the maiden Taphnutia, and Maria the Jewess.[12]

"Merlin?" Lily says. "Like the wizard?"

"I'm not aware of any other Merlins, except for the bird, of course. A small falcon, family *Falconidae*. But according to Agricola, Merlin was not only a real person but an alchemist."

Arizona scans down to footnote twelve, Hoover's footnote on the alchemists, which continues on the next three pages. She reads aloud.

[12] The debt which humanity does owe to these self-styled philosophers must not be overlooked, for the science of Chemistry comes from three sources—Alchemy, Medicine and Metallurgy. . . . Aside from the classics and religious works, the libraries of the Middle Ages teemed with more material on Alchemy than on any other one subject, and since that date a never-ending stream of historical, critical, and discursive volumes and tracts devoted to the old Alchemists and their writings has been poured upon the world. . . .

. . . certain names such as Osthanes, Hermes, Zosimus, Agathodaemon, and Democritus, which have been the watchwords of authority to Alchemists of all ages. These certainly possessed the great secrets, either the philosopher's stone or the elixir.

Arizona stops reading, her eyes wide.

"What's the matter?" says Lily.

"All of the footnotes were added by Hoover, not Agricola."

"So? I don't understand."

"Hoover was a man of science. How could he say that these alchemists *certainly* possessed the philosopher's stone or the elixir of life? Those are just myths. Aren't they, Mr. President?"

37

The Language of the Birds

ARIZONA IS STILL PROCESSING THE REVELATION THAT Herbert Hoover seemed to believe in the great secrets of alchemy, the philosopher's stone and the elixir of life. And her dad's involvement in all this. The tattoo, Titus Canyon . . . it can't all be coincidence, can it? If Hoover was a believer, was Dad, too? Did her dad sacrifice his life to protect the secrets? Secrets of alchemy? That sounds crazy—like, certifiable.

She finds the spot where she stopped in Hoover's footnote on the alchemists and continues reading aloud, riveted.

> Hermes Trismegistos was . . . believed to have possessed the
> secret of transmutation. Osthanes was also a very shadowy
> personage . . . ; there is a very old work . . . in the Munich, Gotha,
> Vienna, and other libraries, by one of this name. Agathodaemon
> was still another shadowy character referred to by the older
> Alchemists. There are manuscripts in the Florence, Paris,
> Escurial, and Munich libraries bearing his name. . . . Synesius
> was a Greek, but of unknown period; there is a manuscript
> treatise on the Philosopher's Stone in the library at Leyden
> under his name . . .

"An alchemical quest through the great libraries of Europe," Arizona says with watery eyes.

Lily sees the change. "What's wrong?"

"Libraries remind me of school. I loved the library. It was the only place I felt safe."

Her train of thought has jumped the tracks.

Lily touches her friend's forearm.

Arizona covers Lily's hand with her own.

Still derailed, she checks the tracker location. But something is wrong with the map.

"There's no blue dot," she says.

"What?" says Lily.

"I can't find the tracker on the map."

She zooms out, scrolls north, but it isn't there. Scrolls farther north, but still no dot. Did she lose track of time? She looks to the menu bar of her Mac. Maybe a little—it's 10:15 P.M. Okay, so she'd taken her eye off the ball briefly, but it wasn't the kind of ball that could be hit out of the park. A thought punches her in the gut, so hard she tastes stomach acid.

"Fuck."

"What's the matter?" says Lily.

"Did they find the tracker and disable it? Even so, the map should show the last-known location."

She bites her lower lip, zooms out again, scans the northern edges of the map as she scrolls northward, past Topaz Lake on the California–Nevada border, all the way up to Lake Tahoe. Still no blue dot.

"Where the hell is it?"

She scrolls south, zooms out, rubs her eyes for relief from the monotonous scanning of the laptop screen. Pans the map to the west, then east, zooms out again.

"There," says Lily.

Well south of Lake Tahoe, still in California. Arizona zooms back in for context. North of Mono Lake but south of Bridgeport. East of Highway 395. The blue dot sits on a small green swatch—labeled *Bodie State Historic Park.*

"Bodie?" Lily says. "The tracker is in Bodie? But Sam said they searched the whole park, right?"

Arizona nods, still looking at the screen. "So either they missed some hiding place like an old mine shaft, which is entirely possible, or Gordon and company weren't there during the search and now they're back. Either way, they're there now, or at least the box is."

She switches to the satellite view, zooms in until she can see the dirt streets, then more, until she can see the individual buildings, preserved in a state of arrested decay. The blue dot is on top of a large building with a distinct shape. She opens the park brochure and looks at the map, nods again.

"The fucking stamp mill, where Mom disappeared." In the satellite image she can even see the remains of the gangling tailings conveyor. "I see you, you bastards." She stares at the dot, a shimmering blue mirage in a desert of pixels. Wait—shimmering? "The dot is pulsing. That means the tracker's still transmitting. They haven't disabled it. I know where they are, and they don't know that I know. I would have the element of surprise."

She dons her lopsided smile.

"You can't be serious?" Lily says.

Arizona pictures riding into Bodie with guns blazing—make that gun, singular—but sees herself outnumbered, outgunned. Shit. She needs a better plan.

"No, not yet at least. We still need something to trade. Leverage. I still need to figure out what they want. Knowledge is power. It's my only real currency."

Arizona sighs and switches back to the poem but struggles to get her mind off Bodie and her mom. Whenever one is lost, it can pay to take a few steps back. She needs to review what they've already learned, to get her head back in the game. She rereads the poem aloud, pausing to summarize key takeaways as she goes:

Verse one: In a collection of old books that included *De Re Metallica,* translated by Herbert Hoover and his wife . . .

Verse two: Some great secret is discovered . . .

Verse three: A secret of alchemy . . . in which Hoover seemed to believe? . . .

Verse four: But the discovery starts a fight, so the secret is hidden . . .

Verses five through seven: Cryptic claptrap.

As she reads verses five through seven aloud yet again, she places her forefinger on her temple and holds it there, as if keeping a thought in place while the glue sets. One line is ringing major bells. Cathedral bells.

"Chartres," she says.

"What?" says Lily.

"*Like the brooding fervor of Chartres labyrinthian fleur.* The labyrinth at Chartres was mentioned in one of the alchemy books I read just before the diving trip."

She opens Fulcanelli's *The Mystery of the Cathedrals* and searches for *Chartres*. The first hit is about the labyrinth.

> . . . the labyrinth at Chartres . . . is composed of a whole series of concentric circles coiling one within another in endless variety. . . . emblematic of the whole labour of the Work, with its two major difficulties, one the path which must be taken in order to reach the centre—where the bitter combat of the two natures takes place—the other the way which the artist must follow in order to emerge.

Arizona searches for *fleur* and finds nothing. *Fleur* is French for *flower,* so she changes her search to *flower* and finds a dozen matches. But none of them relate to the labyrinth. She opens the Wikipedia page for Chartres Cathedral, searches for *labyrinth,* and finds what she's looking for.

"Holy shit," says Arizona. Steepled fingers support her nose as she stares at the diagram of the labyrinth. At the flower at its center. "Six petals, like the Flower of Life. *So many petals on the floor.*"

"And the similarities don't end there," Lily says. "Fulcanelli mentioned the concentric circles of the labyrinth. *Worlds whip 'round concentric rings.*"

"Excellent point," Arizona says, and then, "Wait a second." There's something else about Chartres, too. Some connection she's missing.

Lily waits several seconds. "What am I waiting for?"

Finally she has it. "Birds."

"Excuse me?"

Arizona smiles. "That line in the poem. *A perfect language not of words, but more along the lines of birds.* There was something about that in *The Mystery of the Cathedrals,* too. Hang on."

She switches back to *The Mystery of the Cathedrals* and searches for *birds.*

"Got it! This is from the Preface to the Second Edition, written by Fulcanelli's disciple Eugène Canseliet." She reads aloud.

> . . . Fulcanelli himself confirmed in such a masterly way by rediscovering the lost key to the Gay Science, the Language of the Gods, the Language of the Birds.

Arizona looks at the other search results. "And listen to this one . . ."

> . . . the Language of the Birds, parent and doyen of all other languages . . . is the language which teaches the mystery of things and unveils the most hidden truths.

"And think about all of the bird references in the ciphers." She cites them aloud as her mind races back. "*Lady Bird . . . King-fisher . . . 'fore birds had their say . . . piping bird . . . fledgling secrets . . .* Alcyone, another kingfisher . . . 'The Raven' . . . *with eagle as their king assigned.*"

She switches to her web browser, searches for *Language of the Birds,* and clicks the Wikipedia link.

> In Abrahamic and European mythology, medieval literature
> and occultism, the language of the birds is postulated as a
> mystical, perfect divine language. . . .

"Double holy shit," says Lily.

Arizona looks at the table of contents for the webpage and one word jumps out. *Alchemy.* She clicks on it.

> In Kabbalah, Renaissance magic, and alchemy, the language
> of the birds was considered a secret and perfect language
> and the key to perfect knowledge . . .

Arizona switches back to the poem and scrolls up to verse three.

"What are you thinking?" says Lily.

"We've been so focused on the latter verses because they're so cryptic, but . . ."

"But what?" says Lily.

Arizona raises a finger to the screen, to the top of verse three, and reads two lines aloud:

A perfect language not of words, but more along the lines of birds,
A spagyric Rosetta stone, to stoke the long-cold athanor.

"It was right there all along," says Arizona. "Spagyric—relating to alchemy. Athanor—a furnace used by alchemists. The authors of the poem claim to have found the key to the Language of the Birds, revealing all the secrets of the alchemists. That's what this is all about. That's what they're after."

"They actually believe," Lily says.

Arizona nods. "And there's nothing more dangerous than true believers."

HIJKLMNOPQRSTUVWXY
L   K M N   W X Y

NLHTHDTQGKHRHKCGKH
THE   E   RE   ER   RE

GTNLHBDMNNLHEHMNGQ
   THE   ST THE   EST.

NLUMCGKNDBSGOKFHYH
TH   S   RT   EYE

VHDLGMNAGCHMMCUBUE
  E   H   ST   ESS

LHPKHHNMOMGFNLDNNK
HEGREETS   S   TH   TTR

JKLMNOPQRST UVWXYZ
         K M N   WXYZ

PART FOUR

The highest truths . . . can be
communicated when they are . . .
incorporated in symbols which will
no doubt conceal them for many,
but which will manifest them in
all their brilliance to those
with eyes to see.

—RENÉ GUÉNON,
Symbols of Sacred Science

HTHDTQGKHRHKCGKH
 E E   RE ER   RE

NLHBDMNNLHEHMNGQQKUHF
THE   STTHE   EST   R

UMCGKNDBSGOKFHYHFTM
  S   RT   R   EYL   S

VDLGMNAGCHMMCUBUFPNGNL
  H   ST   ESS   GT   TF

PKHHNMOMGFNLDNNKDFJOL
GREETS   S   TH   TTR

LHKIUIUFPEUKTFGKIHHIL
HER   G   R   R EE

HIJKLMNOPQRSTUVWXY
L   K M N   W X Y

NLHTHDTQGKHRHKCGKH
THE   E   RE ER   RE

GTNLHBDMNNLHEHMNGC
   THE   ST THE   EST

NLUMCGKNDBSGOKFHYH
TH   S   RT   EYE

VHDLGMNAGCHMMCUBUF
  E   H   ST   ESS

LHPKHHNMOMGFNLDNNK
HEGREETS   S   TH   TTR

JNLHKIUIUFPEUKTFGK

38

The Library on Hornton Street

ARIZONA LOOKS OUT THE WINDOW OF THE AIRSTREAM. IN the light of the full moon, the red rocks of the Alabama Hills stand like a terracotta army. She feels the warmth of familiarity, of safety.

She returns to the first line of the poem.

'Twas in Red House on Hornton Street, in the library we adored,

She switches to her web browser, types *Red House on Hornton Street* into the search box, and hits RETURN. Scans the results. Her eyes lock onto the first hit.

The Red House in Hornton Street – London Picture Archive

She clicks on the link.

. . . The house, originally known as Hornton Lodge, was built by Stephen Bird, a well-known local builder and brick maker, in 1835, for his own family. William Conway, art critic and explorer, lived in the house at the turn of the twentieth century. Another notable resident, who lived here in 1907–18, was Herbert Hoover, who later became President of the United States.

With knitted brow and incredulous eyes, Arizona stares at the screen. She makes no sound, moves no muscle while she rereads the sentence.

"When was . . ."

"When was what?" Lily says.

Arizona opens *De Re Metallica* to the title page. Her eyes plunge to the bottom.

London . . . 1912

Thoughts buzz through her mind like bees about a hive. She researches the Hoovers' translation of *De Re Metallica*.

"While living in London, the Hoovers amassed an impressive collection of rare books and manuscripts approaching one thousand volumes, including mathematics, technology, mining, mineralogy, and *alchemy*."

Arizona recites lines two and three of the poem:

We selected, sought, bought, collected, and exhaustively did pore
Over many a quaint and curious volume of forgotten lore.

"The entire Hoover collection was described in a 1980 book titled *The Herbert Clark Hoover Collection of Mining and Metallurgy*. Oh, and check out its alternate title—*Bibliotheca De Re Metallica*."

Lily smiles.

Arizona locates the full text online. She scrolls to the back of the 220-page book. Scratches her head. Goes back to the beginning and looks there. "Seriously?"

"What?" Lily says.

"I mean, I appreciate the scholarly work and all, but no index or table of contents?"

Arizona raises her eyebrows, and furrows ripple across her forehead. She likes the way it feels, so she does it again.

After a lengthy introduction, the bulk of the book is an alphabetical list of authors, brief descriptions of each work, and supplemental notes.

There is no way to peruse the collection without going through every page. Arizona sighs and begins.

Moments later she finds one of the most famous names in alchemy, if not early science—Albertus Magnus, Albert the Great, teacher of Thomas Aquinas. The Hoovers had collected several of his works.

She flips forward a few pages. Avicenna's *Canon*. Roger Bacon's *The Mirror of Alchimy*, which Arizona had read. Basil Valentine's *Last Will and Testament* and three editions of *The Triumphal Chariot of Antimony*, which Arizona had also read.

She skims ahead, looking for Paracelsus, goes too far, and lands at Petrus Peregrinus, also known as Petrus Peregrinus de Maricourt. Her thoughts race back to the second cipher, the one that led her to San Nicolas Island.

> *Some twenty leagues o'er the deep,*
> *A stamp on a marker de Maricourt,*
> *Lest fledgling secrets never shall ye reap.*

The Hoovers had "The Letter of Petrus Peregrinus on the Magnet." Arizona flips back and finds Paracelsus—the Hoovers had a copy of his *Of the Transmutation of Metals*.

She goes back to the beginning and continues, reading aloud names as she goes.

"Thomas Aquinas . . . Robert Boyle . . . Johann Rudolf Glauber . . . William Gilbert's *De Magnete*. Herbert Hoover—*President* Herbert Hoover—owned all of these manuscripts."

"Are you thinking what I'm thinking?" Lily says.

Arizona doesn't respond. She visualizes the connections, the Venn diagram.

Hoover accumulated a vast collection of alchemical manuscripts.

While he lived in Red House from 1907 to 1918.

Their translation of *De Re Metallica* was published in 1912.

There are no other dots to connect, no other conclusions to draw.

"While researching and translating *De Re Metallica*, Herbert Hoover stumbled upon the key to the Language of the Birds."

"President Hoover wrote this poem," Lily says.

"All of these poems."

Hands on her head, as if to keep it from exploding, Arizona stares out the window again. Looks for the familiar, a point of reference. Finds it in the red rocks. Something to keep her grounded while her mind flies.

39

The Adept and
the Journal — Part Five

I N THE OFFICE AT THE STAMP MILL, THE ADEPT SITS BEHIND
Gordon's desk, reading a favorite section of his precious journal.

Wanting to continue my analysis from home, I convinced
myself that an exception to standard document-handling
procedures was justifiable. After all, it seemed impossible to
create a top-secret document by redacting an unclassified
document. So I made copies of both versions, unredacted and
redacted, and smuggled them out. When at work, I continued
to use the ones in my office safe. Until they disappeared.

Not only did the logbook in the safe have no entry showing that the documents had been removed, but all previous
entries for the documents were gone. Yet the log was otherwise perfect, down to my own signature on every entry.
Someone had created a flawless counterfeit log. Someone
with access. I logged in to the computer system to reprint the
documents, but the redacted versions were gone. As if they
had never existed. But I knew differently. I still had a copy at
home.

Within days of the documents disappearing from my safe
and the computer system, I was informed that I had been re-
assigned, to a listening post in a remote location. They said it

was a result of budget cuts and it was either that or early retirement. I chose retirement, which I'm sure was their inten-
tion. That was the end of my career with the National
Security Agency, my security clearance, and my access to their
systems. But it was not the end of my investigation.

In hindsight, I think there was a direct correlation between an epiphany I had, the disappearance of the documents, and my forced retirement. It was as if someone had
been monitoring my progress all along and, until then, I
hadn't learned anything that they didn't already know. Or,
perhaps more likely, that they didn't want anyone else to
know. Although it was protocol, it had been a mistake to keep
my notes in my office safe.

I had successfully unscrambled the twelve hidden sentences and two ciphers from the redacted documents, but
there was one thing that I never understood, and it continued
to haunt me. It was the eleventh sentence:

Just after the Apex of the Sun's way in space, the fire was
set in bodies to burn the Secret, but the fire was not successful.

It was "in bodies" that had nagged at me since I first unscrambled it. Then one day I was looking at the redacted
booklet and noticed something on page six that had previously eluded me. It appeared that one of the redacted words
hadn't been fully redacted. That by itself wasn't unique. From
"quickness" only "quick" had been redacted, and from "key-
stone" only "key" had been redacted. However, in this case it
appeared that an entire word had been redacted with the exception of the S at the end. I switched to my unredacted and
highlighted copy to see what the word was. It was "bodies."

At first I dismissed this as a redaction error, but that felt
wrong. In bodies. In bodie? A place? It didn't take much research to find the answer. The fire that destroyed 90 percent of
the ghost town of Bodie, California, occurred on June 23,
1932. Just two days after the summer solstice. Just after the

Apex of the Sun's way in space. So the eleventh sentence is actually:

Just after the Apex of the Sun's way in space, the fire was
set in Bodie to burn the Secret, but the fire was not successful.

Bodie. *The Secret remains and lies within.* He reflects on the revelation, the catalyst for his journey west. From bucolic Maine to desolate
California, where he founded the new Golden Dawn. Where he recruited his team, Gordon and the woman descended from a member
of the original Golden Dawn. It had been so easy to find like-minded
people. God bless the internet. Not that he believes in God.

Bodie. Where he had installed his team, in the area closed to the
public. Just before the end of the tourist season. Just before the snow
flew, so they could search every surviving building without worrying
about pesky park rangers and tourists.

Then the tattooed man goes to Titus Canyon to retrieve the box
and just weeks later that bitch and her freak daughter show up in
Bodie, no doubt to steal what is rightfully his. But he had turned the
tables on them, on all three of them. The margins of his mouth curl
upward. Schadenfreude—pleasure from another person's misfortune.
And the pleasure is even greater if you cause the misfortune.

His thoughts are broken as Gordon enters, carrying the canvas-
wrapped package.

"Oh, hello, sir," Gordon says, his tone and raised eyebrows betray-
ing his surprise.

But his boss is too busy staring at the package to respond.

"I'm pleased to see you, sir. But I thought I was bringing this to you
in Bridgeport."

Gordon places the package on the desk, closes the door.

"I couldn't wait any longer to see it. Nobody saw me arrive, and
nobody will see me leave."

"Very good, sir. May I?" Gordon motions to the chair in front of his
own desk.

"Yes" is all the Adept says, not allowing his eyes to leave the package.

He carefully unfolds the two layers of canvas, exposing the small dark-colored hardwood box with its brass hinges and two brass clasps.

"Well done," he says with a triumphant grin.

"Thank you, sir." Gordon beams.

The Adept points the desk lamp upward, lifts the box over his head, examines the bottom, and smiles.

"Take a look," he says, tilting the bottom of the box slightly toward Gordon.

"I don't see anything, sir."

"Look more closely," the Adept says, still smiling.

"It's the Flower of Life, sir," Gordon says. "But how did you know it was there?"

"All in good time," he says. The approbation of his acolyte is sunshine on his skin.

He lowers the box back to the desk, turning it to examine all of its surfaces. Stares at it for a few more seconds, releases a sigh of anticipation. He opens the box, then the vial, slides the scroll into his hand, and unfurls it.

"What is it, sir?" Gordon says.

"The remaining clues to the location of the Secret, the key to the inimitable knowledge of the Masters, in the form of an unencrypted poem and another cipher."

The Adept unzips his black computer briefcase, removes a laptop, sets it on the corner of the desk, and turns it on. While it's booting, he retrieves a portable handheld scanner and plugs it into the laptop.

"You hold the scroll while I scan it," he says to Gordon.

"Of course, sir."

When the scanning is done, he opens the PDF file, runs optical character recognition, checks the results against the scroll, and makes corrections as necessary. He double-checks his work and uploads it to the drafts folder of the Proton Mail account.

"Call her and tell her to check the drafts folder," he says to Gordon.

"Yes, sir."

40

Location, Location, Location

ARIZONA AND LILY, STILL PROCESSING THE REVELATION THAT Herbert Hoover wrote the poems, sit at the table in silence. Until Arizona's phone rings. Blocked number. She glances at the time in the upper left corner of her phone's screen—1:07 A.M. She sighs, leans back against the putty-colored cushion, and answers. "What?" she says, with a mixture of disdain and impatience.

"We found something at the coordinates."

"Care to elaborate?"

"Check the drafts folder." *Click.*

Lily flips two birds at the phone, pumps them up and down. "What a dick."

Arizona logs in to the Proton Mail account and clicks on the drafts folder. The new message contains the unencrypted poem and the third cipher, both of which she already has. She logs out and types up a reply in a new document.

Dear Criminal Mastermind,

Carroll's letters is a reference to Lewis Carroll's "The Alphabet Cipher," which described a polyalphabetic cipher (duh). The numbers in the unencrypted poem refer to the six lines that make up the symbols for the elements and the hexagram (double duh). When combined, the lines create a rudimentary alphabet.

Keyword is Alcyone. Decoded third cipher is attached. Feel free
to help, for a change.

Opprobriously, Your devoted jackanapes
P.S. Criminal Mastermind was facetious.

Lily reads over her shoulder and giggles.

"I'll upload it later," Arizona says, "to make them think I'm working
on it." She wonders how long she can put off sending it. She needs to
figure out the poem first, or she'll squander her hard-won lead.

Mojo whines.

"Time for another walk, buddy?"

Mojo and Gus are at the door before Arizona and Lily can stand up.

"I guess that's a yes," Lily says.

"Some fresh air sounds good to me, too," Arizona says. "Good
boys."

The moon has dropped behind Mount Whitney and the sky explodes with stars. Arizona gazes up so long she almost dizzies herself
when she lowers her head. She thinks that if the stars were stones in a
stream, she could walk across the sky without getting her feet wet.
Good boys indeed.

BACK IN THE TRAILER, Arizona returns to the poem. They've puz-
zled out the first three verses for the most part, but the rest remains
opaque. She rereads verse four:

> *Counsel we sought but they just fought, like a lodestone cleft in two.*
> *Use them to aid the sick and poor; lose them, destroy them forevermore.*
> *Now both sides the secrets sought and in the middle we were caught;*
> *In a standard stamp mill—fraught, crushed and broken—we were the ore.*
> *So we hid them, until the hour when man can wisely wield such power,*
> *Where Tad and Mil had lived before.*

She tilts her head to the right as she contemplates. One line stands
out.

"Why a *standard* stamp mill?"

She switches to her web browser, types *standard stamp mill* in the search box, and hits RETURN. Her eyes pass over the first couple of results before locking on the third.

THE STANDARD MILL—BODIE.COM

https://www.bodie.com/history/structures/the-standard-mill/

Bodie. She can't move her eyes from the name. Her head spins. Once she's able to pull her eyes away, they fly back to the poem, to the last line of the fourth verse.

Where Tad and Mil had lived before.

She searches for *Tad Mil Bodie*. Nothing relevant. Cracks her knuckles.

"Tad is short for Theodore," Lily says.

Arizona changes her search to *Theodore Mil Bodie*.

HOOVER HOUSE—BODIE.COM

https://www.bodie.com/history/structures/hoover-house/

Hoover. Bodie. Her eyes bounce between the names like she is watching a tennis match. But surely it can't be Herbert Hoover. She clicks the link.

HOOVER HOUSE

This was the home of Theodore and Mildred Hoover. Theodore was the manager of the Standard Mill and lived in this house for about three years, until 1905.

Theodore was the brother of would-be President Herbert Hoover, who occasionally visited Bodie—long before he was president. But he did stay here at the Hoover home while in town.

"Holy shit," Arizona says. "Hoover actually stayed in Bodie, in his brother's house. But I don't remember a Hoover House there."

"Maybe it didn't survive the fires?" says Lily.

Arizona opens the Bodie park brochure and enlarges the map so she can read the names of the buildings. She needs to confirm her memory before she can move on. One thing at a time. Her eyes tread the dusty streets, shadow her rep-tile search pattern.

Nothing.

She scans the buildings farther from town.

North, past the Parr House . . . Kirkwood Stable . . . Jail . . .

South, past Bodie Creek . . . Brown House . . . Country Barn . . .

East, past the Bottle Works . . . Dog-Face George's House . . .

North again, past the Klipstein House, Burkham, Durham . . . Hoover House.

"No wonder I didn't see it. It's in the area closed to the public."

Her mind is still whirling. She opens a new browser tab, searches for *Herbert Hoover*, clicks on the Wikipedia link, and reads aloud as fast as she can.

> Herbert Hoover served as the 31st president of the United States from 1929 to 1933.
>
> After graduating from Stanford University in 1895, Hoover worked in the gold-mining districts of Nevada City and Grass Valley, California . . .

She blinks, reads it again. "Nevada City? Pioneer Cemetery." Her jaw clenches at the thought of their despoiled home in Grass Valley, but she continues reading.

> In 1908, Hoover became an independent mining consultant, traveling worldwide until the outbreak of World War I in 1914. By then, Hoover was a very wealthy man. . . .
>
> In 1921, Warren G. Harding appointed Hoover as Secretary of Commerce. Hoover was an unusually active and visible Cabinet member, becoming known as "Secretary of Commerce and Under-Secretary of all other departments."

"Under-secretary of all other departments," Lily says with a smile.

Arizona reads on but finds no other Hoover connections. Not to the ciphers. Not to Titus Canyon. Not to San Nicolas Island.

She thinks for two breaths. Another ghost town comes to mind, one in Titus Canyon, of which almost nothing remains—more ghost than town. She types *Leadfield* in the search box and reads aloud:

> Leadfield was an historic mining town in Inyo County, Cali-
> fornia. It is now a ghost town. It is located in Titus Canyon in
> the Grapevine Mountains, in Death Valley National Park.
>
> . . . the townsite of Leadfield at the head of Titus Canyon
> dates to 1925 and 1926. The product of extensive and fraud-
> ulent advertising by the Western Lead Mine Company and
> C. C. Julian, the town boomed in 1925. His advertising posters
> showed steamboats navigating the Amargosa River to Lead-
> field, ignoring the fact that the Amargosa River is dry much of
> the time and does not run within 20 miles of Leadfield.

She titters. Mojo concurs with a chortle-snore. From water and earth, she conjures up an image of the Amargosa River, like a visual alchemist. It's a lot like conjuring up an image of dirt.

"What's so funny?" Lily says.

"Steamboats on the Amargosa. Most of the river's flow is underground—except during flash floods caused by cloudbursts, and even then it wouldn't hold a steamboat."

She reads everything she can about Leadfield but finds no Hoover connection. She returns to the top of the article and rereads the first sentence.

> Leadfield . . . is located in Titus Canyon in the Grapevine
> Mountains, in Death Valley National Park.

Death Valley National Park. The national parks are all about preservation. Titus Canyon was preserved by being included within the park. She follows the link to Death Valley National Park and scans.

> Straddling the border of California and Nevada . . .
>
> . . . protects the northwest corner of the Mojave Desert . . .
>
> . . . salt flats, sand dunes, badlands, valleys, canyons, and mountains. . . .
>
> . . . largest national park in the lower 48 states . . .
>
> . . . hottest, driest, and lowest of the national parks in the United States.

Her eyes backtrack. "Straddling the border?" On her mental map, the border of the park is the state line.

She scrolls through the park page but doesn't see a map. Clicks the link to the park's website, then on *Visitor Guide with park map*. Sure enough, the map shows a large triangle that extends into Nevada. She zooms in on it. Cutting across the southern tip of the triangle is Daylight Pass Road, the road from Beatty into the park. Entering almost exactly at the apex of the triangle is a four-wheel-drive road that appears to lead into Phinney Canyon, close to Grapevine Peak. But it is the third road that catches Arizona's eye. She taps the screen and points.

"Titus Canyon Road," Lily says.

"The only place the park extends into Nevada is in the vicinity of Titus Canyon Road. Where my dad died. Where the box was hidden. Is that coincidence, or was Titus Canyon intentionally included within the park in order to preserve it?"

She checks a few pages on the park's website but can't find what she is looking for. She goes back to the Wikipedia page and finds it.

> Established
>
> Feb. 11, 1933 as a national monument
>
> Oct. 31, 1994 as a national park

"Death Valley was preserved as a national monument in February 1933. But Hoover lost the 1932 election to FDR and inauguration day is January twentieth, so Hoover couldn't have established it. It must have been done by FDR."

Mojo lays his chin over Arizona's foot. She looks at him, scratches the base of his ears with the toes of her other foot. He looks so fulfilled, so untroubled. She smiles and wishes she could live inside Mojo's untroubled mind, if even for a moment.

She returns from her reverie, thinks about the Hoover connections, searches for *San Nicolas Island*, and reads.

> History . . .
> Lone Woman . . .
> Whaling . . .
> Munitions testing . . .
> Geology . . .
> Climate . . .
> Flora . . .
> Fauna . . .

Nothing. No Hoover connection. She looks for the history of the Navy on the island. Surfs from site to site, until she finds History of Naval Auxiliary Air Station, San Nicolas Island.

> In the 1920s or early 1930s, the Civil Aeronautics Administration (CAA) built two emergency dirt landing strips. . . . In January 1933, the CAA relinquished the airstrips as the Navy took over ownership of the island.

Arizona's eyes grow wide.

"The Navy took over the island in January 1933? Hoover was president for the first nineteen days of January. And the survey marker on San Nicolas Island was placed in 1932, when he was president. But still no connection to Leadfield or Death Valley. Unless . . ."

She searches for *inauguration day*, clicks, and reads—like greased lightning, as Dad used to say. She finds it in the first few sentences.

> Since 1937, it has taken place on January 20 . . .

She scrolls down and stops at the heading *Dates.*

The first inauguration, of George Washington, took place on
April 30, 1789. All subsequent inaugurations from 1793 until
1933 were held on March 4 . . .

"FDR's inauguration wasn't until March fourth, but Death Valley
National Monument was established on February eleventh. It was established by Hoover!"

Brow furrowed, she crushes thumbs into her temples and visualizes
the connections again.

In the 1890s, Hoover lived and worked in Nevada City.

Between 1903 and 1905, he visited Bodie while his brother lived
there.

In January 1933, he oversaw the turnover of San Nicolas Island to
the U.S. Navy, preventing subsequent access to the island.

And in February 1933, in the waning days of his presidency, he established Death Valley National Monument, thus preserving Titus
Canyon for the ages.

41.

Back to Bodie

A RIZONA TUGS ON HER EARLOBE LIKE IT'S THE PULL CHAIN for a broken light. Words of the poem skitter through her head. *We hid them . . . where Tad and Mil had lived before.*

In the Hoover House in Bodie, in other words.

It's risky, but there's no other option. That's where she needs to go next.

She downloads the topographic maps for the area and opens the Bodie map. She shows Lily where the stamp mill is, near the eastern edge of the map, then zooms out.

"Bodie Road is out of the question—too exposed. They'd literally see me coming a mile away. And Cottonwood Canyon Road isn't much better."

"Are you sure there isn't another way?" Lily says.

"I'm looking." She scans the area to the north and northwest, the roads from Masonic and Aurora, where Mark Twain had lived for a while. Same problem.

"No, I don't mean another route. I mean an alternative to going there yourself."

She looks at Lily. "The poem's telling us that's the next step. I have to find the secret before they do, so that I have something to exchange for my mom. And they must be in Bodie for a reason, right? Like they somehow know that something is hidden there. Now that they have the scroll, they could crack the code themselves any time. I have to get there, and I have to get there before they figure it out."

"Yes, someone should go to the Hoover House, but it doesn't have to be *you*."

"Who, then?"

"What about Sam, the head ranger? She's already there, in Bodie."

Arizona takes a breath. In. Out. She teeters on the edge of agreeing. Sam *is* there already, and she means well. But she's also a ranger and a responsible adult, and of course she'll object to a seventeen-year-old girl going up against kidnappers by herself. Images of SWAT teams and bloody shootouts and old Waco footage flit through Arizona's head. "No. Nobody else. I have to do this myself."

Her fingertips massage the crown of her head. Like one of the guys in that old comedy duo. Back in the days of moving pictures, black and white. Dad would have known his name. Dad. What the hell was his role in all of this? She grimaces at the hole in her heart, now compounded by confusion—her dad had secrets that he kept from his family, that he took to his grave.

She returns to the map. The area of Bodie that is closed to the public is on a west-facing slope, giving Stephen Gordon and his accomplices a great view in almost every direction. Except east. She opens the adjacent map, Kirkwood Spring, and zooms in until the area just east of Bodie fills the screen. She studies it, visualizes the terrain in three dimensions. It's littered with signs and symbols of mining activity. Mine shafts. Mine dumps. Prospects. Dotted lines labeled *4WD*. She examines each symbol, files it away, moves on.

Lily's eyes move back and forth between the map and Arizona's face, studying the latter more than the former. Her mouth has flatlined.

"I asked you if the authorities aren't better qualified to find your mom. Do you remember what you said?"

"Sure," Arizona says. "That nobody is going to be more motivated than me."

"But the truth is that you don't trust anyone else to save your mom, isn't it?"

"No," she says. *Maybe,* she thinks.

A deep breath. Another.

She returns to the map, zooms out for context. A line snakes east through the hills. She zooms out again, follows it as it rounds a few switchbacks, turns south, and crosses a modern road. Within minutes she learns that it was the Bodie & Benton Railway, built to haul wood for the mines from timber lands south of Mono Lake. It's perfect. With snow in Bodie now, the gentle grade of a railway bed will be easy for the two-wheel-drive Ural. She smiles at the prospect of tracing an old railway route and, even better, sneaking up on those bastards.

But she doesn't have much of a plan after that. She'll need a spot for reconnaissance once they get close. She thinks about Bodie Bluff, northeast of town and the highest point in the vicinity, but it's an obvious spot for them to post a lookout. Since the old railway line ends near Silver Hill, just southeast of town, that seems like a good candidate.

"Okay, I think I've got a plan. Will you watch Mojo for me?"

"No," Lily says, her face a scowl.

"What do you mean *no?*"

"I'm coming with you."

Arizona doesn't know what to say, so she says nothing.

"The only thing you trust me to do is watch Mojo."

"But that's a big deal for me. He's the only family I have left."

"Trust also means letting people help you."

"You are helping me."

"Yeah, by watching Mojo." Her voice is a whip. "What about trusting the judgment of other people? Trust is a two-way street."

"We can't all go, Lily. This approach requires the Ural. If you come with, who will watch the boys?"

"They would be fine in the trailer for a few hours by themselves."

"It'll be more than a few hours. And what if we get caught? Then our dogs starve to death in the trailer? Great plan."

"You're one to talk about great plans," Lily says. "Riding into the enemy camp is just stupid. You shouldn't go at all."

"I have to go. The trail leads to the Hoover House. My mom's life is on the line. I have no choice. But you do."

"That's bullshit."

Arizona looks into Lily's eyes, then away.

"You know what?" Lily says. "I think you don't trust people because you don't respect them. You look down on everyone else. Yes, you're smart, but that doesn't mean other people aren't. Regardless, you're right about one thing. I do have a choice, and I choose not to watch Mojo for you. I won't be party to this arrogant hero bullshit."

Arizona's face is flushed. She bites her tongue for a breath, then another. "Fine, suit yourself. Then I'll just take Mojo with me. At least he won't argue with me."

Lily grabs Gus, storms out of the Airstream, slams the door.

Arizona feels hollow, wonders what she could have done, or said, differently. She thinks about gears again, opens her notebook, and writes.

Square gears can work, so maybe that's not me after all. I don't seem to mesh with anybody. Maybe I'm just a gear with no teeth. Great. I've always felt broken, and now I feel broken in a whole new way.

In hindsight, I think I let my parents insulate me from the world of people, especially Mom with her need to protect. No, I didn't just let them. I *made* them insulate me. I wish I could undo that, but I guess it's too late now. The damage is done.

But there's no more time for introspection right now. It's almost 3:00 A.M., and they'll have to leave soon to be in Bodie at first light.

"Time to gear up for a ride, buddy."

Mojo looks at her but doesn't move.

"Really? You, too? Fuck."

ARIZONA AND MOJO TURN off Highway 395 onto Pole Line Road just as the peaks of the Sierras are aglow from the rising sun. As they ride past Mono Lake and its otherworldly tufa towers, she keeps an eye on her GPS. She programmed in key points of the railway line, since everything is buried under a blanket of snow. Even without the snow, the rails and ties were probably long gone.

There is nobody else on the road as they approach the virtual intersection at 6,800 feet. "Hang on, buddy," she says to Mojo, who sits up in the sidecar, dapper in goggles and jacket. She turns left onto the snow and heads northwest into the hills to begin the fifteen-mile cross-country journey to Bodie.

As she approaches the mile mark, she slows and keeps her eye on the GPS again, so she won't miss the right turn as the railway grade climbs diagonally up the slope. Once past the turn, the cut into the side of the hill is easy to follow. She takes in the views of Mono Valley and Mono Lake.

At about 7,400 feet, the rail grade takes a sharp left turn before winding its way up to the first of the switchbacks. The two-wheel-drive Ural handles the snow with aplomb and they make good time, pass the second switchback at 7,800 feet and up to the high point at 8,400 feet. Evidence of intense mining activity is everywhere—old roads and rusted remnants of equipment, now coated in rime ice. Arizona spots Bodie Bluff off to the right. But if she can see it, then a lookout up there can also see her if he's scouting in the right direction at the right time. Moments later Bodie Bluff disappears behind the safety of Silver Hill. She breathes a sigh of relief, turns right, and climbs the southern flank of Silver Hill until she knows they're near the top.

She shuts off the bike and puts a forefinger across her lips, even though Mojo doesn't understand the shush gesture. She dons her pack, covers the motorcycle with a white tarp she brought, and climbs to the top of Silver Hill, crouching as they get close. At the top she drops to her belly in the snow, pulls off her pack, retrieves her binoculars, and starts her recon.

The Standard Mill is easy to find due to its shape and size, and just south of that is the Hoover House with a metal roof and intact brick chimney. People are coming and going from the mill and two of the smaller buildings nearby. Although she doesn't observe any activity at the Hoover House, seeing firsthand how close it is to the mill—less than two hundred feet—puts a knot in her stomach. If she approaches from the south, she should be able to use the house itself and neighboring buildings as cover.

She looks at Mojo, lying patiently in the snow in his insulated jacket. She isn't sure that bringing him was the best idea, but Lily wouldn't watch him, and she selfishly wanted his company, anyway. Lily. She thinks of the fight and the accusation that she doesn't trust people because she doesn't respect them. It had hurt. Still does, now that she thinks about it. Her parents told her that sometimes the truth hurts, especially when we're lying to ourselves. Is this one of those times? Lying to oneself seems particularly stupid. She starts to feel lightheaded, but this isn't a good time for that, so she buries the thoughts in the snow. To be dug up later, no doubt.

She surveys the town, but the mill and adjacent buildings are the only places with activity. She is torn about where to leave the motorcycle. Approaching on foot seems much stealthier, but if they have to beat a hasty retreat, she wants the bike close by. Running uphill in the snow to retrieve the bike doesn't feel like the recipe for an expeditious getaway.

She decides to play it by ear as they get closer to town. She coasts the bike down to the saddle on the north side of Silver Hill, tells Mojo to stay in the sidecar, hops out, and creeps over to take another look through the binoculars. The wind has picked up, bites her face and hands, sends riffles of gooseflesh across her skin. She sees a couple of people moving about near the mill—presumably guards making their rounds—but thinks she can traverse the exposed area quickly enough to justify the risk. She times their movements, goes back to the bike, and waits for the next window when the guards will have their backs turned. She coasts the bike down into town and pulls in behind Dog-Face George's House.

She covers the bike with the white tarp again, tells Mojo to wait, and creeps to the southwest corner of the house. She signals for Mojo to come—two fingers curled twice—and then runs to the Selhorn House, two hundred feet to the west, peeks around the corner again, and makes the hundred-yard dash north through the thickening wind to the Burkham House. They are only a hundred feet from the Hoover House now, a hundred yards from the mill. Peering from behind the Burkham House, she scans for activity near the mill, but the view is blocked by the Hoover House. Blocking the line of sight was, after all, the plan.

"Okay," she says under her breath, "there's no time like the present."

She runs as fast as she can, stopping only to stretch apart the strands of the barbed-wire fence for Mojo. At the back of the Hoover House, she drops to her knees to catch her breath. Her heart is racing, as much from fear as from running through the snow, her lungs gulping in the thin air more than one-and-a-half vertical miles above the sea.

She tests the back door. It's locked, but that's little deterrent considering the age of the structure. Fingers wedged behind the thin wooden door, she pulls as hard as she can. The upper hinge comes off the frame and the door judders around the lower hinge, dislodging more screws from the hundred-year-old wood. She pulls the door just enough for Mojo to go through and follows him inside.

42

The Hoover House

ARIZONA GIVES MOJO A TOOTHBRUSH-SHAPED TREAT AND tells him to stay near the door. It's a relief to be out of the wind, although it sounds even louder inside as the gale whistles through every crevice in the drafty old home where President Hoover once slept, albeit before he was president. It is a large house compared with others in Bodie and, unlike houses in the public area, appears to have been mostly emptied of furniture. *That should make it easier to search*, she thinks.

She explores the house to get the lay of the land, cautiously approaching each of the north-facing windows, which provide an excellent view of the stamp mill two hundred feet away. Guards move about near the mill, but they aren't rushing toward her. She lets out a deep breath, checks on Mojo, gives him another treat, and begins examining each room.

The recurring annoyance of not knowing what she is looking for etches another grimace on her face. Yet in her mind's eye she sees some of the possibilities. Angels with features like eagles—*angels aquiline*. Symbols for the four elements—*elements, but not those you think*. An arching corridor. Concentric rings. *"These are a few of my favorite things,"* she sings under her breath, parodying *The Sound of Music*.

In what she presumes had been the dining room, she squeegees a forearm through the thick pall of dust on the leaf table but finds nothing. She gets down on the planked floor, crawls under the table, and examines its underside. Still nothing. The walls are next. She moves quickly, eyes scanning up and down as she walks around the room. Then the floor, up one narrow row and back down the next, as if vacuuming up the decades of dust. She hopes she won't miss something buried beneath it all but doesn't think she has time to search the whole floor on hands and knees. Ceilings are last—same as the floors but with head tilted back forty-five degrees.

Five rooms later, she is nearing the end of the house and her patience. Just two more rooms to go. She is in a child's bedroom, based on the single remaining piece of furniture, a small wooden dresser. She scans the walls. Nothing. Floor, zilch. Ceiling, zip. She examines the top of the dresser, then its front and sides. Nada. She rotates it away from the wall and examines its back. Bupkis.

As she wonders whether to move the dresser back—her logic says it's pointless, but her need to put things back where they came from has a different opinion—she notices something on the floor where the dresser had been, where the dust isn't quite as thick. A mark on a floorboard. Not a scratch from the dresser being moved but something deliberate, circular.

She brushes away the dust with her fingertips, as if excavating some archaeological find. Then changes her mind and brushes with abandon, kicking dust into the air and her nose. She sneezes twice, worries that the sound is too loud. But the wind is still wailing. "Bless me," she says under her breath, as she looks down through the dust-filled air.

A simple flower has been carved into the floor.

Just the scribbling of a child. Graffiti scratched into the floor of a bored child's bedroom. Sigh.

Her mind races back to one line of the poem. *So many petals on the floor.*

The projection screen in her head displays a different image. The labyrinth at Chartres. The flower is close to a perfect match.

It reminds her of Lily-like-the-flower, but she brushes away the thought like so much dust. She can't think about their fight right now.

She pushes on the flower, hoping it will open some secret panel, then chuckles at herself. Two inches past the stem of the flower is a joint between two floorboards, but there is no other joint between the petals of the flower and the wall, so it doesn't seem like the board can be lifted out. She tries to pry it up with her fingernails anyway, first along the sides, then at the joint between floorboards. But rather than moving up, the board slides lengthwise, its far end disappearing into the wall, leaving a hole four inches wide.

She fetches her headlamp from her pack and peers into the hole but can't see anything. Reaches in and feels around but can't reach far. As she pulls her hand out, her wrist catches, and the short floorboard opens like a trapdoor and slaps against the wall. She looks in again but sees only dirt. She slides her arm in at a shallow angle until her elbow is through the hole, allowing her to expand the area she can reach. Nothing.

She pulls her arm out as Mojo ambles in, bored and curious about the noise. His perfect tracks parallel her own, like the footprints on a treasure map. She rubs his head and dust flies off.

She inserts her other arm, gropes around in the other direction. Her fingers touch something smooth and round like a small log, a couple of inches in diameter. She digs along its edges, gets fingers underneath. It is light, too light for a log, and comes up easily. Grasping it near the end, she pulls the object through the hole. It's a two-foot piece of bamboo. It isn't what she expected, but she doesn't know what would have been.

She stares at the short bamboo pole for a moment before thinking to look at the ends. Both ends have the natural seals of bamboo knots. It is just a piece of bamboo. She brushes the dirt off. There are two more knots near the center, but they are surprisingly close to each other. She scratches at the area between them. Her fingernail catches in a crack. A seam. With a hand on each side of the seam, close to the center knots, she twists and pulls. As the two halves separate, she sees that they're hollow, like some kind of tube. But she glimpses something inside the piece in her left hand—a piece of paper. It's a document holder!

She doesn't have time for reading now, but she can't resist a peek. She removes the single sheet of paper and unfurls it just a couple of inches. Printed in the upper left corner is:

DEPARTMENT OF THE INTERIOR
U.S. GEOLOGICAL SURVEY

She slips the topographic map back into its tube, closes the trapdoor, and pushes the small dresser against the wall. Unlike with the box in Titus Canyon, she doesn't return the tube to its hiding place. She is done cooperating.

It's time to go, but she has to plan their departure so they won't be seen by the guards. With Mojo in tow, she discreetly scans the view from each of the north-facing windows again. There are two people near the mill. She pulls the binoculars out of her pack and rests them on the dusty windowsill while she adjusts the focus. Both figures are turned away. The taller one is gesturing, perhaps giving orders. The shorter one has the brown pants of a park ranger. The tall one turns toward the Hoover House. Arizona sees his face for only a second, but it is all she needs. It's the face of Stephen Gordon.

She is tempted to race after him, shotgun blasting away, but the better part of valor tells her that killing him won't get Mom back. She stares through the binoculars. The shorter person turns and Arizona's heart sinks. It is indeed a ranger. Sam Yeats. Arizona slumps to the floor, back against the wall.

"You double-crossing witch," she says, too loudly if not for the howling wind. However, she says it not with anger but matter-of-factly, almost entirely devoid of emotion. The razor edge of rage has been blunted by the sledgehammer of betrayal. Again.

Sam never searched for Mom at all. She didn't have to, because she knew where Mom was this whole fucking time. Arizona thinks of Lily, of their argument about trust. *See, Lily? I was right. Nobody can be trusted.*

She resumes her perch at the window and waits for Gordon and Yeats—she is no longer Sam—to go back inside the mill. When they're both safely out of view and she can't see anyone else, she and Mojo head for the door.

43

The Chase

S HE IS LYING ON THE COT UNDER TWO BLANKETS, HAND-cuffed to the frame, when she hears footfalls approaching. Gordon steps in and closes the door behind him. She doesn't look at him.

"Meal time," he says. "I brought you a warm breakfast since it's cold in here. I'll get you another blanket, too."

"A sleeping pad would be better. The cold is coming through the cot, so another blanket probably won't help." Her voice carries the weight of helplessness, of resignation.

"Okay," he says as he unlocks her wrists so she can eat. "I should be able to find a sleeping pad."

She knows the routine. She sits, stretches her arms over her head, and rubs her wrists where the handcuffs dig in. She wants to use the handcuffs to throttle Gordon's neck—*snuffocate him,* as Arizona would say. But it wouldn't matter. Her legs would still be locked to the cot, and he probably doesn't have that key on him.

He hands her the tray, which looks like it was stolen from a cafeteria, and she sets it on her lap. She unfolds the white paper napkin and overlaps it between the edge of the tray and the small part of her lap that's uncovered. She surveys the items—a plastic bottle of water, a spoon, a bowl of oatmeal, half an apple, and a couple of slices of sourdough bread. As she moves each item to the appropriate place, one side of her mouth lifts and she thinks of at least two traits that she passed to her daughter—the need for order and her lopsided smile.

Gordon is watching her—with what strikes her as a combination of curiosity, sympathy, and amusement—when the door is flung open.

"She's here!" shouts the man at the door.

"What the hell are you talking about?"

"The girl! Come, quick!"

He rushes from the room and slams the door behind him.

She hears people yelling, mostly men but at least one woman. Seconds later she hears what sounds like a motorcycle firing up, or maybe it's a snowmobile. Or both. She hears gunshots and her stomach moves to her throat.

ARIZONA AND MOJO ARE just fifty feet from the motorcycle when she realizes something has gone wrong. She hears shouting and the revving of a small engine. She wonders if it's a snowmobile but doesn't dare look back. Rounding the back corner of Dog-Face George's House, she tears the tarp off the bike. "Mojo, sidecar!" Moments later the Ural is skirting the western verge of Silver Hill at full throttle.

Over the wind she hears the racing of the other engine and thinks it's getting closer. She also hears what sounds like gunfire but dismisses it as a backfiring engine—until, a second later, something buzzes past her left ear. Snow flies and whirls behind them, but the Ural is no match for a snowmobile. With the snowmobile gaining and the lack of cover in the wide-open terrain, they don't have much time. Another bullet whizzes by. Fuck.

But there is one thing the Ural can do that a snowmobile can't—ride through water almost two feet deep. If she can find a stream crossing wide enough and deep enough, maybe they can get away. Cottonwood Creek. She races toward Cottonwood Canyon Road, one mile south. The winding folds of the canyon will also minimize the amount of time that they are exposed to a clean shot by their pursuer, or pursuers. She thinks they're being chased by a single snowmobile, but she isn't sure and doesn't know if the driver has a passenger, a gunsel.

The motorcycle strains for traction as it climbs up the small ridge before Cottonwood Canyon. Another bullet zips past. She plunges into the canyon as steeply as she can, races down at full throttle, trying to eliminate the snowmobile's line of sight. They are above tree line but dropping fast, and Arizona catches glimpses of a copse of cottonwoods. Another creek comes in from the left and she veers to the right.

As they round the corner, she sees a thicket of small trees and larger trees ahead. They speed around the first grove. A bullet strikes a small tree. As they round the second copse, the air cracks again, followed by a yelp from Mojo. Arizona looks over at the sidecar and sees blood. Concentric circles of fear radiate out from her, like ripples on a pond of panic. Or is it rage? No. It's both. They crossed a line with Mojo, her brother and best friend. All that's left of her family.

The next grove is large enough to provide good cover, so halfway through she turns sharply to the right and doubles back, until they are only yards from their own tracks. She kills the motorcycle, removes her helmet, grabs the shotgun, and waits behind a large black cottonwood, her cheek against its gnarled gray bark. She doesn't have to wait long. No gunman, just the driver. Her hands are shaking and her eyes are blurry, but she aims and fires. He tumbles off the snowmobile as it clips a tree and rolls over.

Arizona has fired the shotgun many times, but never without ear protection. While she was prepared for the recoil, she wasn't prepared for the auditory assault, for the ringing in her ears. A devastating cacophony of bells swing ceaselessly in the belfry of her head. Her hands fly reflexively to her ears as the gun falls to the snow, the hot barrel hissing in protest like a petulant tomcat. But hands over ears don't help, so she wraps her arms around her head and squeezes as hard as she can, as if trying to crush her own skull. She collapses onto her knees and stays that way, unable to move or think. Slowly, mercifully, the internal clamor subsides. She sits up, picks up the gun, and takes three more slow breaths. The acrid smell of gun smoke hits deep inside her head, olfactory salt to the auditory wound.

She stands and walks the short distance to the unconscious pursuer, who is bleeding from his right leg. Her eyes and brow screw themselves into a fierce squint. "You shot my dog, you son of a bitch!"

She imagines aiming the shotgun at his chest.

Imagines pulling the trigger, as if in a dream.

Seeing him jerk from unconsciousness.

Seeing the pain, the defeat in his eyes before they slowly close for the last time.

Seeing his wretched body go limp.

She doesn't fire, of course. Still overflowing with rage, she stares at the man for what seems like an eternity. Clipped to the chest pocket of his parka is the mic of a two-way radio. She grabs it and presses the push-to-talk button.

"Hey, Gordon, do you read me? Over." She counts to five and tries again. "Arizona to asshole, you have a man down. Over."

"You killed him?" comes through the radio.

"You're supposed to say *over*, dumbass. Never mind, just shut up and listen. Your man isn't dead, but he is bleeding pretty badly. I might have hit his femoral artery. He's in Cottonwood Canyon. You should probably hurry. Over and out."

She drops the mic and starts back toward Mojo. The snow scrunches, squeaks beneath her boots. She stops after two steps and looks back at the man. There is so much blood. She's never shot a living thing before, just targets and clay pigeons. She doesn't want him to die. But she didn't have a choice. She takes a moment to process, to center herself by engaging her senses. The creek purls. Individual crystals of snow and ice reflect the blue sky. The last cottonwood leaves, heart-shaped and yellow, rustle as they cling to the branches like drops of honey. She takes a deep breath. "I wish I could stay," she says to the moment, "but I can't. Mojo needs help."

She walks back to Mojo, who is barely conscious. She finds entrance and exit wounds on his right hind leg. She runs her eyes across the outside of the sidecar, then her bloody fingers across the bullet hole. He has an exit wound, so no bullet inside but possibly shrapnel. He can survive this if she can get him help ASAP.

She grabs the first aid kit from a saddlebag and bandages her best friend's leg as best she can within the confines of the sidecar. Her shaking hands make it all the more difficult. Her entire body is trembling, like she's a human tuning fork. She covers him with an emergency blanket, scrubs the blood off her hands with tree bark and snow, wishing the fear would wash away, too. Never has she been so scared that she couldn't stop shaking. Until now.

"Hold on, buddy," she says as they begin the ride to Bridgeport. "Please."

44 •

The Operation

THE RIDE TO BRIDGEPORT TAKES FOREVER. ARIZONA CAN'T tell if Mojo has lost consciousness or not, but there's nothing she can do for him anyway. Other than worry, that is. And she's doing plenty of that. But during the long, cold ride, her worry has lots of company. Myriad thoughts and feelings swirl about like the snow behind the motorcycle. She's pretty sure that the loudest of them is guilt, made manifest in her pained breaths.

Mojo was shot, and it's undeniably her fault. She put him in harm's way. Meanwhile, she drove away Lily—the one friend she ever made—and now she's alone again. But if she'd brought Lily instead, would Lily be the one at risk of bleeding out? Should she have not gone at all, just played nice with the kidnappers and hoped for the best? There seems to be no right answer.

She thought she could play Indiana Jones and be a hero, but this isn't a movie. This is real life, and people, or dogs, could die.

She pulls up to the veterinary clinic door, mind still swirling, jumps off, and runs inside.

"Please, I need help! My dog has been shot!"

The receptionist hurries around the counter and follows Arizona outside. She bends over the sidecar and examines Mojo, who barely opens his big brown eyes.

"Let's get him inside. Then I'll call the surgeon."

They struggle to pry his immobile seventy pounds from the sidecar and rush him inside. The staff tracks down the surgeon, who says he can be there in half an hour. They give Mojo some pain meds and clean and examine his wounds.

There is nothing Arizona can do except wait. She hates waiting. It feels so useless, so powerless. She asks if there is a restroom she can use, goes in, cleans the blood off her hands, and does a cursory job of mopping the blood from her clothes with wet paper towels. She takes a seat in the waiting room, then flips through a stack of magazines to take her mind off Mojo, and Mom, and her own stupidity. She picks up a *National Geographic* and starts thumbing through it, before remembering the map.

She runs out to the motorcycle and retrieves the bamboo map holder from the sidecar. It is stained with Mojo's blood. A shiver of empathy—or is it guilt?—cascades across her skin. She goes back to the restroom, wipes the blood off the map holder, and sits down in the waiting room again.

She removes the map and unfurls it completely. In the upper right corner it reads:

NEVADA–ARIZONA

BOULDER CANYON QUADRANGLE

Near the center of the top margin it is stamped:

ADVANCE SHEET

SUBJECT TO CORRECTION

The most prominent notations, however, have been done by hand. Someone has drawn numbers on the map, all with circles around them and some with arrows pointing to specific locations or geographic features. The numbers range from one to twenty-five or so. But the numbers aren't the only annotations. Someone has also drawn in the boundary of Lake Mead and labeled it, with *MEAD* trailing off into the right-hand margin.

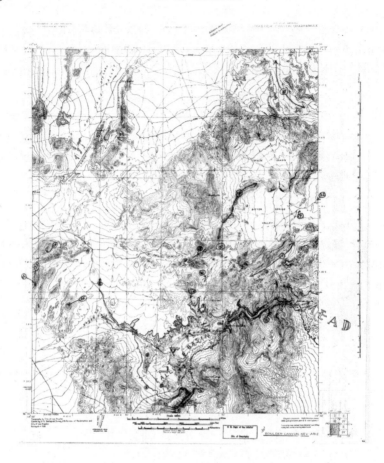

Arizona scans the margin of the map for a date and finds it in the lower left—1926. That's well after Tad and Mil had left Bodie. Hoover wasn't president yet, but he was secretary of commerce. And undersecretary of all other departments.

A veterinary technician comes out and tells Arizona that the surgeon has arrived and is prepping for surgery. She looks at the clock. Only twenty-three minutes have passed since they arrived. It's going to be a long wait.

She thinks about Mojo going under the knife, and her eyes close under the weight of the thought. It is more than she can bear. Her whole body quivers. She thinks of the Hippocratic oath. *First, do no harm.* Surgery feels like adding insult to injury. She knows it's not that simple, but that's how it seems in the moment. She feels powerless. *Focus on the map,* she tells herself. *That's something you can do.*

She starts to study the annotated numbers on the map—in order, of course. She finds number one on the left-hand side a little more than halfway down, finds number two close by, and keeps counting. Six . . . seven . . . eight. Number eight is near the bottom edge of the map, centered left to right. The adjacent text reads *Upper Black Canyon Dam Site.* As she reads the words, time stops.

Black Canyon.

Lake Mead.

This is a planning map for a dam.

For the *Hoover* Dam.

Her eyes still point at the text but are focused on the middle distance, the map a blurred background to the memories that play in her mind. The family had spent a week kayak camping in the Black Canyon, just downstream from the dam. When she first saw Lake Mead on the map, she didn't make the connection, but now the memories come flooding back.

By design, the dam had dramatically transformed the area upstream, submerging the deep canyons of the Colorado River, Virgin River, and hundreds of small side canyons, entombing river-level settlements, ranches, forts, mills, and ferries hundreds of feet below the surface of the new hundred-mile-long lake. Yet downstream the Black Canyon wasn't dramatically different than it had been for eons, with dark vertical walls and numerous hot springs bubbling up in its feeder canyons.

Their trip had started at Willow Beach, a dozen miles downriver from the dam but twice that by road. They had paddled upstream against the mostly gentle current, quickly learning the times of day when the current was stronger as more water was released to generate electricity. They hopped from side canyon to side canyon, paddling just a few miles most days, and camped on the gravel-filled washes where the side canyons met the Colorado River. They stayed one or two nights in each spot, explored slot canyons, soaked in hot springs.

On the day when they were closest to the dam, they had paddled right up to the chain of buoys that prevents boats from getting too close, but that was close enough, anyway. From the surface of the river, they had a breathtaking view of the dam rising dramatically above. They saw massive torrents of water being released. Heard the thunderous roar. Felt the current beneath their kayaks. Although Mojo was usually comfortable in a kayak, Arizona recalls with a smile his unease with the roar of the released water and the jitteriness of the kayaks in the resulting current.

It had been a marvelous trip, and Arizona happily devours the sweet memories for some time before they turn bitter. No, *bitter* doesn't do it justice. Tainted? Defiled? Infected? By Dad's death, Mom's captivity, Dad's secrets, Mojo's suffering, Arizona's guilt.

Her thoughts are interrupted by the veterinary technician again. "I wanted to let you know that the operation went well. The surgeon will be out to see you shortly."

She looks at the clock. Another hour has passed.

Five minutes later, a middle-aged woman comes out in scrubs. "Hi, are you Arizona?"

"He's okay?"

"He's a lucky boy. The bullet missed the bone, barely glanced connective tissue, and missed the major arteries and veins."

"And no complications? Will he be able to run again? There isn't much that he likes more than running."

"Yes," the surgeon says with a smile. "He'll have a limp for a while, but he's young and strong. I expect he'll make a full recovery. Dogs are incredibly resilient."

"Thank you, Doctor." Arizona smiles and lets out a long sigh.

"You're very welcome. By the way, how did Mojo get shot?"

"A hunting accident," Arizona says without hesitation. Lying to the surgeon is harder than lying to Gordon but easier than lying to Lily. Interesting.

The surgeon winces. "I see. Take care, Arizona. Someone will be out shortly to give you follow-up instructions."

Bodies are so fragile, Arizona thinks. *Yet also remarkably resilient.* Her curious mind appreciates a good paradox, even one balanced on the edge of a knife.

———

THREE HOURS LATER, back at the *Gunga Din* campsite in the Alabama Hills, she unlocks the Airstream door, leaves it open, and goes back to the bike to get Mojo.

Lily runs up and hugs her, like the argument never happened.

"You're not mad at me?" Arizona says. Her arms, still at her sides, seem just as confused as she is.

"No, I've been worried about you."

Arizona feels her arms tugging against her confusion, succumbs, and lets them slide up Lily's back.

"You've been gone forever," Lily says, still holding Arizona.

"Less than twelve hours, actually," Arizona says, "but it feels like twice that. Could you give me a hand with Mojo?"

Lily pulls away and looks into Arizona's eyes. "Why? What happened?"

Arizona sighs, doesn't want to have this conversation now. Or maybe ever. She doesn't want to admit that Lily was right, that it was a dangerous plan. She braces herself for conflict.

"They shot him, but the surgeon said he'll be okay."

"Fuck!"

Lily rushes to help without saying another word. Prying his semiconscious body from the sidecar is beyond awkward, and they stumble and almost fall while carrying him into the trailer. They place him on the bed, less gently than Arizona would like, and she kisses his forehead.

"Can you tell me everything?" Lily says.

"Later? I'm exhausted. I'd like to lie down with Mojo."

"Of course. Can Gus and I stay here?"

Arizona hesitates. "You're really not mad at me anymore?"

"No, I'm not mad. A little frustrated that you put yourself in danger, but not mad. I'll understand if you need some alone time, but I'd like to stay if that's okay."

Arizona nods. "Stay. I'll see you in a bit."

"Thank you," Lily says. She squeezes Arizona's arm gently and takes Gus out of the bedroom.

Arizona closes the privacy curtain and sits on the edge of the bed to decompress—slowly, just like scuba diving. She thinks back through her day. Betrayal. Bullets. Blood. She opens her notebook and writes.

I've been thinking about gears again. Pairs of gears have gaps between the teeth. When the drive gear changes direction, that gap must be closed before force can be applied in the new direction. The resulting lapse in motion is called backlash. How perfect is that? I'm the drive gear now, and I'm changing direction. I'm the external force. There will be backlash. There will be gnashing of teeth. But not mine.

She closes her notebook, curls up next to Mojo, and falls asleep almost instantly.

45 •

Backlash and Bête Noire

O N THE AIRSTREAM'S QUEEN BED, MOJO PUSHES AGAINST
Arizona with his strong front legs. She opens her eyes. With her
face so close to his, perspective makes him look like a Picasso painting.
She likes Picasso, can relate to seeing the world through a unique lens.
Mojo pushes again with his cubist legs.

"Hey!" she says, before she sees his bandaged rear leg. A small
amount of blood has wept through his bandage, and the ruby reminder
of the violation makes Arizona's stomach twist. "Sorry, buddy. You
sleep as long as you need to."

She kisses him on the crown of his head and swings her feet over
the edge of the bed. But as she sits there, something gnaws at her center. Something both past and present. She scans her memory and her
body.

Dad's death, just weeks ago. She holds the thought long enough to
recognize the sensations, the hole in her heart that is so familiar now.
And the confusion over the secrets Dad kept. But neither of those was
what she felt moments ago.

Mom's captivity. The feeling is similar to that for Dad, but the hollow space inside her seems slightly smaller. Because there's hope? She
can still save Mom, in theory. She was so close to Mom in Bodie,
probably less than a football field away. Should she have tried to free
her and ended this thing for good? She holds on to the question, lets
it hang in her head for a minute, but still doesn't have an answer.

The fight with Lily. Butterflies in her belly. Prickled skin. Parts of her are cold, other parts warm. The hole is there again, small but certain. It's all very confusing, so she moves on.

Mojo's injury. Her face flushes, her muscles tense. She's pretty sure that's anger and guilt but, again, those impressions aren't the ones she had noticed.

And she shot someone. She tilts her head, searches herself. Visualizing all the blood raises hairs on her arms and neck. But otherwise there isn't much she can find. Interesting. Opposing sentiments that cancel each other out? Is that even a thing? Denial? Regardless, it's still not what was gnawing at her.

Which brings her back to Lily, to their fight when she was planning the trip to Bodie. Those feelings are the closest. And now she has to plan another trip, to Hoover Dam. And she has to go alone again. Clearly she was right about the danger, and she can't expose Lily to that. But how will Lily react this time?

Fear? Is that what this is? Fear of telling Lily that she's going off alone again. Fear of her not understanding. Again. Fear of consequences, of losing her newfound friend, of inevitability. Fuck.

Sunlight streams past the edges of the blinds. It is day outside, but which day? Her internal clock has sprung its mainspring. She looks at her phone to check the time and date. October 20, 4:30 P.M. Same day, and she slept for only an hour. Shit. She needs meaningful sleep but doesn't think she has time for it. She's stressed, anxious, trying to get ahead and stay ahead. Time spent sleeping strikes her as time wasted. Regardless, she's wide awake now, so she gets up and opens the privacy curtain.

"Hey, sleepyhead," says Lily. "Feel better after your nap?"

"Maybe a tiny bit."

Arizona puts the kettle on, cleans the French press, and scoops coffee in a spoonful at a time. The first coffee grounds skitter about like water bugs in the freshly rinsed pot. It's a disconcerting thought, but on the other hand, bugs are a good source of protein.

As the expanding metal of stove and kettle creak to life and the

heat of the burner warms the kitchen, she catches Lily up. The trip to
Bodie. The Hoover House. The narrow escape. Mojo's surgery. The
planning map for the Hoover Dam.

"You've had one hell of a day," Lily says.

"Yeah, feels like several."

"So is Hoover Dam the next stop?"

Arizona nods. "Seems likely."

"When?"

"Not sure yet. I took a tour of the dam with my parents, but I need
a refresher. I've gotta do some research and see if I can glean anything
else from the puzzle poem, too."

"Can I help?" Lily says. "Sounds fun."

"Sure, but you have a strange idea of fun."

"Takes one to know one." Lily winks.

"Let's see if the Hoover Dam epiphany gets us any further with the
poem."

Arizona wakes up her Mac and they scroll through the poem.

"The first four verses seem pretty clear now," says Lily, "but the rest
is as clear as mud."

"Agreed." Arizona reads the last three verses aloud.

The grandest theater of Rome, the Pharaoh's stately catacomb,
Athena's hilltop temple home, resplendent monuments of yore.
Like the brooding fervor of Chartres labyrinthian fleur,
Elements, but not those you think, delineate the contour;
Follow the arching corridor, through earth which wind and water bore.
So many petals on the floor.

Formed in Creator's loving hands, some say that when He made the lands
From shifting circles in the sands, He commanded who each was for:
Two for the angels aquiline, one for the beasts so anodyne,
With eagle as their king assigned, whence he was to rule and soar;
The closest two were made for man, our zealous penchant to explore;
The last His, for us to watch o'er.

The arc of the sky draws your gaze; one for repose in waning days,
One for the flare of summer's blaze, and one to guide you theretofore.
Worlds whip 'round concentric rings, summers fall and winters spring,
But always up extend the wings, a celestial semaphore.
By that Heaven that bends above us—by that God we both adore—
The secrets are safe forevermore.

When she's done, Arizona taps her finger on the screen, on the longest line in verse five:

Follow the arching corridor, through earth which wind and water bore.

"*Through earth which wind and water bore,*" she says. "It's a canyon. The Black Canyon, where Hoover Dam was built."

"*Follow the arching corridor,*" says Lily. "Corridors within the dam itself?"

"Could be. It is an arch dam, after all. Look at the previous line."

"*Elements, but not those you think, delineate the contour,*" Lily says.

"Yeah. The elements that come to mind are the four classical elements, three of which—earth, wind, and water—are even mentioned in the next line."

"But it explicitly says *not those you think,* so the first thing that comes to mind is probably wrong. Or do you think that's more misdirection, a red herring?"

"I don't know." Arizona tilts her head to the left, to the right, then grasps a passing thought as if it's a log floating down her stream of consciousness. "*Delineate the contour . . . arching corridor . . . shifting circles . . . arc of the sky . . . concentric rings.* That's at least five geometric references in three verses."

"And?" says Lily. "Tell me what you're thinking."

"Out of habit, I capitalized the first letter of every line in the poem. *Elements* with a capital E. But maybe capitalization actually matters?"

"I don't understand."

"Euclid wrote one of the most influential works in the history of math. It served as the primary text for teaching geometry for two millennia. It was commonly referred to as *Elements of Geometry*, but its actual title was just *Elements*. Is that it? Is it Euclid's *Elements* that delineate the contour? Geometry?"

"Huh," Lily says. "In which case, do you think that *follow the arching corridor* could mean something else?"

"Maybe. In geometry, three points define a unique circle, a unique arc. So are we supposed to follow a path or arc through three points? But if so, what three points?"

"Let's move on to the next verse," Lily says. "We can always come back to that one."

Arizona reads the sixth verse aloud, reads it again, and shakes her head. Self-reproach sets into her face and stays as if chiseled in stone.

Lily notices the change. "What's the matter?"

"I'm just really frustrated."

"With me?"

"No, with myself. I'm used to being able to solve puzzles, but I'm totally clueless. I feel so stupid."

"You're like the opposite of stupid, AZ. And we're making progress, even if it's slow."

Mojo whines.

"Sorry, buddy," Arizona says as she fetches a pain pill. "This will make it hurt a little less, for a while at least."

She rolls the pill into mozzarella cheese and manages to get a brief tail wag while he gobbles it down. She gives him two more bits of cheese and they turn their attention to the last verse.

The arc of the sky draws your gaze; one for repose in waning days,
One for the flare of summer's blaze, and one to guide you theretofore.
Worlds whip 'round concentric rings, summers fall and winters spring,
But always up extend the wings, a celestial semaphore.
By that Heaven that bends above us—by that God we both adore—
The secrets are safe forevermore.

Arizona shakes her head.

"Multiple geometry references before," says Lily. "Astronomy now?

Arc of the sky . . . worlds whip 'round . . . celestial semaphore . . . Heaven that bends above us."

"That's it, Lily! You're a genius."

"I am?"

"Stars! If the first two lines refer to stars, *one for the flare of summer's blaze* would be the sun."

"And *one to guide you theretofore*," Lily says, "would be the North Star?"

Arizona nods.

"But what about *one for repose in waning days?*"

"Once again, I have no idea. Shit."

She rereads the verse, gleans nothing else, and exhales a long and exaggerated sigh, as if she'd forgotten to breathe for a minute. "Wait," she says.

"Wait what?" says Lily.

"*Follow the arching corridor* . . . a path through three points."

"So you're thinking that *the arc of the sky* could be a path through three stars?"

"Exactly," Arizona says. "But even if that's right, and even if we knew the third star, how do we follow a path through the stars? Double shit."

Arizona's phone interrupts them. Blocked number.

She looks at the phone but can't answer yet. Part of her wants to give Gordon a ration of shit about shooting Mojo. *You shot my dog, and now you want me to take your fucking call?* But an even bigger part of her is afraid for Mom, afraid of the consequences of her own actions. She lets it ring two more times, then picks up.

"Yes?" she says.

"What were you doing in Bodie?"

"Research."

"Care to elaborate?"

"No, not really."

"This isn't a game, Arizona. We still have your mother, and after your little escapade, you're lucky she's alive."

Arizona swallows, then opens her mouth to speak, but nothing comes out.

"Although I see where you get your tenacity. She's tried to escape at least twice and is probably still trying, I imagine."

Arizona smiles at the idea of Mom trying to escape. "How do I know she's still alive?"

"Would you like to speak with her again?"

"Of course."

"Okay, I'll put her on briefly."

Seconds pass, and then Arizona hears her mom's voice. "Honey? How are you?"

"I'm fine. More important, how are *you*?"

"I'm okay, tired of—"

Mom is cut off.

"Satisfied?" says Gordon.

After a pause she says, "It sounds like her."

"Yes, because it is her. She's fine. So, did you find something in Bodie?"

"A desideratum." She hopes he doesn't know the word. *Oh, is that beyond your ken? Read a fucking book.*

"What sort of needful thing?"

Arizona hesitates. "A bamboo tube." She strings out her answers, from frustration—with herself, with Gordon, with the whole fucking situation. She needed to get a step ahead of them and stay a step ahead, but she screwed up, was found out. Can't really hold out now.

"Where was it?"

"Hidden, under the floor in a house."

"And where is it now?"

"I have it."

"And what was inside?"

Arizona hesitates again. "A map."

"You're making this harder than it has to be."

"Yes, I am."

He sighs. "What kind of map? A map of what?"

"A topographic map, U.S. Geological Survey, 1926, Boulder Canyon quadrangle."

"How did you find it?"

She hesitates again but can't think of a good lie. "I decoded the third cipher." Shit. So much for staying a step ahead.

"I see. Send it to me, along with the map."

"I don't have a scanner in the Airstream, asshole."

"Take pictures with your phone."

"Fine. And then we're done? I mean, if all you wanted was the map and decoded cipher, can I have my mom back now?"

"No. The map and cipher aren't the endgame, merely steps along the way. We'll let you know when we're done."

Yeah. She knew that but had to ask all the same.

He pauses, changes the topic. "Thanks for not killing our man."

"Don't thank me. I missed," she lies.

"He wasn't even supposed to be shooting at you. You're too valuable."

"So, what, it's okay to kidnap people, and kill people, but just not me?"

"That's not what I meant," he says. "And we haven't killed anyone."

"You killed my father, fuckwad! You said so in your note."

Lily gives her a thumbs-up, and she wonders if it's for *fuckwad* or her attitude in general.

"We said that his death could have been avoided, not that we killed him," Gordon says.

"Oh, I get it. You're just too cowardly to admit it."

"We found another blood trail. You were hit?"

"My dog."

"I'm sorry. Is he okay?"

"He'll live," Arizona says, "not that you care."

"I'm not . . . we're not evil. We merely believe in something greater than ourselves, greater than all of us."

"The Language of the Birds," she says. "Alchemy."

He chuckles. "Alchemy is one name for it, although that term conjures unflattering connotations. What we seek is nothing short of the potential nobility of the race of men—and women. Time is the intangible governor of all our acts, the nemesis of the human race. What if we had more time? What if everyone lived long enough to fulfill their Great Work, their magnum opus? How much better could the world be?"

"Yeah, utopian dreams work out all the time. You know that the Thousand-Year Reich ended after only twelve years, right? With millions dead. It sounds to me like you already drank the Kool-Aid, and, yes, the reference to Jonestown is intentional."

"This is different," he says without hesitation.

"You used the word *nobility*. Noble utopian dreams beget ignoble dystopian nightmares. It's simple human history."

"I'm disappointed. I had hoped you'd understand."

"I'm happy to disappoint you," she says, then hangs up.

Arizona's hand is shaking. Lily places her own over it.

She wants to scream, to purge the anger and frustration. But she got caught, and now she has no choice but to give Gordon what he wants. Fuck.

She opens a new document.

Dearest Bête Noire,

Map and decoded third cipher are attached.
P.S. Fuck you.

Arizona uploads the message as Lily nods her approval. Then Arizona does something she's never done before. She opens her notebook and shows Lily one of her entries—the one about *backlash*.

"You go, girl," Lily says with a smile.

Arizona looks at Mojo, whose big brown eyes seem to reflect the resolve in her own. As do Lily's.

46.

The Booklet and
the Bobblehead

I'T'S JUST AFTER 6:00 P.M. ARIZONA'S COFFEE MUG IS EMPTY, but so is the pot. She fills the kettle again and goes outside for a few minutes. Lily and Gus follow.

The sun is behind the mountains but daylight still masks the stars, even in the eastern sky. The air is sharp and clear. They stand on the edge of the small canyon next to camp, listening to the stream burble, until the kettle screams for attention.

Back inside, Arizona opens the Wikipedia page for Hoover Dam and they read everything.

Design, preparation, and contracting. Hoover, as secretary of commerce, had been integral in the planning stages.

Labor force, river diversion, groundworks.

Rock clearance, grout curtain, concrete.

The 112 deaths during construction.

Dedication and completion.

The art deco design work of Gordon B. Kaufmann, the Navajo- and Pueblo-inspired artwork of Allen Tupper True inside the dam, and the external artwork of Oskar J. W. Hansen.

Hansen's dedication plaza, on the Nevada abutment, contains a sculpture of two winged figures flanking a flagpole. Surrounding the base of the monument is a terrazzo floor embedded with a "star map."

"Holy shit," Arizona says. "A star map. That's how we follow a path through the stars!"

Lily smiles, puts her hand on Arizona's shoulder, and squeezes.

Arizona looks into her friend's eyes and smiles back.

"So, we're back in business?" says Lily.

"Well, now we know where the path is. But so far we still have only two stars—our sun and the North Star. That would give us a straight line, but not an arc of the sky."

"We'll find the third star," says Lily. "Let's keep reading."

"Agreed." Arizona switches her search to *Oskar J. W. Hansen* and finds plenty of information on the dedication plaza, now called Monument Plaza. But most pictures just show small pieces of the star map.

She changes her search term again, runs through several before she spots one of the results from *Oskar J. W. Hansen Bureau of Reclamation.* The thing that catches her eye is the publication date—1936.

HOOVER DAM MONUMENT PLAZA SAFETY ISLAND:
OSKAR J. W. HANSEN . . .

Oskar J. W. Hansen via US Bureau of Reclamation. Publication date 1936-02-25.
https://archive.org/details/SafetyIsland

She clicks the link. The top portion of the screen becomes a document viewer, with a description below:

Drawings for Hoover Dam Monument Plaza (originally called Safety Island)

"Drawings. Blueprints," Arizona says. "Now we're talking."

There's something alluring about old blueprints. Page after page of desk-sized sheets. So simple, yet so complex. No color to distract the eye. Blue on white, or white on blue. The aroma of ink and paper, just like with books. Okay, the digitized ones not so much.

Her attention shifts to the words RELATED DOCUMENTS, followed by a single link:

HOOVER DAM MONUMENT PLAZA SCULPTURES
COMPLETE BOOKLET

> This is an out of print booklet produced to explain the sculptures at the Hoover Dam. . . . Much of the text of this booklet was written by the artist himself, Oskar J. W. Hansen.

Arizona downloads the booklet and opens it. Each page of the digitized booklet is two adjacent pages of the original, complete with fold and staple marks.

Sculptures
at
Hoover
Dam

She flips past the combined front-and-back-cover page and scans the foreword.

> *Rising from a black polished base is the flagpole, 142 feet high, flanked by two winged figures. . . . Near the figures, and elevated above the floor, is a compass, framed by the signs of the zodiac.*

"A compass," Lily says, "invented by Petrus Peregrinus de Maricourt."

"And framed by the signs of the zodiac, which the alchemists used to represent the twelve steps of the Great Work. Is that just weird serendipity?"

Surrounding the base, upon which rest the figures, is a terrazzo floor.
Inlaid in the terrazzo is a star chart, or celestial map. . . . Thus our
pole star (Polaris), indicating the true obliquity of the North Pole of
the earth . . .

"Polaris, the North Star," says Lily.

"*One to guide you theretofore,*" says Arizona.

Mojo's jowls flap as he snores. Gus whistles through his short nose. Together they sound like a cartoon dog.

Arizona finishes the foreword, flips to the next page, and freezes, eyes locked on the title of the booklet's first section:

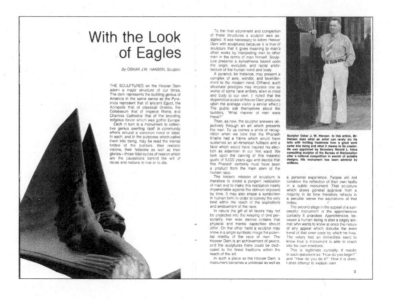

"With the look of eagles," she says. "Aquiline. *Two for the angels aquiline.*"

She reads aloud from the opening paragraph:

The dam represents the building genius of America in the same
sense as the Pyramids represent that of ancient Egypt, the Acropolis
that of classical Greece, the Colosseum that of Imperial Rome, and
Chartres Cathedral that of the brooding religious fervor which
was gothic Europe.

Then recites part of the fourth verse:

> *The grandest theater of Rome, the Pharaoh's stately catacomb,*
> *Athena's hilltop temple home, resplendent monuments of yore.*
> *Like the brooding fervor of Chartres labyrinthian fleur . . .*

"Pyramids, *the Pharaoh's stately catacomb*," Lily says. "Acropolis, *Athena's hilltop temple home*. Colosseum, *the grandest theater of Rome.*"

Arizona nods. "The booklet even uses the words *brooding fervor* in reference to Chartres."

"There are too many connections to be coincidence," Lily says.

"Agreed. It's like the booklet was written to contain clues to the secret."

"But who could hide cryptic clues within a government document?" Lily says. "Oh, never mind. Duh. The president could. President Hoover."

While trying to process the connections, the revelation, Arizona looks out the window. Night has fallen. All she can see is her own reflection, but she is taken aback by its expression. Bewilderment? Disapproval? She lowers the blinds to prevent more intrusions from her judgmental doppelgänger and reads on. Farther down the same page:

> *. . . a sculptor may show in a single symbolic image the potential*
> *nobility of the race of men.*

"*The potential nobility of the race of men?*" Arizona says.

"What about it?" Lily says. "Other than the purple prose, that is."

"I swear that Gordon used that exact phrase."

She reads the next sentence:

> *The Hoover Dam is an achievement of peace, and the sculptures there*
> *could be dedicated to the finest traditions within the reach of the art.*

"Not art," Arizona says, "but *the* art."

"As in alchemy, the Great Work."

She finishes the page and flips forward. The top of the next page has an illustrated aerial view of the entire plaza.

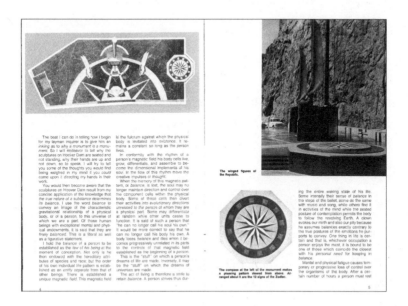

Arizona zooms in and can see some of the constellations on the star map, but not in enough detail to be useful. Then the concentric rings around the flagpole catch her attention. She taps the screen and recites two lines.

Worlds whip 'round concentric rings, summers fall and winters spring,
But always up extend the wings, a celestial semaphore.

"*A celestial semaphore,*" Arizona says again. "Of course. The winged figures."

"I get the celestial part," says Lily, "because they sit above a star map, but semaphore?"

"A semaphore is a way to send messages by holding your arms or flags in certain positions according to an alphabetic code."

"Oh, and they have their wings straight up, like they're sending a semaphore," Lily says.

Arizona nods and continues reading aloud.

*There is established a unique magnetic field. This magnetic field is the
fulcrum against which the physical body is levitated into existence. . . .
In conformity with the rhythm of a person's magnetic field his body
cells live, grow, differentiate, and assemble to become the dimensional
implements of his soul.*

"Okay," Arizona says, "my mom is an artist, so I know firsthand
that they can be a little out there. But what are the odds that an artist
would talk at length about magnetic fields?"

She finishes the section and flips to the next. As she reads, one line
jumps out:

*On this star map, the center of our Sun is shown as the very center of
the flagpole.*

"The flagpole represents the sun," says Lily.
"One for the flare of summer's blaze." Arizona smiles.
She pages forward again.

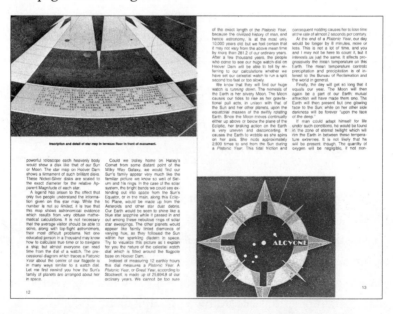

Her eyes lock on the picture in the lower right. She blinks, questions her eyes. At first she isn't even sure what she's looking at because
the picture, unlike most of the others, doesn't have a caption.

"Is that part of the star map?"

She switches to her web browser, opens a new tab, searches for a word—a name, really—and follows the most promising link.

"Alcyone is also a star?" Lily says.

"Apparently. Halcyon days. *One for repose in waning days.* It's the third star!"

She continues reading, rapt.

I made the Diorite base of the monument describe an arc through the central field of this celestial watch dial.

"Diorite," says Arizona, "contains magnetite, the most magnetic naturally occurring mineral on earth. And an older name for magnetite was lodestone."

"*Counsel we sought but they just fought, like a lodestone cleft in two,*" Lily says.

"Exactly. Hang on a sec. I think Fulcanelli mentioned lodestones, too."

Arizona opens *The Mystery of the Cathedrals* and searches for *lodestone.*

. . . the lodestone, that virtue shut up in the body, which the Wise call their Magnesia.

"Magnesia," Arizona says, "was the alchemists' name for a mineral used to make the philosopher's stone."

Lily shakes her head in disbelief.

"And I think Fulcanelli's disciple, Eugène Canseliet, also mentioned magnetism."

She opens *Alchemy and its Mute Book* by Canseliet and searches for *magnet.*

A mere thirty years ago the main argument used against alchemists was that they did not have the means to provide a sufficiently high degree of heat. Today it is recognised that

**the real agent of transmutation at the heart of the mineral
realm is *magnetism*. This magnetism unquestionably must be
activated by a certain external energy source.**

"An external energy source," Lily says. "Hoover Dam."

Arizona remembers a fact from all the Hoover Dam history she's
just read. "Not only does the dam generate a massive amount of energy," Arizona says, "but electrical generators are more accurately referred to as electro*magnetic* generators. It's entirely possible that when
Hoover Dam was built, its generators had some of, if not *the,* most
powerful magnets in the world."

"So are we saying what I think we're saying? That Herbert Hoover
unlocked the secrets of alchemy and built the dam specifically to power
some alchemical process?"

Arizona's head is swimming, too, and she pieces the thoughts together as she speaks.

"I don't know. That all sounds insane, right? But we know Hoover
was a believer, and that seems to be what the poem's telling us." She
gestures at the laptop, where the booklet stares back at her. "I don't
know how else you'd explain this."

"Regardless, the booklet has to be Hoover's work, right?" Lily says.

"Agreed. It's brilliant, actually. All these arcane references hiding in
plain sight, but without the encrypted poem, they'd just be written off
as the ramblings of an artist, as has no doubt been the case for almost
one hundred years now, since the dam was built and the booklet published."

Arizona nods in thought, head on a spring like a bobblehead, while
she navigates back to the Monument Plaza drawings and downloads
them.

47

The Drawings and
the Arc of the Sky

THE AIRSTREAM IS RUNNING OUT OF NECESSITIES, SO ARIZONA takes the truck into Lone Pine. It's a good excuse for a little solo time. Time to think about—and summon courage for—telling Lily that she's going to Hoover Dam alone.

She opens the front passenger door, puts the bag of groceries on the seat, and slides the pizza box onto the floor. Mojo could perhaps be trusted with groceries, but the margherita pizza will not be risked. Alas, it is just habit and Mojo is still recuperating in the trailer, with Lily and Gus.

It's a little after 8:00 P.M. The sky is dark, full of stars, except where the mountains blot them out. She drives slowly on the loose dirt of Movie Road to keep the dust from coming in through the open windows. It's been less than twelve hours since she and Mojo were racing through the snow. Alabama Hills, a vertical mile lower than Bodie, feels like a different world. She acknowledges the *Tremors* residual boulder with a faint smile. Carries the groceries in and puts them away.

Coffee and Coke.

Dog food.

Fixings for breakfast burritos (a misnomer if ever there was one—good anytime, not just for breakfast).

They sit outside and wolf down the pizza, then head inside and get back to work.

She wakes up her laptop and opens the set of Monument Plaza

drawings that she had downloaded after they read the booklet. She pages through to get the lay of the land, as Lily looks over her shoulder. The first page shows the entirety of Monument Plaza and includes a legend with forty-three numbered items.

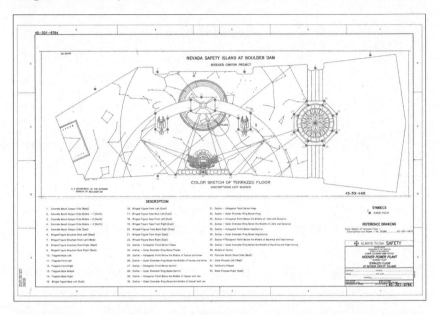

The overview is followed by detailed drawings of the flagpole, floor construction, the compass, several smaller features on the star map (including Polaris, Alcyone, and other star clusters), and a set of comprehensive drawings for the entire plaza.

Half of the drawings date back to the 1930s, and most of those are attributed to the sculptor, Oskar J. W. Hansen. The rest, with one exception, are from the 1950s. Arizona returns to the first page, which is dated 2009 and seems the most useful with its broad view and legend.

"Polaris and the flagpole-sun are clearly labeled," Arizona says. "But I don't see Alcyone."

"Since it's a map and you're like a map genius, can't you just look up the location of Alcyone on the web and then locate it on the star map?"

"I haven't studied celestial maps at all. And yes, looking back, that feels like quite the oversight."

"Could you study up online?"

"Sure, but that would be slow. Maybe we can find Alcyone on one of the other drawings."

Doubtful that the smallest seeds will bear fruit, Arizona suggests that they dispose of them first. They scour the drawings of the compass, flagpole, floor, and star clusters. While the drawing of the Alcyone cluster shows plenty of detail, it doesn't provide any context for Alcyone's location within the star map. Predictably, nor do the others.

"Nothing left but the big drawings," Arizona says. "This is going to take a while."

To make out the smallest details on the blueprint-size documents, she zooms way in. But then they can see only a small portion of the overall drawing. They start in the upper left, carefully examine everything on the screen, and scroll down a tiny bit to the next segment. When they get to the bottom, Arizona scrolls back up to the top, over a smidge, and repeats, ad nauseam. It's like searching the Hoover House, without the dust or sneezes, although the memory tickles her nose.

They read every word they can make out. She zooms in even more to try to make out writing that isn't otherwise legible, but it often still isn't.

Something North Pole of the Milky Way.

Meridian of the autumnal equinox.

Star cluster behind the arched base. Is that Alcyone?

Meridian of the winter solstice.

Vega.

Galactic equator.

As they finish the first sheet, Arizona rubs her eyes and moves on to the second.

"Look," Lily says, "the images overlap, so we can skip the left part of the sheet."

Arizona turns and stares at Lily.

"What?" says Lily. "No can do?"

Arizona shakes her head. "Not my nature. Sorry."

"Okay, suit yourself."

Arizona rescans the left half of the image but finds nothing they haven't already seen, so they continue.

The great something in Andromeda.

Capella.

More star clusters near the front edge of the star map.

Alpheratz.

Meridian of the vernal equinox.

"Alcyone!" says Lily. "There it is." It's barely legible, on the far-right side of the star map, almost to the compass. "What are these lines that connect it to other stars?"

"I'm pretty sure that's the constellation of Taurus. I remember from when we looked it up that Alcyone is the brightest star in the Pleiades cluster, which is part of Taurus."

Another revelation erupts from Arizona with a snicker.

"What's so funny?" Lily says.

"In astrology, Taurus is late April to late May, the time of year portrayed by many alchemical texts as optimal for the Great Work."

Lily shakes her head.

"Let's see if we can find Alcyone on the 2009 overview now," Arizona says.

She scrolls up to the first page and zooms in on the area of Taurus.

"Alcyone is there." Lily points. "Unlabeled but definitely there."

"Cool. Let's draw the arc that connects the three stars—*the arc of the sky*."

Arizona adjusts the zoom level so she can see all three stars—the flagpole-sun, Polaris, and Alcyone. Remembering her geometry, she draws the triangle that connects the centers of the three stars, the first step in drawing the arc, or circle, that passes through any three points.

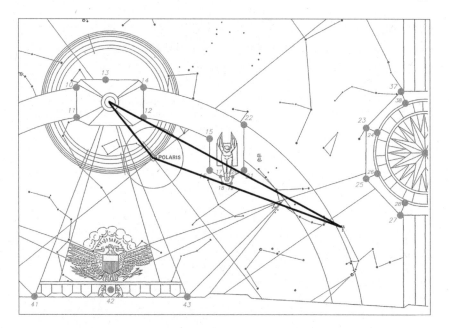

She shakes her head. "The triangle is obtuse, just like the alchemists' writing."

Lily groans.

Arizona strains to remember the next step. *Come on, Pythagoras,* she thinks. But that reminds her of Dad, and a grimace of pain shoots across her face.

"What's the matter?" Lily says.

"I was thinking about Pythagoras, and that reminds me of my dad. There's a great quote from *The Martian* by Andy Weir—*I'm traveling ninety kilometers per day as usual, but I only get thirty-seven kilometers closer to Schiaparelli because Pythagoras is a dick.*"

Lily giggles.

"I remember sharing that quote with my dad. He laughed but then launched into a full-throated defense of Pythagoras. I rolled my eyes."

Lily places her hand on Arizona's.

"Oh, now I remember. Perpendicular bisectors."

The three perpendicular bisectors of a triangle always meet at a single point, which is the center of the circle that passes through the three points. She finds the midpoints of each side of the triangle and draws perpendicular lines through them. She pastes a circle onto the

drawing, moves its center to the point where the three bisectors inter-
sect, and resizes it until it passes through the three stars.

"There it is," Arizona says, "*the arc of the sky.*"

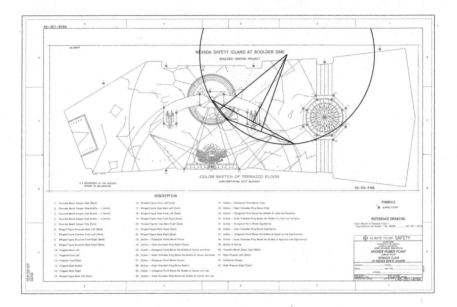

"But what the hell does it mean?" says Lily.

Arizona examines the arc, follows its course. "To the right of Alcyone, it passes through the compass. And one part of it is almost a
mirror image of the arched base on which the flagpole and winged
figures sit."

"Is any of that significant?" Lily says.

"I have no idea." She keeps her eyes on the screen. "I think we've
done all we can on paper. It's time to pay the dam a visit."

"So we leave in the morning?"

Arizona's eyes don't leave the laptop.

Lily waits, but Arizona won't look at her.

"I see," Lily says. "You're going alone again, aren't you?"

Arizona nods.

They sit in silence for what seems like forever.

"You took Mojo with you to Bodie because I wouldn't watch him,"
Lily says, "and then he got shot. Do you blame me?"

"No," Arizona says. *Maybe a little, briefly,* she thinks. "You didn't shoot him, and I know you were worried for me. It's just . . ." She wishes the last two words hadn't come out.

"It's just what?"

Arizona stares at the floor. "You complicate things."

"But not in a good way, I guess?"

"I don't even know what that means. When is more complicated good?"

"In relationships, because they're complicated by definition. Take one imperfect person and put them with another imperfect person, and things get more complicated. That's kind of the nature of relationships, AZ. But there are supposed to be more pros than cons. As Hillary Clinton says, it takes a fucking village."

"Yeah, my parents told me something like that." She lifts her eyes to Lily's. "I guess I'm just not good with people. Maybe I never will be."

"Well, one thing's for sure. You'll never get better at relationships if you keep pushing people away."

"I'm sorry."

"Are you?"

"Yes," says Arizona.

"I'm sorry, too." Lily stands. "I hope you find what you're searching for." She kisses Arizona on the crown of her head. "Goodbye, Arizona-like-the-state." She fetches Gus and leaves.

Arizona looks at Mojo, whose eyes ask: *Where are they going?*

She wants to run after them, wants to say so many things to Lily. But what's the point? Lily would just tell her that she doesn't trust people, that she's refusing help again, putting Mojo in harm's way again. But it's not like that. Is it?

"Goodbye, Lily-like-the-flower," she says to the air.

ARIZONA BREATHES. IN AND OUT. One, two, three, four times.

She opens her notebook and writes.

I said goodbye to Lily.

It's probably for the best. I seem to be a magnet for hurt.

    Dad. Mom. Mojo.

And I'm better on my own, anyway. More focused.

It's funny. I was always a loner but never lonely.

In hindsight, I didn't even know what loneliness was.

    Until recently.

There's a hole

where I used to be whole.

Loneliness is

a destitute soul.

How do people live with this kind of pain?

I take it back. It's not funny at all.

She slides the notebook away, the page watermarked by teardrops.

48

The Adept and
the Journal — Part Six

- - - - - - - - -

THE ADEPT THUMBS PAST THE FINAL LACUNA AND READS the last page.

While I have made no conscious effort to hide my feelings while writing this journal, I have also not gone out of my way to share them. If they were evident, so be it. They have wandered far and wide, from unquenchable desire to obtain and use the Secret for selfish aims, to hope for more selfless goals, to harrowing fears—fear that the Secret might fall into the wrong hands, fear of the unknown, fear of my own weaknesses. The progression of my thoughts and feelings with regard to this discovery has been anything but linear, and I have experienced each of these emotions in turn more times than I can count.

Although I admit that the progression was not linear, that does not mean that there was no progression at all. Though I have been adrift in confused seas, with each passing day the time dedicated to desire and hope—be it for selfish or selfless aims—has waned and fear has waxed. Finally, through this circuitous route, I have come to a place of stability.

I believe that the author was correct. I agree that it is best to hide the Secret until the hour when man can wisely wield

such power. We are indeed still treading with uncertain emotional steps the paths of youth in springtime.

Therefore, I too have decided to hide my knowledge, or at
least some of it. I have decided to destroy key pages of this
journal.

The Secret remains and lies within.

I found my way, and you will have to find yours. Just as the
Masters of yore would have wanted it.

Masters of yore, he thinks. Soon to be supplanted by the Masters of
tomorrow. The rise of the new Golden Dawn.

He catches himself wearing the smile of a confident man and wipes
the sanguine grin from his face. Yes, he has come far in his quest,
bridged so many of the chasms in his knowledge, but it is still no time
for smugness. Not quite yet, but soon. Very soon.

He closes the journal, until next time.

49.

Hoover Dam

ARIZONA SWINGS HER LEGS OUT OF BED JUST AFTER 6:00 A.M.
She steps outside. Lily's van is gone. *How do I fuck up? Let me count the ways,* she thinks. But it's too late now.

While she waits for the kettle to boil, she pulls the batteries out of all three GPS trackers. She's done being watched.

They pull out of the *Gunga Din* campsite before seven o'clock. She turns to get a final glimpse of Mount Whitney, its face veiled by clouds of white lace and silver filigree. A veil feels fitting, but it should be black to match her mood. There is a thin rigid line where her mouth used to be.

She'll leave the trailer just outside the tiny town of Shoshone, California, where she and her parents had boondocked before. It's beautiful, remote, and only two hours from the dam. The first half of the drive retraces the route to Titus Canyon, but instead of going left on Scotty's Castle Road, they stay on the Death Valley Scenic Byway through the commercial center of the park, the aptly named Furnace Creek. Then past Twenty Mule Team Canyon, up over Travertine Point, and down the straight and easy grade into Death Valley Junction, population 4. From there it is just twenty-seven miles south to Shoshone, population 31, a veritable metropolis by comparison.

In Shoshone they pass the small RV resort, the filling station that doubles as the general store, the post office, the tiny museum, and the venerable Crowbar Cafe & Saloon, where they will go for at least one burger while in the area. With town behind them, they motor the last five miles of pavement, turn onto a nondescript dirt road, and, after two miles of slow going, pull off the road into a flat and gravelly spot that they will call home for the night.

Even though Arizona has taken the Hoover Dam tour before with her parents, more information is always better, so she checks the tour descriptions and schedules. The comprehensive dam tour is an hour long and starts every half hour from 9:30 A.M. to 3:30 P.M.

She unhitches the Airstream and unloads the Ural—with the motorcycle on top, the truck is too tall for the parking garage at Hoover Dam. Takes Mojo for a slow, limping walk through a nearby wash, then grabs snacks, water, and a couple of Cokes for the road. She helps Mojo into the truck—he puts his front paws on the threshold of the open door and she lifts his rear end in—and starts the drive to Hoover Dam. She chooses an alternate route through the tiny town of Tecopa, because it will take them past a small grove of Joshua trees that the family had explored just months ago. Although she can't take the time to stop and walk among the alien-looking trees (which always remind her of the Truffula trees in *The Lorax*), she still wants, or perhaps needs, the connection to happier times.

The two-hour drive is uneventful other than delays on the southern verge of Las Vegas, which seems to Arizona to be in a permanent state of construction. She pulls into the parking garage and drives past several spots until she finds one that she can confidently squeeze the F-150 into. She cracks the windows, puts Mojo on leash, and takes him for a short walk inside the parking garage. He pees on a car tire, albeit awkwardly with his wound. Arizona looks around to make sure nobody else sees.

Back at the truck, she pours water into a bowl, gives Mojo a treat, and pulls a couple of chew toys out from under the seat to remind him that they are there. "I'll be back soon, buddy," she says while admiring the beauty of his square boxer head—a *bucket head*, as Mom calls it. She kisses him on the forehead and locks the truck.

As she walks toward the visitor center, she thinks about what Lily said. *Take one imperfect person and put them with another imperfect per-*

son, and things get more complicated. Is that why she can show physical affection for Mojo but not for people? Because Mojo is perfect and people aren't? Mojo never complicates anything. *You'll never get better at relationships if you keep pushing people away.*

She goes into the visitor center, purchases a tour ticket, and catches the ten-minute introductory film. There is nothing in it that she doesn't already know. She assembles with the other ticket-holders and waits for the tour to begin.

"Good morning, everyone!" the guide says with a chipper voice. "Gather 'round, please. You're about to take a seventy-second elevator ride down five hundred thirty feet—that's about fifty stories—through the rock wall of the Black Canyon. We'll exit the elevator into a tunnel drilled in the 1930s for the construction of the dam, and then we'll take a short walk to our first stop, the Penstock Viewing Platform. Please, follow me."

The group follows the guide through the art deco elevator entrance. The seventy seconds feel like an eternity. She remembers saying to her parents that elevators must have gotten much faster since they built the dam. It isn't fair that even good memories hurt now.

Standing in the rear of the elevator, she distracts herself from the memories by surveying the other tourists. Her eyes scan from feet to face, one person at a time. She is assessing a middle-aged man two rows in front of her (sensible white walking shoes, jeans, blue nylon anorak) when he turns and intercepts her gaze. She averts her eyes. Was he watching her?

They debouch from the elevator like sheep from a paddock and follow the guide to the Penstock Viewing Platform, where he resumes his memorized lines. "Welcome to the Hoover Dam Power Plant. You are now on top of one of four thirty-foot-diameter pipes that can transport nearly ninety thousand gallons of water each second from Lake Mead to the dam's hydroelectric generators. This animated display shows some of the complexities of the construction of the dam and also how it operates. . . ."

After looking at the display, Arizona lowers her eyes and scours the floor for signs of Anorak Man. The sensible white walking shoes are ten feet away, on the other side of the group, but pointed directly toward her. Or are they just pointed at the display? After all, everyone on the other side of the group has to face her. Such is the nature of a circle.

After a few minutes the guide says, "Okay, now we'll take a shorter elevator ride up to the Nevada Power Plant balcony. Please, follow me."

The group follows the guide into and out of the elevator again. "This is the Nevada Power Plant balcony. The balcony gives you a panoramic view of the six-hundred-fifty-foot-long Nevada wing of the power plant and eight of the dam's seventeen massive generators. . . ."

The guide rattles on, the group trooping behind him. Arizona stays at the back of the pack, behind the blue anorak. Better to observe than to be observed.

The second half of the tour explores passageways within the dam itself. The group winds through tunnels to the inspection galleries, peers out of air vents in the downstream face of the dam, and feels the breeze rising from the river below. They navigate myriad other tunnels throughout the massive structure while the guide discusses the purpose of each. *Follow the arching corridor.*

Unfortunately, the tour doesn't help solve the puzzle. Arizona wonders if she missed key information while focused on Anorak Man and scolds herself for the distracting fixation. She sets off to examine the visitor center and other public areas.

Exhibit gallery. A speed tour.

Observation deck. Audio presentation about the dam and its surroundings.

Old exhibit building. The original visitor center, which had also been used as headquarters for soldiers protecting the dam during World War II.

Nevada Intake Towers. Audio presentation about the artwork incorporated into the towers and the role of the towers in power generation.

She takes detailed pictures everywhere for later reference. Investigator rather than tourist. But still she hasn't noticed anything revelatory, and there's no more sign of Anorak Man.

She's saved Monument Plaza for last, hoping that one or more things from the tour and exhibits might help her see something in it that she otherwise wouldn't have. She stops at the edge of the plaza to get her bearings.

She was here once before with her parents, but then it was just . . . artwork at a dam. Now it's steeped in mystery, every object humming with hidden meaning. She smiles as she takes it all in—winged figures, star map, compass rose. Tourists mill about, admiring the art, blissfully unaware that the objects of their admiration are actually clues to long-lost secrets, hidden in plain sight.

She looks at the most prominent features of the plaza, the winged figures. Officially known as the Winged Figures of the Republic, the striking bronze sculptures sit on the ends of a black arched base (made of diorite, she recalls) with the massive flagpole at the center. She takes pictures from every angle. Their parallel wings extend straight up thirty feet. *Always up extend the wings, a celestial semaphore.* The two statues appear to be identical, both male. That figures. She shakes her head and thinks of Lily again for some reason.

She walks to the flagpole and reads the inscription, written in an art deco font:

> IT IS FITTING THAT THE FLAG OF OUR COUNTRY SHOULD FLY HERE IN HONOR OF THOSE MEN WHO, INSPIRED BY A VISION OF LONELY LANDS MADE FRUITFUL, CONCEIVED THIS GREAT WORK AND OF THOSE OTHERS WHOSE GENIUS AND LABOR MADE THAT VISION A REALITY

Two words jump out. *Great Work.* Magnum opus.

She turns and looks at the raised octagonal base of the compass, visualizes a long sweeping arc—*the arc of the sky*—then looks down. Encircling the flagpole, out to a radius of about ten feet, are a number of concentric circles. She thinks of the concentric circles of a cipher disk, then the concentric circles of the labyrinth at Chartres, pointed out by Fulcanelli. Then of the poem.

Worlds whip 'round concentric rings.

Behind her is the flagpole, representing our sun—*one for the flare of summer's blaze.*

She walks along the arc of the sky until she reaches the outermost of the rings. There, at her feet, is the Little Dipper.

At the end of the dipper's handle is Polaris, the North Star—*one to guide you theretofore.*

Intended to represent the night sky, much of the floor is blank black stone peppered with constellations, classically drawn with lines connecting the stars.

As she continues along *the arc of the sky,* she thinks of Lily, of one of their walks, of imagining that if the stars were stones in a stream, she could walk across the sky without getting her feet wet.

Lily, like the flower.

She stops again, at Alcyone—*one for repose in waning days.*

In her mind's eye she sees the obtuse triangle that connects Polaris and Alcyone with the flagpole-sun.

She continues to the compass, framed by the twelve signs of the zodiac, which the alchemists used to represent the twelve steps of the Great Work. She walks counterclockwise around the compass, takes pictures of each zodiac sign. She pays particular attention to the areas where a small section of the arc of the sky intersects with the compass. Interesting.

She turns back toward the flagpole and again visualizes the long sweep of the arc of the sky.

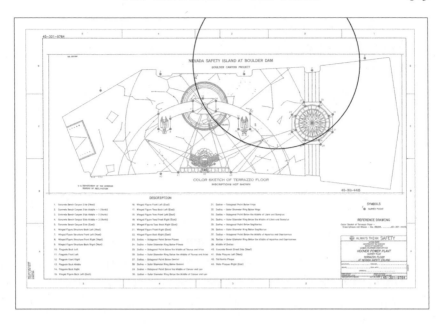

After creating the arc on the drawing of the plaza, she had desperately looked for meaning and noted that the arc is almost a mirror image of the arched base on which the winged figures sit. But now, standing here in person, without the clutter of all the other lines on the drawing, she sees how together the two opposing arcs form a common shape—a leaf, or . . . a petal.

On her phone she calls up a diagram of the plaza with 'the arc of the sky' circle and visualizes another arc tracing the arched base.

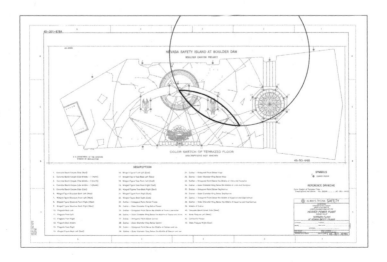

So many petals on the floor.
Petals of a flower.
A flower, like Lily.
A flower, on the floor of the Hoover House.
A flower, on the floor of a cathedral, at the center of a labyrinth.
A flower, on the terrazzo floor beneath her feet?
Is it possible?
She recalls the sixth verse of the poem.

Formed in Creator's loving hands, some say that when He made the lands
From shifting circles in the sands, He commanded who each was for:
Two for the angels aquiline, one for the beasts so anodyne,
With eagle as their king assigned, whence he was to rule and soar;
The closest two were made for man, our zealous penchant to explore;
The last His, for us to watch o'er.

Shifting circles. As in overlapping circles? That's exactly how the Flower of Life is drawn. Start with one circle, pick any point on it, and use that as the center of a second circle. Then each point where a circle crosses the first circle is used as the center of yet another circle. After seven circles, including the original one, you have the basic Flower of Life in the center.

In her mind's eye she sees a giant petal, on which perches one of the winged figures.
She looks at the other winged figure, pictures another petal.

The artist himself described the winged figures as having *the look of eagles.*

But they also look like angels.

Two for the angels aquiline.

She pictures a third petal, walks to the front edge of the star map, halfway between the winged figures, stops and looks down. She is standing on the Great Seal of the United States.

At its center is an eagle.

One for the beasts so anodyne, with eagle as their king assigned.

She walks past the second winged figure, then around the arched base until she is directly behind the flagpole.

Turns her back to the flagpole, pictures three more petals, and scans her surroundings.

She walks to where one of the petals meets the canyon wall, turns, and flops down onto a bench before her knees give out.

A bench. *The closest two were made for man.*

She sits motionless, trying to absorb the entirety of the revelation.

The arc of the sky is the circle that passes through the three stars.

But drawing that circle is just the first step.

The first of six overlapping circles that form a six-petal rosette.

The Flower of Life.

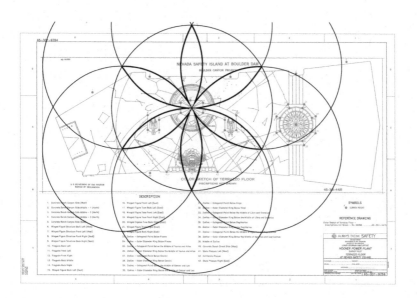

The entire Flower of Life maps perfectly onto Monument Plaza.

And five of the six petals appear to be occupied.

By two winged figures, an eagle, and two benches.

Holy fucking shit.

Thoughts and feelings spin around her head, like electrons around a nucleus.

Is the secret real?

Is it hidden here somewhere?

If so, where?

Did her dad know?

Did he die to protect it?

She is lost in the woods again. Last time, her father saved her. Who will save her this time?

A tear runs down her cheek, falls to the star map, lands on a constellation she doesn't recognize.

HIJKLMNOPQRSTUVWXY
L   KMN   WXY

NLHTHDTQGKHRHKCGKH
THE   E   RE   ER   RE

GTNLHBDMNNLHEHMNGQ
   THE   STTHE   ES T

NLUMCGKNDBSGOKLHYH
THS   RT   R EYE

VHDLGMNAGCHMMCUBU
E   H ST   ESS

LHPKHHNMOMGFNLDNNK
HEGREETS   S   TH   TTR

JKLMNOPQRSTUVWXYZ
            KMN   WXYZ

PART FIVE

I write so that this mighty secret
may not be lost in the mists of time,
nor perish in the torrents
of the years; but that it may shine with
the rays of the true light,
far from shipwreck and
from the multiplicity of fools.

—BASIL VALENTINE,
Tinctures of the Seven Metals

HTHDTQGKHRHKCGKH
E   E   RE   ER   RE

NLHBDMNNLHEHMNGQ
THE   STTHE EST   R E

UMCGKNDBSGOKFHYHTM
S   RT   R EYE   S

DLGMNAGCHMMCUBUFPNON
H ST   ESS   GT T

PKHHNMOMGFNLDNNKDTJOU
GREETS   S   TH   TTR

LHKIUIUFPEUKTFGKIHHIL
HER   G   R   R   E

HIJKLMNOPQRSTUVWXY
-             KMN   WXY

NLHTHDTQGKHRHKCGKH
THE   E   RE   ER   R E

GTNLHBDMNNLHEHMNGC
   THE   STTHE EST

NLUMCGKNDBSGOKFHYH
THS   RT   R EYE

VHDLGMNAGCHMMCUBUF
E   H ST   ESS

LHPKHHNMOMGFNLDNNK
HEGREETS   S   TH   TTR

JNLHKIUIUFPEUKTFGK

50

Rose of the Winds

- - - - - - - -

S HE SITS ON THE BENCH FOR ANOTHER MINUTE, GATHERING her thoughts. As the epiphany slowly releases its grip on her brain, she stands up, snaps a few more pictures, and heads for the parking garage.

She kisses Mojo and whispers, "I think we're closer to getting Mom back, buddy," as if testing the sound of the words, the veracity of the thought. He wags his little tail. He doesn't know what *closer* means, but he knows the word *Mom*. "I'm sorry you've been cooped up in the truck all day. We'll stop at the Crowbar for burgers, with bacon." Mojo wags his tail again. He knows the word *bacon,* too.

During the drive to Shoshone, she tries to process all she has learned. Tries to picture a bird's-eye view of Monument Plaza, with the Flower of Life superimposed. But visualizing while driving is like taking her eyes off the road—*safety first,* she reminds herself—so the visual analysis will have to wait until she's back in the trailer, looking at the drawings of Monument Plaza.

While at the plaza, she cracked much of verse six, although maybe not all of it. She thinks about the entirety of the poem.

Verses one to three: *De Re Metallica,* Herbert Hoover, a great secret of alchemy . . .

Verse four: The secret is hidden, Hoover House in Bodie . . .

Verse five: Hoover Dam, Chartres, so many petals on the floor . . .

Verse six: Monument Plaza and the Flower of Life . . .

Verse seven: The arc of the sky, more Monument Plaza references . . . and?

What is she missing?

And then there are the questions that make her head spin—questions about Dad.

So many questions. So few answers.

Her phone rings, and she glances to see who's calling. Sam Yeats, the turncoat. She wouldn't take Sam's call even if she wasn't driving.

By the time they get to the Crowbar Cafe, she needs a break. She is all thunk out. Or maybe it's her feelings, rather than thoughts, that have worn her out? She can't tell the difference.

She ties Mojo's leash to an unoccupied table out front, swings open the squeaky screen door, and steps inside. The aroma of greasy food settles over her like a favorite shirt just out of the dryer. She orders two burgers with bacon, retrieves Mojo, and they poke around the pocket-sized museum while they wait.

"Here you go, miss," says the waitress, who doubles as bartender, as she hands the grease-stained paper bag to Arizona.

"Thank you," Arizona says.

Back at the truck, she checks the time on her phone and sees that she has voicemail. She taps PLAY.

"Hi, Arizona. It's Sam. I need to speak to you as soon as possible. I have some things to tell you. I haven't been completely forthright with you but for reasons I hope you'll understand. Please call me and give me a chance to explain. I hope I'll hear from you soon, before it's too late."

Haven't been completely forthright. Talk about an understatement.

Arizona tosses her phone onto the passenger seat and starts the truck. Less than twenty minutes later she and Mojo are eating burgers inside the Airstream. Just the burger patty for Mojo, plus the bacon, of course.

It's been a long day for both of them—busy and emotional for Arizona, boring for Mojo. After dinner they take a walk through the sand and gravel washes, wind their way between the aromatic creosote bush, silver sagebrush, and desert holly saltbush. After a minute of stiffness, or soreness, Mojo seems to limber up, then marks the swollen stem of a desert trumpet as if it were a fire hydrant. Arizona stops to revel in the ornate skeleton of a dead cholla branch, hollow like the bones of the red-tailed hawk that screeches high overhead. The sun has reclined, bathing the eastern mountains in warm canted light, flattening the western ones into silhouettes.

Back at the Airstream, Mojo curls up on the daybed and Arizona sits down at the table. She's still thinking about Dad, but it's so fatiguing that she pushes those thoughts away for now. The feelings linger like a bad taste in her mouth, confused and conflicting, but at least she can distract her mind, or so she hopes. She imports her Hoover Dam pictures to her MacBook, then looks at her drawing of the arc of the sky. She creates another copy of the drawing and adds more arcs— more circles—all with the same radius.

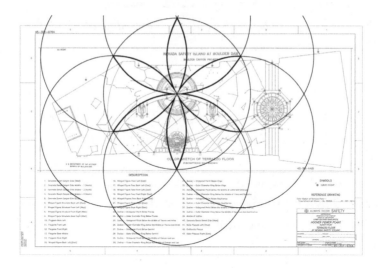

A bigger-than-life Flower of Life. And, sure enough, the winged figures, eagle, and two benches all rest on petals.

She shakes her head as if she still can't believe it. Questions she asked herself at Monument Plaza return.

Is the secret real?

Is it hidden there somewhere?

If so, where?

She reads the whole poem again and confirms that nothing in the first five verses seems to be nagging at her. But there's something about those last two verses.

> *Formed in Creator's loving hands, some say that when He made the lands*
> *From shifting circles in the sands, He commanded who each was for:*
> *Two for the angels aquiline, one for the beasts so anodyne,*
> *With eagle as their king assigned, whence he was to rule and soar;*
> *The closest two were made for man, our zealous penchant to explore;*
> *The last His, for us to watch o'er.*

> *The arc of the sky draws your gaze; one for repose in waning days,*
> *One for the flare of summer's blaze, and one to guide you theretofore.*
> *Worlds whip 'round concentric rings, summers fall and winters spring,*
> *But always up extend the wings, a celestial semaphore.*
> *By that Heaven that bends above us—by that God we both adore—*
> *The secrets are safe forevermore.*

The last His, for us to watch o'er. At Monument Plaza, she thought that five of the six petals were occupied. But she was wrong. There it is, right in the poem. The last petal, directly behind the flagpole, is for the Creator.

That completes verse six, but what about the last verse?

Lines one and two give us the arc of the sky.

Line three, the concentric rings on the star map, around the flagpole-sun.

Line four, the winged figures.

Line five was borrowed from "The Raven."

Line six just says the secrets are safe.

She rereads lines five and six several more times but gleans nothing. Unless . . .

Her thoughts go back to the first two ciphers, which seemed to lead to two dead ends—Malachi's grave and the survey marker—until she *combined* them.

Maybe line six doesn't just say that the secrets are safe but, combined with line five, it says *where* the secrets are safe.

Then *by that Heaven* could be a reference to the star map.

And *by that God* could be a reference to . . . the Creator? To the sixth petal.

Is that where the final secret lies?

She recalls Fulcanelli's *The Mystery of the Cathedrals*, where she first learned of the Language of the Birds. And where it was also referred to as the Language of the Gods.

This is crazy, she thinks. *Alchemy is just bullshit, a cosmic joke with a bad punch line.*

A phrase and a question drop into her head with a loud thud, like a large book falling in a quiet library. Deliberate obfuscation. It was the alchemists' modus operandi. What if they had sullied their own reputations just to hide their secrets? It would be the greatest obfuscation of all time.

In which case, the secrets of alchemy would be . . . real?

She thinks of Herbert Hoover, who was no fool. By all accounts he was a highly intelligent man. If he believed that the secret was too dangerous to expose—which seems irrefutable now—then maybe she can't expose it, either? But she has to expose it to save Mom.

Is she damned if she shares information and damned if she doesn't? Or, more to the point, is the world damned if she does and her mom damned if she doesn't?

There has to be another way. She closes her eyes to think. Breathes in and out. Once. Twice. She pictures the *Gunga Din* campsite in the Alabama Hills. She is at the fire ring, holding a hammer.

Her phone rings. So much for thinking. It's Sam Yeats again. Arizona feels her temperature rise as she pictures Sam and Gordon talking in Bodie.

She hesitates, then answers. "I saw you and Gordon together in Bodie. So whatever you want to say, you should probably just save your breath."

"I understand. I wondered whether you had seen us together."

"So why are we talking?"

"Please hear me out. Things aren't what they seem. I'm not actually a park ranger."

"No shit." She thinks about hanging up, visualizes slamming an old-fashioned phone into its cradle.

"Arizona, I'm an undercover federal agent."

"Like FBI? Bullshit."

"Secret Service, actually."

"Double bullshit."

"Gordon has a boss, who arrogantly calls himself the Adept. I've been trying to get him to expose himself, to come out of hiding. It turns out he came to Bodie unannounced, to get the box, but he left before I even knew he was there."

"I'll give you an A for effort, but I still don't believe you. I'm going to hang up now."

"No, wait! Help me set a trap for him, Arizona. Help me and we can free your mom and this will all be over."

"Why would you be coming to me now and not when this all started? Just for the sake of argument."

"Because they're getting close, and I only have one chance left. I think the Adept will show himself once more if he believes he can retrieve the secret safely. After that he'll be gone. You're their conduit. I need you to give him the bait."

"Why would I possibly believe you? Why would I trust you?"

"I'm not asking you to trust me. I'm asking you to *think*. If this is all a lie on my part, some kind of elaborate ruse, what would be my endgame? How could what I'm asking you to do possibly benefit the people you think I'm working with?"

Arizona is silent, so Sam speaks again. "And what do you have to lose?"

Arizona takes a breath. Then another. "I don't know. I need to think."

"I appreciate that," says Sam. "Maybe that's a start. Please consider what I've said, and do it quickly. Time is of the essence."

Click.

Her head is spinning from circular thinking. Sam's question is a good one—if she's lying, what's her endgame?

Arizona thinks back to just before Sam called. She had closed her eyes to think. To think about another way. A way to avoid exposing the secret but still save Mom.

She closes her eyes again. Images from the last several days run through her mind.

She sees herself at the *Gunga Din* campsite in the Alabama Hills, about to hammer the GPS tracker she found on the Ural. She thinks of magicians, sleight of hand, misdirection.

She remembers sitting here in the Airstream, puzzling over the unencrypted poem, "Halcyon Days." The first two lines of the second verse. An upturned vessel becomes a foundering ship rather than Pandora's box. Artful misdirection—an apt description of the writings of alchemists.

And later still, looking at the final poem with Lily. *Elements, but not those you think, delineate the contour.* More misdirection.

Misdirection. Deliberate obfuscation. What better to use against wannabe alchemists?

But how?

She feels another itch, another nagging thought. She looks at the last verse again. It points to two of the prominent features of the plaza—the star map and the winged figures. But no mention of the compass?

She returns to her arc of the sky drawing, zooms in so she can see the arc from flagpole through compass:

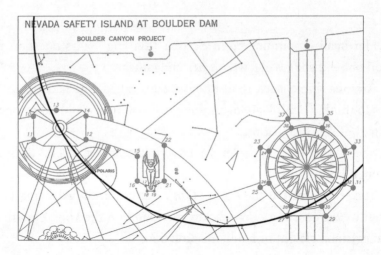

The arc goes right through two of the numbered points on the compass, 27 and 32. She notices the small arrow on the inner ring of the compass that indicates north, just below point 36. The two points that the arc passes through appear to be due south and due east. Interesting.

She opens her notebook and writes.

Switches to her computer. Downloads a map of Lake Mead and scours it.

Back to her notebook.

Back to computer.

Draws a line on the Lake Mead map.

Writes in her notebook.

Creates a new document on her computer.

Computer to notebook.

Notebook to computer.

When she finishes, there is still one more thing to do, if she can summon the courage. She picks up her phone.

"Hello?"

"Lily, it's Arizona. I wanted to apologize, and I could use your help if you're still willing."

"You're asking for help? Are you sure?"

"Yes, I'm sure. And I really am sorry."

Half an hour on, they've caught up and hatched a rough plan.

But Arizona still has another phone call to make.

"Hey, it's Arizona."

"Well, hello. It's good to hear from you, young lady."

"Thanks. I, uh, have a story to tell you. And a favor to ask . . ."

AN HOUR PASSES BEFORE she hangs up. She feels empty, physically and emotionally drained. But the work is mostly done anyway. She turns off the lights and curls up on the bed with Mojo, who, with Arizona's help, had moved there some time ago.

On the table, her notebook is still open:

> Compass. Rose of the Winds.
> Direction. Misdirection.

> Old Senator Mill. Senator Sargent.
> Callville. Anson Call. Port of Call.

> Basil Valentine. Perfect.

> This might actually work.

51

The Multiplicity of Fools

T HE EARLY MORNING SUN, STILL LOW ON THE EASTERN horizon, shines through the windows of the Airstream. Arizona has just finished feeding Mojo breakfast when her phone buzzes and dances on the counter. Blocked number. It's about time.

"What?" she says.

"Any progress on the map?"

"No."

"What about on the poem?"

"No."

"No progress at all?"

"Some."

"On what?"

Arizona hesitates. She has rehearsed the biggest lie, wants to get it right. "There was something else in the bamboo tube. One last cipher."

"What! Do you think we're playing games here? How do you know it's the last one? Upload it."

"Cipher text or plain text?"

"You've already decoded it?"

"Yes. I've explained in writing." She hangs up and uploads her message. But she is immediately overcome by an array of symptoms— sweaty palms, heavy chest, muscle aches, chills.

What if it doesn't work?

What if they know it's all a lie?

What if something goes wrong?
She has caught a case of the dreads.

GORDON CHECKS THE DRAFTS folder and clicks on the new message. He doesn't notice the lack of sarcastic salutation.

> Below is the decoded fourth and final cipher, which was
> hidden with the map in Bodie.

———————————

I write so that this mighty secret may not be lost in the mists
    of time,
Nor perish in the torrents of the years;
But that it may shine with the rays of the true light,
Far from shipwreck and from the multiplicity of fools.

You have come too far to founder now on the skerries of this
    closing rhyme;
Sergeant from the first sailed with privateers,
From the doomed port of call to the old miller's bight,
To sepulcher secrets where nevermore the raven mewls.

Only an adept can divine the secrets of a language so sublime.
The heavens show the way to new frontiers;
Rose of the winds, beyond the twins, there set your sight,
And at long last silence their derisions and ridicules.

———————————

The words *this closing rhyme* clearly indicate that this is the final poem. The entire first verse is a quote from Basil Valentine's *Tinctures of the Seven Metals*. Before I elaborate on the meaning of the rest, I need to share what I learned from the third cipher.

Gordon reads on, amazed, as Arizona lays out the logic for drawing the arc of the sky on the floor of Monument Plaza, with the sun, Alcyone, and Polaris as its key points.

When you add the arc of the sky to a drawing of Monument Plaza (originally called Safety Island), you get this:

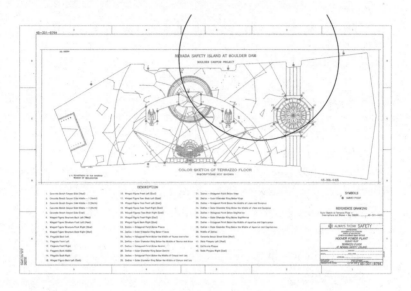

There is one other line of the third cipher that provides an additional clue:

> *Counsel we sought but they just fought, like a lodestone cleft in two.*

Lodestone should bring to mind Petrus Peregrinus de Maricourt, who invented the compass. Note that the arc of the sky cleaves the compass in two. Zooming in:

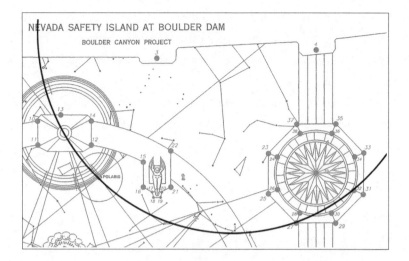

The arc passes directly through two of the numbered points on the compass, 27 and 32. The compass is framed by the twelve signs of the zodiac, and the descriptions of numbers 27 and 32 are:

27. Zodiac—Octagonal Point below Gemini
32. Zodiac—Outer Diameter Ring below Virgo

Those are the key clues in the third cipher.

Now that we have some context, we can return to the fourth cipher. We'll start with the third verse:

> *Only an adept can divine the secrets of a language so sublime.*
> *The heavens show the way to new frontiers;*
> *Rose of the winds, beyond the twins, there set your sight,*
> *And at long last silence their derisions and ridicules.*

The heavens show the way to new frontiers refers to the star map and the arc of the sky (duh).

Rose of the winds is another name for a compass. Recall that the arc passes through the compass below Gemini and Virgo. So we sight our compass beyond the twins of Gemini, at the second point where the arc crosses the compass, below Virgo.

The final clues necessary to find what you seek can be found in the second verse.

However, I will not explain those clues until you bring my mom to Monument Plaza and release her to me. We will meet at the compass, at a time of my choosing.

P.S. You're still an asshole.

52

The Exchange

A T NOON THE NEXT DAY, ARIZONA SITS ON A BENCH AT
Monument Plaza. *The closest two were made for man.* It's a sunny
day, as it often is on the Nevada–Arizona border, and the wings of one
of the winged figures cast shade across the bench. Her pack is slung
loosely over one shoulder, rolled documents sticking out from the top.
She has a clear view of the compass and everything behind the arched
base on which the winged figures sit. With her back to the canyon
wall, nobody can sneak up on her. The plaza is busy with tourists, and
a security vehicle is parked less than fifty feet from the compass. It's a
good setup for the exchange.

She sees Gordon and Mom as they approach the stairs between the
compass and the canyon wall. Sam was right—the Adept isn't here. Or
at least he's not showing himself. *It's the smart way to do it,* Arizona
thinks. Why risk getting caught at the exchange, when you can keep
to the shadows till your henchman has the final clue in hand?

Gordon holds Mom above the elbow, like a blind woman being
guided, but with a tight grip. His other hand is in his coat pocket, close
to Mom's back. They stop before the first stair and scan the area like a
family looking for a lost child. They climb the five steps, stop and scan
again. Arizona smiles at the sight of her mom, stands up and steps
away from the bench, out of the shadow of the winged figure. They see
her and start moving toward her. She raises her hand like a crossing

guard stopping traffic, palm facing them, then points to the compass, indicating that she will join them there.

In her head she has already run to her mom. If it were only that easy. Her legs are rubber, every step an effort, like a toddler learning to walk. She wonders if she looks as unsteady as she feels. She almost wobbles into a gray-haired gentleman making his way toward a bench. It is the longest fifty feet of her life. She stops five feet from her mom and Gordon.

"Let go of her arm," Arizona says. She looks into Gordon's eyes and doesn't look away.

"First, I believe you have something for me," he says. He raises his caterpillar eyebrows but doesn't let go.

Arizona's eyes are still locked on his. "Let go of her, and take your other hand out of your pocket."

"Give me what I came for. Until that happens, why would we give up our leverage?"

He said *we*. Is the Adept here somewhere after all? Or is Gordon just a good soldier, speaking for the cause?

"There are two reasons," Arizona says. "First, that was the deal and I, unlike you, am trustworthy. But second, and more important, I'm not alone."

"I think you're bluffing."

"Feel free to test that theory," Arizona says. "Part of me would really like to watch you die."

"What if I'm not alone, either?"

"I don't see how it would change the equation, assuming you want the two things I expect."

"And what two things might those be?"

"Your precious secret," she says, "and to not die today."

"I'm afraid you've overplayed your hand," he says.

"Listen up, Deputy Dork," she says. "Either hand my mom over to me right now, unharmed, or things stand to get messy."

"I applaud your tenacity," he says, "but I've already called your bluff."

"You think I'm bluffing? Do you see the man I passed as I walked over here, seated on that bench?" She motions with her head. "I'm pretty sure he sees you."

Gordon looks over at the man with gray hair, who has his hands inside his own jacket pockets and stares directly back.

"I assure you that he knows how to use what's in his pockets," Arizona says.

Gordon's eyes return to Arizona, but he doesn't let go. "So, we have a standoff," he says.

"No, we really don't," says a female voice from behind Gordon.

Gordon starts to turn.

"Don't turn around."

Something jabs him in the back.

"It's a bluff," Gordon says. "That's too big to be a gun."

"You're half right," says Lily. "The shotgun is inside my telescoping fishing-rod case, and you owe me a new case since I had to cut a hole for my trigger finger."

"Still think I'm bluffing?" Arizona says. "I shot one of your guys before, with that same gun. Do you really think we'll hesitate this time? And especially if it's you?"

Gordon doesn't reply, as if considering.

"I'm still waiting for you to release my mother," Arizona says.

"How do I know you'll hand over the final clues if I release her?"

"Because I gave my word. Beyond that, you have no guarantees. It's entirely possible that none of us will walk away from this. Except my dog, who you already shot once anyway. Oh, and your boss, since he's too cowardly to show up."

Gordon squints, suspicious, and Arizona realizes her mistake.

"What makes you think I have a boss?"

"You strike me as more henchman than inspirational leader."

"They shot Mojo?" says Mom. "What kind of assholes shoot a dog? Is he okay?"

"The kind standing next to you," Arizona says. "But Mojo will be fine."

"Okay, I'll play along and release her," Gordon says. "But my hand stays in my pocket."

Arizona nods and he releases Mom, who rushes to her daughter and embraces her. Arizona hugs Mom with one arm as she holds her pack and keeps her eyes on Gordon.

"Mom, I don't feel comfortable with you being this close to him, so please give us a little more room. But don't go anywhere—I don't want to lose you again."

"I won't go anywhere, honey," Mom says with a smile as she steps a few paces away.

Arizona swings the pack off her shoulder, pulls the rolled documents out, and steps up to the compass. Gordon follows, hand still in pocket.

"Here's a summary of the final clues," she says as she hands him a piece of paper. "Read it, and then I have one last document for you."

He takes the paper and reads it:

Recall the second verse of the final cipher:

You have come too far to founder now on the skerries
    of this closing rhyme;
Sergeant from the first sailed with privateers,
From the doomed port of call to the old miller's bight,
To sepulcher secrets where nevermore the raven mewls.

The middle two lines are the key.

In line two, *the first* refers to the first cipher. Therefore, *Sergeant from the first* is Senator Sargent, who was buried in Pioneer Cemetery.

Doomed port of call refers to Callville, which was a settlement, fort, and steamboat port on the Colorado River. It was established in 1864 by Anson Call and was submerged under 400 feet of water when the Hoover Dam created Lake Mead.

The old miller's bight is the final clue. In addition to being a loop of rope, a bight is also a curve in a coastline, river, or other geographical feature.

Recall the following line:

Rose of the winds, beyond the twins, there set your sight . . .

Also recall that *rose of the winds* is another name for a compass and that the arc of the sky passes through two points of the compass, below Gemini and Virgo. *Beyond the twins* is obviously a reference to the twins of Gemini, so we sight our compass beyond Gemini, at the second point where the arc crosses the compass, below Virgo.

Follow that bearing from Callville to where the secrets have been sepulchered and *where nevermore the raven mewls.*

Notice the small arrow on the inner ring of the compass that indicates north, just below point 36. If you look closely at the drawing, where the arc of the sky crosses the compass below Virgo, you'll discover that it's due east. Therefore, one might think that from Callville we would sight due east. However, the compass at Monument Plaza is aligned with magnetic north, not true north. Unfortunately, the earth's magnetic poles are not constant, so magnetic declination for a given location varies over time (duh). The 1926 topo map that was hidden in Bodie specifies a magnetic declination of 16 degrees east, but a recent NOAA marine chart for Lake Mead shows it as low as 13 degrees 15 minutes east.

I found something at a declination of approximately 15 degrees south of east (105 degrees from true north) that fits with all the other clues in the final cipher.

Gordon finishes reading and says, "What did you find?"

Arizona unrolls a larger document, a map, and holds it open on top of the compass. There is a diagonal line drawn across the lower panel.

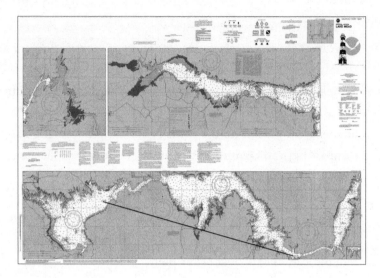

"This is that NOAA marine chart for Lake Mead," Arizona says. "Marine charts are particularly useful for aquatic environments for numerous reasons, including that they show things that are submerged."

Gordon's eyes widen.

"Here's Callville," she says, pointing to the left end of the line, "shown as *Fort Callville* on the map, and this line is one hundred five degrees from true north."

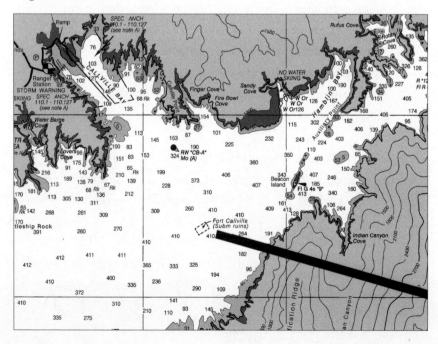

"So follow this line *from the doomed port of call to the old miller's bight* and remember that *Sergeant from the first* refers to *Senator* Sargent and that bight is also a curve in a coastline or river."

She runs her index finger along the line and taps the end point.

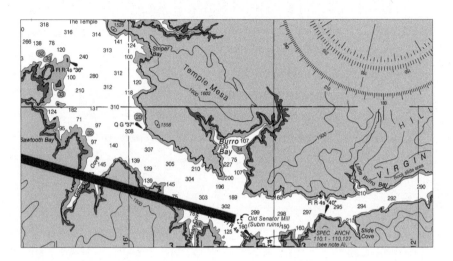

He nods. "You're an impressive young lady."

"Use it in ill health," she says.

He lets out an arrogant chuckle, removes his hand from his pocket, and rolls up the map.

He looks into Arizona's eyes.

She looks straight back. For a moment she wonders if this is really the end, if he'll just walk away and take the bait to his precious leader. "It's time for you to leave," she says. "Go now, and never mess with my family again."

He pauses, his eyes still on hers, then turns and walks away.

Arizona lets out a ten-second sigh as her mom embraces her again. The gray-haired man approaches. Lily lowers the fishing-rod case.

"Lily, Marty, this is my mom, Amelia. Mom, these are my friends, Lily and Marty."

"You've been making friends?" Mom says as she smiles and extends her hand to each of them. "It's very nice to meet you both. Please, call me Amy."

"Nice to meet you, too," says Lily.

"The pleasure is ours," Marty says. "You have an extraordinary daughter."

"Yes," Mom says, "yes, I do. I'm curious what you were going to do if he didn't let me go."

"I'm afraid I would have had to use this to the best of my ability," Marty says. He reaches into one of his jacket pockets. Pulls out a whistle.

"Formidable," says Mom.

"Indeed," Marty says with a smile.

Lily stands next to Arizona, takes her hand.

Tourists and a warm breeze murmur, like bees on a flowering hedgerow. Arizona hears only her heart.

53

Over and Out

TWENTY-FOUR HOURS LATER, TWO DIVERS SURFACE NEAR a chartered boat moored above the submerged ruins of Old Senator Mill. It is what the agents have been waiting for. Two teams speed in, one from Virgin Canyon to the east and one from Temple Basin to the northwest. Each team comprises two patrol boats running side by side and a helicopter one hundred feet above the boats. It is a classic flanking operation, and there is nowhere for the Adept to go.

Secret Service agents, led by Sam Yeats, board the boat without incident, zip-tie wrists behind backs, read Miranda rights, and escort them onto two of the four patrol boats.

Just as Sam anticipated, the chance to safely retrieve the prize was enough to lure the Adept into the open.

"What did you find down there?" Sam asks him.

"Nothing," he says, seething.

"That's probably good for you," she says. "Otherwise, we'd have to charge you with tampering with government property, too."

"Or maybe illegal salvage," another agent jokes.

IN BODIE, TWO HELICOPTERS and a dozen black SUVs move in from multiple directions. All roads have been barricaded, and the helicopters maintain surveillance from the air. It would have been almost as swift as the simultaneous operation on Lake Mead, but a couple of men try to flee on foot before realizing it is hopeless. Everyone is in custody within ten minutes. No shots are fired.

It is over.

Sam calls the family with the news and schedules a debriefing for the next day.

Arizona makes one last entry in her notebook.

> Sam says the guy I shot is going to be okay.
> Good. They don't deserve death.
> Prison. A cage.
>
> Time for a new notebook. This one is full.
> Time to be with my family, Mojo and Mom. And my friends.
> Over and out, for now.

54

The Debriefing

ARIZONA AND HER MOM TAKE SEATS IN AGING OFFICE CHAIRS that face a metal desk. Sam, who sits behind the desk, has turned off the fluorescent lights for Arizona, leaving the room lit only by natural light from the open awning windows. Sounds of traffic drift in from the street below. Mojo curls up on the institutional flooring between Arizona and Mom, who both wear dazed expressions, still emotionally processing all that has happened.

"Okay," says Sam. "You probably have lots of questions, so fire away."

Arizona and Mom look at each other, both granting tacit permission for the other to go first.

"Okay, I'll go," says Arizona. She turns to Sam. "Your last name isn't Yeats, is it?"

"No," Sam says with a chuckle. "My last name is McKee. My relation to W. B. Yeats was a cover to help me infiltrate the group. You see, W. B. Yeats was a member of the Hermetic Order of the Golden Dawn."

Arizona nods. "I probably should have made that connection."

"Other well-known people were purportedly members, too," Sam says.

"Yeah," says Arizona, "Sir Arthur Conan Doyle and the mystic Arthur Edward Waite, who among other things was the co-creator of a popular deck of tarot cards."

"Also Bram Stoker, author of *Dracula*," says Sam, "if memory serves. But I assume you have questions more pressing than that."

"Yes," Arizona says. But she hesitates, afraid to ask the question. Two slow breaths, in and out. "Did they kill my dad?"

"We obviously wondered that, too. They admit to surveilling your family, and even to following your dad into Titus Canyon because they thought he was there to retrieve the box, but they claim they didn't kill him."

"Of course they'd say that, though," says Mom. "They wouldn't want a murder charge added to the list."

"Fair enough. However, the truth is that we haven't been able to find evidence that his death was anything other than an accident."

"So we don't know for sure?" says Arizona.

"No, and I'm sorry. I know that's probably not what you want to hear. I expect it would be easier to blame them rather than bad luck."

"Maybe," says Mom, "but only easier in the short term. Anger isn't exactly a healthy thing to carry around for long, if at all."

Arizona nods but looks at the floor, at a distracting crack in the tile. She does want someone to blame for her dad's death, but maybe Mom is right.

Sam waits patiently.

Arizona raises her head. "Why did all this happen? Why us?"

"That's a great question. I wondered that myself, and ultimately you provided the answer."

"I did? How?" says Arizona.

"By getting the Adept to expose himself. We now know his identity—Peter Emerson. Once we learned that, the pieces of the puzzle finally came together. Most of them, anyway."

"I don't understand," says Mom.

"Peter Emerson is the son of Margaret Emerson, who I think you both know as Maggie."

"Maggie?" Arizona says. "Who worked with my dad?"

"That's right. She was a colleague and friend of your father at the USGS, and they kept in touch after her retirement. The catalyst for all of this was actually a journal that Maggie had and that Peter found."

"A journal?" says Mom.

"Yes, this is going to sound a little crazy, but bear with me."

"Sure," says Arizona, "we're getting used to crazy."

"No doubt." Sam smiles. "The journal is incomplete, with a large number of pages torn out. It was purportedly written by someone who worked at the NSA, the National Security Agency."

"What?" says Arizona.

"The author of the journal claims to have found documents that were redacted in such a way as to create a hidden message and two ciphers. Specifically, the documents related to the artwork at Hoover Dam's Monument Plaza."

"What was the hidden message?"

"Twelve cryptic sentences that seem to tell a tale of someone who stumbles onto a great secret." Sam flips papers, then reads her notes. "*The ancient key to interpreting and understanding the Great Work.*"

Arizona nods. "You said two ciphers. But there were three that I had to solve."

"That's right. The first two ciphers, which were hidden within re-dactions of the drawings for Monument Plaza, were still in the jour-nal, along with their solutions. That's where the Adept, Peter Emerson, got them. The third cipher wasn't in the journal, at least not after pages were torn out, but it was mentioned in the journal. As was the box in Titus Canyon. And Bodie."

"Bodie. So that's how they knew that something was there?" Ari-zona says.

"Correct, but they didn't know where exactly. And you beat them to it."

"The map in the Hoover House."

Sam nods. "You asked why all of this happened to your family. So, here's one possibility. We don't know where Maggie got the journal, but—"

Arizona interrupts. "What do you mean you don't know? What does Maggie say?"

Sam sighs. "Unfortunately, we can't ask her. She died earlier this year. She fell down a flight of stairs and broke her neck. However, in light of Peter's actions, local authorities may open an investigation into the circumstances surrounding her death."

"Are you saying that Peter might have killed her?" says Arizona.

"We don't know, but it does seem possible."

"My God," says Mom.

"Indeed," says Sam. "As I was saying, we don't know where Maggie got the journal. But one possibility is that it was written by your father."

"But . . ." Arizona can't form a thought, much less words. She takes two deep breaths and tries again. "But you said the journal was by someone who claimed to be in the NSA. My dad was a cartographer. Are you saying he was a spy?"

"No, but what if he wrote it as fiction? I understand he had considered a career as a writer."

Arizona's jaw slackens as the statement hangs in the stagnant office air. There's no way this was just a story. After all she's done, all she's seen, it isn't possible. When she finally speaks, it comes out as a whisper. "What about the box in Titus Canyon? And the map in the Hoover House? Those are real."

"Yes," says Sam, "but what if I told you that we analyzed the physical evidence—the box, the scroll inside, the bamboo tube, and the map—and none of it dates back to Hoover's time. What if I told you it's all just about twenty years old?"

Arizona feels her pulse pounding in her neck. She scrabbles for more evidence, hears her voice rising as she speaks. "And the booklet, all the alchemy references and mystical language? Are you saying that's a fake, too?"

"No, the booklet's real. And it's quite a bizarre artifact, no question. My guess is your dad came across it somehow and thought the same thing, so he used it as the jumping-off point for his story."

"And he . . . what, wrote this imaginary journal, planted all this fake evidence?"

"It's a possibility. And if he did write it, he might have sent it to Maggie just to solicit her opinion. There are some reasons to believe that it's his invention."

"Such as?" says Arizona.

"Your dad had numerous interests that are also key elements of the journal and the ciphers. Numerous enough to make one wonder if they're just coincidences."

"How so?"

"Well, the ciphers borrow from some of your dad's favorite authors, who I understand became some of your favorite authors, too."

Arizona thinks back to the ciphers. "Lewis Carroll. Robert Louis Stevenson. Edgar Allan Poe."

Sam nods.

"But they were all hugely popular in their day," says Mom. "That's hardly conclusive."

"True. But what about the ghost towns, maps, and survey markers? Your dad loved ghost towns, right? And maps and survey markers were squarely within his area of expertise. And then there are the prime numbers, old-school poems, and a journal, for that matter. All interests of your dad. Also, he came from the world of science and your mom from the world of art. I understand that he loved the nexus of those two worlds. The art at Monument Plaza is one such nexus of science and art. Alchemy is another."

Arizona stares in disbelief. "Come on. You really expect us to believe that he did something this elaborate, just for *fun*?" She's on the verge of shouting by the time the sentence is over, but even as she says it, the doubt creeps in. Creating puzzles wasn't exactly out of character for her dad. Still, this seems about five bridges too far.

"Arizona, I understand that hearing these things might be very frustrating. I'm sorry. But what's the alternative? That Herbert Hoover discovered the secret to eternal life? That he built the entire Hoover Dam to power some alchemical process? I know you're a fan of Sherlock Holmes, so you probably know his famous dictum—*When you have eliminated the impossible, whatever remains, however improbable, must be the truth.*"

Arizona hesitates while she processes all that Sam has said. "The box seemed older than that to me. Can I see it?"

"No, sorry. It's all been logged in as evidence."

"And the Adept, Peter Emerson, believed everything in the journal was real?" says Mom.

Sam nods. "The combination of the journal and the physical evidence wove a convincing tale." She looks to Arizona. "You saw that for yourself." She pauses. "I can't say too much about Peter, you understand. But it seems that he is highly distrustful of government and prone to believing conspiracy theories. For someone like him, this was a spark to a flame."

Sam goes on. "Conspiracy theories can be incredibly comforting. They let us believe that there's pattern and purpose behind the world around us. They let us build stories and narratives and attribute events to logic and cause and effect. The truth is much scarier. Our lives are ruled by random chance, fate, luck—whatever you choose to call it. And luck can be good or bad, serendipitous or calamitous. The event that set all this in motion—your dad crashing in Titus Canyon, while they were watching your family—was, quite possibly, coincidence. Just bad luck, with tragic consequences."

Arizona is staring at the floor. She looks up at Sam, opens her mouth to speak, then closes it. Lowers her head again, diverts her attention to the stupid crack in the floor.

"I'm sorry, Arizona. I know that's hard to accept. But it's a crazy universe, and strange things happen. Flip a coin enough times, and it'll eventually come up heads fifty times in a row."

But Arizona isn't resisting anymore. She feels . . . deflated. Like an empty balloon.

Her mom reaches out and takes her hand. Arizona clutches it tightly.

"I've kept you here long enough," Sam says, "but I do have one last question before you go." She is studying Arizona.

"Sure," Arizona says.

"Just curious, but did you ever solve the last piece of the puzzle? Figure out where the secret was supposedly hidden?"

Arizona hesitates, searching for the right answer, then shakes her head. "But if there's no secret, nothing to find, then it doesn't really matter, does it?"

Sam looks at her for an extra second, then smiles. "I guess you're right."

Sam rises from her chair. Arizona and Mom follow suit.

"Conspiracy theories can be seductive, Arizona," Sam says, "but don't let yourself get pulled in. The bad guys are in prison. Your mom is home safe. The story is over, with a happy ending. Forget all this craziness. Let it go. Go live your life. Go be happy."

Arizona nods.

Sam extends her hand. "Thank you. To say you've both been helpful would be an understatement. And again, I'm very sorry for your loss."

They shake Sam's hand.

"Let's go home," Mom says. "I understand we have some cleaning up to do."

55·

Epilogue

Six months later

THE AIRSTREAM IS PARKED IN THE SAME PLACE IT WAS ON Dad's fateful morning. The last place they saw him seems like a fitting spot to spread the last of his ashes.

It's springtime in Death Valley, and the winter rains have created a rare superbloom. The creosote bushes are covered with small yellow flowers. Large pink blossoms adorn the prickly pear cactus.

Arizona and Mom are building a small rock garden for the ashes, a place to come and visit with their memories of him. Arizona is mostly quiet, wandering around, looking for exactly the right rocks, admiring the surprising geological diversity of the desert, as Dad would have. Mojo, fully recovered now, wanders through the sandy wash next to camp, short boxer nose to the ground, looking for lizards or the elusive desert hare.

Mom is crouched down, positioning rocks just so, when Arizona puts a hand on her shoulder. She turns and looks up at her daughter.

"Mom, maybe I should go to school somewhere closer? I could commute and live at home with you. I hate the thought of you being alone."

Mom stands, pulls Arizona into a hug, then steps back and looks into her eyes, hands on her daughter's shoulders. "That's sweet, honey, but who's being overprotective now?" She smiles. "I'll be fine. Stanford is only three hours away, and I'm a grown woman. And it's where you belong. It's what your dad would've wanted."

Arizona covers Mom's hands with her own. "Are you sure?"

"Yes, honey, I'm sure."

LATER, IN THE SLANTING light of late afternoon, Arizona sets up camp chairs as Mom puts the finishing touch on the rock garden—a small flamingo sculpture she made out of wood and bare wire (plastic wouldn't be environmentally friendly). In the distance, dust rises from the dirt road. As the dust cloud approaches, it's preceded by an old VW camper van that is going a little too fast. The van circles and stops a short distance from the Airstream. Lily hops out, walks around the van, and opens the door for Gus. Mojo comes to see what the ruckus is and then, after hugs and head scratches for everyone, leads Gus back into the sandy wash.

"How's your dad?" says Arizona.

"He's doing so much better," Lily says. "It was a good visit, so I stayed longer than I planned."

"Awesome," says Arizona.

"That's wonderful, Lily," says Mom. "I'm so happy for you both."

"Thanks. Me, too," Lily says with a smile. "Okay, let's get this party started!"

IT'S ARIZONA'S KIND OF PARTY for sure. Just four other souls, all of whom she loves, and two of whom are dogs. It's perfect, other than Dad's absence, of course. There's still an empty feeling in her chest when she thinks of him, but the empty spot no longer aches quite as much. It's a celebration of life, but not just Dad's life—a celebration of life in general, of life itself.

Camp chairs arranged on the smoke-free side of the fire, dogs at their feet, they spend the evening chatting and laughing to a backdrop of music from Arizona's phone. The playlist is Dad's, although Arizona and Lily have taken a few liberties to bring it into the twenty-first century.

They share stories of family, friends, places, activities. Mom seems herself again, smiling, laughing, a sparkle in her eyes. Arizona notices, and smiles, too. Mom really will be all right.

They talk about college—Lily is already back at UC Berkeley, and Arizona starts at Stanford in the fall. She still can't quite believe it. Just months ago the thought of venturing back to school, of leaving her bubble, was terrifying. Now she's . . . excited? Yes, she's excited! Maybe because now she knows there are people other than her parents who understand her, who accept her, who love her. And she'll find even more.

"So," says Lily, "you know Stanford is Herbert Hoover's alma mater, right? That's just a coincidence?" She winks.

Arizona laughs. "Yes, just a coincidence. It's where my dad went, too. Although I think they do have an original copy of *De Re Metallica* in the Hoover collection. How cool would that be to see?"

Lily laughs. "You're such a nerd, AZ. But you know I mean that with all due affection, right? I still like nerds."

"Yes, I know." Arizona smiles.

"Speaking of Hoover," says Lily, "when I come to visit, we should launch a bunch of paper airplanes from the observation deck of Hoover Tower."

"Ooh, great idea!" says Arizona. "We'll totally do that!"

Mom laughs and rolls her eyes as if picturing the scene, the skies of Palo Alto filled with paper airplanes. "On that note, I think I'll call it a night and leave you two alone to hatch your evil plans."

Lily does her best evil laugh and twists her imaginary villain mustache.

Mom hugs them both and heads into the Airstream.

ARIZONA AND LILY TALK and laugh for another hour. Lily has just risen from her chair to turn in for the night when "Suspicious Minds" by Fine Young Cannibals starts playing.

"I love this song!" says Lily. "One last dance! Good night, AZ."

"Good night, Lily-like-the-flower."

Lily scoops up Gus and dances past the campfire—just as Arizona pictured shortly after they met—singing along as she disappears into the night. Based on Lily's gyrating leg, Arizona is pretty sure she's doing the Elvis version.

Arizona lets the song end, then turns off the music.

But a line from the song echoes in her head.

And we can't build our dreams
On suspicious minds

She watches the fire. As the flames finally shrink, then gutter out, leaving only glowing coals, she thinks of a line from a poem—*and each separate dying ember wrought its ghost upon the floor.* It's from "The Raven," which was co-opted for the third cipher.

The gears of her mind hum, consider possibilities, calculate probabilities.

Suspicious minds. She thinks of Sam's comments about conspiracy theories and her last, oh-so-casual question—*Did you ever solve the last piece of the puzzle? Figure out where the secret was supposedly hidden?*

Not that it matters, of course. Right?

She lifts her pack off the ground, next to where Mojo is lying, warm and content.

Pulls out her laptop. Looks at the last two verses of the poem, the first of which describes the six petals of the Flower of Life:

Formed in Creator's loving hands, some say that when He made the lands
From shifting circles in the sands, He commanded who each was for:
Two for the angels aquiline, one for the beasts so anodyne,
With eagle as their king assigned, whence he was to rule and soar;
The closest two were made for man, our zealous penchant to explore;
The last His, for us to watch o'er.

The arc of the sky draws your gaze; one for repose in waning days,
One for the flare of summer's blaze, and one to guide you theretofore.
Worlds whip 'round concentric rings, summers fall and winters spring,
But always up extend the wings, a celestial semaphore.
By that Heaven that bends above us—by that God we both adore—
The secrets are safe forevermore.

She goes over her conclusions, for the hundredth time.
Two for the angels aquiline.
The petals at four o'clock and eight o'clock, where the angels "with the look of eagles" sit.
One for the beasts so anodyne, with eagle as their king assigned.
The petal at six o'clock, signified by the eagle.
The closest two were made for man.
The benches on the petals at ten o'clock and two o'clock.
Leaving one petal—*The last His, for us to watch o'er.*
The petal belonging to the Creator, at twelve o'clock.
Which also happens to be directly behind the flagpole.
And then the final clue, the last two lines of the poem:

By that Heaven that bends above us—by that God we both adore—
The secrets are safe forevermore.

She thinks back to the revelation she had on Monument Plaza, all those months ago. If *by* means *near*, then *that Heaven* is a reference to the star map, and *that God* refers to the last petal, the Creator's.

Scientia donum dei est, Arizona thinks. *Knowledge is the gift of God.* In hindsight, it makes perfect sense. In Fulcanelli's *The Mystery of the Cathedrals*, the Language of the Birds is also referred to as the Language of the Gods. Where else would you hide the secrets of a divine language but with God?

In other words, the key to the Language of the Birds is buried beneath the sixth petal, behind the flagpole. Or at least that's what the poem says.

She closes her eyes.

Her mind slows and she thinks about her life. All she has been through. All she loves.

Family. Friends. Books. Discovery.

She thinks about patterns.

Order to entropy.

Tempest tossed to halcyon days.

The end of one chapter, or book, to the beginning of another.

Eyes still closed, she brings a hand to her neck and cradles the figure-eight pendant between her thumb and finger. A wave rolls from the pendant through her fingertips, up her arm, past her heart. But the wave is warm now.

She opens her green eyes, sharp as razors, and looses a crooked smile.

THE END

Author's Note

IT WAS WIDELY REPORTED THAT IN THE SPRING OF 1933, shortly after leaving office, President Hoover spent a great deal of time touring California and Nevada, including trips to Gold Country, Death Valley, and a fair amount of fishing (Hoover was an avid fisherman). Whether he visited Pioneer Cemetery in Nevada City, or the old Hoover House in Bodie, or explored an old mine in Titus Canyon, or caught a large fish just off San Nicolas Island, I cannot say. I also cannot say whether his Secret Service code name was Kingfisher.

Herbert Hoover and his wife, Lou Henry Hoover, did translate *De Re Metallica*. The footnotes I quoted are real, including the statement that particular alchemists "certainly possessed the great secrets, either the philosopher's stone or the elixir." As to whether Hoover truly believed, I leave it to the reader to draw their own conclusions.

With but a few exceptions (Malachi's tombstone, the stamps on the survey marker, and of course the journal), all the places, artwork, books, documents, drawings, manuscripts, survey marker descriptions, and websites referenced herein are real.

In particular, the one dozen bizarre sentences discussed in the journal can indeed be constructed using excerpts from a booklet about the Hoover Dam sculptures. And when the Flower of Life is drawn on Monument Plaza, the winged figures, eagle, and benches do in fact fall on five of the six petals. The booklet and drawings can be found here:

https://archive.org/details/HooverDamMonumentPlazaSculptures CompleteBooklet

https://archive.org/details/SafetyIsland

I did not make up the Language of the Birds or the Flower of Life. Their places in mythology predate this novel.

Sadly, the terrazzo floor at Monument Plaza, including the star map, was torn up in 2022. The U.S. government claims that it will be restored. To the best of my knowledge, nothing was found beneath it.

There's an admonition near the end of the alchemical text *Mutus Liber*—*Lege, lege, lege, relege, labora et invenies.* It translates roughly as:

Read, read, read, read again, work and discover.

—K. A. MERSON

Acknowledgments

T HIS BOOK AND MY HEART ARE DEDICATED TO MY WIFE, Kristi. Without her unwavering support, the book would simply not exist. But writing a book doesn't get it published, and I will be forever grateful to Oli Munson, my literary agent at A.M. Heath in London, and Julian Pavia, my editor at Ballantine/Penguin Random House. Thank you both for believing in me and this story. It's truly an honor to work with you. And I would be remiss in not recognizing all the other wonderful people at both A.M. Heath and Ballantine/Penguin Random House.

Angela Cheng Caplan, it's so great to have you on the team. It would be a dream to see this story on the screen.

Thank you and hugs to all my writing friends, who are also my beta readers, and most of whom I met through courses at Curtis Brown Creative. Your camaraderie remains as invaluable as your feedback. It's difficult to imagine navigating this journey without you.

And to my alpha readers: my wife, my dad, my sister-in-law Carol, and my dear friend Nancy.

Stephen King, thank you so much for your stories and for your book *On Writing*. It was *On Writing* that inspired me to take this effort seriously.

Andy Weir, for demonstrating how science and math writing can be eminently accessible.

Blake Crouch, for your stories that blend—and bend—genre so seamlessly.

Stieg Larsson, for your inspirational heroine in *The Girl with the Dragon Tattoo*.

I'd also like to thank the following, in alphabetical order: Bodie .com, California State Parks, everyone at Curtis Brown Creative, DuckDuckGo, Herbert Hoover Presidential Library, Hoover Institution Library & Archives at Stanford University, The Manuscript Academy (and Danielle Chiotti at Upstart Crow Literary) for excellent querying advice, Nevada County Historical Society, National Park Service, The Novelry (and Tash Barsby in particular) for valuable manuscript feedback, QueryTracker.net for making the daunting process of finding and querying literary agents slightly less painful, United States Geological Survey, literary agent Abby Saul for the nicest rejection letter ever written, Kenneth Whyte for his excellent book *Hoover: An Extraordinary Life in Extraordinary Times*, Wikipedia (Wikipedia excerpts have been edited for brevity and/or clarity), and John Yorke for his remarkable analysis of story structure in *Into the Woods: A Five-Act Journey Into Story*.

ABOUT THE AUTHOR

K. A. MERSON is a vaguely reclusive writer who lives in the foothills of the Sierra Nevada mountains, along with a patient spouse, a malevolent boxer dog, and an Airstream trailer.

This book was set in Caslon, a typeface first designed in 1722 by William Caslon (1692–1766). Its widespread use by most English printers in the early eighteenth century soon supplanted the Dutch typefaces that had formerly prevailed. The roman is considered a "workhorse" typeface due to its pleasant, open appearance, while the italic is exceedingly decorative.